Caught in the Lye

By Marilyn McGriff

Marimac Enterprises
2016

Copyright © 2016 Marilyn McGriff

All rights reserved. No part of this book may be reproduced in any form or by any electronic or mechanical means, including information storage and retrieval systems, without permission in writing from the publisher, except by a reviewer, who may quote brief passages in a review.

To inquire about
- permission to reproduce selections from this book
- making bulk purchases
- scheduling the author for speaking engagements

mmcg844@gmail.com
Marimac Enterprises
720 E. 7th St. #308, Saint Paul, MN 55106

This book is a work of fiction. While real placenames have been used to provide a setting for the novel, their characteristics and descriptions are fictional. The characters, incidents, and events are products of the authors's imagination and are used fictitiously. Any resemblance to actual events or persons, living or dead, is entirely coincidental.

Library of Congress Catalog Card Number: 2016914574
ISBN: 978-0-692-77626-1 (paperback)

Photo of the author by Wes Peterson

Printed in St. Cloud, Minnesota by Sentinel Printing Co.

Caught
in the
Lye

{ Acknowledgments }

Little did I know when I would go with my mother to the Day locker to get meat or vegetables from our rented freezer drawer, that years later I'd be using that setting for a local history mystery.

I'm grateful to the story tellers of Isanti County (Minnesota), whose stories I've heard over the years have now found their way onto these pages – perhaps in a different time frame or a different context and certainly with different characters, all fictional.

Thanks to my friends and colleagues who offered input, feedback and encouragement. Thanks also to those who indulged me when I dominated the conversation with reports of the novel's progress.

Particular thanks go to my editors and proofreaders: Natalie Miller, Karen Gleeman, Susan Heineman and Ana Martina. Your skills coupled with your critiques have been invaluable.

Thanks also to to Renee Vaughan and Ed Gleeman for cover design consultation; to Sandy Peterson for permission to print excerpts of *Growing up in the Lutefisk Ghetto;* and to Nick Dimassis for suggesting the book's title.

A final word of appreciation goes to all the readers. May you enjoy this tale, but be careful that you don't get "Caught in the Lye." And keep telling stories. You all have them. And they are waiting to be heard!

Prologue

When a dried cod is soaked in an alkaline solution, it will undergo lots of changes when it is rehydrated.

- The oil in the skin and the muscles is quickly converted into soapy fatty acids.
- The muscle proteins are denatured and lose their firmness.
- The connective tissue, the delicate membranes between the muscles, is destroyed.
- The high alkalinity charges the muscle fibre proteins with positive electricity, making them repel each other and weaken their bond, resulting in a flesh with jelly-like consistency.

It is this "jelly" that holds the lutefisk together while it is soaking in the alkaline solution. Even the bones will be softened and turned to a gelatinous consistency on prolonged exposure. Of course, how far these chemical processes proceed depends on the strength of the alkaline solution, its temperature and the length of time the fish is kept soaking.

It is important not to let the fish soak for too long, or its fat will start to saponify, i.e. convert to soap. This is why even the commercially produced lutefisk must be handmade, each batch being controlled by a trained professional with a long experience in the process.

As soon as the producer believes the fish are sufficiently rotted in the alkaline solution, he removes them and rinses the fish in fresh water to remove the lye. If the soaking time is too short, the fish will turn into jelly and disintegrate when cooked; if too long, it will become too hard and firm. Especially during the first days, the soaking water is changed daily. The basicity of the final product has a pH of around 10.5 to 11.

Excerpted from *The Science of Cooking* by Peter Barham. Springer, 2001

{ 1 }

It was late afternoon on Christmas Eve at the Day Fish Company. Bob, one of the owners, and Ivar, a long-time employee, were finishing up with the day's tasks. Jack, the other owner and Bob's brother, had just left for the day. Ivar, looking up from where he was wielding a mop, said, "Why don't you go on home, Bob? I can lock up. There ain't goin' be any more customers this afternoon anyway. Unless maybe somebody needs a last minute bucket of herring. If people are having lutefisk tonight, it should already be heading for the oven."

"You're sure then, Ivar? I'll owe you. And I'll take the cash box so you won't have to worry about that."

Bob slipped off his big rubber boots, put on his Sorels, tucked the cash box under his arm and headed towards the door. With his hand on the knob, he turned back to Ivar and asked with a twinkle in his eye, "So is Marcie planning something special for supper for you two tonight?"

"Na, she headed to Iowa this morning to see her folks."

"What? You're not spending Christmas Eve by yourself, are you?"

"Yah, but it wouldn't be the first time."

"Well, if you get hungry, you can come on over to my place. You know there'll be no shortage of food there, the way Edith cooks up a storm for all the grandkids."

Ivar nodded and began walking towards the mop rack. Bob

went through the door, slamming it shut behind him to keep out the 0-degree Fahrenheit weather. He climbed into his Ford 150 truck he'd parked next to the fish company earlier in the day. He hoped the 10-year-old vehicle would still start.

For the last three years he'd wanted to get a new truck. His share of the proceeds from the fish company that he shared with his brother was certainly adequate, but Edith managed to always find something that took a higher priority in the Brewer household than a new pickup truck. He wondered though if this might be the year. They had rehydrated more bales of dried cod than ever before and sales had been good. There had been a record number of folks who had made the intentional journey to the fish company, and the bulk sales of lutefisk to restaurants and churches had been brisk.

Any exact figures would have to wait until February when they wrapped up the five-month lutefisk season and turned all the paperwork over to their accountant. Time was when Jack's wife Dorothy took care of all the bookkeeping, but it soon got to be too much for her—not just because the business had grown beyond her accounting capabilities but also because her health started failing. She had died three years ago after losing the battle with Parkinson's disease.

Jack's drinking escalated a bit after her death, and Bob, together with several of the guys in the neighborhood, tried to keep a close eye on him to make sure his drinking didn't get out of control. They figured if they all drank together there'd be less chance of Jack trying to drown his sorrows alone. However, the two brothers were a bit notorious for getting "happier" as the Christmas holidays approached. Christmas Eve was the pivotal point for the lutefisk business. Business was slow when they opened up in October and most of their time was spent getting a healthy bunch of fish processed to meet the November and December demands. November was taken up primarily with supplying the lutefisk for scores of church dinners where lutefisk was both the main entrée and a persevering symbol of Scandinavian heritage.

When December rolled around, the number of walk-in customers increased. They'd buy a hunk or two of the fish and maybe a pail of pickled herring, both of which could be purchased at any of the supermarkets in the larger towns. But the fish company offered a fair amount of local color. It was the only business in a so-called crossroad community that had thrived at one time. Certainly the two proprietors and their sole employee Ivar contributed to the appeal. Customers were greeted with a "Goddag," a sort of generic Scandinavian "hello," and if the customer responded in like manner, a conversation of sorts would commence in either Swedish or Norwegian until all known words were used up—usually within a minute.

If new customers wanted to see how the lutefisk process worked, the guys were only too eager to show them. After driving to this remote location, seeing the modest building and experiencing a humble sales area, those new customers were already primed not to expect a gleaming work area. Following Bob or Jack behind the counter and through the doorway of vinyl strips, they could see all there was to see—a dozen or so large stock tanks that held the hunks of fish in various stages of processing—from slabs of dried cod to quivering masses of ready-to-cook lutefisk.

As much as those new customers wanted to partake of an experience brimming with local color, they were never prepared for the odorous challenge that greeted them at the main door of the fish company. But serious lutefisk lovers overlooked the smell as long as they were able to walk out the door with their hunk of fish that would complete their holiday festivities. By necessity the processing area was kept quite cool, and so was the temperature of the small sales area. Needless to say it was not a place where customers would hang out for any longer than it took to make their purchases. Even though their visit was short, it was long enough for their clothes to absorb the ambient aroma. Thus, it was quite impossible for any such visit to be kept secret.

Whether it was because of the chilly working conditions, the continual bombardment to the olfactory nerve or a need to pass the time in between customers, the bottle of schnapps in a desk drawer of the adjacent heated office was used more and more frequently during the Christmas season. There was a subtle acknowledgment that during the season when the fish company was open, any monitoring of Jack's drinking was put on hold.

It had been a tradition for as long as Jack could remember that Bob and Edith hosted a Christmas Eve meal for the family. Years ago it had just been the four of them. Then it was six with Bob and Edith's two children. Now that they had grown up and each had a spouse and two children, the group had grown to twelve. With no children of his own, Jack had been a favorite uncle to Bob's kids, and both he and Dorothy had enjoyed watching them grow up. Now alone, Jack was still included as a part of his brother's family, and he found he was looking forward to joining them on this Christmas Eve.

There was a time—before Jack and Bob had started the fish company—that Edith fixed lutefisk for Christmas Eve as it was the *plat du jour* for every household in the neighborhood where the inhabitants were steeped in their Norwegian or Swedish heritage. She seemed to have a knack for preparing lutefisk so it stayed flaky and didn't become a gelatinous white blob. Nowadays, Edith declined to serve lutefisk because she said she'd smelled so much of it lingering on Bob's clothes when he came home from the fish company, she'd already inhaled her share.

Ending the tradition of serving lutefisk at the Christmas Eve meal in the Brewer household had coincided not only with the success of the fish company but also with the introduction of Bob Jr. and Christine's spouses. Not being Scandinavian, they weren't familiar with the lutefisk tradition, but they had learned the lore quickly and were certainly aware their father-in-law had a peculiar smell for several weeks around Christmas time. As adults, Bob Jr. and Christine also admitted they had only tolerated the fish when they were kids to please their folks and out of fear that if they didn't eat at least a forkful, some presents might be withheld. They'd heard that in some of their friends' houses, such a threat was actually made.

The Brewers maintained the custom of opening their presents on Christmas Eve. Once the meal was finished, the men adjourned to the living room while the women took care of any leftovers and washed up the dishes. The kids occupied themselves by trying to guess what was in the various packages under the Christmas tree, struggling to remain patient until the appointed time. The signal that the present-opening would soon commence was when Edith took off her apron. Then she'd say, "Karen, why don't you hand out the presents this year?" The grandkids had been waiting in suspense to see whom their grandmother would choose.

Once the grandkids were old enough to read the names on the tags attached to the presents, Edith had taken it upon herself to choose one of them for the gift delivery. It was now a firmly implanted tradition in the Brewer household.

As the presents were opened, there were the usual squeals of delight from the children. There were also a few "oohs" and "ahs" from the adults as well as the predictable "Oh, Bob, you shouldn't have," when Edith opened whatever new kitchen gadget he'd heard about, most likely from querying the customers at the fish company. Jack had long ago given up trying to give his nieces and nephews or the next generation any three-dimensional object as they already had too much "stuff," in his opinion, so he opted instead to give a little cash to each of them. More recently, he discovered gift cards were always welcome.

While Jack enjoyed being together with Bob's extended family, he soon began to tire from all the whirring of the new toys. And the mechanical voices coming from some of them grated on his nerves and bothered his hearing aid. "I'll be going on home now," Jack said, as he headed to the hooks in the front hall where he'd hung his jacket. "You all enjoy yourselves, and maybe I'll see you tomorrow at the Johnsons.'"

Edith piped up over the din of her grandchildren's playing, "Hey, kids, your Uncle Jack is leaving."

The kids stopped long enough to holler out in unison, "Goodbye, Uncle Jack."

Then as they turned back to their toys, Edith once again piped up, "And…?"

From the grandchildren came another united cry, "Merry Christmas, Uncle Jack." Then Jack, grinning, was out the door, and the Christmas Eve festivities continued at Bob and Edith's.

{ 2 }

Christmas Day dawned crisp and cold but sunny. Time was when the churches in the area had early Christmas morning services called *Julotta*. Old-timers relate how those who lived close to the church, probably within a mile or two, walked in the dark carrying torches to light their way while others arrived at the church in sleighs, well bundled up against the cold. Following the 6:00 a.m. service, they would all head back home so the men could feed and milk the cows. Meanwhile the women were busily getting ready for the big Christmas dinner to be served around noon—sometimes just for the family but often together with neighbors or relatives. As in most Scandinavian communities, there was no lack of relatives close by. When immigrants came to the area, they often looked for land close to those who had come before them, and in many instances those first settlers had written to their relatives in Sweden or Norway, encouraging them to leave their homeland to seek a more prosperous life in the "new land."

Now several generations later, the Scandinavian character of the community had dissipated to some extent. The first generation immigrants were long gone, and many of their children had sought greener pastures elsewhere. Some would say that those from the succeeding generations who had stayed in the area were the less adventuresome. Indeed, those moving into the community from outside often discovered that the remnants of clannishness still existed.

Jack well-remembered *Julotta* services as a kid, but by that time the horses and sleighs (and the torches) were a thing of the past. He remembered he thought it was a bit cruel for his mom to wake him and Bob up so early on Christmas Day and bundle the family together in the 1947 Chevy for the five-mile drive to the church. If he was going to get up that early on Christmas, he'd rather use the time to further examine the toys he'd gotten the evening before. By the time he was a teenager, the early morning service had been abandoned much to the dismay of the older folks, but Jack did not share their sentiments.

Jack must have been dreaming about Christmases of the past because he woke up even earlier than his usual 7:00. It took him a minute to remember he not only wouldn't have to go to *Julotta*, he also wouldn't have to go to the fish company because it was a holiday.

He lay in bed a few more minutes before deciding he may as well get up. While there were no new toys that needed examining, he remembered that for some time he had planned to fix the faucet in the kitchen sink that had developed an annoying drip. Maybe he'd tackle that project now as he had a block of time to work on it before the Johnson gathering in the afternoon.

Since he lived by himself, it was easy to let things go, so there were numerous projects needing attention: a screen door had a rip in it but that could wait until summer; a couple of light fixtures were on the blink and probably needed new switches; and the whole place could use a good cleaning. Marcie, Ivar's lady friend, had offered to be his cleaning lady, but Jack thought she'd had too much of a twinkle in her eye when she mentioned it, and he was afraid she was interested in more than just the dust bunnies under the bed. However, now that the busiest part of the lutefisk season was over, he'd maybe think about doing some serious cleaning and maybe even getting some paint to spruce the place up a little bit.

Chapter 2

It took him a while to find the new faucet he'd bought at Walmart several weeks before. Then he gathered up the necessary tools, turned off the hot and cold water supply lines to the kitchen sink, and he was ready to begin his project. The plumbing jobs he'd tackled at the fish company were pretty straightforward as the pipes, hoses and faucets were all exposed and within easy reach. This job, though, required that he get part of his body into the cupboard under the sink. After clearing out the array of cleaning supplies that obviously had not been used for some time, he sat on the floor and leaned forward into the cupboard to reach the pipe that connected to the faucet. After bumping his head a few times and cursing as many times, he accomplished the task. He eased himself out, removed the old faucet and installed the new one. On the trip back into the cupboard, there were as many head bumps and curse words, but he managed to reconnect the pipe to the new faucet. He maneuvered himself out of the cupboard, but when he tried to stand up, he felt a sharp pain in his spine. He cursed a bit more while he slowly got upright enough to try the new faucet. He was pleased there were no leaks and no drips once the faucet was turned off, but instead of beams of success radiating from his face, there were only grimaces of pain.

Not surprisingly, the project had taken longer than he had anticipated. He wondered if he should even go over to the Johnsons,' but he figured if he was going to be in pain, it would be better to be among friends. And maybe, he thought, they'd have some libations to help ease the discomfort. For now, he headed to the bathroom in a stooped position, found some ibuprofen pills in the medicine cabinet and downed a couple. He left the tools lying where they were and collapsed into the recliner in the living room, turned on the TV to see if there were any early football games and promptly fell asleep.

When he woke up, he was surprised to discover he'd slept for over an hour. He gingerly lowered the footrest and tried to stand up. The ibuprofen had indeed taken the edge off the pain, but his back wouldn't quite straighten out. As he took a few steps, he glanced at his reflection in the mirror on the bathroom door and thought to himself that his posture resembled Ivar's. For as long as he'd known him, Ivar was always a bit bent over. That, combined with his bony frame, lent a sort of scarecrow image to the guy. "No chance I'll ever be mistaken for a scarecrow," thought Jack as he patted his not-so-small paunch.

Jack checked his watch and discovered it was almost time to head over to the Johnsons' so he changed his shirt--with some difficulty because of his uncooperative back. He put on his jacket, also with a little difficulty, found his hat and gloves, grabbed a six-pack of Coke and a bucket of pickled herring from the refrigerator and went out the door. Again with some difficulty, he climbed into his truck which started on the first try in spite of the below-zero weather.

The Johnsons lived only a mile away, and when he rolled up their driveway he saw a half dozen cars already there. He recognized most of them—the Olson's, the Carlson's, the Berglund's, his brother Bob's, of course, and he figured the others belonged to Johnson family members. Ivar's car wasn't there yet, but he was notorious for being late. No doubt he and Ivar would be the only "singles" there, but as long as no one started thinking of them as a couple, he was just glad they were included in the neighborhood gatherings.

Jack stepped slowly out of his truck and made his way up the walk to the house. He walked extra carefully as the last thing he needed was to slip on the patches of ice dotting the walk. A cacophony of "Merry Christmas" and "Ho, ho, ho" greeted him as he opened the door. He grinned and then grimaced as he reached up to put his hat and jacket on a hook. Then came another grimace when Pete Olson slapped him on the back. Pete noticed it and said, "Whoa, what happened to you? One too many barrels of lutefisk?" And then he laughed in his big hearty laugh. So Jack

Chapter 2

had to explain about his morning amid a few "Gee, that's too bad" comments but there didn't seem to be much sympathy.

Since it appeared that all had been imbibing the "Christmas cheer," Jack decided to open one of the cans of Coke he'd brought. He took a swig and then spied the rum bottle so he topped it off with the slightly less toxic liquid. He didn't even have a chance to feel a little buzz from the concoction before Valerie Johnson declared it was time to eat. "Wait a minute," Bob said, "Hadn't we better wait for Ivar?"

"Oh, he'll be along, you know how he never quite keeps track of time," Jack said.

"You don't suppose he got waylaid with Marcie, do you?" piped up Pete.

"Shush," said his wife.

And under her breath, Abby Carlson said to Rose Berglund, "She's not coming along with him, is she? The way she looks at all the men, why, they're likely to have a heart attack right on the spot."

Jack had gotten the picture of how the women felt about Marcie, so he quickly interjected, "Marcie's down in Iowa with her folks so it will just be Ivar." The women all seemed to breathe a sigh of relief, and the men acted like whatever Jack had said didn't concern them at all.

There were too many people to fit around the Johnsons' table so the meal was served buffet style. That way the men could eat in the living room while they watched football on TV. The women would stay in the kitchen and eat at the table. As usual there was more than enough food. Everyone had brought side dishes to go along with the big ham Valerie Johnson had baked. It was from one of the pigs the Johnsons had raised. So there were scalloped potatoes, a lime Jell-O mold, buns (homemade by Rose Berglund) and Abby Carlson's perennial hot dish of French cut green beans, cream of mushroom soup and canned fried onion rings. For dessert there was Josie Olson's angel food cake with frozen strawberries she'd picked last summer.

   The same meal could have been on any number of Christmas dinner tables in the upper Midwest, regardless of ethnic background of the diners. Two items at the Johnsons' offered clues that there was at least a notion of Scandinavian background being honored. Those would be the pickled herring Jack brought and his sister-in-law Edith's lefse. Just last year Einar and Valerie Johnson's new son-in-law, Hector Espinoza, had been introduced to lefse for the first time. As Einar tells it, "Yah, he thought it was pretty good, but he did wonder why people were putting butter and sugar on their tortillas."

   Throughout the meal Jack kept looking at his watch and wondering why Ivar hadn't shown up. "Guess I'd better call him," he said to himself as he pulled his cell phone out of his pocket and punched in Ivar's number. It went straight to voice mail which was no surprise because Ivar wasn't quite used to such modern technology.

   "Just a damn nuisance," Ivar had said after Marcie had insisted he should have one—

   "So she could get ahold of him in case of an emergency," she'd said.

   Jack didn't leave a message, but once he'd eaten hearty portions of everything, he took his plate out to the kitchen and announced to the women he was going to go check on Ivar. "I'll have my dessert when I get back," he said.

   As soon as he had gone out the door after grabbing his jacket, hat and mittens, Abby Carlson muttered, "I bet Ivar hit the bottle a little too hard last night, and right now he's sleeping it off. Well, if that's the way he wants to celebrate Christmas, all alone and drunk. . . ."

   Rose Berglund broke in, "Don't be too hard on the guy. He's got a heart of gold and would probably give you the shirt off his back if he thought you needed it worse than him."

   Abby came back with, "And we know who he gave his shirt

to now, don't we?" The other women assumed Abby was referring to Marcie, but they didn't want to mar the Christmas festivities by fueling the gossip fires.

Then Josie Olson piped up directing her comments more to Edith than to the others, "Your Bob, and Jack too, of course, deserve a lot of credit for giving Ivar his job at the fish company. Once he quit farming, he didn't have much to look forward to. His job there makes him feel useful again."

Edith replied with a bit of a twinkle in her eye, "Well, you have to admit there aren't many guys out there who would want to work where it's damp, chilly and smelly."

That brought a chuckle from the rest of the women as they began putting the food away and getting ready to wash the dishes. "I'll make up a plate and set it aside for Ivar," Rose said.

{ 3 }

As Jack headed towards Ivar's farm, he turned on the radio and discovered a previously recorded episode of *Prairie Home Companion*. Jack just shook his head wondering about the humor those city slickers saw in life in rural Minnesota. He thought that if they came out here and spent a few weeks doing some real work, they might not be so eager to poke fun.

On the five-mile drive, he passed by many farms that now were owned by only a few farmers. The houses were mostly new, built within the past 20 years, usually on a few acres that had not been sold off to the "big guys"—the farmers who had bought up these farms to add to their corn and soybean acreage. Occasionally there was a farmstead left over from the time when Jack was growing up. Then the norm was for folks to have 80 to 120 acres, a good share of which was in pasture for the dairy cattle. And the rest was devoted to raising oats, corn, and alfalfa—the feed for those cattle. The sale of their milk provided the income for the farm to survive. But gradually the cows disappeared, mainly due to stricter regulations for handling milk. A lot of farmers opted to get out of the dairy business rather than suffer the expense of installing a pipeline system that carried the milk directly from the cow to a refrigerated bulk tank.

What Jack saw now were only the corn and soybean fields, albeit covered with snow—no pastures, no cattle, and no barns except for a few that were in various stages of disrepair. He wondered what happened to those current crops once they were harvested. He didn't think they did much to help out the local economy—not like those farms of his youth that sustained a number of small communities like Day, where the fish company was located.

Of course, the fish company was not an original business. If people wanted lutefisk back in the days when the town had a general store, feed mill, garage, tavern and hardware store, they made it themselves. They'd buy a hunk of dried cod at the general store, set it to soak in water in their own lye water solution made from water and wood ashes (of which there were plenty as everyone had a woodburning stove. After the fish had plumped back up, they'd rinse it and cook it.

Some of the old-timers recalled that the stacks of dried cod outside the store were a magnet for the local dogs. They'd sniff the cod and promptly lift their legs, letting a stream of urine mark the territory.

Jack and Bob's business was headquartered in a former locker plant that had been part of the cooperative creamery in Day. While most small communities had creameries, Day was a bit unique in that it also had a facility where farmers could rent locker storage to keep frozen meat, vegetables and fruit. Once the creamery was no longer viable due to the decrease in dairy farmers, it closed, together with the locker. The buildings stood empty for a few years until Jack and Bob spied them and decided to set up their fish company. They doubled the size of the locker plant building by constructing an addition to the rear of it. The fish tanks were in that addition; they used a part of the original freezer space for a walk-in cooler; and they kept the office area intact. They used the creamery building next door for storage, but it was beginning to deteriorate—like the other remaining buildings in the town.

The general store was now two apartments; both the tavern and the feed mill had burned, the feed mill years ago and the tavern more recently after standing empty for several years; the hardware store eventually had to be razed; and the garage was close to falling down. But the houses where the feed mill owner and the garage owner had lived were still occupied as was the butter maker's house. At any one time the population might be 24, but the number fluctuated regularly due to breakups of marriages or partnerships, with new partners moving in—and often quickly moving out—and a few adult children moving back in with their folks.

Jack slowed down well before the four-way stop sign not only because the road was just a bit icy but also because the dogs of Day were a constant hazard. There weren't quite as many dogs as people in the town, but they had a nasty habit of lying in the street just waiting for a car to come by so they could bark at it and chase it. They were more of a nuisance in the winter time, probably because there was more traffic through the town due to people coming to the fish company. During the summer, they usually just napped in the street and sometimes didn't even raise their heads when a car came by. Occasionally a car horn's honking would rouse them and they'd move off to the side of the road. These were not rogue dogs like one would see in third-world countries; they all had homes but preferred to keep company with their own kind.

Today, fortunately for Jack, the dogs were absent from the street. Most likely they had decided so spend the holiday at home, where undoubtedly there would be plenty of scraps from the Christmas table. Jack put on his signal to turn left to continue to Ivar's place, when he noticed Ivar's truck was sitting at the fish company in the exact same place it had been the day before. He slammed on the brakes, skidded a bit and had to back up to turn into the fish company. "What the hell?" he said to himself. He was going to be pretty pissed if Ivar was in there sleeping off a hangover.

Jack turned off the engine, and grabbing his keys, he climbed

Chapter 3

out of his truck. He was just about to put the fish company key in the lock on the door when he saw it was not latched. He pushed it open the rest of the way yelling, "Ivar, what the hell do you think you're doing?" No answer, so he headed to the office area, sure he'd find Ivar sound asleep on the sofa. No Ivar there, but Jack did notice Ivar's coat was hanging on its usual hook, so that pretty much ruled out the possibility someone had come by and picked him up. Even if that were the case, he wondered why the hell Ivar had left the damn door unlocked. He yelled again, "Ivar, Ivar!" He walked back through the customer area and proceeded through the door of plastic strips into the fish tank area. "Ivar, are you in here?" he called. Just then he saw something awry in the number two fish tank, the one that held the prime lutefisk, soon ready to be rinsed of the caustic solution it had been swimming in for several days.

There in the tank lay Ivar, like one over-sized hunk of cod doing the dead man's float. "Oh my God," shouted Jack, "what happened?" Then realizing that Ivar wouldn't be answering him, he reached for his cell phone and called Bob.

When Bob answered, Jack tried to tell him what had happened, but Bob could hardly hear him with all the noise from the TV and the shouts of the guys who were either cheering over a score for their team or revealing their intoxication (or both). Bob could tell that Jack too was pretty excited so with the phone to his ear he moved into the hall and asked Jack to repeat himself. "I found Ivar in one of the fish tanks," Jack yelled.

"What? Is he dead?"

"What do you think? Of course, he's dead."

"Which tank is he in?"

"The number two. If you're going to choose a tank to fall into, that one would be the worst."

Bob, in a state of shock and semi-inebriation, thought for a minute and then asked, "Do you think you can save the fish in that tank?"

"Christ, Bob, don't you think we ought to first get Ivar out of that tank? I don't think I can lift him myself with this bum back, and then what would I do with him? No undertaker is going to want to even touch him."

"Okay, Jack, the football game is just about done here so I'll come on over and see what I can do. I'll make up some excuse as to why I've got to leave. I don't think it'd be a good idea to let the news out yet that Ivar is swimming with the fishes." He hung up and went back into the living room to discover he'd missed the last touchdown that solidly gave the win to the Minnesota Vikings.

Jack thought about what Bob had said about getting the fish out of the tank. He also thought it was good the main part of the lutefisk season was over, and it was also a good thing this hadn't happened a month earlier. Any fish they were preparing now was gravy, so to speak, to fill the retail trade and have a bit more on hand for any straggling customers who maybe hadn't had their fill at either the lutefisk dinners or at their holiday meals. Once the word got out about Ivar's demise, any customers would no doubt wonder if their fish had been commingled with a corpse.

"Well, what the hell," Jack said to himself, and then wondered if he should mix up a new batch of soaking solution in one of the empty tanks and transfer the fish into it or try to siphon the solution from the tank where Ivar lay. He decided on the first option. The solution was cheap and pretty easy to mix—it was the fish that was valuable. Each year the price of dried cod had risen, and the brothers had to raise their lutefisk prices accordingly. So far that hadn't kept customers away, probably because most of their customers were senior citizens who had a fair amount of discretionary income. The diners at any of the lutefisk dinners too were by and large part of that gray-haired swarm and didn't seem to mind that the price they paid to eat lutefisk would have bought them a walleye dinner or maybe even a small steak at a nice restaurant. Jack and Bob were well aware

Chapter 3

their business had an expiration date probably in the not too distant future, but they figured they'd be ready to retire by that time anyway.

Jack put on his rubber apron and boots and began running water into the empty tank. One of the reasons Jack and Bob had decided on this location for their fish company was that there was plenty of good water from the well that had served the creamery. When the water level reached the half-way mark on the tank, he turned off the hose and brought over the barrel with NaOH handwritten in big letters on a homemade label. It had been Bob's idea to cover up the original labels of "caustic soda" and "lye" that were in parentheses below the chemical formula designation. He figured customers might not be so eager to buy lutefisk if they knew that such a corrosive substance had been part of the recipe. If any customers were savvy enough in chemistry to know NaOH is the symbol for sodium hydroxide, the chemical name for lye, they had probably decided that tradition trumps terminology. And any who were versed in Nordic languages knew "lutefisk" meant "lyefish."

Jack carefully measured the lye crystals into a plastic container. Then just as carefully he lowered the container into the tank, submerging it before emptying its contents to minimize the fumes. Using the stirring stick, a wooden oar that had once propelled Ivar's row boat, Jack stirred the mix, checked it with a ph-strip and pronounced it ready to receive the fish from their tank of tragedy.

During these preparations, Jack had almost forgotten the reason why he was doing them. But once he donned his long, heavy duty rubber gloves and walked back to the fateful Tank No. 2, he was quickly brought back to reality. As he peered into the tank where Ivar lay, he grimaced and hoped Bob would get there soon so they could figure out what to do. Leaving him much longer in the tank would certainly not do him any good. "What in the world happened to you?" Jack asked as he reached into the tank and retrieved the first hunk of fish. "Did you have a heart attack while you were cleaning up yesterday? You seemed fine when I left, and I figured you'd be leaving soon after. All you had to do was put the smoked fish back in the cooler, straighten up the counter and maybe sweep out the office. I didn't expect you'd even have to come back here. What went wrong?"

As Jack straightened up with the fish in hand, his back didn't want to cooperate, and he almost dropped the fish back in the tank. But with a little effort he stood almost upright and took the fish over to its new home. "Boy, I don't know how much of this I can do. Bob is going to have to get the fish that are deeper in the tank. Let me try one more," he thought to himself. As he fished for the next hunk and bent down to grab it, he had a major spasm in his back which caused his knees to buckle and he started going headlong into the tank. He released the fish and his arms went quickly to the bottom of the tank where they supported him in an upside down "v" position unable to move. His nose was just inches from the soaking solution which meant it was also just inches away from Ivar's backside. What was worse, however, was that his plunge into the tank had caused a near wake, and some of the solution had splashed him on the face (thankfully not in his eyes). Furthermore, the turbulent solution had rippled over the top of his rubber gloves and was seeking to settle around his fingers. A string of expletives exploding from his mouth prevented him from hearing Bob open the door.

The sight greeting Bob when he came into the back room caused him to yell, "Christ, almighty, don't you think it's a little late for any kind of resuscitation?" At that, Jack flew up out of the tank into a standing position, but only for an instant when his back decided otherwise. He quickly let his body fall forward, this time outside the tank, and muttered more expletives. "Well, Merry Christmas to you too," said Bob. But when Jack managed to pull off his gloves, and examine his hands, Bob saw the red spots and figured out what had happened. He quickly got a pail of water for Jack to dunk his hands in.

"I got some on my face too," Jack said, and Bob fetched more water and a washcloth they kept around for just such emergencies. As he applied cold water to his face, Jack explained what had transpired.

"Okay," said Bob, "First let's get you off that floor and then we'll tend to the fish, and then we'll tend to Ivar." Jack tried to sit up but thought better of it and rolled himself up to hands and knees.

When Bob got hold of him under his armpits to get him into a standing position, Jack hollered out and said, "That's not going to work. Just let me crawl over to the office." With that he took off and managed to get alongside the couch in the office where he was able to hoist himself up and collapse on his back. Bob came in and took off Jack's boots. He then rummaged around in the desk drawer and pulled out a bottle of Jim Beam. He took a swig and handed the bottle to Jack.

"You just lay here and rest up a bit. Let me take care of the fish," Bob said. He took another generous swig, recapped the bottle and put it back in the desk. Jack tried to relax and found the warmth of the whisky actually helped. As he heard Bob sloshing around with the fish, he even closed his eyes for a bit but opened them abruptly when he heard, "Christ almighty, you'd better get in here." Jack sat up carefully, pulled on his boots and then stood up with only a minor catch in his back. As he pushed aside the plastic strips in the doorway, he found Bob leaning over the tank where Ivar was reposed and examining something on Ivar's head.

"What's going on?" Jack asked.

When Bob looked up, his face was almost as white as the fish in the tank.

"Come and look at this," he said.

Jack hobbled closer to the tank but didn't want to bend down for fear he wouldn't be able to straighten himself back up. But even in his almost upright position he could see what had caused Bob's outburst. There on Ivar's head was an obvious bruise. It was near the top of his head and had been covered by his cap so Jack had missed it. But with all the sloshing in the tank with the fish removal, Ivar's cap had slipped forward a bit exposing what certainly appeared to be a blow to the head.

"So it wasn't his ticker that gave out," said Jack as he stood gazing at their employee who now was not only dead but mysteriously dead. "What do we do now?"

"Jesus, I don't know," Bob said as he stood there scratching his own head. "We'll have to call the sheriff, but I hate to mess up anyone else's Christmas. Let me finish transferring the fish and then let's try to get him out of that tank. If we can just lay him on the floor, he'll keep till morning as cool as it is in here, and then we can let the sheriff know."

"But," Jack said, "how are we going to explain that he's been moved from the place where he died?"

"Well, we don't know for sure that he died in the tank. Maybe that blow killed him, and whoever hit him then tossed him into the tank."

"Now wait a minute. Don't you think it's possible Ivar bumped into something around here, got a bump on the noggin that made him a little dizzy and then he fell into the tank?" Jack asked somewhat half-heartedly.

"Look around. Do you see anything sticking out from the wall that Ivar could have run into? As slow as he moved, he couldn't have banged into anything with enough force to cause that kind of a bruise."

"Okay, then I was just trying not to think about the alternative. Who would want to kill him anyway? I don't see anything else out of place, but I did think it was awfully fishy the door wasn't locked when I got here this afternoon. Let me take a closer look around while you handle the fish move."

Jack shuffled off back to the customer area and stood in one

Chapter 3

place letting his eyes roam around the room—to the supply of lingonberry jam on the counter, the various signs listing prices, and finally the box of smoked fish. "What the hell," he said to himself, "Ivar was supposed to put the box in the walk-in cooler. If he didn't get to that, it means that whoever came in here must have arrived shortly after Bob left. Jeez, I wish we'd stuck around a bit longer. Maybe Ivar would still be alive or who knows, maybe we'd be lying dead in fish tank too."

He opened the door to the walk-in cooler with a bit of trepidation, peered in and looked around, but he didn't see anything missing or out of place. With the door open he walked back and got the box of smoked fish. As he was about to enter the cooler with it, he made a mental note of the number of fish in the box. Keeping a strict inventory of supplies on hand was not a strong point for either Jack or Bob, but when Jack had helped himself to a fish the day before to take to the Christmas Eve supper, he had noticed there were six fish in the box minus the one he took. Now there were only four. He went ahead and put the box in the cooler, then ambled over to the counter to see if Ivar had left a note about the sale of a smoked fish. Jack had taken the customer sale book with him, being quite certain there wouldn't be any more sales of anything so late on Christmas Eve. No note was anywhere in sight. Jack considered the idea that a destitute customer might have come in for a smoked fish and when he couldn't pay, he and Ivar got in a scuffle and Ivar got the worst of it. He thought that wasn't very likely because if someone couldn't pay, Ivar would most likely have given the guy what he wanted and stood the cost himself.

Just then Bob came through the plastic strip door and asked Jack if he'd found any clues that might point to a motive or a suspect. "Nope," said Jack, "only one smoked fish I can't account for."

"Since when do you keep track of the smoked fish?" Bob asked. Jack then explained how he knew one was missing, and

Bob just shook his head thinking to himself that now he not only had a corpse on his hands but an aspiring Inspector Clouseau.

"I got all the fish moved, so let's see if we can now move Ivar."

"You're sure we won't get in trouble for tampering with the evidence or whatever they call it on CSI?"

"Think about it Jack. You know what that lye solution does to the fish. I hate to think how Ivar's face looks even now after almost 24 hours. Another night in there and it's definitely not going to be a pretty sight." Jack and Bob both thought about that image for a bit and then Bob continued, "It would be different if it wasn't Christmas. Any other day I'd have called the sheriff immediately. But, given the circumstances, I'd say that getting Ivar out of that tank is the right thing to do."

"All right, then. My back seems to have limbered up a bit, thanks to our friend Jim, so let's get it over with."

Jack grabbed his long rubber gloves and followed Bob through the plastic strip door into the fish processing area.

"So how are we going to do this?" asked Jack as he stood on one side of Ivar's tank with Bob on the other.

"Well, how about if you grab him by the straps on his bib overalls, and pull him up as far as you can and then I'll grab one of his legs and get it over the edge of the tank. Then we'll see how it goes."

"Okay, here he comes," said Jack as he pulled on the back of the overall bib. As Ivar came close to the surface, Bob reached in, grabbed a leg and began maneuvering it so it would clear the rim of the tank.

Then he stopped and said, "You know, it would be easier if we turned him over. Then his leg would bend the right way to get it over the rim."

"Oh jeez, Bob, I was hoping we wouldn't have to look at his face."

"Well, you're going to have to look at it sooner or later. Come on, give me a hand. Get over on this side of the tank so we can

Chapter 3

each grab on to his far side arm and flip him over."

They got into position and both started reaching across the tank. Bob got hold of Ivar's arm and was waiting for Jack to do likewise when he heard a sort of yelp. As he turned to look at Jack to see what was the matter, he realized Jack's reach was far short of finding Ivar's arm and was dangerously close to finding a landing somewhere in the middle of the tank. Bob quickly let go of Ivar's arm and just as quickly put his own arm around Jack's waist and pulled him up. Coming back upright so rapidly made Jack yelp even louder. So Bob eased him back down so he could rest in a stooped position with his hands on the rim of the tank.

Jack took some deep breaths and gradually raised himself to a near upright position, muttering all the while. Bob just stood by shaking his head but soon he said, "Okay, here's another idea. How about if we leave Ivar in the tank, but drain out the lye solution he's swimming in and replace it with fresh water?"

Jack thought for a minute and then agreed it was a good idea. Bob surmised, "That way we haven't really tampered with any evidence, and the sheriff probably isn't going to do any kind of chemical analysis. If that blow knocked Ivar out, then he'd have drowned even in fresh water."

"Yah, but there's just one thing," said Jack, "What about Ivar's face? If it's as bad as I think it is, that's going to be hard to explain."

"Well, let me think. For all we know, whoever hit him on the back of the head might have hit him in the face too, so maybe his face was banged up before he went into the tank."

"Ivar's face was never much to look at anyway. But being homely is no reason to get dunked in a bath of lye," quipped Jack.

"I never said it was, and I doubt that's why he ended up like he did. Let's get this tank drained and get out of here."

Bob reached down and loosened the drainage valve on the tank and the solution spewed out and found its way to the floor drain with a little help from both Bob and Jack using big squeegees on poles. When the flow was down to a mere trickle, Bob tightened the valve again as Jack unwound the hose hanging from the fresh water tap along the wall. He managed to drag the hose across the floor and began letting the water run into the tank.

"Here you go, Ivar," he said as the water started to rise up around the still body. "May you rest in peace."

Just as Jack started to head back towards the office to join Bob and their friend Mr. Beam, he heard a strange noise coming from the direction of Ivar's tank. He walked back over to it thinking there was something wrong with the hose, and then he heard it again. There didn't seem to be any problem with the hose so he turned his head slowly and did a 360-degree turn, eyeballing the entire room. Nothing seemed amiss, but once more there was the strange sound which he now had determined was definitely coming from the tank.

"Bob, Bob," he called, "Get in here."

Bob came running into the fish room with the whisky bottle in his hand. Thinking that once again Jack's back had caused him to fall, stumble or whatever, he was a bit surprised to see Jack standing by Ivar's tank with his hand to his heart and white as a sheet.

"I-I-I-Ivar might not be dead," Jack stammered.

"What?" Bob exclaimed.

Then Bob heard the strange noise also. "Shit, Jack, it's Ivar's cell phone."

"How the hell can that thing be ringing after being underwater all this time?"

"Remember? He always kept it in a Ziploc bag in his shirt pocket with just the vibration thing—said it gave him a little thrill when it rang."

"Well, don't you think you should fish it out and answer it?" asked Jack, knowing he wouldn't be able to bend down far enough to reach it.

Chapter 3

"Hell, no. Talk about tampering with evidence. Let the sheriff's boys deal with it." He cocked his head, listening for another ring. When he didn't hear one, he said, "There, it's gone to voice mail."

"Are we about done here, Bob? This place is starting to give me the willies."

"Yah, not much more we can do around here today. But let's make sure we're on the same page for tomorrow. We'll get here as usual tomorrow morning when we make this awful discovery of Ivar in the fish tank. We call the sheriff and wait. No word to anyone about this before that. Are you clear on that, Jack?"

"Sure, but how are you going to explain why you left the Christmas gathering?"

"Oh, I'll think of something. You must have been trying to fix something and needed help because of your back."

"All right then. Let's make sure the door is closed tight and locked. And, Bob, would you mind following me to my place? I don't know of anyone that's got it in for me, but then I didn't know of anyone who had it in for Ivar either."

Bob rolled his eyes a bit but nodded his head and said, "Sure thing. Take a couple of ibuprofen and go to bed early. I'll see you in the morning."

With that, they each got into their trucks and headed down the road. When they pulled into Jack's place, he got out, walked up to the house, turned on the light and disappeared inside. After a few minutes, he came back on the porch, waved to Bob, giving him the "all clear" sign. Bob waved back, turned around and headed back to the Johnsons' hoping he could persuade Edith it was time to go home.

{ 4 }

THE NEXT MORNING when he woke up, Jack was surprised that he'd slept so well. He eased himself out of bed and discovered that he could stand up pretty straight. After his usual Cheerios with sliced bananas and a piece of raisin toast with peanut butter, he called Bob, and they decided to meet at the fish company in a half hour.

Bob got there first but he decided to stay in his truck until Jack arrived. Best to go in together just in case. Bob wasn't prone to getting spooked, but finding Ivar dead led him to wonder a bit. Maybe ghosts from Christmases past had decided to inhabit the fish company as in the Dickens tale. Or maybe a sea troll had hitched a ride from Norway with the dried cod intent on some sort of misdirected revenge. And then there's always the Huldra, the troll-like creature disguised as a beautiful woman who lures men to their doom. That would be fitting for Ivar, Bob mused and smiled a bit at the thought.

There was also the possibility that Marcie had somehow played a role in Ivar's demise. Sure, she had said she was going to Iowa, but had she really? For all he knew Ivar had a life insurance policy listing Marcie as sole beneficiary. Or maybe Ivar had drawn up a will, leaving everything to her. Bob had tried to caution Ivar about being taken advantage of, but Ivar always said, "Nah, she's not like that. She's a big help and we get along real good."

Chapter 4

He was quickly jolted out of his reverie when Jack started pounding on the truck window. "Jeez, for a minute, I thought you'd bit the dust too," Jack said.

"Guess I was just a bit reluctant to go back in there," Bob said as he climbed down out of his truck.

Both were relieved when the door was still securely latched. They went inside and together they walked into the fish processing area. Once they had seen Ivar in his repose, they turned around and walked back to the office. Bob sat down at the desk and Jack sat down on the couch. "Well," said Bob, "I guess we'd better get it over with. I'll call 911 even though at this point, it's not really an emergency." "Yah, but they don't know that," said Jack.

"Okay," Bob said with his hand on the telephone receiver, "How do you want to play this? We got here this morning and found him, right?"

"Sure, let's go with that and see what happens."

Bob made the call and explained the situation to the dispatcher. She said she'd send someone right out from the sheriff's office. Bob thanked her and hung up the phone.

"So what do we do while we wait?" Jack asked.

"Hell, I don't know. Go grab a magazine or something. I'm going to count the receipts from Christmas Eve. Never got a chance to do that yesterday."

Twenty minutes later they heard two car doors slam, and Bob went to the door to let the sheriff in. He knew Sheriff Erickson, of course, but he hadn't met the young fellow with him.

"Morning, Bob," the sheriff said as he walked through the door. "I hear you have a situation here. I brought along our new deputy, Nick Nordin, in case we need some help figuring out what happened." Nick meanwhile had visibly recoiled from the strangest smell he'd ever encountered. He didn't say anything but looked as though he may have to retreat outside to catch his breath or give up the scrambled eggs he'd had for breakfast.

Bob shook both their hands and Jack came out of the office and did likewise.

"Okay, let's see what you've got," the sheriff said.

They all ambled into the fish processing room while the deputy looked around incredulously, keeping the back of his gloved hand against his nose.

"We found him just like that," exclaimed Jack as they approached the tank. "It's Ivar Peterson, right?" asked the sheriff.

"We thought maybe he'd had a heart attack and fell into the fish tank," Bob said, "but then we noticed that wound on the back of his head, so we're thinking someone did him in."

The sheriff looked at Bob a bit skeptically, but as he bent down to get a closer look at the back of Ivar's head, he had to agree it looked like he'd been clobbered with something,

"So when did you last see him alive?" the sheriff asked.

"Christmas Eve. Jack left about 4:00, I left a few minutes later, and Ivar said he'd lock up. He also said he was spending Christmas alone as his girlfriend was with her folks down in Iowa," explained Bob.

"Girlfriend, eh?" said the sheriff raising his eyebrows. "Like live-in girlfriend?"

"Technically she was keeping house for him," Jack answered.

"But you think they were also playing house?" the sheriff interjected, giving Jack a sly smile.

"She just showed up one day a few years ago and moved right in," Jack continued. "Ivar seemed to like the attention, but several of us warned him she might rob him blind and just disappear one day. We never could get a handle on Marcie's past—only that she said she had family in Iowa."

"So you don't even know that for sure?" the sheriff asked. Without letting them answer, he said to his deputy, "Guess you'd better pay her a visit when she gets back."

Deputy Nordin made a note to that effect. When he took his hand away from his nose so he could retrieve his notebook from

Chapter 4

his jacket pocket, he noticed the smell really didn't bother him as much. Thank goodness for olfactory fatigue--or in this case total olfactory exhaustion, he thought.

"How long do you think before we can get him out of that tank?" asked Jack.

"We thought it would be best to wait for you guys before we moved him."

"Good idea," said the sheriff. "But I can understand why you might want to. That is lye you use in the lutefisk process, isn't it?"

With this question Deputy Nordin almost dropped his notebook. The sheriff, seeing his astonishment, offered the explanation that his new deputy had just moved to the area from Spearfish, South Dakota, and he wasn't familiar with lutefisk.

"Look," said the sheriff, "normally, I'd have to advise leaving the deceased where he met his demise in order to avoid destroying any evidence; but in this case, leaving him where you found him is no doubt doing the destroying."

Jack and Bob stole glances at each other and then Bob said, "Well, I can certainly help you guys lift him out of that tank. Jack's got a bum back. But you're both going to need rubber aprons and gloves. And I'd advise boots too. We've got all that stuff."

Jack rounded up the supplies, and the two authorities got prepared. Then Jack asked, "So where are you going to put him? You can't just lift him out and plop him on the floor"

The sheriff looked around and seeing a couple of empty tanks, said. "How about turning one of those empty tanks upside down so we have a sort of table to lay him on?"

The sheriff, his deputy and Bob tackled the job. After a few grunts and groans, they got the tank turned over.

Then they turned their attention to Ivar. The sheriff, feeling as though he was the strongest of the three, got on one side of the tank while Bob and Deputy Nordin got on the other. While

Deputy Nordin had fears that when he grabbed hold on one of Ivar's legs, it would come off in his hands, he didn't have to worry. Ivar was still solid dead weight, and in spite of his weighing only 160 pounds, it did require some huffing and puffing to get his torso out so it was resting on the rim of the tank. With the sheriff grabbing Ivar under the arms and the other two each getting a leg, they were able to maneuver him over to the upturned tank. Jack was standing by, eager to see what kind of damage had been done to Ivar's face.

He heaved a sigh of relief when he saw that Ivar was still recognizable, albeit dead, and when he stole a glance at Bob, he noted he seemed relieved as well.

Putting fresh water in the tank had definitely been the right thing to do.

As Ivar lay there, the reality finally began to sink in that their good worker, neighbor and friend was actually gone. The sheriff seemed at a bit of a loss to figure out what to do next. He circled the makeshift bier several times scratching his head while his deputy looked every bit as bewildered. Surely this can't be their first homicide case, Bob thought. Jack, whose favorite TV shows were any of the various CSI's and who read every crime novel he could get his hands on, was thinking the forensics team should be called in, and the medical examiner should examine the corpse.

Then the sheriff stopped his circling and asked, "What the hell is that?" as he pointed to a piece of clear plastic that was barely visible above Ivar's waistband.

"Quick, Nordin, get your camera and take some shots of this."

Nordin had left the camera in the squad and he hurried outside to retrieve it. The fresh air was a relief, and he took a few deep breaths as he located the camera in the glove compartment. When he returned to the scene of the crime, the smell hit him again but not quite as bad as that initial encounter.

In the meantime, Bob and Jack had moved closer to the body so they could get a better look at the mysterious plastic. "Oh,"

Chapter 4

Bob said, "That's just his cell phone."

"Cell phone?" the sheriff asked incredulously. He was about to pull the package out of Ivar's pants, when Nordin told him to wait so he could get a few camera shots before the scene was disturbed. The sheriff continued, "Why the hell is his cell phone in a plastic bag and what the hell is it doing in his pants?"

"The first question is easy," Bob said. "He thought it was a good idea to protect it in case it fell out of his shirt pocket into one of the tanks. Uh, I can't answer the second question."

"Is it on?" asked Deputy Nordin.

"Seems to be," answered the sheriff. After looking a little more closely, he said, "Looks like there's at least one message." Then becoming almost ebullient, he said, "You hardly ever get better effidence than this."

Bob and Jack again exchanged glances but Deputy Nordin just shook his head. Having been on the job only a few months, he was still getting used to several of the sheriff's words being slightly off.

As he removed the phone from the plastic bag, Nordin asked, "Uh, Sheriff, don't you think we should take it into the office and log it as evidence?" Nordin asked.

"Well, sure, but I'd like to know now who was calling Ivar. Besides, it looks like the battery is getting low. You guys know if there's a charger around here?"

"Not for that phone. Ivar always took it home to have Marcie charge it. She's the one who convinced him in the first place to get the thing. Ivar thought it was kind of silly," responded Bob.

"Okay, then," the sheriff said, as he flipped the phone open and pressed the button for voice mail.

He listened for a bit, nodding his head, and then suddenly his face turned red, and he snapped the phone shut.

"So what'd you hear?" Jack asked. "You look like you're either scared or blushing."

"The person didn't identify herself, but I assume it was that

33

Caught in the Lye

Marcie woman. First she said she'd gotten to Iowa okay and then she got all mushy, saying some pretty raunchy things to her lover boy here," the sheriff said as he glanced over at Ivar, who didn't seem like a natural recipient of such sexually explicit language, even when he was alive.

Deputy Nordin chimed in, "Well, the message seems to confirm what you guys said, that she'd gone to Iowa to see her folks. When did she leave that message?"

"According to the voice mail center, it was 4:15 p.m. December 24."

"That checks out," said Bob. "She must have called right after I left."

"While you were still here, I don't suppose you noticed if Ivar's cell phone was sticking out of his pants?" Nordin asked with an amazingly straight face.

"Actually," Bob replied, "I'm pretty sure I saw that he had it in his shirt pocket." Then he added, "Sheriff, check the other calls on that phone—both incoming and outgoing."

The sheriff flipped the phone open again and punched the "calls" button.

"No outgoing calls, but there are a couple more that came in.

"Well one would be me," Jack said. "I tried calling him Christmas Day when he didn't show up over at the Johnsons'."

"3771?" asked the sheriff.

"Yup," replied Jack.

"There's another one on the 25th. Same number as the one with the sizzling message. Guess she was just checking up on him. Of course, you know," continued the sheriff, "that message hardly counts as an alibi. She could have been calling from anywhere."

Just then Deputy Nordin, who had been circling around the tank where Ivar lay, called out to the sheriff, "I think he had more than the cell phone in his pants."

The sheriff turned red again and said, "Uh, what do you mean?"

Chapter 4

Nordin had noticed a mysterious bulge in Ivar's trousers. It seemed to be big enough to extend beyond his groin and partway down his thigh. He snapped a few pictures and then feeling the crime scene had already been compromised, he set the camera aside and undid the fly, opening Ivar's pants wider. There between his underwear and his pants was wedged the second foreign element that only deepened the mystery of what had happened to poor Ivar.

The sheriff, Bob and Jack closed in around the corpse to get a closer look. "Well, I'll be damned," Jack exclaimed. "So that's where the stray smoked fish landed. If you ask me, it didn't get there on its own."

Nordin stifled a "duh" but he left the fish where it had landed. Bob and Jack stepped back, shaking their heads while Nordin and the sheriff conferred about what to do next.

"By rights," the sheriff said, "we ought to call in the coroner to make an official declaration of death, but I think we're all agreed there's no question about our friend here being dead."

"Uh, that's not exactly the point," Nordin interjected. "I'm pretty sure that when a homicide is suspected, the coroner's office has to be notified in order to conduct an inquest."

"Yah, yah, yah, and then what they'll do is turn everything back over to us so we can figure out what happened here," the sheriff rebutted.

"At least you'd better call the office and get some advice on how to proceed," Nordin suggested.

While the sheriff made the call, Jack and Bob went back to their office to gather their thoughts. Bob started to reach for the bottle of Jim Beam but Jack cautioned him he'd better wait until the authorities were gone.

"I hope it isn't long," Bob said. "We'll no doubt have some customers stopping by, and they'll wonder why there's a sheriff's car here."

"I put a 'closed' sign on the door, but I'd say this could take a while." They could hear the sheriff on the phone describing the situation and then some protests as though he didn't like what he was hearing. Finally, he hung up, muttering about those sons of bitches.

"So what's the deal?" Bob asked.

"Back in the old days, I could call the coroner and he'd let me fill in the death certificate and give me full reign to do any investigating that needed to be done. But now, there's a regional medical examiner and special investigators who run the show out of Anoka. (He gave a sneering emphasis to the word "special.") They want to see the scene of the crime, check for fingerprints and all that stuff. So it's up to them now, and they're probably not going to be too happy when they find out the rearranging we did in order to get Ivar out of the tank where he met his demise."

"How long will it take them to get here?" Bob asked, thinking of his friend Jim waiting there in the office.

"Well, fortunately, they've had a slow couple of days so they said they are going to head right out. It shouldn't take more than 40 minutes or so."

Just then the sheriff's radio broke in, with the dispatcher wondering if they could head towards Braham where a car had run off the road and was on its side in the ditch.

The sheriff was only too glad to be gone from the premises before the more elite crew arrived. He motioned to his deputy to come with him and was out the door without another word. Nordin, on the other hand, shook hands with Jack and Bob and said he'd no doubt be back.

With the authorities gone, Jack and Bob again retreated to the office and this time they didn't hesitate to get quite well acquainted with Mr. Beam. With the reality of the last few days beginning to sink in, they each began blurting what had come to their respective minds:

"Who the hell would have done such a thing?"

Chapter 4

"What's Ivar ever done to deserve this?"

"What if whoever did this has it in for us too?"

"Who's going to give him a funeral?"

With that last outburst, they looked at each other and realized it would probably be up to them to take care of any funeral arrangements. Ivar had no spouse, no children, and his only sister, who had died in the 1980s, never had children either. There might be some distant cousins somewhere, but Ivar had never talked about them. And then there's Marcie—hardly next of kin and furthermore, a possible suspect.

When they heard a commotion outside, Jack looked out the window. He saw two men putting on their Hazmat gear. "Christ," he said, "We've got guys in bunny suits. What next?"

{ 5 }

As the two investigators came through the door, Jack and Bob ambled out from the office, none too steadily, and introduced themselves. Without shaking hands, the one investigator said, "I'm Ed, the medical examiner, and this here is Stan, the crime scene expert."

"You guys look like you just came in from outer space," Jack said.

"Yah, we get that a lot," Ed said. "We don't like wearing these things much but we have to whenever we're dealing with hazardous materials." Jack and Bob stole a look at each other, no doubt thinking they'd been dealing with hazardous materials for years with no such suit.

"Let's get to work," Stan said. "Where's the body?" Jack and Bob ushered the guys into the lutefisk processing area. The investigators looked around and quickly spotted Ivar on the upturned tank. "Ed here will determine if there's need for an autopsy. While he's looking over the body, why don't you bring me up to speed on what's gone on here."

Jack explained how he and Bob had discovered the body and how they'd called the sheriff when they saw the wound on the back of Ivar's head. Then Bob continued with how they'd fished Ivar out of the tank, and how they uncovered both the cell phone and the stray fish stuffed down Ivar's pants.

"Okay, at some point you both may need to make a formal

Chapter 5

statement, but for now we'll examine the crime scene to see if we can get any clues." With that, Stan opened up the case he'd been carrying and laid out an array of tools. Jack eyed them with considerable interest, comparing them to the tool kits he'd seen on countless television crime shows. Not wishing to be interrupted, Stan assured Jack and Bob they were not needed at the moment and could go back to whatever they were doing previously.

They retreated to the office, and decided maybe they shouldn't go back to what they had been doing before the investigators arrived. Instead they sat quietly for a few minutes, both pondering the state of affairs they now found themselves in.

Meanwhile, Stan was busy dusting for fingerprints and looking for other clues that might help to explain what had gone on in this remote part of the county. As he bagged the cellphone to take back to the office, he muttered, "Idiot."

"What's that?" Ed asked, looking up from where he was examining the corpse on the overturned tank.

"Oh, I was just wishing the sheriff wouldn't have done quite so much stumbling around here so the crime scene could have been left more intact. I found a few prints on the cell phone but I'm pretty sure they'll end up being the sheriff's. That stray smoked fish certainly didn't have any fingerprints. And there was absolutely nothing on either tank – the one where victim is now or on the one where he was caught lying."

"No pun intended, right?" asked Ed with a bit of a grin.

"Right, and I suppose you're going to put in your report that there was suspicion of foul play too," retorted Stan.

"Given this place, it could hardly be anything but. I've experienced a lot of different aromas over the years—decaying bodies, burned flesh and numerous other putrefactions, but nothing quite like this. I'm pretty eager to get out of here so if you're about done, I'll finish up my report and we can take off."

"But Ed, don't we have to take the body in for an official autopsy?"

"Uh, I'm going to bypass protocol on this one. I got enough information from the exam I did right here to know that cause of death came from a blow to the head. Whether that killed him outright, it's hard to say, but it was at least severe enough to knock him out before he went headlong into the tank. If you're going to end up head first in a tank of lye, it would be good to be either unconscious or dead, I'd say."

"By the way, Stan, you didn't find anything that could have been used as the murder weapon, did you?"

"Nope. I mean that smoked fish is pretty hard, but I don't think it could have delivered a lethal blow. And besides, it was stuffed in his pants before he died."

"So what do you make of it? Pretty strange, if you ask me."

"Well," Stan replied, "Strange things stuffed into a victim's pants generally indicate a motive with sexual implications.

"So you're thinking the murderer was a woman?" asked Ed.

"That would be my guess . . . or maybe two of them."

"Why do you say that?"

"Let's say our victim was being threatened, chased, or whatever after some kinky stuff had gone on, and as he heads into the back room he gets hit on the head and he falls into the tank. But I don't think his whole body would have ended up in there, so unless the murderer was a pretty hefty gal, she would have needed some help to get the rest of the body over the rim of the tank."

"Yah, I see your point, but the cellphone and fish being stuffed into his pants seem like more of an anger thing — like maybe the stuffer had been rejected and this was the retaliation."

Packing up his tools, Stan said, "Could be, but I think we're done here. Let's get back to the office and finish up our reports so the boys in Cambridge can get going on finding who the murderer is. I'll bring the guys here up to date on what we know

Chapter 5

so far and tell them they can go ahead and call the undertaker."

"Okay, I hope they don't have to do anything today that requires use of a knife or any other sharp object. It seemed to me they both had been hitting the bottle pretty hard before we got here."

"I wonder what proof alcohol you need to overpower the aroma of rotting fish," Ed quipped.

* * * * *

The sheriff and his deputy made quick work of the call regarding the car in the ditch. The driver was unhurt, there was no evidence he'd been drinking. He explained that he'd hit an icy patch on the road and lost control. The car suffered some front end damage and the liquid leaking out of it indicated a punctured radiator. The sheriff called for a wrecker and let the guy sit in the squad car while they waited. As he got into the car, he said, "Phew, you guys been to the fish company?"

Erickson said only, "Yup," and no more questions were asked. Instead there was some chitchat about the weather and how each had spent their Christmas (with Nick not being able to add much as he had been on call both Christmas Eve and Christmas Day—not having anything else to do). When the two truck arrived, it easily got the car out of the ditch, and prepared to tow it back to town with the driver riding in the truck's cab. Just as the two law enforcement officers were getting ready to head into town themselves, the sheriff's cell phone rang.

"Hope whatever this is can wait until we get some coffee and pie," the sheriff said to Nick as he answered the phone.

The caller was Ed, the medical examiner, and he filled the sheriff in on his and Stan's findings at the fish company.

"Okay, thanks," said the sheriff. "I'm going to be turning the case over to Deputy Nordin as I'm still up to my ears in that drug bust from last month."

He hung up and told Nordin that both the medical examiner and the crime scene investigator would be getting in touch with him as he was now the primary investigator on the case.

"Okay, Sheriff," he said. "I'll take it from here—just as soon as I get that coffee and pie."

With a grin from the sheriff, the two continued towards the Park Café in Braham. The drug bust the sheriff had referred to was etched in Nick's memory. He was still pretty new to the sheriff's office and was still getting adjusted when one afternoon the sheriff had burst into his office and said, "Come on, Nordin. This is going to be a big one!" Nick grabbed his jacket and followed the sheriff out to a van that was the first vehicle in what appeared to be a convoy.

"What's all this?" asked Nick as he began clambering into one of the rear seats of the van.

The sheriff, settling himself into the passenger seat in the front of the van, said he'd explain on the way. Judging from his huffing and puffing after the hurried exit from his office, Nick hoped the sheriff wouldn't expire before he had a chance to offer details of the mission.

Nick greeted Scott, the driver, another deputy, but he didn't recognize the fellow who shared his seat. He put out his hand and introduced himself and got the response: "Glad to meet you. I'm Joe Clark with the DEA."

DEA? thought Nick. The inclusion of a federal agent coupled with the array of official vehicles all heading out of Cambridge could only mean this was no ordinary exercise.

The sheriff, having caught his breath a bit said, "Yah, Joe's been on the pot patrol for a long time now. He knows or can find out where every patch is in all of east central Minnesota. "

"So anybody want to fill me in?" Nick asked.

The sheriff then briefed him on a suspected marijuana operation of considerable size in the northern part of the county. Numerous plants of a suspicious nature had been sighted during

Chapter 5

the routine flyovers conducted by the Bureau of Criminal Apprehension. It was the BCA's contention that the acreage in question was being used for commercial production of marijuana. While the farm's electrical use had not indicated any unusual spikes (after being monitored by the local electrical cooperative), and after no further evidence was collected to confirm that sales of marijuana were being conducted from the farm, the BCA suggested to the sheriff it would helpful to get a warrant so the premises could be searched. With a little luck, that search would turn up further evidence regarding the more serious offence of growing marijuana with intent to sell.

When Nick asked about the guys in the other two vehicles, the sheriff said that the one directly behind them was Frank Billings from the BCA together with his dog Snoop.

"He prefers to travel alone," Joe chimed in. "Guess the dog's sniffer stays sharper." Rounding out the convoy was a vehicle with two sheriff's deputies from Kanabec County. When Nick looked puzzled, the sheriff explained that the farm in question straddled both counties.

They parked the vehicles on the road just before the long driveway leading to the house. The strategy was that the first vehicle would proceed up the driveway, and the sheriff would go to the house alone with the warrant. Billings would go halfway up the driveway but would stay put until the sheriff gave a "go ahead" signal. When that happened, Billings, Snoop, the DEA guy, Scott and Nick would zoom in to conduct a thorough search and presumably assist with arrests. The two Kanabec County officials would remain on the road to watch for anyone who might be running away from the premises.

The lead vehicle was just about to enter the driveway when a Dodge Caravan came from the other direction and signaled to turn into the driveway. "Oh great," Scott said. "No doubt we've been made."

"Yah, you're darn tootin,' it's great!" exclaimed the sheriff.

"We might have ourselves a buy going down and we'll get both the customers and sellers and the contraband to boot. Let's go!"

So leaving a trail of dust behind them, two of the vehicles bearing a host of law enforcement personnel, sped up the driveway. The suspected drug customers had not yet had time to get out of their van as Scott pulled up on the passenger side, Billings pulled up on the driver's side, and the Kanabec County deputies had stayed back blocking the driveway so the Caravan would not be able to get out.

Just then the van's front passenger window lowered, and a young woman peered out with a puzzled look on her face. "Is that you, Scott?" she asked. Scott, who recognized the woman as one of his high school classmates, had no choice but to acknowledge his identity. At the same time this reunion was taking place, Nick had peered into the Caravan and noticed a stack of "Watchtower" magazines on the lap of one of the two other passengers.

"What's going on?" asked a rather bewildered sheriff. Nick leaned forward towards the sheriff and whispered, "Jehovah's Witnesses."

The sheriff stifled a response that included a number of expletives, set his jaw and concentrated on looking straight ahead. Scott assured his classmate that she and her party were in no danger but it might be best if they postponed their visit until the next time they were in the area. He radioed to the Kanabec County car and without giving any details asked if they would kindly allow the visiting van to return down the driveway. Once the van was gone, Nick informed the officers in the two other vehicles why the drug bust had gone bust.

The warrant, however, was served, the warrantees (a young couple renting the farm and trying to make a go of it) were very cooperative, and no evidence of marijuana processing or dealing was found, and a search of the cornfield yielded only corn.

As far as Nick knew, the case was closed so he wondered why

Chapter 5

the sheriff had used it as an excuse to turn the fish company incident over to him. He wondered if it just wasn't an easy out for the sheriff so *he* wouldn't have to go back to the fish company.

* * * * *

Jack and Bob were relieved to have all the officials gone with no apparent suspicion that Ivar's body had actually been discovered a day earlier than what their story indicated.

"But we're not out of the woods yet," Jack said. "The white suits said we will probably need to make a formal statement. So we'd better get our stories straight because they'll no doubt want a statement from each of us. For all we know, we might be considered as suspects."

"Nah," Bob cut in, "I, at least have an alibi that Edith can confirm. You, on the other hand . . . ."

"Now wait just a minute," Jack exploded.

"Take it easy, Jack. I was just kidding. But I can't help but think that Marcie is somehow involved. I wish I knew what she knew of Ivar's finances. He once told me he didn't really need this job, but he liked to come here and meet the folk, and he said it gave him something to do. So he must have some sort of nest egg tucked away and his farm has got to be worth something."

"Well, since they aren't, uh I mean *weren't* married, she's not really entitled to anything, at least legally, is she?" asked Jack.

"Particularly if she's a murderer." Then Bob looked at his watch and said, "You know, she'll most likely be checking in here when she gets back so I say we should call the undertaker and get Ivar out of here before she shows up."

"Good idea," agreed Jack. "We've got fish to take care of and I guess we'd better get used to doing it ourselves. We can probably manage it for now. I'm sure glad this didn't happen before Christmas."

"Yah, maybe we'll wrap up this season a little early and then think about who we can hire for next year. Funny thing though how there aren't many guys out there who are beating down the door to work in a cold and smelly place."

Jack, who was pre-occupied with trying to find a number for the undertaker in the telephone book, murmured an "ah huh" and said, "How the hell do you even find an undertaker—there's no listing in the Yellow Pages."

"Try looking under Funeral Homes. You know, that gal who works at the funeral home in Braham lives just down the road. At least that's what Edith said. I guess she found that out when she went to old man Jesperson's funeral a couple of weeks ago. Edith said she was surprised that women were in that line of work."

"Well, that'd be handy—maybe cheaper too if she could come on by and take Ivar off our hands. I don't suppose you know her name."

"No, but you can find out easily enough by calling the place in Braham."

Jack, who finally had success with the telephone book said, "Found it. Big ad. Says they offer funeral and cremation services. Don't you think that's what we want—cremation, I mean. Who knows what Ivar would have wanted, but he sure isn't going to object."

"Sounds good to me but before we do anything too hasty, let's see what the funeral home has to say."

Jack was about to lift the handset when the telephone rang. He checked the caller id before he answered and whispered to Bob, "It's Marcie. What should I tell her? Or shouldn't I even answer?"

"We have to tell her sooner or later. Find out where she is and take it from there."

When Jack answered the phone, Bob pushed the speaker button so he could hear too. They discovered that Marcie was at Ivar's place. She said Ivar wasn't there and it looked like he

Chapter 5

hadn't been there for a while. There were dirty dishes in the sink and the Christmas presents he had for Bob's grandkids were still there too. She also said she'd tried calling his cell phone several times and there was no answer.

"When did you get back from Iowa?" Jack asked. "Ivar told me you were going to spend Christmas with your folks."

"Yeah, but I left early this morning. I wanted to stop in St. Cloud and catch the after-Christmas sales but when I couldn't reach Ivar, I got worried and I came straight here."

Jack and Bob looked at each other and Bob nodded, giving the go ahead to Jack to tell her the news.

So Jack started in by saying, "Uh, I'm afraid we have some bad news. We found Ivar here at the fish company this morning. Um, he was dead."

"Oh my God, my poor Ivar. What on earth happened?" exclaimed Marcie, stifling a sob.

"Well, near as we can tell, he somehow ended up in one of the fish tanks when he was cleaning up around here on Christmas Eve after Bob and I had left." "So you mean he drowned in that awful stuff you soak the fish in?"

"Well, we think he was dead before he went in there."

"Like a heart attack or something?"

"Um, most likely 'or something,'" Jack said, exchanging glances with Bob who was drawing an imaginary line across his throat to signal that Jack needed be careful in what he said next.

But Jack just shrugged his shoulders and continued relating to a now hysterical Marcie what they and the investigators surmised as to how Ivar had met his demise. He also explained that they'd talked to the sheriff, but he left out anything about the cell phone and the smoked fish. He did say, though, that the sheriff was already in the process of lining up some suspects. Bob rolled his eyes at that last statement.

"Well, I sure hope they catch the bastard who did this," sobbed Marcie. She then asked through her sobs, "Where is he now? Can I see him?"

Bob shook his head and Jack, not knowing quite what Bob had in mind, said, "Ugh, I'm a little choked up myself. Bob's right here and I'm going to the phone over to him."

Bob frowned at Jack but took the phone. "Yah, Marcie, terrible thing. We're working with the funeral home in Braham so we'll let you know when Ivar is ready for visitors. You take care now, you hear?"

With that, he hung up, knowing the next thing they had to do was call the sheriff and let him know Marcie was back in the area (assuming she had really left).

"Well, what did you think of that?" asked Jack.

"Hard to tell," Bob responded. "She's a cagey one, and I've seen her turn on her tears before. Guess we'll let the sheriff check out her alibi."

Bob called the sheriff's department and was told by Sheriff Erickson that Deputy Nordin would be handling the case. He said he'd relay the message and assured Bob that Nordin would be contacting Marcie real soon. "I've got her number, you know. Took it off that cellphone we found there on the corpse," he said. Then he ended with, "You guys have a good day now. Hope the next time I see you it will be under better circumstances."

Bob just shook his head while he hung up and then he handed the phone over to Jack and told him to go ahead and call the undertaker. Jack dialed the number and heard some clicking sounds after it rang, then no more rings, but after a few seconds a woman answered, "Megan Perry. How may I help you?"

"Uh, I was calling the funeral home. Must have the wrong number," Jack said.

"No, I'm one of the undertakers on call today so you do have the right number. Are you needing assistance with the death of a loved one?" she asked.

"That's right. I'm Jack Brewer from out at the Day Fish Company, and my brother Bob and I need to arrange a funeral

Chapter 5

for a friend of ours who passed away. Say, you aren't the undertaker who lives out this way, are you?"

"Yes, indeed. I'm buying the Greene place just south of Day."

After a few more pleasantries, Megan got down to business and gathered a few details. After hearing that the person who was now in need of her services had succumbed at the fish company and that there was no apparent immediate family, she said she was available to stop by and pick up the body and could also help them with the funeral arrangements. She did verify with Jack that he had the paperwork that gave the "okay" to proceed.

{ 6 }

Megan Perry had begun working with the Stone funeral home in Braham just four months earlier. It was her first appointment after receiving her degree in Mortuary Science from the University of Minnesota. Being a farm girl herself (growing up near Sleepy Eye), she was glad to land a job in another small town. It didn't take her long to find a farm for sale that had a decent house and a pole building. She'd spent the fall working on fences and building a couple of stalls in the barn for her two horses she was finally able to reclaim from her folks. When they brought the horses, they included the dog who had been a mere pup when Megan went away to college. It didn't take long before she adopted a few cats who had strayed to her place. She was already planning a garden for the next spring, and she had hopes of reclaiming the pasture acreage in order to raise a few grass-fed beef.

Megan drove by the fish company every time she went to work in Braham but had never stopped in. Lutefisk was not in her family's tradition, and she knew of it only from jokes she'd heard about it. Upon moving to east central Minnesota, however, she began to see its importance in the local culture. Even the cafés in Braham and the other towns around served it at holiday time. At several churches where she had assisted at funerals, she saw posters for their lutefisk dinners. She also had noticed in the weeks before Christmas there was considerably more traffic past

Chapter 6

her place. When she mentioned that observation to someone, she was told it was due to the lutefisk lovers making their pilgrimage to Day.

As soon as she hung up the phone after talking to Jack, she took off her coveralls and changed into the standard uniform for her line of work—a black pants suit with a tailored blouse (a decision she'd soon regret). She knew this first contact with the bereaved was crucial. She had to be sympathetic and businesslike at the same time. More than once she had encountered some skepticism about her abilities in what was generally considered a man's occupation, so she had to be particularly careful to present herself in a professional and confident manner.

Her plan was to drive up to the fish company, meet the proprietors, offer her condolences, take a quick look at the body, make sure the death certificate was in order, and initiate the preliminaries for the funeral arrangements. Once she had the information she needed to proceed, she'd call her associate, Wes, and ask him to bring out the hearse to transport the body to the funeral home.

Judging from her conversation with Jack, she figured that he, his brother and the deceased were over 50 years of age. Their day-to-day dealing with a major icon of Scandinavian heritage indicated they must be pretty traditional. Thus, she assumed the brothers would opt for a standard funeral, that is one where the body was embalmed, placed in a casket, viewed by mourners, memorialized at a service either in a church or at the funeral home, and then interred in a cemetery, most likely in a family lot.

But Megan knew only too well that there were now many variations to the "standard" funeral, something her boss, Mr. Stone, couldn't quite fathom. He'd been in the funeral business for almost forty years and seen funerals evolve from solemn and sacred occasions to events that bordered on festive. Yet, he had no choice but to go along with whatever the clients wanted. First,

Wes, Stone's assistant, had to talk him into accepting the idea that women could be pallbearers (if only honorary); Wes had also suggested it would be a nice touch to have a photo of the deceased printed in the memorial leaflet; and it wasn't long before he was encouraging Stone to expand their services to include videos of the deceased's life.

Because the pastors were in charge when a funeral was held at their respective churches, the funeral home had no control over what occurred at the actual service. But there was no mistaking Stone's dismay at some of the musical selections. Megan and Wes had both heard him rant: "What ever happened to the old funeral hymns like 'Rock of Ages,' and 'Just a Closer Walk with Thee'? Nowadays you're just as likely to hear 'On the Wings of a Snow White Dove' or that Rose song."

He also ranted about the practice of impromptu remembrances shared by those attending the funeral, and he was adamant that providing balloons was not one of the Stone Funeral Home services. Stone also had trouble accepting that the women of the churches often were not willing to prepare and serve a funeral lunch. He'd been told that many of the older women were no longer able to take on that responsibility and that many of the younger women were either working during the day or were simply not interested. "How much work can it be to throw together a few dozen sandwiches and some bowls of Jell-O?" he'd ask whoever was listening. "Next thing you know, they'll want us to provide catering services as well," he would grumble.

It was no secret that Wes would one day take over the business, and the old man was deferring more and more to him. When the former assistant moved on to be an associate at a funeral home in a northern suburb, it was Wes who had advocated for bringing in a woman as the new assistant. The old man just rolled his eyes and shrugged his shoulders giving Wes a "whatever" look. As it turned out, Stone seemed to genuinely like Megan, and he could find no complaints with her work.

Chapter 6

Wes had told Megan that a few years earlier, he had suggested that maybe it was time to consider installing a crematorium. Predictably, there was considerable sputtering from Stone, but when Wes enlightened him that they were losing business because they were not able to offer cremation services, Stone relented. Wes had already scouted an empty building in the next block, and it was a relatively simple task to retrofit it to accommodate a cremation chamber. However, neither Wes nor Stone had anticipated the growing popularity of cremation as a choice for disposition of a corpse. As the only crematorium within a radius of 20 miles, it became a destination for bodies handled by a number of funeral homes. Soon there were several cremations each week, sometimes two a day. While this new venture was quite lucrative for Stone's business, there was one major downside, and it was not long before there were complaints about degradation of the air quality in the downtown area during those times when the cremation chamber was in use.

When those complaints reached the ears of the city council members, an ultimatum was handed down to Stone—close the crematorium or move it to the fledgling industrial park on the edge of town. Stone, not wanting to create enemies of those who one day would require his services, would have likely closed the crematorium and gone back to business as usual. But under Wes' advisement, Stone took on the additional expense of having a building constructed in the industrial park which could house the cremation chamber. Luckily, Stone had been leasing the downtown building which the owner reclaimed for expansion of his exercise facility that advertised hot yoga, saunas and massage with hot rocks.

Megan drove the short distance to the fish company and noted the "dogs of Day" were maintaining their positions at the intersection of the two roads that formed the nucleus of this once-bustling community. Because she lived in the neighborhood, she knew to watch out for them, but she was concerned that someone unfamiliar with the territory might not heed the four-way stop sign and hit one or more of the dogs who didn't have time to get out of the way.

She pulled up to the fish company, grabbed her leather portfolio, and climbed out of her car. But before she even got to the door, she noticed a strong "fishy" smell. She also noticed the "closed" sign so she decided to knock. The door was soon opened, and she quickly introduced herself so whoever was at the door would know she was not a lutefisk customer. "Come on in. I'm Bob Brewer and this is my brother Jack. He's the one who called you." She stepped through the door and immediately knew that the smell she'd heard people laugh about was no laughing matter. Bob put out his hand, but Megan's free hand was already up against her nose.

Bob pulled his hand back and said, "Let's go to the office and get started." They invited Megan to sit on the sofa which the brothers used for on occasional cat nap if business was slow. If they got a quick break when business was brisk, they lay on the sofa for a few minutes to rest their feet after tromping around on cold concrete. Occasionally, they'd get a little too familiar with Mr. Beam, and more than one customer reported they had had to rouse one or the other of the brothers from a sound sleep on that couch in order to buy their lutefisk. While those customers could have helped themselves, most would not have risked grabbing a hunk of lutefisk from the wrong tank and getting splattered with lye. Not only that, the customer base that had developed over the years was genuinely grateful for having the opportunity to buy lutefisk directly from the manufacturer.

Bob took the chair behind the cluttered desk, and Jack sat on a folding chair he'd brought out from behind the door. That left Megan alone on the couch with plenty of room for her attaché case which held some brochures about the funeral home's services, a checklist of questions to ask so the funeral details could begin and a packet of tissues in case the bereaved needed

Chapter 6

them. In this instance, however, it was Megan who made use of a tissue.

Once her olfactory nerve hit the fatigue threshold and she wasn't quite so overcome by the fish smell, Megan had a chance to look around the office. Its clutter and its overall shabbiness, combined with the grimness of the salesroom, the cold clammy environment overall *and* the smell were good indications the place was sorely in need of some better business practices. She wondered what kind of a funeral the two brothers could even afford.

But putting on her best business persona, she got ready to go through her preliminary interview, realizing this case was a bit unusual. Normally a body is delivered to the funeral home and then the funeral director meets with the family members or whoever was going to be making the funeral arrangements (i.e. paying for them). It was only because she lived nearby that she had circumvented those regular procedures.

She asked to see the death certificate. As she looked it over to get the full name of the deceased, her eyes strayed to the "cause of death" blank. She gave a start when she saw the word "homicide." "Excuse me," she said, "I wasn't aware there was some criminal involvement in this death. I need to call my superior to find out...."

Before she could finish, Bob jumped in with, "All that's been taken care of." He handed her the papers from the medical examiner releasing the body. "The county sheriff's department is handling the investigation, but apparently they don't need the body anymore. So he's all yours."

Megan looked over the papers and determined that indeed arrangements could proceed. But then the thought struck her that maybe either one of the brothers, or perhaps both, were murder suspects. For all she knew, the sheriff was on his way there to arrest them. And here I am, she thought, alone in a creepy smelly place with one dead guy and two seemingly alive guys who make their living by selling rotting flesh. At that moment she just wanted to get out of there, so she said, "Listen, you are certainly under no obligation to have the Stone Funeral Home handle the arrangements. If you--"

But Bob cut her off saying, "No, no, we're sure. They took care of Ivar's mother and sister and probably his dad too for all I know."

"Yah, that's right," chimed in Jack. "And the sooner you can get him out of here, the better. We'd like to get things back to normal."

"Normal? thought Megan as she began to gather up her things. Out loud, she said, "Unfortunately, I can't transport a corpse in my car." For once, she was glad she had a small car. "I've got to run into Braham, and my associate and I will come right back with the hearse to take him off your hands."

"How long do you think that will take?" asked Bob.

"We should be back within an hour," replied Megan or not, she thought, if the sheriff doesn't give me the 'all clear.'

With that, she was out the door. She was barely into her car before she had speed-dialed Wes at the funeral home to fill him in on what had happened. He was a bit surprised at how shook she seemed because she normally had a pretty cool head. He said he'd have the hearse ready and waiting by the time she got there.

"Okay," she said, "I'll be there in fifteen minutes." She then hung up and floored her six-year-old Mazda Protégé as she headed east on County Road 4. Then she decided she'd better slow down as she approached the S-curve that seemed to harbor icy patches even when the rest of the road was clear. Her decrease in speed also allowed her to take a few deep breaths and regain her composure somewhat for the rest of the trip into Braham.

{ 7 }

As soon as Wes hung up the phone, he locked the front door of the funeral home and went out the back door to the garage where the hearse was parked. After backing it out of the garage, he took a spray bottle and a couple of cloths from the console cubby and began to polish the windshield. Depending on how much time he had, he'd do the headlights and the tail lights too. It wasn't so much that the hearse needed any extra cleaning (with its regular and almost obsessive cleanings, it was close to being the main support of the carwash in town). Instead the touch-ups were a ruse to foil the funeral home's busybody neighbors who assumed the only reason the hearse was out of the garage was that it was about to pick up a body.

A couple of busybodies whose houses had windows in view of the garage would even speculate about who was going to be getting a ride in the hearse. To deflect that speculation (if not anticipation), Wes began to randomly polish the hearse, sometimes when he was indeed going to pick up a body but other times when business was a little slow. Mr. Stone was actually quite pleased that the hearse was getting some extra attention without even asking that it be done, and he was even more pleased that he didn't have to pay for it.

In his years of working at the funeral home, Wes had dealt with a homicide only one other time. That one was the victim of what was first thought to be a deerhunting accident, but upon further investigation it was discovered that the two people involved had had a running feud for years. It didn't take long for the authorities to change the cause of death from accident to murder, particularly when the widow, upon hearing of her husband's demise, exploded with. "He'd never go hunting with that son of a bitch."

"Geez," he thought to himself, "Megan didn't even tell me what condition the corpse is in. From the way she was acting, it must not have been a pretty sight."

Just then Megan's car pulled up. She got out, grabbed her attaché case and headed over to where Wes was taking care of one last smudge.

When she got within a couple of feet from him, he wheeled around and said, "What's that smell?" He was just about to apologize, thinking maybe whatever had caused her to be so upset had also upset her bodily functions.

She seemed to acknowledge as much by saying, "This suit is ruined!" "Do you have anything you could change into?" Wes asked.

"What would be the use of that? Anything else I'd put on would get ruined too." Before Wes could offer any kind of consolation, Megan exclaimed, "It's that damned fish company. Anything and everything that even goes near the place reeks to high heaven. Here, take a whiff of my case," she said as she handed him the leather attaché case she'd received from her parents when she graduated from the U. "I bet it smells just like the place too. But I can't tell because I smell the same." Wes took the case and walked a few steps so he'd be outside the sphere of Megan's aromatic emanations. Then he held the case up to his nose. The cough he uttered gave Megan her answer, and tears began to well up in her eyes. This was a side of Megan Wes had never seen before. She'd been a rock when dealing with the grief and sorrow that goes with the funeral business. Wes thought it was strange that the loss of an outfit and a brief case could elicit such an emotional response.

He tried to think of something to say that would be sincere but wouldn't bring on a full sob scene, so he opted for the phrase he often used when folks had experienced a more significant loss: "Please accept my sincere condolences."

It was a phrase Megan knew well, and hearing it applied to her situation did bring her attention back into focus. She sighed and said, "Before I get into that hearse and endanger the upholstery, I've got to call the sheriff. I need to get some sort of official word that lets the fish company brothers off the hook for offing their employee."

Even though this wasn't a true emergency, she dialed 911 and was patched through to the sheriff's department. "Deputy Nordin here," a voice said. How can I help you?"

Megan identified herself and said she was about to head out to Day to pick up a corpse at the fish company. "I just wanted to make sure...."

But Nordin cut her off. "I need to put you on hold for a second."

Before Megan could protest, she heard the click and then only silence. On the other end Deputy Nordin's suspicions were aroused, having heard a woman first of all identify herself as an undertaker and secondly ask about the situation in Day. He wondered if this could be that Marcie babe trying to squeeze him for information. He turned to Deputy Bruce Hokanson who was also on duty and asked if there was a woman undertaker in Braham by the name of Megan.

"So which are you more interested in, if the undertaker is female or if her name is Megan?" Hokanson asked, chuckling. Then when he saw that Nordin was not amused, he said, "Yes, indeed right on both counts."

Nordin went back to the phone and resumed the connection saying, "I'm sorry, what was it you needed?"

Megan then said she just wanted to confirm it was safe to

pick up the body, seeing as how it had been a crime scene. Nordin assured Megan that the body was good to go.

"But maybe you could do me a favor," Nordin added. "Let me know the details about the funeral. I would like to be there and scope out the crowd--just in case any suspicious characters show up."

"Sure," Megan said. "Is this the best number to reach you?"

"I'll give you my cell number. Got a pencil and paper?"

"Sure thing," Megan replied, as Wes handed her the attaché case and she quickly found a pen and her notebook. She jotted down the number and hoped she would remember to call Nordin amid all the other details that went with planning a funeral.

Making a face while she closed up her case, Megan said to Wes, "If I smell this bad from only being in that place a few minutes, how bad must the corpse smell? After working in that place all fall and then spending time with a bunch of rotting fish, his odor must be off the scale."

Wes merely stifled a smirk at the pun Megan had uttered unknowingly. She continued, "If we put him in this hearse, even if he is in a body bag, you'll have a real cleaning job on your hands--maybe for years to come." "What do you suggest?" Wes asked.

"I was in such a hurry to get out of there I didn't get a whole lot of details about the funeral--only that there was no immediate family and that the Brewer brothers were presumably in charge of any and all arrangements."

"Hmm," said Wes, thinking again it was quite unusual for Megan to be so inattentive to basic details. "Let's go on out there and get to work. May as well have two suits to send to the dry cleaners."

They got into the hearse with Wes driving. Neither spoke until they were three miles out of town. Megan broke the silence. "I may have an idea."

"About a powerful new kind of air freshener?" Wes asked

nonchalantly.

"No, silly." Megan replied. "What would you think if we didn't bring the body to the funeral home?"

"So, what, we're all of a sudden out of the funeral business?" Wes asked.

"No," Megan replied, "But since Ivar's whole life seemed to revolve around the fish company, and with no family to speak of, why not let his friends and neighbors come to the fish company to pay their respects."

"Interesting idea, but I doubt Stone would go for it."

"But you were telling me how unhappy he was when he had to deal with the guy who fell into the sewage lagoon because he thought the stench would permanently taint the embalming room. I'd say this case is on par with that one."

"True," Wes replied, "but there will still be the matter of taking the corpse to the crematorium after any so-called visitation."

"So you must know someone who has a pickup truck."

"Geez, Megan!"

"Okay, let's focus first on trying to put some dignity into the situation. Now that I know the Brewers aren't suspects, I should be able to ask some decent questions in order get a better idea of what kind of a funeral they would like to provide for their longtime, loyal employee."

"All right, I'll leave it up to you, then, to suggest the onsite visitation. If they go for it, it will be all your idea. If they don't go for it, I'll tell Stone I tried all sorts of ways to avoid having the corpse brought to the funeral home," Wes said with a twinkle in his eye.

"Gee, thanks."

As they pulled up to the fish company, Jack's face could be seen in the office window. Obviously waiting for them, he opened the door and stepped out, indicating he wanted to speak to them. Wes rolled down the window, and Jack nervously asked him if he could please pull ahead a little farther so the hearse wouldn't be immediately visible to passersby. Wes complied, turned off the engine, and they went inside. Megan was just as taken aback by the smell as she had been earlier, but her primary attention was focused on Wes as he reacted with obvious aversion to the attack on his olfactory nerve.

While Wes was attempting to regain his professional composure, Megan introduced him to the Brewer brothers. They went into the office, and this time Megan and Wes squeezed onto the sofa. Bob took the desk chair and Jack the same folding chair. Megan reviewed with them what she knew so far. "So am I right that Ivar has, er, had no immediate family?" Both brothers nodded. "And what about a pastor? Was he a church-going guy?"

Jack jumped in with "Hell, no. Oh, in his early years he might have gone to Sunday School and was maybe even confirmed, but it's been years since he darkened the door of a church, except maybe to go to somebody's funeral."

Bob added, "He just naturally had a big heart that didn't come from anybody preaching to him."

That was all Megan needed to hear to broach the idea of holding the visitation for Ivar right there at the fish company. She put forth her rationale—that the fish company had pretty much been Ivar's whole life and everyone who knew him associated him with that place. Wes merely nodded his approval as he tried to find a comfortable position on the lumpy and sagging sofa.

Megan admitted the proposal was a bit unusual but under the circumstances, it seemed the most prudent way to proceed. That the proposal carried a considerable reduction in cost seemed to be the most significant factor in the brothers' decision to give their initial approval. With that, Megan asked Wes if he could go out to the hearse and find the necessary forms in her briefcase. Her query had a two-fold purpose--to give Wes a break from the smell and to avoid having to bring her briefcase back into the fish company.

Chapter 7

Megan was well aware that no form in her briefcase would include an option for an *in situ* visitation. Not only was this one to be exactly at the site where the death had occurred, but the death carried with it questionable circumstances. She had been so intent on getting the venue changed to the fish company that she had not really thought out any of the details. She knew time was of the essence. Judging from the current temperature in the place, it was about the same as in the cold storage facilities where some bodies were kept for burial in the spring after the ground thawed.

A "regular" funeral would usually be held four or five days from the date of death. Since this was already day three as far as she could tell, and there had been no embalming Megan thought the visitation should occur on Wednesday at the latest. That would allow for the word to get out through the regular channels, aka the grapevine. Then, those who wished could don the clothes they usually reserved for trips to the fish company and pay their respects to a guy whom they assumed would always be there.

Along with the forms Wes brought in from the hearse was the generic checklist of any and all possible items that could be included in a proper sendoff -- beginning with the type of casket and ending with the color of balloons to be released at the grave site (over Stone's objections.). Each item carried a suggested price, so the total cost of a funeral could be easily calculated by adding up the numbers next to the check marks. The standard procedure was to get the necessary information from the party paying the bill, proceed through the checklist, provide an estimate of costs based on what was checked and then request a signature. Inevitably there would be some consternation exhibited upon hearing the cost estimate, so of course, there was room for negotiation. In a small town the financial resources of the deceased were usually known (at least generally), so the caring funeral planner would have a pretty good idea of which items on the checklist could be ignored and which could be adjusted.

In this case the number of check marks would be minimal, so Megan opted instead to make suggestions as to how best to undertake this unusual situation. Megan surmised that the word "dignity," which the Stone funeral home used liberally, would soon become a relative term. No amount of euphemism could deem this setting "dignified." Yet apart from that anomaly, the planned visitation would bear considerable similarity to one held in the funeral home on the eve of a more traditional memorial service.

Megan's first suggestion was that any notices, whether written or oral, should emphasize that the event at the fish company would be the sole opportunity to wish Ivar well on his next journey. "Wouldn't you agree?" she asked Wes while giving him a look indicating he had better not disagree. Bob Brewer seemed to catch on to what Megan was driving at.

"I see what you mean," he said. "While practically everybody for miles around knew Ivar or at least knew who he was, there probably aren't that many people who would be coming here without buying anything."

That hadn't been exactly Megan's point, but before she had a chance to clarify the fact that mourners needed to understand that this event was not a prelude to a funeral—it WAS the funeral, Wes cleared his throat and then in his best funeral planning voice laid out his idea for the logistics of the event. "There's not much room here for a crowd, assuming there will be one, so it will be best if folks come in and go directly to the fish room, file around the tank where Ivar is laid out, proceed back into the customer area and exit. We can provide instructions for the mourners and keep the line moving. We can also hand out our standard memorial folder with a few details about Ivar."

Megan nodded her approval at the same time wondering how she would gather enough details about Ivar's life to warrant a memorial folder. But she put that thought aside for later and said, "Wes' plan also offers us the opportunity to observe everyone

Chapter 7

who comes by. Sheriff Nordin has asked our help in keeping an eye out for any suspicious characters."

"And what about us?" asked Bob.

Megan deferred to Wes, who said, "I'm thinking there's no real need for you to be here. We want to keep any chit-chat to a minimum and make it a solemn occasion for those who mourn Ivar's passing. "

Jack, who had been sitting quietly by with his head bowed in either some sort of meditation or drowsiness, suddenly said, "I have an idea. Why not have everyone go to the Dusty Eagle after the wake or whatever we're calling it?"

"That was next on my list," Megan said. "I think it's an excellent idea. There may be those who aren't available for the event here." What she was thinking, of course, was that there were those who would rather not become tainted with the smell of lutefisk but who would still like to pay their respects. "You guys could serve as the hosts there, and we'd have extra folders to hand out." She paused briefly and then continued, "Speaking of the memorial folder, what can you tell me about Ivar? Do you even know his birthdate or where he was born or how long he'd lived in the area?"

The next few minutes were taken up with Jack and Bob offering as much as they knew about Ivar. They only had a guess about his age – somewhere around 80—but they did know his birthday was October 14 because they always celebrated it when they were gearing up for the annual fish processing business.

"I think he was born in the house where he lived and never lived anywhere else. He took care of his mother for a number of years after his dad died, and when she was gone, he just stayed on."

"That's good," said Megan. "I can work up something that will reflect how he's been a long-time member of the community, but if you think of anything else that could be included, let me know by tomorrow night at the latest. I'll give you my cell phone number. Any examples of what you said earlier about his 'big heart' would be good to include. And I really should have a firm birth date."

"Okay," said Bob, "but I have some questions. How much will all this cost?

And what do we say when someone asks us about how Ivar died?"

Wes, who had been looking over Megan's shoulder while she was jotting notes quickly added some figures in his head — costs for the cremation, of course, 100 memorial folders and the fee for transporting the body to the crematorium. There'd be no need to charge for the current trip — call it a joy ride. Rather than give the two brothers a firm figure, though, he said, "We ought to be able to do this for less than $2500."

He saw Bob's eyes get big and was afraid he might protest when Jack said, "That's a helluva lot cheaper than what I had to come up with for Dorothy's funeral."

Since cost was not apparently going to be a factor, Wes continued, "As for what to say about how Ivar died, I suggest you ask Deputy Nordin for some advice on that one. It shouldn't be a problem during the visitation here as Megan and I will keep people moving. If anyone asks us, we can refer them to Nordin also. Of course, I'm sure tongues will be wagging, so by the time folks get to the Dusty Eagle, there will no doubt be plenty of questions and you'd better be prepared."

"Okay, then," Megan said. "I guess we all know what our jobs are." She handed Bob her card with her cell number, shook hands with both brothers and started for the door, eager to get out of there. At the same time, she was dreading that she'd have to come back to the place again in a couple of days. Wes also shook hands with Bob and Jack, and soon both he and Megan were out in the fresh air.

{ 8 }

By the time Wes and Megan left the fish company, it was dark. While there was still a streetlight to indicate there had at one time been some sort of town here (Megan had at times wondered who paid the electric bill for the light), its beam did not reach the driveway alongside the fish company where the hearse was parked. At least the light from the fish company office window allowed Wes to find the door handle, and once he opened the door there was light enough for Megan to find her way to the other side.

"Well, we made it," Megan uttered as she sank down into the seat and breathed a sigh of relief.

"Yes, indeed. I guess this is where it would be appropriate to say, 'Uffda,'" Wes responded as he backed out of the driveway. Just as he began to turn onto the road, they both heard a yelp and a simultaneous thud.

Wes yelled, "What the hell was that?" as he slammed on the brakes.

Megan groaned, "Oh no, those damn dogs."

They were both getting out of the car when the door to the fish company opened and Bob and Jack came out to see what had happened. At first they didn't see anything, but when the ever-vigilant Wes shone his pocket penlight under the hearse, Bob looked underneath and verified that indeed there was what appeared to be a lifeless form of a dog.

"Jesus," said Wes.

"Oh don't feel too bad," said Jack. "I can't tell you how many times I've come close to hitting one of those dogs that insist on laying out here in the street."

Since the dog was well under the car and out of reach, Bob told Wes, "I think if you crank the steering wheel the other way and back up real slow, we'll be able to get the critter out, so we can take a better look at him. Jack, you keep watch for any cars coming."

Wes got back into the hearse and did what he was advised. He stopped when Bob held up his hand. With the help of the streetlight and the hearse's headlights, Bob could see that the dog belonged to Pat Brown, who lived in the apartment above what had once been the general store. Bob glanced up at the apartment windows, and noticing they were all dark, said, "I think he usually gets home around six. I suppose the dog was out here waiting for him." Seeing light in the other three houses in the town, he surmised, "I guess this pooch's pals had already gone home for the night."

"Say Bob," said Jack, "you know, if we're not going to be open until after this wake or whatever were calling it is over, we've got some work to finish up yet tonight. We'll keep an eye out for Brown, and when he comes home, we can tell him what happened. How about if we put the pooch inside for now?"

"Well okay, I just hope Brown doesn't wait too long to get back here. I don't fancy having that dog in there any longer than necessary."

"It might be good company for Ivar," Jack replied. Megan and Wes looked at each other and rolled their eyes. Jack continued, "I think Ivar was sneaking a few dog treats to these mutts. That's probably why they hung around the fish company."

"Gee, I have never run over a dog before. I feel just awful. What should I do?" asked Wes. "I really can't hang around until

Chapter 8

Brown gets home. But you tell him to give me a call, and I'll gladly offer some compensation or something," said Wes.

"Oh, you don't need to worry about that," offered Jack. Looking at the dog, he said, "This guy wasn't likely to win best of show. He was probably some stray that was wandering around until Brown took him in. It was an accident after all, wasn't it?" He glanced over at Wes who was about to protest, but then Jack assured him he was just kidding.

Bob then grabbed the dog by his hind legs. Jack held the door open, and all three disappeared into the fish company.

Megan and Wes got back in the hearse and headed for Braham. Neither one said anything for a while. Finally, Wes said, "Well, that was something."

Megan thought to herself that that was classic Wes. They had just spent a very strange afternoon and had what were no doubt a couple of unique experiences in their respective careers in the funeral business. She could have added some more descriptive comments but said only, "I guess today might be chalked up to those circumstances that don't get covered in mortuary science school."

She continued, "It may be that our clothes are ruined for good, but until we trash them completely, we may as well keep them as is and put them on again for when we have to go back on Wednesday. I'll just hang my suit on a hanger in the screened porch so it can at least air out. What about you? Do you have some place to hang yours? Or maybe I should ask if you have another suit you could wear for regular business tomorrow?"

"Of course I have another suit. And yes, my back porch will work just fine. We better both hope though there aren't any mink around who might think the smell will lead them to an easy dinner."

"The other thing, and I don't know why I didn't think of this before, we need something to drape over both Ivar and that fish tank he's resting on. And I may have just the ticket."

Oh boy, thought Wes. This ought to be good. "Dare I ask what you have in mind?"

"I must have a half-dozen quilts my grandma made for me, presumably for my hope chest, and each one she gave me was uglier than the last. How about if I bring one of those, and it will actually serve two purposes as we can use it to wrap around Ivar when we remove him from the premises."

"Sounds like a plan to me," replied Wes.

Back at the fish company Bob deposited the dog in the room with the fish tanks (and Ivar). Then he called home to tell Edith that Ivar had met with an accident and that yes, he was dead. After Edith got over her initial shock, she switched into her neighborhood action mode and asked how she could help. Bob explained about plans for the event at the fish company and the gathering afterward at the Dusty Eagle. "You need to get that telephone tree thing going," he said. "Call everyone you know and tell them to call everyone they know. Oh, and call the Dusty Eagle and tell them there's going to be a big crowd on Wednesday. They can help get the word out too. Oh, and one more thing – I'm not exactly sure of Ivar's birth date so if you know somebody who knows, get that too. And when you call people, jot down anything they say that could be used in the obituary."

Bob reached in the desk drawer for the bottle of Jim Beam and helped himself to a healthy swig. Jack was in the back room checking the tanks of fish to determine which ones needed attention. At first he tried to avoid looking at Ivar, but then he thought, what the hell, so he started up a rather one-sided conversation with him. As Bob came through the plastic strip door to see how he could help Jack, he thought perhaps Mr. Beam had messed with his hearing. But no, there was Jack talking away in some sort of trip down memory lane. Bob cleared his throat to let Jack know he was approaching, and Jack cleared his throat in return, saying, "Uh, I was just checking these tanks. We need

Chapter 8

fresh water in this one, but the rest should be okay until things get back to normal."

"If that's possible," muttered Bob. "Here, I'll give you a hand. You start the drain going, and I'll get the hose rigged up. "

Just then Bob's cell phone rang. He headed back to the office, not wanting to be interrupted by either Jack's conversation or the banging around with the fish tanks.

"Hello," he said.

"Deputy Nordin here," the voice on the other end of the line said. "Sorry to bother you, but I'm wondering if you have an address for that Marcie woman."

"Do you mean local, or where her folks supposedly live?"

"Local, for now. I want to question her and see if her alibi holds up."

"Well, she did call here earlier today and said she was at Ivar's place and had wondered if we'd seen him. We had to tell her the bad news. Gee, I hope we didn't say too much."

"She'd find out sooner or later. I think I'll take a run out there tomorrow and maybe catch her off guard."

"Good idea. By the way, we decided to leave Ivar right here and let people come by and pay their respects. The funeral home in Braham is in charge, and everything is all set for the day after tomorrow at 4:00. Then afterwards folks will get together at the Dusty Eagle. Should be a good send-off. About the only thing that would ruin it is if Marcie is there blubbering away about her beloved Ivar." Bob paused for a second and then continued, "Say, since she's a suspect in this thing, or at least a person of interest, as they say on TV, do you think you could arrest her and put her in jail for a couple of days so we won't have to worry about her?"

"That would be highly irregular, but I see what you mean. I suppose I could get by with it on the grounds that I'd be checking out her alibi."

"That's it! And to my way of thinking you're not stretching the law, not even one little bit."

"I'll see what I can do. A lot will depend on how the meeting with her goes. I'll keep you posted." When he hung up, Nordin wondered why he had said that. He was under no obligation to let the fish company brothers know anything about the investigation.

Bob took another healthy swig of Jim Beam and then went to check on Jack's progress with draining the tank. Apparently Jack had gotten weary of the lopsided conversation he'd been carrying one as all was quiet except for the gurgling of the drain as the lutefisk liquid disappeared to some unknown point under the floor. Bob handed the bottle to Jack who took considerably more than a nip, and the two proceeded with their fishy business.

They were just about done when there was a rap on the door. Bob and Jack glanced at each other and then Bob said, "I'll get it." He opened the door and was relieved to see it was someone he knew but then not so relieved when he realized it was Pat Brown, the dead dog's owner.

"I saw there was a light on and just wanted to tell you how sorry I am about Ivar," Brown said. When Bob looked a little surprised, Brown continued, "I got a call on the way home from my girlfriend who works at the Dusty Eagle."

Wow, thought Bob, this telephone tree thing is really working. Aloud, he said, "Uh, thanks. But I'm afraid I have some bad news for you. You know that dog of yours who has a habit of lying out in the street? Well, a black dog on a black street...."

Before he could finish, Brown interjected, "How bad is it?" Bob, trying to look sorrowful, said, "He didn't make it. It happened about an hour ago so we brought him in here until you got home."

While Brown looked around for his former pet, he said, "I figured it would happen sooner or later. The only other option was to keep him tied up while I was away. I figured it was better to let him run free and spend the days with his pals even though it might mean he'd come to this kind of an end."

Chapter 8

Just then Jack poked his head through the plastic strips to see what was going on. When he realized it was Brown who had stopped by, he quickly ducked back into the fish tank area. He bent down to grab hold of the canine corpse and dragged it across the floor out into the customer area. When he stood up, as quickly as he could, he said, "Kind of ironic, don't you think?" Jack asked, "for an undertaker to run over a dog? It sort of flies in the face of the friendly service they're always advertising."

"Undertaker?" asked Brown.

Bob explained what had happened and assured Brown that the dog's death was instant.

"Let's just put him outside. I'll go get my wheelbarrow, and you guys can go on home. The ground is probably too frozen for me to dig a hole for him, but I've got that big brush pile I was going to burn on New Year's Eve so Sport here can just be added to it."

Jack, holding the door for Brown to get the dog back outside, said, "Good idea. It's sort of like killing two birds with one stone."

With the dog taken care of, the fish tanks in good order, and the arrangements for Ivar handled, it was time to call it a day at the fish company. The brothers grabbed their jackets, made sure the "closed" sign was still on the door, turned out the lights, shut the door and locked it securely behind them and headed home.

When Wes and Megan got back to the funeral home, Wes parked the hearse in the garage and they went inside. Mr. Stone was there, and they were no sooner through the door when he said, "Whew. Smells like you guys have been out lutefisk hunting." Megan then realized she and Wes were the embodiment of the tales she'd heard how the lingering odor on lutefisk customers is clear evidence of where they have been.

They then proceeded to fill Stone in on the day's happenings, but they neglected to mention the part about the demise of the dog. They related details about the suspicious death, Ivar's loyalty to the fish company and his lack of any known relatives.

To prime Stone about their rather irregular plan to hold the wake at the fish company, they perhaps overemphasized the risk of permanently sullying the funeral home if the corpse were brought there. Wes reminded Stone of the sewage lagoon victim. Stone frowned, scratched his head for a moment (which he often did when he was faced with having to make a decision) and then told them it was undoubtedly a good idea because the visitation for old man Engstrom was scheduled for Thursday at the funeral home. "That will be a big one, and you know how fussy his wife is. She'd wouldn't be happy if the place smelled like leftover lutefisk. I was just on my way out to go pick him up down at the hospital, so I'm glad you guys got the hearse back here. It's good to go, right?"

Megan and Wes looked at each other before Megan said, "You tell us. I imagine we left a little lingering aroma, but we couldn't exactly tell."

"I'll get that air freshener and spray it around real good," said Wes. "That should at least take the edge off. And when you get back, leave the windows open. In fact, you might want to drive down to Cambridge with the windows open, so bundle up."

{ 9 }

THE NEXT MORNING Nordin reported to the sheriff's department at his usual time of 8:00, wearing a spare uniform. He reviewed his notes from the day before and put a call into the medical examiner's office to inquire when his report would be ready. He was told it would be faxed yet that morning.

He needed to call that Marcie woman to make an appointment to meet with her but he wanted to see the ME's report first. From what he'd heard about her, she might have already skipped town with a carload of Ivar's stuff. He took the chance that he'd soon see the report, so he picked up the phone and punched in the number that had been in Ivar's cell phone memory.

He wondered if she'd even answer when she saw that the call was coming from the sheriff's department, but after three rings she answered.

"Yes," she said abruptly.

"Uh, this is Deputy Sheriff Nick Nordin, and I'm the head investigator handling the Ivar Peterson case...."

Before he could continue, she interrupted, "And just what are you doing to find whoever it was that did in my poor Ivar?" Then she started sobbing.

Nordin, ignoring her question, said, "Well, it seems like you knew him better than anyone so I'd appreciate any help you could give me in tracking down some leads. How about if I stop by this afternoon—say about two o-clock?"

Amidst her sobs, she replied rather sweetly, "I'm pretty distraught right now. Can't this wait for a few days?"

"I'm sorry, ma'am, but in these types of cases, it's always best to. . . ." He was going to say, 'strike while the iron is hot' but he quickly decided to respond instead with "act as quickly as possible." Then without letting her come up with an excuse, he said, "I'll see you at two this afternoon."

As Nordin was checking his other messages, Sheriff Erickson poked his head in the door and without even saying good morning he asked, "So how's it going in Department of Fish and Wildlife this morning?" Then he laughed heartily at his own joke.

Nordin was not amused and just answered matter-of-factly, "I'll know more after I see the medical examiner's report, and I made an appointment to visit the deceased's so-called girlfriend this afternoon."

"That oughta be interesting. From what we know already, she's quite the lady." As he said, "lady," he made quotation mark signs with the index fingers of both hands. "Sure you don't want one of the other deputies to ride along in case she gets a little frisky?" He laughed again.

Nordin replied, "I think I can handle this, Sheriff."

The sheriff ambled on down the hall to his own office, and while Nordin was getting his second cup of coffee for the day, his cell phone rang.

It took him a moment to recognize the name "Perry" on the caller ID. By the third ring, he answered with a simple, "Hello" instead of with his official voice.

"Sheriff Nordin?" the caller asked.

"Yes, this is Deputy Nordin," Nick replied.

"This is Megan Perry with the Stone Funeral Home. I wanted to call and tell you about the funeral arrangements for Ivar Peterson."

And even though the Brewer brothers had already filled him in, Nordin let Megan describe the details. While Nordin had

Chapter 9

never met her, he liked the sound of her voice, curt and businesslike. It was a young voice, he figured, perhaps even belonging to someone under thirty, and he wondered how he could find out if she was married or had a significant other. But for now, he decided he'd better play the deputy sheriff role and be professional.

"Thanks for the update," he said. "I know I said I would be there to make a few observations, but I think I would be too obvious at the fish company."

"Okay," Megan said, "But folks are bound to ask questions about how Ivar died. Any tips for how we should respond?"

"The less said, the better," replied Nordin. "You could say something like 'the cause of death is under investigation' or 'the authorities are looking into it'. And, of course, if you notice anything really suspicious, you can always give me a call. I am thinking of dropping by the Dusty Eagle in my civilian clothes to eavesdrop on a few conversations."

"You won't have any trouble telling who was at the wake and who wasn't," Megan said.

It took Nordin a few seconds to figure out what she meant and then he said, "Oh, because of how they smell, you mean?"

"Exactly," said Megan.

"Will the funeral home be represented there?" asked Nordin.

"No, our job is done once all the mourners leave the fish company and we remove the corpse for cremation. I suppose I could stop by the Dusty Eagle though, just as a neighbor. I do go there occasionally for a burger since I live out that way."

"Okay, maybe I'll see you there. I'll be one of the fresh-smelling ones."

"After a hot shower and a total change of clothes, I might be too," Megan said rather whimsically.

When Nordin hung up, he realized he was actually looking forward to the quasi-investigation where he might discover something much more interesting than leads to who murdered

Caught in the Lye

Ivar Peterson.

As promised, the medical examiner's report came by fax at 11:30, so Nordin had time to read it and grab some lunch before he headed out to interview the only lead so far, Ivar's girlfriend Marcie.

The report didn't reveal anything new for Nordin. Death was caused by a blow to the back of the head with a blunt object. Time of death was listed at approximately 5:00 p.m. on December 24. However, Nordin suspected the time had been determined more by what the Brewer brothers had told the medical examiners than by any concrete forensic evidence—lying in lye was not conducive to providing reliable indications of rigor mortis, body temperature or state of decomposition.

On the way out to the interview, he thought about how different the northern part of the county was from the southern part. Erickson had told him when he came on board at the sheriff's department that most of his work was going to be south of Highway 95. That's where the concentration of new homes was, and Erickson maintained that the folks living there were not from the same stock as the farmers they displaced had been.

"Hell, they work in the cities, spend a couple of hours on the road each day, they're bushed when they get home, and meanwhile their kids are running rampid. Soon one of the neighbors is callin' the sheriff, either because some of their stuff is missing and they're blaming the rampid kids or they think those same kids are smoking dope or worse. Then before you know it, all the stress gets to the parents and they start bickering and fighting and *they're* callin' the sheriff."

Erickson had continued his diatribe with, "When I started as sheriff, it was just me and one deputy and now look at us. We've got ten deputies, a bunch of investigators and some patrol sergeants. . . . " From talking to the other deputies, Nick knew the workload in the department had indeed increased over the last few years. He had certainly seen a few "rampid" kids in his

Chapter 9

shifts as deputy, and he'd been called in on a few domestic abuse cases. They were mainly in the southern part of the county. That's why it seemed a bit odd that the only murder investigation of the year and the largest drug bust (however bungled) were both centered around the northwest quadrant of the county, which was the least populated.

Nordin chuckled a bit to himself when he thought about the sheriff's department Christmas party a couple of weeks ago. The county coordinator had been invited, and she found it obligatory to make a few remarks, applauding the good work of the department. She couldn't help but use the opportunity to recite her standard mantra of how great it is to live and work in the county. To emphasize her point, and in an effort to be jocular, she turned to Sheriff Erickson and asked, "So how many murders or other violent crimes has your department handled this year?" Erickson, knowing how to play the game, puffed out his chest and replied, "Not a one, ma'am." The group assembled broke out in wild applause and cheers— but Nordin remembered seeing a few gritted teeth and hearing barely audible groans from some of the deputies.

As Nordin pulled into the driveway at Ivar Peterson's farm, he drove rather slowly so he could get an idea of how the farm was laid out. He first saw a barn that had seen its better day. He wondered how long it had been since it had been a viable farm building. Then further up the driveway he saw the house where Ivar had lived all of his 82 years. It looked sturdy enough, but the paint was peeling and a side porch was listing pretty badly like it soon might come loose from the main part of the house. There were a few other outbuildings that appeared to have been a granary and a chicken coop. While both were still standing, they looked quite forlorn. The whole setting didn't match Nordin's idea of a little love nest, so he was even more curious about the woman he'd come to interview. May as well get it over with, he thought as he stepped from his squad car and headed toward the house, taking time to jot down the license number of the car parked close to the house.

Before Nordin could even knock on the door, it was flung open by the inhabitant. Marcie eyed him up and down and said, "You must be Nordin." And then looking beyond him out towards his car, she said, "You come alone?" Before Nordin could answer, she continued, "I thought maybe they'd send a whole posse. The sheriff's department is kinda known for being a little overenthusiastic."

Nordin wondered if her assessment was from personal experience, or if she just wanted to catch him off guard. Rather than explain that yes, he was alone, he handed her his business card and said, "I'm Deputy Nordin. As I mentioned in our telephone call, I'd like to ask you a few questions about Ivar Peterson. May I come in?"

Now it was Marcie who was taken off guard as she wasn't expecting either such a young deputy nor one who actually had some manners. She motioned to him to come inside, and she pointed to a chair at the kitchen table. Since the only impression he'd had of his prime suspect came from the messages left on Ivar's cell phone, he knew only that she could certainly reel off a bunch of so-called sweet nothings and that her language was replete with sexual connotations reminiscent of almost steamy romance novels.

From the Brewer brothers he'd gathered she was considerably younger than Ivar, and that alone had been fodder for gossip around the neighborhood. Now that Nordin had come face to face with the woman, he could see that yes, she was definitely younger than Ivar's 82, but he was unable to tell which of life's decades she fit into. At one time, Nordin surmised, she may actually have been quite attractive, but now her face bore a severity indicating she'd seen some rough times. Nordin's colleagues in his previous job in South Dakota would have described her as "ridden hard and put away wet."

Chapter 9

Of course, being questioned by someone in law enforcement doesn't exactly lend to the softening of anyone's countenance, but as Nordin sat across the table from the woman he'd come to interview, he was more than a little uncomfortable by her set jaw and piercing eyes. He wondered for an instant if he should have brought another deputy with him.

Then, as if a switch had been turned, she put her head in her hands and began to sob. "Oh boy," thought Nordin, "This is like something out of Law Enforcement 101." He remembered his instructor saying that the first thing a suspect will do is turn on the tears in an effort to gain your sympathy. So Nordin did what he'd also been instructed and said, "I know this is a difficult time for you, but I do need to ask you a few questions."

Marcie stifled a sob, and said, "I know what you're thinking. You think that . . . ."

But Nordin cut her off in order to get back on track. While he was tempted to give her a line about how he was interviewing several people who had known Ivar, and she was just one of many persons of interest, he got right to the point and asked, "Where were you on the afternoon of Christmas Eve?"

Marcie seemed to straighten up a bit at such a direct question and said, "I was in Iowa."

"Where in Iowa?" Nordin asked.

"Near Cedar Falls."

"And what time did you leave from here?"

"As soon as Ivar left that morning to go to the fish company."

"Can you be more precise?"

As quickly as the tears had started, they had stopped. Now there was just impatience in Marcie's voice when she answered, "Seven minutes after nine, that's A.M."

Nordin ignored her sarcasm and proceeded to ask when she had arrived in Iowa and if she had stopped anywhere along the way. He also asked if there were people in Iowa who could verify she had been there, and he added, "Of course, I'll check all the information you've given me."

"Of course," Marcie replied with a sneer.

"It shouldn't take more than a couple of days. In the meantime, I'd like you to come with me."

"What?" Marcie exclaimed. "Are you arresting me?"

"Let's just say I'm detaining you temporarily. You'll be released just as soon as your alibi checks out."

"Can you do that?" asked Marcie who had risen from her chair and was looking as if she was going to make a run for the door.

Nordin, also rising, realized he was in a precarious position, not only because Marcie might escape but also because the proffered detainment was a ruse suggested by the Brewer brothers to keep her away from any of the so-called funeral arrangements for Ivar. He was somewhat astonished at his quick reply: "It's a good idea that you be kept in a safe place for a few days. Whoever murdered Ivar is still on the loose and could be coming after you next."

Marcie eyed Nordin suspiciously from where she stood. Then she challenged him with, "Okay, but you'll find that everything I've told you is true, and while you're at it, you find the bastard that killed Ivar." With that she grabbed her coat, and said, "Let's go."

Nordin was a little taken aback at her compliance because he'd assumed he'd have to cuff her. Nick followed her out to the car and watched as she willingly got into the back seat. She sat with her arms clasped in front of her and put a scowl on her face. As Nick headed down the driveway, he radioed that he was bringing in a detainee. On the way into Cambridge, he observed Marcie in the rearview mirror, and he wondered if her sullenness was from grief or guilt. He'd have a better idea once he checked her alibi.

{ 10 }

With Marcie safely behind bars (and it certainly had seemed as though she was familiar with the procedures for being admitted to a jail), Nordin's task at hand was verifying her whereabouts on the afternoon of Christmas Eve. But first he stopped by Sheriff Erickson's office and filled him in on his interview with Marcie and try to explain why he'd brought her in as a detainee.

Erickson stroked his chin and said, "That's not the way we usually do things around here, but like you say, she very well could be a suspect. How long you thinking of keeping her?"

Nordin replied, "She'll be free to go when and if her alibi checks out. I'm going to get started on that yet this afternoon. I plan to be done by tomorrow evening so I'd say she could be released sometime Thursday morning." He hesitated only briefly before adding, "It's too bad she'll miss the send-off for Ivar."

Erickson looked at him rather quizzically. But then thinking back to his and Nordin's visit to the fish company and remembering both the obvious disdain the Brewer brothers had for Ivar's lady friend and those steamy cell phone messages she'd left, he began to laugh heartily. "I see where you're coming from, Nordin. Pretty clever. The Brewers and the whole community out there should be mighty thankful they can pay their respects without having some floozy hanging around."

Thinking his chat with the boss was over, Nordin turned to

leave but then Erickson said, "Thursday morning, ay? Well I just might have to find an excuse to visit the dining room before then so I can get a look at the dame who sends such mushy messages."

Nordin rolled his eyes as he left Erickson's office and headed back to his own. The next order of business was for Nordin to call the gas station where Marcie said she had stopped near Austin. Luckily the station had video security, so the manager said he would check for cars like hers from about noon to 3:00 p.m. on Christmas Eve.

Nick also called the number Marcie had given him for her mother in Hudson, Iowa. That call revealed some surprises. The woman who answered said, "No, Marcie's mother is not here." Her voice was ragged and rough, indicating she had most likely smoked a few too many cigarettes.

"Do you know where I can reach her?" Nordin asked.

Amid either a laugh or a cough (Nordin couldn't tell which), she said that that might be difficult as Marcie's mother had been dead for 15 years.

"I see," said Nordin. Then he proceeded to explain why he was calling.

"Oh yes, she was here all right," the woman said. "Is she in some kind of trouble?"

Nordin thought it was odd Marcie hadn't let the woman know about Ivar's untimely passing, but instead of answering the woman's question he asked, "Do you remember what time she got to your place?"

"Hmm. I'd say it was about four in the afternoon."

"On Christmas Eve, right."

"Yup, that's right."

"Were you expecting her?"

Again, the cough/laugh, "If you mean, did I invite her, no, but she has a habit of showing up at the damnedest times. And then leaving without even saying goodbye."

"So when did she leave this time?"

Chapter 10

"She was gone by the time I got up the day after Christmas."

"And she hasn't checked in with you?" Nordin asked, wondering if Marcie had called the woman to substantiate her alibi.

"Nope, and I probably won't hear from her until the next time she shows up on my doorstep."

"Do you have any idea why she said this was her mother's number?" Nordin asked.

"Well, seeing as how you're a cop, I'm thinking she didn't want to let you know right off the bat we'd done time together."

That explains a lot, Nordin thought. Then he said, "I think I have everything I need. Thanks for your help."

"No problem, but tell Marcie that the next time she needs me to vouch for her, [cough, cough] I'd rather not be referred to as her mother. She's older than I am, for God's sake."

Nordin hung up the phone and wondered if what he had just heard was the truth. Of course, even if it was, Marcie's alibi didn't rule out the possibility she had an accomplice who actually committed the murder. But what was the motive? And what about the items found in Ivar's pants? Or was that all a ruse to get them off track?

Nordin called Bob Brewer to assure him he wouldn't have to worry that Marcie would be at the wake for Ivar. Brewer thanked Nick, who didn't think it was necessary to go into detail about where Marcie was or how long she'd be there. He thought Brewer sounded rather subdued, if not exhausted, and he wondered if that was because Brewer was mourning the loss of a friend or the loss of business that could have been generated during the days when the fish company was closed.

The wake was set for 3:00 to 5:00 on Wednesday. Wes had assured Megan he'd handle the transportation of the corpse to the crematorium, and while she wondered what kind of a scheme he'd planned, she didn't ask. On Tuesday, she'd been in touch with Edith Brewer, who had offered a few details about Ivar

Peterson's life. She'd even found a picture of Ivar which Megan was able to include in the memorial folder. Since Edith didn't have the means or the expertise to send the photo electronically, she drove into Braham to deliver the photo to the funeral home. Megan digitally scanned the photo while Edith waited and then placed it into the memorial folder template. She already had formatted the brief biographical information about Ivar, so she ran off a copy for Edith's approval. Edith said it was a nice tribute, and as she turned to leave, Megan said, "I wish I had known Ivar. He was practically a neighbor."

"He worked hard all his life, and if he had any faults it was that he was too good-hearted and easily taken advantage of. When that Marcie woman appeared on the scene, Bob tried to tell him she was trouble, but Ivar just grinned and said it was about time he had a good-looking housekeeper."

This was the first Megan had heard about any woman in Ivar's life. She tried to stifle her surprise and asked as innocently as she could why this Marcie hadn't been involved in any of the funeral plans.

"On the way into town Bob called me and said he'd just talked to the deputy who told him not to worry about Marcie making a scene at any of the funeral doings because she was safely locked up in the county jail."

"So she's a suspect then?"

"Hah, she's more than a suspect if you ask me," replied Edith. "I'm betting dollars to doughnuts she is the one who did in poor Ivar."

Now, more than ever, Megan was eager to get to the Dusty Eagle the next night and see what kind of information she could get from the deputy. There was a possibility he wouldn't want to talk to her for fear of jeopardizing the case, but it wouldn't hurt to ask him a few questions.

* * * * *

Chapter 10

When Megan and Wes arrived at the fish company Wednesday afternoon, Bob Brewer was there to let them in. Wes had driven the hearse from the funeral home in Braham, and Megan had come from just down the road in her own car. She had retrieved her suit from where it had been hanging in the porch and she wrinkled her nose a bit as she put it on. Although most of the smell had dissipated, there were still indications it had been somewhere in the vicinity of dead fish. Now as she again entered the fish company, she wondered if she might have to go shopping for a new suit.

Bob had looked around to make sure the place was the same as he had left it on Monday, which now seemed like an eon ago. When he was satisfied all was copacetic (save for the corpse laid out on an overturned stock tank), he advised Megan and Wes to make sure the door was locked when they left. He turned to go and then inquired when they thought they'd have the bill for him. "Should be in a couple of days," Wes said. "I double-checked with the crematorium and their fee is $2300. Another $250 should take care of it, but you'll get an itemized statement."

Bob, reaching for his check book said, "How about if I give you a check now for $1200? I'd like to spread the cost over both this year and next if possible."

"'s fine," said Wes, so Bob proceeded to write the check which Wes deposited in his pocket.

"Thanks a lot," Wes and Bob said at almost the same time.

"I'll be on my way then," said Bob. "I hope everything goes well here."

Before he was out the door, Megan remembered the memorial folders. She handed him a bunch for distributing at the Dusty Eagle. "If there are any left over here, I'll bring them along with me." And as an afterthought, she said, "Oh, and Deputy Nordin asked if we'd keep an eye out for any suspicious characters."

Bob replied, "Well, the main one is sitting in the jail down in Cambridge."

Because Megan had not had a chance to fill Wes in on the woman in Ivar's life, he was a bit bewildered by Bob's statement. Megan gave him a look which said,

"Tell you later."

Then Bob was gone, and it was just the two of them (and Ivar) waiting for the mourners to arrive. Megan and Wes quickly went into the fish tank room where Ivar lay at rest and they draped Megan's quilt over the corpse. She had chosen one of two log cabin quilts her grandmother had made for her. This one looked like it had been an experiment as there were several places where the "logs" didn't quite join together squarely. They positioned the quilt so only Ivar's head and part of his chest were showing. Megan said that most likely the bib overalls, the flannel shirt and the seed cap were his standard uniform. As they arranged the quilt, Megan started telling Wes about the woman in Ivar's life when they heard a car drive up. Megan quickly took her post at the door where she would hand out the memorial folders. Wes had produced the funeral home's standard basket as the receptacle for any condolence cards. He had placed it on the counter that was normally used for sales transactions. "That basket will have to be burned," said Megan.

"Oh, we've got a bunch of them," Wes said, "Stone buys them by the gross and they're part of the funeral package."

"Fine," said Megan. I'll take this one along with me to the Dusty Eagle to collect any cards that folks might bring there. I'll also take the guest book." It was another part of the "funeral package" and had been placed on the counter next to the basket.

Wes was to stand at the entrance to the fish tank room and direct the mourners to file past Ivar's body in an orderly fashion. They had no idea how many people to expect. In addition to some of the loyal lutefisk customers and neighbors, there was always the possibility of curiosity seekers.

There wasn't much Megan and Wes could do in the way of other logistics. The place was what it was, and it certainly didn't

Chapter 10

lend itself to any kind of comforting atmosphere. Someone had contacted the funeral home about where flowers could be delivered. Wes had told the caller that the ones making the arrangements had requested no flowers. That was a blatant lie, but he couldn't fathom how flowers would enhance the venue, and he was sure they may very well begin to droop once they were brought in to the fish company.

The first mourners who arrived were an older couple who apparently were not strangers to the fish company because they did not even flinch when they entered the place. Megan greeted them warmly and handed them a memorial folder. Before she had a chance to direct them to where they could view Ivar, she got her first opportunity to dodge questions about Ivar's demise. "Was Ivar really murdered?" the woman asked.

Megan calmly replied, "The authorities are considering it a suspicious death. I'm afraid I can't tell you more than that."

The woman glanced at the memorial folder and saw the death date was listed as December 24. "That was Christmas Eve," she exclaimed. Then to her husband she said, "Carl, we were here on Christmas Eve day. Ivar certainly looked okay then. What a shame. The place won't be the same without him."

Megan, now in her dual role of funeral director (formally) and investigative assistant (informally), inquired, "What time were you here, then?"

"It must have been about three o'clock. I always serve lutefisk on Christmas Eve, and I want it as fresh as possible. In fact, Ivar always lets me go in the back room and pick out exactly which hunk I want. He fishes it out of the tank and wraps it right up for me." Then realizing she was speaking in the present tense, she gave a little gasp.

Megan in her formal role put a hand on her arm and said, "I'm so sorry. And it means a lot that you came to pay your respects." She then directed them to the very back room where the woman's prime lutefisk had been soaking just a few days earlier. From this brief conversation Megan had surmised that the couple lived in the community. She made a mental note to pass the information on to Mr. Nordin.

As more mourners arrived, Megan successfully deflected any questions about how Ivar died. A few of the mourners lingered a while in the customer area after they had been to view Ivar, and Megan kept a keen ear to their conversations. The gist of them though echoed the first woman's thoughts of "What a shame," "The place won't be the same without him," and "Whenever I came here, I knew I'd see Ivar."

By 4:45 there had been 35 people who came to pay their respects, and none of them had appeared to either Megan or Wes as particularly suspicious. If there were any so-called curiosity seekers, it hadn't been obvious, and they were quite sure Jack and Bob would recognize all the names written in the guest book.

As they heard the last car pull away, they also heard a much louder vehicle. Wes grinned and said, "That'll be Fred." Megan assumed he was the guy Wes had solicited to transport the corpse to the crematorium. Wes opened the door and the noise from Fred's pick-up truck was almost deafening. *It's enough to wake the dead*, Megan thought and then quickly dismissed that notion from her mind.

Fred turned off the engine, jumped out of the truck and came inside. "Whew," he said, "This place stinks! I knew I should have worn my old clothes."

Megan looked a little bemused as she glanced at his greasy bib overalls and ragged Carhartt jacket.

Fred laughed at his own statement and said, "Okay, let's load 'im up."

Wes and Fred made quick work of wrapping the quilt snuggly around Ivar, securing it with some baling twine Fred just happened to have in his truck. Then they brought Ivar out and slid him onto the bed of Fred's pickup. As Fred closed the tailgate, he said, "Yup, he's not goin' anywhere." Then to Wes, he said,

Chapter 10

"I'll follow you into town and we can make our deposit."

Wes and Megan went back inside to make sure nothing was amiss. Megan took the remaining memorial folders and the basket of cards. She had noticed all had been addressed to either Bob or Jack with the exception of one which was addressed to Marcie. She'd be sure to tell Deputy Nordin about that. It took a while to find the light switches, and after turning off the lights, they both checked the door after them to make sure it was securely locked. They had had the foresight to leave their coats in their respective vehicles, so they hurried the short distance to where they had parked.

Fred fired up his truck and backed out of the driveway onto the street. Wes cautiously put the hearse in reverse and more slowly than necessary made his way the short distance to the street. His caution was needless, however, as any of Day's dogs that might have been lying there would have been scared away by Fred's noisy truck. Wes headed to Braham with Fred and his cargo following. Megan drove the short distance to her place, thinking how good it would feel to get out of her stinky clothes and have a nice hot shower.

{ 11 }

Megan headed to the Dusty Eagle at 6:30. She felt quite refreshed after her shower. She had shampooed her hair three times before she no longer noticed any residue from the fish company. Her suit was again in the porch airing out before she took it to the dry cleaners, and she'd decided to deliver it herself to the cleaning establishment in Cambridge rather than risk contaminating the firm's truck which made regular stops in Braham.

After her first visit to the fish company, she'd put her undergarments in a sealed plastic bag and left it in the porch as well. She added her current duds to the same bag to wait for a time when they'd be washed separately, apart from her other laundry. She put on a clean pair of jeans, a turtle neck sweater and wound a bright turquoise scarf around her neck. A quick look in the mirror revealed an image which defied the stereotypical look of a mortician. Megan hardly ever wore perfume (the instructor in her business management course at the U had been adamant that one should never wear perfume when meeting with clients, the live ones, that is, because so many people are either allergic or otherwise averse to the synthesized scents found in all but the most expensive perfumes). But for this social occasion, she spritzed her neck and the inside of her wrists with an herbal aromatherapy body mist called Sensual Serenity.

Unfortunately, when Megan got in her car, there was that all

Chapter 11

too familiar odor that had emanated from her previous clothes. With the engine running, she left the heat off, opened the windows and turned the fan up to its highest setting. Then she went back inside her house for her bottle of body mist. She was about to liberally spray the entire interior of the car when she noticed the basket of cards and the leftover memorial folders. "Shit," she said, realizing they were also contributing to the "all too familiar odor." Until she got rid of that basket, no amount of air freshener would do much good. She laid the bottle on the seat and hoped she'd remember to use it on her way home. For now, she left the windows down about an inch, cranked up the heat and headed down the driveway for the three-mile trip.

The Dusty Eagle was about the only business that still existed in the town of Dalbo. Once it had been considerably larger than Day, and because of its location on a state highway, its viability had persisted longer than most of the other so-called crossroads communities. It had a feed mill, creamery, hardware store, grocery store, the bar, of course, but it also had a post office which still was in operation although the open hours had been greatly reduced. There was no longer a Dalbo postmark as all the outgoing mail was routed through Cambridge. Any incoming mail addressed to Dalbo was either put into one of the post boxes inside the post office or sent out with the mail carrier to be delivered to residents on the Dalbo rural route.

When the number of dairy farmers decreased to the point that having a local creamery was no longer viable, some enterprising residents of the community started a cheese factory. Within a short time, the operation had grown to be a major employer in the area, but buyouts and succeeding mergers resulted in a drastic downsizing. The thought of converting the business into a lutefisk processing plant had apparently never been considered, and by that time the fish company in Day was adequately serving the needs of those desiring that commodity.

Once the standard cash crops of corn and soybeans were being grown, the services provided by local feed mills had become obsolete, and they too began disappearing from the local landscape. With no services to draw the local residents, most who had at one time been farmers, it wasn't long before the other commercial establishments closed as well. The highway running through the town no doubt was a factor in the bar being able to survive. Perhaps the name itself attracted a few folks passing through. Of course, it hadn't always been called "Dusty Eagle." But for years a stuffed golden eagle has sat on a perch above the bar gathering dust. The story is told that one night the owners and several customers were discussing possible names for the establishment that would be more interesting than just "The Dalbo Bar." One gazed, perhaps not too clearly, at the taxidermied specimen and said what he thought was a non-sequitur, "Eagle's dusty."

"That's it," exclaimed another customer. The owners weren't so sure, but it wasn't long before the bar was being called the Dusty Eagle in honor of the bird that had long been an observer from its lofty perch. In time a glass case was made for the bird so it was no longer dusty, but the name stuck.

When Megan pulled up to the Dusty Eagle, she had to park a few hundred feet away. She wondered if the crowd of folks had come because of Ivar or if they thought this was a karaoke night. Not a karaoke fan herself, she'd noticed a lot of cars around the place on those nights when she drove by.

A few smokers were gathered outside the front door, but they stepped aside as she approached. A din greeted her when she walked through the door. She saw Bob Brewer standing at the bar. As she was about to give him the basket of cards and folders, she noticed someone had compiled a nice display of photos of Ivar. When Bob spotted her, he said, "It took me a minute to recognize you without your business garb on." Then as he took the basket and set it on the bar next to the display, he said, "Pretty nice, don't you think? Edith put that together—with the help of

Chapter 11

quite a few of the neighbors."

Megan agreed it was a nice tribute. "Lotsa people," she said. And then she added, "There were about 35 people who stopped by the fish company."

"And Ivar?" Bob asked.

Megan replied, "All taken care of."

"Well, that's that then. Can I get you a drink?"

"Sure," Megan replied. "I'll have a vodka gimlet on the rocks."

While she was waiting for the drink to arrive, she looked around the room, wondering if Deputy Nordin was among the crowd. The guys definitely outnumbered the women, and she figured most of them had stopped in on their way home from work. There were also a few couples in snowmobile suits partially undone, and she recognized a few others who had been at the fish company. When Bob handed her her drink, she asked him if Deputy Nordin had happened to stop by. "Yup, he's down there at the end of the bar." Then with a twinkle in his eye, he said, "Funny thing. He was asking if you were here. Guess you two had better get acquainted."

Megan blushed, and after thanking Bob for the drink, she threaded her way through the crowd and was thinking about how she should introduce herself to the handsome deputy. She figured she may as well be direct, so she put out her hand and said, "Hi, I'm Megan Perry. You must be Deputy Nordin."

"Indeed I am, but please call me Nick," he said, and then added, "Sit down," as he patted the empty bar stool next to him.

"So how did it go at the fish company?" he asked.

Megan proceeded to fill him in, mentioning the couple who said they had been at the fish company earlier in the afternoon of Christmas Eve. "I don't know who they were, but I remember the woman called her husband 'Carl.' The couple seemed like regular customers. Oh, and there was a card addressed to Marcie. The person who gave it is sitting over there in the second booth—the woman with the bright red hair. You might want to check with Bob or Jack on both counts." She took a sip of her drink, and then said, "Of course, I don't want to tell you how to handle the investigation."

"Right," Nick said. "You probably wouldn't want me to give you advice about the funeral business either." Then he looked straight at Megan and gave her a big smile that would have charmed even the most callous and resistant. Meg was neither, and while she did hope to get married one day, she was most intent at the present to get her career underway and to direct as much of her time and income as possible into her little farm.

Nick, meanwhile, was pleasantly surprised that the business-like voice he'd heard on the telephone belied the physical presence of the woman sitting beside him. He had not even thought about being involved with anyone since he moved to the county, still smarting from his experience in Spearfish. The other guys in the sheriff's department were only too eager to try to "fix him up," but Nick had always declined. He was also aware that there had been buzzing about the possibility of his having a questionable sexual preference.

"So, what can you tell me about the investigation? Wes, my partner, er ah, colleague at the funeral home said it's pretty unusual to handle a homicide victim, so naturally I'm a bit curious. And I got even more curious when Edith, Bob's wife, said Ivar had a girlfriend but that she was locked up in the county jail thanks to the efforts of one Deputy Nordin."

When Nick didn't answer immediately, Megan was afraid she'd overstepped her bounds and wished she'd kept the conversation to comments about the weather or the Minnesota Vikings (neither of which particularly interested her).

Finally, Nick said, "Yes, the big, bad Deputy Nordin did put a woman behind bars yesterday, but the official word is that she is being 'detained' for her own protection."

"Well, according to Edith Brewer, your detainee is, in her

Chapter 11

opinion, the primary suspect," Megan said.

"Hmm, then it could be she's also being detained so that her alibi can be checked out."

Just then one of the guys in a snowmobile suit maneuvered his way onto the barstool next to Megan. His corpulent size plus the added bulk of the winter gear required more than the normal bar stool space and Megan was forced to scoot her stool just a bit closer to Nick's.

Nick, noticing that Megan's drink was almost empty, asked if he could get her another. "No thanks," she replied. "Since I didn't have supper before I came here, I'd probably fall off the bar stool if I have any more to drink."

"That could be disastrous," Nick said, "particularly if you fell towards him." He motioned to the burly guy on her left.

"Yes, I might start a domino effect." The thought of everyone at the bar toppling over caused both Megan and Nick to laugh.

"We'd better get you something to eat. I've heard the burgers here are pretty good. Is that okay?"

"Sure," Megan said.

"Okay. I'm going to make a trip to the men's room and then I'll try to flag down a waitress and maybe do a little eavesdropping on the side. Save my place."

Not a chance that I'll let anyone else take it, thought Megan.

Since it took a few minutes for Nick to return, Megan checked her cell phone to make sure there weren't any messages that might mean she'd have to return to work that night. Seeing none, she breathed a sigh of relief and hoped her luck would last.

When Nick returned, he said, "The kitchen is being a little overworked right now because of the crowd, and it will be at least a half hour before we get any food. Will you last till then?"

"Oh, I'll make it, but you know, I was thinking that I've got some pretty good leftover lasagna in my fridge, and I've got salad-makings too. There's plenty for two unless you need to stay here and do more sleuthing."

Megan had been a little surprised at her own forwardness in inviting Nick over when she hardly knew him, but he seemed interesting enough to warrant getting better acquainted, and the noise in the bar did make it difficult for any real conversation. As deputy sheriff, he would have his reputation to uphold, so she shouldn't have to worry about any irresponsible behavior. Morticians' reputations were somewhat more dubious, however.

"I didn't hear anything very interesting on my way to the john, and it wasn't difficult to figure out which folks had been at the fish company, but I think I'm done here, and yes, I'll take you up on your offer of lasagna. The noise in here is starting to get to me." He gave her arm a little squeeze and said, "I'll wait for you outside."

As Megan was putting on her coat, she caught Bob Brewer's eye. He and Edith were at one of the tables. Megan made her way over to them and after she thanked Edith for the display of photos she'd put together, she asked them too if they knew the red-haired woman. Neither one recognized her, and when Megan told them about the card addressed to Marcie, Bob said, "I'll get her name from the card and give it to Deputy Nordin. He may want to talk to her. By the way, where is he?"

Megan blushed a bit and said, "He just left, but I'm sure he'll be in touch."

Then Edith piped up, "He's a cutie. I might even turn to a life of crime if I could count on being arrested by him."

"Good luck with that," Bob said. And then he leaned over and planted a little peck on his wife's cheek.

Megan, thinking that this had been a most unusual day (and it wasn't over yet), waved a quick goodbye and headed for the door.

As she walked towards her car, she didn't see Nick anywhere. She began to wonder if he'd had cold feet and taken off for Cambridge. Then just as she was about to open the door of her trusty Mazda, some headlights flashed just across the street from

Chapter 11

where she had parked. She waved to him and started to get into her car. That old familiar smell met her, and she turned on the interior light to look for the body mist she'd tossed onto the seat before she left home. Not seeing it, she rummaged around and felt it underneath the seat but she couldn't quite reach it. She got out of the car and with a little effort found the bottle. Before she got back into the car, she liberally sprayed the interior. Nick meanwhile was wondering what the heck she was doing, puzzled by the motions she was making with her hands. But soon she was back in the car, started it up and after making a u-turn, she was headed home. Oops, she thought to herself, I suppose that was illegal—making a u-turn on a state highway. But like Edith Brewer, she wouldn't mind being arrested by the 'cutie' who was now following her.

Megan couldn't tell if the spritzing she'd done with the body mist had helped or not, but she certainly hoped she hadn't picked up any of the residual lutefisk odor that was hanging around in her car. With the headlights of Nick's car visible in her rearview mirror, she drove the three miles to her place and turned in the driveway. Nick followed, and when they simultaneously got out of the car, he said, "Nice place. But what were you doing in your car back there at the Dusty Eagle?"

"Don't ask," Megan replied. "Let's just say that I hope I never have to smell lutefisk ever again."

Nick laughed and said, "I know what you mean. Unfortunately, I'll no doubt have to go back to the fish company to continue the investigation. But I'm going to ask if I can go without my uniform."

"That oughta be interesting," Megan said as she gave him a rather coy smile, and opened the door, "Welcome to my humble abode." They were greeted by her rather boisterous golden retriever whose tail was wagging vigorously until he realized Megan wasn't alone. He uttered a low growl, but Nick took off his glove and dropped his hand so the dog could sniff it, and when he seemed satisfied that Nick was not a threat, either to him or to Megan, he wagged his tail and then went back to his doggie bed.

After they hung up their coats, Megan told Nick to make himself at home while she got the lasagna heated up. "Sorry I don't have any beer," she said as she had noticed he was sipping on some sort of draft beer earlier. "How do you feel about wine? I just have a box of Malbec."

"I can tolerate it," he said. "But only a small glass. I'm driving, you know." To himself he said, "Or at least I think I will be."

Megan brought out the box of wine and two glasses. She poured them each a modest amount and then went back into the kitchen. Nick looked around the cozy living room while also noticing the little gallery of photographs on the wall, presumably family pictures, the dog as a puppy, and some horses.

He realized he knew very little about this woman who had captivated his interest, but so far he liked what he did know, and from the smells coming from the kitchen, it appeared she was also a good cook.

Over the lasagna, which Nick had declared to be "a cut above," a tasty salad of greens with a dressing Nick liked, but didn't recognize, and garlic toast, Nick and Megan shared tales of where they had each grown up, their college experiences, and how they had each ended up in Isanti County (although Megan felt Nick was a bit reticent regarding his recent past i.e. the job he'd had in Spearfish).

After a couple of hours Nick yawned and said he'd better be getting back to his home, an apartment in Cambridge, Megan had discovered. "I've got to work tomorrow, and then it's my turn to be on call all weekend."

"I've got to be at a visitation tomorrow at the funeral home, and then I'll have to be at the big funeral Saturday. You're lucky you have a rotation for being on call. In my job, it's either Wes or me.

Chapter 11

Nick retrieved his coat from the hook near the back door, and then he told Megan how much he'd enjoyed himself. "I'm really glad I decided to come out to the Dusty Eagle. In case you haven't figured it out, I didn't expect to find out much there that had to do with the investigation."

"But now because of your new association with the local funeral home, you at least have some people to interview—Carl what's his name and the red-haired woman who addressed the card to Marcie."

"Right," said Nordin. Then he put an arm around Megan's shoulder and drew her to him. He'd intended to just give her a little good night kiss, but from the way Megan responded, the kiss turned out to be rather prolonged. It was abruptly broken off when Megan started giggling.

"Was it something I did?" asked Nick.

"No, no no. I liked what you did. But I got to thinking about how different it would be to kiss someone who's worked all day in the fish company. Can you imagine that Marcie woman greeting her lover with open arms as he comes through the door? She must have been either pretty desperate or else Ivar's charms were well-hidden."

"Boy, I sure hope you don't have to deal with any more lutefisk-related deaths. They could be devastating to your love life."

"I'm sorry," Megan said. "It won't happen again." This time their kiss lingered until each decided it was best to stop before something happened that neither one of them was quite prepared for.

"I'll let you know when I'm back this way to get the formal statement from the Brewers. I'll probably wait until early next week. So you'll be hearing from me."

"I'd like that," Megan said and watched as he headed towards his pick-up. She gave him a little wave and closed the door against the cold. Then leaning against the door, she sighed and

Caught in the Lye

said to Pepper, "Well, what do you think of that? An honest to goodness prospect who's both cute and polite and even intelligent." Pepper looked up, thumped his tail on the floor a few times and went back to sleep.

{ 12 }

When Nick arrived at the sheriff's office at 8:00 Thursday morning, he discovered a message waiting for him from the gas station in Austin where Marcie had said she'd stopped for gas. The message was from Joe, the owner, who requested that Nick call him back. He quickly did that and discovered the security video tape did indeed reveal a car matching the description of the one Marcie was driving. The time stamp was 1:30 p.m. December 24. When Nick inquired if there was any footage of the driver, Joe replied that yes, there was a pretty good image of a woman getting out of her car. "I can send it to you if you want," Joe said, but Nick said he didn't think that would be necessary. "Is there anything in particular you recall from the image? Approximate age, size, coat style, things like that?"

"She seemed to be somewhere between 30 and 50, and I guess that won't probably help you much. She looked fairly slim and seemed to be wearing a plaid coat, more of a jacket." So far the description matched Marcie, and indeed she had been wearing a plaid jacket when he picked her up for her "detainment."

"Thanks a lot," Nick said. "I'll check with my boss to see if we want a copy of that footage, so hang onto it for a week or so just to be on the safe side."

Nick went into Sheriff Erickson's office and told him the news that Marcie's alibi checked out. "I don't see how we can legally hold her any longer."

"Yah, you're right," said Erickson. Then he added, "But you know what that means—it means you've got to find out who did commit the murder. Do you have any more leads?"

"First I'm going to talk to the Brewers. I need to get their formal statement anyway, and maybe they can shed some light on anyone in Ivar's past who might have cause to kill him."

Nordin turned to go but then turned back to the sheriff. "You know, I just don't get it – what is the fascination or whatever you'd call it with this lutefisk stuff? You know as well as I do how the stuff smells, and I can't believe it would taste much better."

Erickson sat back in his chair and folded his hands over his large midsection, striking a rather pensive pose. He thought for a moment. "You know, Nordin, since you're new to the area, I think it might be a good idea to pay a visit to our so-called local historian. She might be able to help you make some sense out of this lutefisk custom, and I'll bet she'd fill you in on a few other customs around here."

"All right," said Nick hesitantly. "Uh, so how do I get ahold of her?"

"Her name is Madeline Moriarty. She lives about halfway between Cambridge and Day, so maybe you can drop by when you're in the neighborhood. Her number should be in the book. You can tell her I recommended her. You're not the first rookie I've sent her way, but I can't recall if any of the others needed to talk to her about lutefisk."

"Okay, then. Guess I'd better go tell Marcie she's free to go."

Nick headed over to the jail and told the deputy on duty that day, that Marcie could be released. "So does she get a ride home courtesy of the county?" the deputy asked.

Nick replied, "Find out first if there's someone she could call to come and pick her up. If there is, that will serve two purposes. First, we'll get Marcie out of our hair, and secondly, you can take

Chapter 12

particular note of who comes for her. Try to get a name too because I'll want to talk to her as part of the investigation."

"Will do," said the deputy as he began pulling out the release papers from a file.

Nick walked out to his vehicle, hoping he wouldn't have to be the one who took Marcie back to her place. He liked Sheriff Erickson's suggestion about getting some insight into the local lore, so he pulled out his cell phone and pushed 411 to get the number for Ms. Moriarty. After four rings the call went to her voice mail. A woman with a rather sultry voice said, "You've reached Madeline's voice mail. Here's your historical tidbit for December: Rural Free Delivery was started in December of 1901. Now leave me a message."

Just as Nick was starting to identify himself, Madeline herself answered with a simple, "Hello."

Nick told her who he was and why he was calling. She chuckled and said, "So Sheriff Erickson thinks I can clue you in about lutefisk? He should know that anything I'd tell you would not be from personal experience. I can't stand the stuff, but I've got a few things in my files since it's a pretty important Scandinavian tradition around here."

When Nick asked when it would be convenient to stop by, Madeline replied that her schedule was pretty open. Thinking to himself that it might be a good idea to get some background on the local culture before he revisited the Brewers, Nick asked rather boldly if that afternoon would work.

She replied that it would and it would also give her some time to dig out the information she had about lutefisk. After she gave him directions to her place, they said goodbye and hung up.

On the way to Madeline's a few hours later, Nick thought about the person in Spearfish who was Madeline's equivalent in knowing about the local history and lore. The man had more than once been helpful in providing background to Nick and his colleagues when they'd encountered a controversy between ranchers and the Bureau of Land Management.

He turned off the paved road onto a gravel road and soon spotted a mailbox with "MM" on it in bright red letters. He didn't see a house, but he turned in the driveway that was almost like a tunnel with tall pine trees on either side. Finally, after a quarter of a mile, there in a break in the forest he saw a modern log home. Aside from the garage there were no other outbuildings, so he assumed this was a fairly new homesite and not an original farmstead. He noticed two doors and wondered which one he should go to. He'd learned long ago that folks living in rural areas rarely used their "front" doors with the so-called back door being the entrance of choice for both the residents and any visitors. In the wintertime the choice was pretty obvious as a shoveled path would lead to the door of choice. In this case the path led to the back door.

He was barely halfway up the path when the door opened, and he was greeted by Ms. Moriarty. Because of the isolation of her place and because of a stereotype that exists about local historians, Nick was expecting a reclusive, wizened woman whose posture indicated years of poring over archival documents. What he saw instead was an upright woman, perhaps in her sixties, whose welcoming smile and greeting belied any indication of either seclusion or social isolation.

"You must be Deputy Nordin," she said, putting out her hand.

"Please call me Nick," he answered. As he shook her hand, her firm grip surprised him.

"Come on in. You a coffee drinker?" Madeline asked.

"Sure, I haven't quite had my quota today," Nick replied.

They walked into an inviting kitchen, but she told him to go on into the dining room where she had some folders laid out on the table.

"Go ahead and look through that stuff. I'll be with you in a minute."

Nick sat down, but before he began his perusal he glanced

Chapter 12

around. He had expected Madeline's house might be filled with antiques, but he once again had to shift his thinking from those stereotypical images. He also quickly observed that in spite of its log construction, there was nothing rustic about the place. The exposed logs served as an interesting backdrop to the eclectic décor that was a pleasing combination of contemporary and traditional. Framed photographs of various scenes were displayed on one wall combined with woven hangings, one of which he knew was from the Southwest. On another wall were posters with motifs and words he assumed were Scandinavian, and on a shelf unit there were a number of wooden figures that all appeared to be hand-carved. Two large abstract paintings took up most of yet another wall.

As he was settling himself at the table, Madeline appeared with a tray of two steaming cups of coffee and a plate of chocolate chip cookies.

"Help yourself," she said. Nick didn't have to be told twice, and he quickly discovered the cookies were almost better than those his mother used to make.

"I have to ask," Madeline continued, "if your interest in lutefisk has something to do with the demise of Ivar Peterson. I heard he was discovered in a tank of the stuff and maybe had some help getting there."

"Yes, unfortunately," Nick replied. "I don't know what else you've heard but we're treating his death as suspicious, and I've been placed in charge of the investigation. I'm fairly new around here, and this lutefisk tradition or whatever you call it has me pretty baffled."

Madeline laughed heartily and said, "Well, I've lived here practically my whole life, and it baffles me too. I've never understood why lutefisk has persevered when there are so many other Scandinavian traditions that have either been forgotten or overlooked. I take it you're not Scandinavian. Your name sounds like it could be."

"It could be," Nick replied, "but the truth is I don't really know. My dad was adopted and got the name Nordin from his adoptive parents. And where I grew up in the middle of South Dakota there were a lot of Germans, so before I came here I'd never even heard of lutefisk."

"I do have Scandinavian roots," Madeline said. "My father's mother came from Norway, but she always said that she grew up on the west coast of Norway and had access to fresh fish so why would she want to eat lutefisk?'"

At this both Nick and Madeline laughed. Then Nick, turning serious, asked, "How well did you know Ivar Peterson?"

Madeline told him that Ivar had been a fixture in the community, a sort of local color character, and that image became enlarged once he started working at the fish company. The place had become a social outlet for him. He enjoyed meeting the customers, and the customers had come to think of him as an integral part of their lutefisk shopping experience. "It won't be the same without him," she said.

Nick then asked how well she knew the Brewers. Madeline replied she really didn't know them at all. "They don't live in the county, so they're a little bit out of my territory," she said.

"Did you know Ivar had a girlfriend?" Nick asked, thinking he was perhaps straying a bit from his stated mission.

"Oh, yes, everyone knew that. You'd see them over at the Dusty Eagle. She'd get him to dance, a rather humorous sight. He was a bit stooped and had hawklike features, but they both wore bib overalls and seed caps. I have to say he seemed pretty happy. I don't want to meddle in your police business, but did I hear that the girlfriend is being considered as a suspect?"

Nick had to think again how he should respond to this question, but he figured there was no harm in telling her that Marcie had been cleared of any suspicion. "So now I'm back to square one," he said.

"As you know, we don't get too many 'suspicious deaths'

Chapter 12

around here, so I'm sure you'll find somebody who knows something. And I'll keep my tentacles out too."

"I'd appreciate that. Now let's see what you've got on lutefisk."

Madeline opened the file folders that revealed several newspaper clippings about the Day Fish Company, some cartoons about lutefisk, a few computer printouts and one small book called *Growing Up in the Lutefisk Ghetto*.

"This was written by a local woman. I think it will give you the best picture of what lutefisk means to the community around here." She handed the book and a few more pages from her file to Nick, who seemed a bit bewildered, not knowing if he was supposed to read them right there or take them with him. But then Madeline said, "Read them at your leisure. I'm in no hurry to get them back. Here, you might as well take the whole folder, and you'll no doubt find out more about lutefisk than you'd ever wanted to know." Nick thanked her and tucked the folder under his arm. He rose from the chair and thanked her again for the coffee and cookies.

"Do come back," she said. "I think there is a lot more I could tell you about what makes this county tick. And I'd like to learn more about you too. Next time you come I'll try to have some lefse along with the cookies."

"What's that?" Nick asked.

Madeline laughed, "There should be something about it in that material, and I can guarantee it's much more palatable than lutefisk."

"Can't wait," Nick said with a little roll of his eyes that caused Madeline to laugh heartily. Then he got into his truck and headed back to Cambridge, eager to settle down in an easy chair and get some lutefisk lore. Before he could begin his reading, however, he needed to stop by the jail and make sure Marcie was no longer there.

As he walked in, the deputy on duty said, "She's gone... and good riddance too."

"Did she give you any trouble?" Nick asked.

"Nah, there's just something about her that gives me the creeps. It's pretty obvious she's no stranger to jails, and regardless of her alibi, I'd put money on it that she had something to do with that Ivar guy's death."

"I'm inclined to agree," Nick said, "but with no real evidence, I had no choice but to release her. I'm going to keep an eye on her though."

"It's more likely she'll be keeping an eye on you," the deputy said. "I saw the way she looked at the other guys around here, even me. But that roughness around the edges doesn't hold much appeal."

"Well, Ivar Peterson apparently saw something that he found appealing. They'd been together for several months."

"Maybe his eyesight wasn't too good, and she probably flattered him. Just from her language around here, I bet he heard things from her he'd never heard before."

"So," Nick asked, "how did she get home?"

"She made a call and about 20 minutes later a beat-up 1980-something Chevy pulled up and Marcie got in. And yes, I got the license number," the deputy said as he handed a piece of paper to Nick. Before Nick could ask if he'd gotten a look at the driver, the deputy added that all he could see was that it was a woman with a lot of red hair. "They were out of here before I could get her name."

Hmm, thought Nick. That's gotta be the woman Megan pointed out at the Dusty Eagle—the one who had also been at Ivar's wake at the fish company. Aloud, he said, "Thanks," as he headed to his office.

When he found Bob Brewer's phone number, he called to set up an appointment for Monday so he could get his and Jack's formal statements. Bob said they both planned to be at the fish company, so they settled on a 10:00 a.m. meeting. Nick told Bob about the red-haired woman, but Bob could only verify that her

Chapter 12

name was no doubt Leslie as that was the signature on the sympathy card addressed to Marcie.

On his way to his apartment Nick thought about calling Megan but then he remembered she had to be at a wake (or visitation as she called it) that evening. Probably just as well because if she were free, he'd have to decide if he wanted to spend an evening with her or reading about lutefisk.

Once home, Nick changed from his deputy's uniform into a sweatshirt and jogging pants. He looked at his mail—only two bills and the local weekly paper. Then he looked through his refrigerator to see what there might be for supper. He found a frozen pizza, a can with a few peach slices, and a 7-Up. While he was waiting for the pizza to bake, he glanced at the newspaper. There was an interview with Sheriff Erickson regarding Ivar Peterson. There weren't many details, only that it appeared to be a suspicious death. There was no mention of any "detainee," and when he'd been asked if there were any suspects, Erickson had replied that the case was under investigation and that the sheriff's department was devoting considerable time and manpower to apprehend whoever the perpetrator was. On page eight of the paper Nick found Ivar's obituary, the same one that had appeared in the memorial folder. Since it was after Christmas, there wasn't much else of interest, so Nick tossed it aside and ate his somewhat meager and not very appetizing supper while he watched the six o'clock news.

{ 13 }

Then it was time to get serious about reading through the material Madeline had lent him. Nick settled himself into the recliner, one of the few pieces of furniture that he'd brought with him from Spearfish. It, the small dining table, a couple of chairs, a bed, a chest of drawers and his clothes, of course, were about all that would fit in the small U-Haul trailer he pulled behind his pick-up. He'd debated about bringing the recliner because it dominated the living room, but it was a comfortable place to relax at the end of his workday. Because he had the recliner, he figured he didn't need a sofa. He made himself comfortable and opened Madeline's folder. He decided to start with the little book Madeline had pointed out, *Growing Up in the Lutefisk Ghetto.*

The first chapter called "Eat, Eat, Eat" started right out with a description of lutefisk. Nick read,

> *People either like lutfisk or they hate it. I hate it. I struggled to learn to like the reconstituted dried cod fish for forty years or more but finally gave up. I am 100% Swede and having been told by my fainthearted mother that I should be afraid of thunderstorms, I thought perhaps Thor, the Scandinavian God of Thunder would be kind to me if I ate lutfisk, so I tried. Apparently Thor wasn't even listening.*
>
> *The Swedes spell it lutfisk, the Norwegians, lutefisk, and the Danes ludefisk. In English it translates to lye-fish. And in the*

Chapter 13

Scandinavian countries few of the natives, except the real old-timers, know what it is! Of course, they can eat cod, what they call stock fish, fresh every day so there is no need to preserve it by drying the fish.

There is no middle ground when it comes right down to it. Even the biggest enthusiasts say that in the kettle of the wrong cook, it can turn into a disgusting quivering, slimy mound of gelatinous gloop.

At this description Nick wrinkled his nose and shuddered, but he continued reading:

What starts out as a simple old cod fish, swimming in the cold waters off the Norwegian fjords, is caught and dried into hard stiff filets which will last forever. Then before eating, it is necessary to be reconstituted by soaking in water and more water. At one time, in order to hurry up the process, lye was added to the water. Some say it has little or no real taste (others vehemently disagree) but the peculiar smell will be remembered for a lifetime.

Year after year, numerous roving bands of eager white-haired Scandinavians search out churches, America Legion Clubs and the few exceptional restaurants which serve these lutfisk suppers throughout the Christmas season. It is a dying tradition, however, and the prices of these out of the ordinary meals have gone up to about the price of a good lobster dinner.

I remember when I was a child and we used to go to Grandma and Grandpa's festive, warm and inviting home every Christmas Eve. Lutfisk was traditionally served on that special day. What a wonderful time we all had! It was an occasion we looked forward to all year. All the aunts and uncles and cousins were there. This was the only occasion that we saw some of the out-of-towners. We could hardly wait to open the enormous pile of gifts under that fantastic Christmas tree but not until after we had all eaten our supper. Every year we had to wait for some of our cousins to get there because they went to the German Lutheran Church and had their Christmas Eve services much too late, according to us waiting Swedish Lutherans.

The meal was wonderful, with mashed potatoes and gravy, salads, pickles, relishes, cranberries, and vegetables, homemade rolls and breads, potato sausage and other meats such as ham or turkey. It seemed that my aunts tried to out-do each other in all the magnificent and special desserts. But before we ate any of that feast we would have to eat a token taste of lutfisk, served with white gravy and melted butter on a boiled potato. We ate it obligingly, whether we liked it or not because after that we could eat everything we wanted. Some of us grandchildren actually liked this time-honored Scandinavian ethnic fish but most of us kids however, like me, did not. My five-year-old brother Steve was not fond of it either and one year as we waited for him to choke down the smelly morsel of fish, suddenly with lots of apparent discomfort and a terrible repulsive noise, he just happened to hurl it back up onto his plate right after he'd managed to swallow it. Everyone stared at him and there was absolute silence for several seconds; suddenly reality set in and we screamed and ran from the table - or continued eating, based on how strong a stomach we had. After that unpleasant incident Grandpa said we didn't have to eat lutfisk at Christmas if we didn't want to.

While Nick was grateful for the description of lutefisk, he had to agree with Madeline that it seemed peculiar to hang on to this particular Scandinavian tradition when so many others had gone by the wayside. He hoped he would never be subjected to having to taste it as he was afraid he'd have a similar experience to Steve in the story. The rest of the chapter dealt with other types of food from the author's childhood, and as Nick read, he discovered quite a few things about life in another era, many of which reminded him of stories his grandfather would tell.

Chapter 13

Now I am a fish lover and I eat just about any fish there is except lutfisk. One of the enjoyable adventures for me as a child was staying up at Sugar Lake near Glen, Minnesota every summer. It was a wonderful walleye lake and I always caught fish. We also had a lot of success when we went to Mankes on Spectacle Lake. We would dig in the heavy clay ground for worms to use for bait and catch hundreds of sunfish in the cold clear water of that deep lake. Dad would always tell me to dig lots of worms so we'd have some "extras" and could leave them with Bobby (Manke). He told me that it was probably hard for anyone to find worms down in the sandy soil by Spec Lake. I always wondered if that was true or not.

I remember many nights in the summer 'us kids' and perhaps a few cousins or neighbor kids would go to the creek and catch a gunny sack half-full of bullheads. If we caught a northern or walleye, crappie or anything else, we would throw it back – this was before "catch and release" was ever heard of. When we went there we planned on fishing for bullheads only. We had a well-worn path going to our favorite fishing hole. It was one of the few places in "The Crick" as we called it, where there was a hard gravel bottom; most other places had a few feet of water but many feet of mud below that so it was almost impossible to walk, wade or swim across Stanchfield Creek anywhere else.

We would come home and sit outside by the pump and skin and clean the bullheads. We'd try to be careful so we didn't get poked with a sharp fin. Our parents would usually be in bed by then but we would come in and start frying bullheads in hot grease in the middle of the night. I often try to imagine what kind of mess Mom woke up to when she started cooking breakfast the next morning. In the winter we would have a fish house out on the frozen lake. We would eat many big northern pike from the lake. To this day, a twenty pound northern doesn't impress me as we ate hundreds of them that weighed much more than that.

Rated right up there next to lutfisk, at least for me, was the smelly tullibee or "white fish" as we called them. Every year, in late autumn my father and a couple of his cronies would go up to Liberty Beach on the east shores of Lake Mille Lacs and seine for this multitudinous fish. I'm sure he had a great time fishing, eating and celebrating with his friends. When they had about half a ton of the revolting things they would come home where we humble assistants would help clean them. Some years we cleaned all of them in the nice balmy Indian Summer weather of November but usually we would be outside helping clean them during a blinding sleet storm with our frozen little fingers. Then Dad would get busy patching the seining nets, merrily getting ready for the next fishing trip.

He would soak hundreds of fish in a special brine and smoke them in our ample smoke-house. These were usually very good and most of them were given away to friends, neighbors and relatives. Mom would fry some of the fresh fish in grease and some she would boil in salt water. The rest were preserved in big Red Wing crocks down in the cool basement, with layers of fish and salt.

When Mom decided to cook some for a meal, she would soak them in water until the salt was gone. Later she would cook them and serve with a milk gravy or boil them in water or fry in grease and then she'd salt them all over again. My parents seemed to enjoy this with boiled potatoes. I don't remember that we had this real often but either way, it tasted about the same to me...about one degree above lutfisk and definitely not a favorite of mine.

We usually ate very well when I was growing up...like most farm kids during that era. When Mom and Dad grew tired of eating fish, our meals were normally huge servings of home grown meat--roast beef or pork, steaks pounded with flour and fried tender, big fat pork chops, delicious chicken or Swedish meatballs, gravy and plenty of home grown vegetables, bread

Chapter 13

and potatoes--always potatoes-- fried potatoes, mashed, baked, scalloped and boiled potatoes. We drank gallons of milk at meals - never "pop" as that was almost unheard of and if we did get any it was orange, 7-Up or root beer.

We also ate lots of pheasants. During the fall of the year we probably had ringneck rooster almost as often as eating chicken. One of my brothers would usually shoot them with the .22 when the bird was sitting between the corn rows. Old Pat was good at flushing up birds too and always went with us hunting. When we were quite young, the only shotgun we were allowed to use was old Long Tom--a 12 gauge single-shot. It kicked like a mule and if you didn't hold it really tight up against your shoulder it would fly up and hit you in the face, I remember getting a nosebleed because in the excitement of the hunt I forgot how it would jerk when you pulled the trigger.

Our parents had coffee with the dessert after each meal. We always had a dessert but it was usually something simple such as home canned sauce--peach, rhubarb, raspberry, blueberry or strawberry. Sometimes we'd have rice pudding or tasty "krem" which was a Scandinavian dessert made from grape juice and cooked with a thickening so it was like a pudding. We had abundant fruit trees so we ate countless desserts made of apples and pears. On Sunday we usually had a seasonal pie, apple and pumpkin in the fall and rhubarb in the spring, always with lots of home-made whipped cream.

Breakfast was bacon, ham, side pork, salt pork or sausage with fried potatoes, eggs and cooked cereal such as oatmeal, Malt O'Meal or Cream of Wheat. About the only cold cereal we ever had was cornflakes, puffed wheat or that dreadful shredded wheat. Often we had pancakes or French toast and ate it with lots of butter and warm maple syrup. We also ate a lot of bread or toast with homemade jam, jelly or preserves.

Our noon meal was called "dinner" and our evening meal, as

in the Bible, was called "supper." Once in a while we had "hot dish" which was macaroni, hamburger and tomatoes baked in a casserole dish. In the winter we ate a lot of soup--vegetable, pea or bean soup with chunks of fat ham. We never knew what pizza was back then, and about the only seasonings used were salt, pepper and cinnamon. But our favorite meal was when our parents would go to town and get home too late for Mom to start a regular supper. Then she would buy Wonder bread and ring bologna for the evening meal. What a treat! Who wanted roast beef or steak when you could have bologna and store-bought bread!

Each year before Christmas and just after butchering a hog, we would help our parents concoct home-made potato sausage. It was an all-day project and almost everyone helped grind or mix or peel potatoes or do something to make this important and traditional Scandinavian treat of ground meat, potatoes, onions and seasonings.

Most of our meals were meat, potatoes, bread and vegetables... lots of vegetables. I was not a vegetable lover. I ate corn on the cob but not canned corn. I didn't eat cabbage, broccoli, spinach or most any green vegetable. And I never liked tomatoes or squash or cooked carrots or any yellow vegetable either. My mother informed me that I would end up with some horrible disease because I didn't eat my vegetables. I did like rutabagas, however, and that was always a great bewilderment to my parents because most of my brothers and sisters didn't eat them. I could make an entire meal on that superb vegetable!

My younger brother couldn't pronounce my name as "Sand," when he was learning to talk and he called me "Nanny". Eventually everyone called me by that name--except my father. Instead of just calling me "Nanny" like everyone else, he embellished it and always called me "Rutabaga Nanny" for years.

I remember my grandfather coming over one fall with a big

Chapter 13

sack full of something. We couldn't wait to see what was in that gunny sack. As young grandchildren we just knew that Grandpa would bring us something wonderful! We tore at the burlap bag to get a look. My brother looked in and saw what it was and started to cry. I looked in and joyously yelled, "It's rutabagas!"

Mom always told us that we should "eat as if we were eating with the queen--then if we ever had to eat with the queen, we would know how to act." We never had the audacity to ask where in the world we would ever meet up with the queen. Then one year cousin Ardys was voted both queen of Princeton for the centennial celebration and also homecoming queen so we got to eat with a queen at last, although I don't think this was the queen my mother was referring to. "The queen is here! The queen is here!" my brothers would sardonically yell to each other whenever the bewildered Ardy would come around.

It was explained to us that we should always be helpful, supportive and kind to our neighbors. Our parents always stressed that we must be thankful for what we had and to try our best to leave this world a better place than when we came into it. (Excerpted from Growing up in the Lutefisk Ghetto by Sandra Sjoquist Peterson, Snapdragon Press, 2001.)

As a fisherman himself, Nick really enjoyed reading about the author's fishing experiences, but the term "tullibee" was new to him except for what he'd read about the USS Tullibee, the submarine that sank in the Pacific in 1944 when a torpedo doubled back and hit the very sub that had launched it.

Paging through the rest of the book, Nick saw that it was mostly about the author's family. He laid it aside and decided to browse through some of the other items in the folder. As he leafed through them, he realized that Madeline had been collecting tidbits about lutefisk for years, and he had to wonder what lay in her many other files. There were several newspaper clippings about the Day Fish Company. Most were from the local paper but he found one from the Minneapolis *Star Tribune,* and even one that was written in a foreign language, presumably Swedish.

He noticed that one article referred to the place as a "small shop with a stink twice its size." He saw photos of the Brewer brothers with Ivar, and he learned a bit about the town that Day had once been. One article had quite a description of the process of turning dried cod into lutefisk, and another even had recipes for how to prepare it. A slightly wrinkled placemat with "Love that Lutefisk" inscribed on a heart was among the folder's contents. There was also a piece of an article written by a musician who said he was off to his first lutefisk gig of the season. He wrote, "I am coating the steel reeds on my accordion with protective anti-rust goop. Unfortunately, there is no protection for my fiddle. It will have to just tough out the exposure when we pass close by the lutefisk vats...."

Then there were various notes on scraps of paper that had apparently been written by Madeline perhaps waiting for a time when they could all be organized into some sort of treatise or exposé on lutefisk. Several of them referred to issues at lutefisk dinners when the uninitiated were confronted with lutefisk for the first time. One such newcomer to lutefisk looked at his plate being dished up and turned up his nose (thinking that was the appropriate response) when all that was on the plate was a boiled potato. A new volunteer at a lutefisk dinner was convinced that there was something wrong with the fish and didn't think it should be served. A similar note referred to an incident at Ann Sather's restaurant in Chicago (famous for Scandinavian cuisine and legendary cinnamon rolls). A customer there had ordered lutefisk, but when it came, she decided she didn't like it so she sent it back. However, the waitress chastised her saying, "Don't order something if you don't know what it is."

Then Madeline had two items on a sheet of paper that simply said, "Overheard." One was about a fellow named Midnight Swanson who waited too long to get his lutefisk for Christmas

Chapter 13

Eve so there was no longer any available at the local store. "Oh well," he said, "I guess I'll just have to eat venison." The other told of the food inspector who made his annual trip to the fish company. Nick's eyes went wide on reading that because he couldn't imagine what kind of criteria one would use to evaluate either the place or the product. The note indicated that the food inspector knew to dress in old clothes for the assignment, but while he was there, the designated employee from the Isanti County Government Center stopped in to pick up the herring, smoked fish and other orders for all the other government employees. He recognized the food inspector and chided him a bit for dressing so sloppily while being on the job. The food inspector looked at the courier's leather jacket and replied, "This must be your first time here." Nick could only imagine the fate of that contaminated jacket.

But Nick's favorite of all the notes was the scrap of paper with a cheer for the Braham basketball team: "Lutefisk and lefse tack ska du ha; Braham High School, yah, yah, yah." He next picked up *The Lutefisk Handbook*. But after a few pages of the jokes, cartoons and tips for non-culinary uses, he decided he'd had enough of lutefisk for one night.

Before he turned in, he decided it was not too late to call Megan. She answered on the second ring, and he was glad to hear her voice. They chatted a while, and then Nick asked her what her plans were on Monday because he planned to be out in her area to talk to the Brewers again. She said she should be home since it technically was her day off. "Why don't you stop by if you get a chance? I'm going to be spending most of the day out in the barn building a couple of stalls and fixing up a workshop. I can probably use some help."

"Okay, but I'd better warn you that I'll no doubt be coming from the fish company." Megan laughed and said that there wasn't much in the barn that he could contaminate (except herself, she thought). Nick said that he thought his meeting with the Brewers shouldn't take more than an hour although he was thinking of asking one of them to go with him over to Marcie's to ask for her help in tracking some possible leads.

"Maybe I can figure out something for lunch. We could have a picnic in the barn," she said chuckling.

"Sounds good," Nick replied. "I'll give you a call if there's a change in plans."

Megan was pleased that Nick had called. She wondered if any relationship would ever be more than his stopping by while he was on duty (and getting a free meal). Maybe Monday's visit would give her a clue.

{ 14 }

Although Saturday was New Year's Eve, Nick had been invited to help his friend Bill at the DNR patrol a few lakes earlier in the day to make sure that all the ice fishermen had their proper documentation. Since he didn't have to meet Bill until 1:00, he took advantage of the morning to finally wash out all the clothes he'd been wearing on his trip to the fish company—all except for his hat, boots and overcoat. He'd been leaving them out on the balcony each night, and the cold air had seemed to freshen them up. Everything else he'd put in a plastic bag, waiting for a time when both he and the communal laundry room in his apartment building were free. After their washing, the shirt, pants, socks, underwear and even his gloves had no lingering fish smell, and after sniffing the washer, he declared that his wash load had left no aromatic trace in the machine either.

Meanwhile Megan had washed out her underwear by hand Friday morning, and before she left for the funeral home, she made a trip to Cambridge to drop off her suit skirt, jacket and blouse at the dry cleaners. As she laid the plastic bag with the tainted clothes on the counter, she inquired of the clerk if dry cleaning removed odors. The clerk eyed her suspiciously as she recognized Megan as an undertaker from a funeral she'd attended a couple of weeks earlier. "What kind of odors are we talking about?" the clerk asked, thinking that perhaps some embalming fluid or worse had come in contact with the clothes. As she opened the bag and caught a whiff, she said, "Oh, we've dealt with this kind of odor before. This is lutefisk, isn't it. I bet you've been to the Day Fish Company."

Megan admitted the clerk was right on both counts, and she hoped the clerk wouldn't ask why she went there wearing her good suit. The clerk said that indeed their dry cleaning process would take care of the odor and Megan would have the suit back as good as new. "You're just lucky you weren't wearing a fur coat. We had one lady come in who made the mistake of shopping for her lutefisk in a jacket with a mink collar. We could clean the coat all right, but there was nothing we could do with that collar. We removed it for her, offered our regrets and sent her on her way. She was pretty upset until she decided she could maybe use the collar as bait to catch a few more mink so she could get a new collar. I assured her no self-respecting mink would even come near that bait. About the only thing she could hope to catch would be a skunk and then she'd have a whole other set of problems. At any rate, she won't be donning any fur the next time she goes shopping for lutefisk." Megan said she'd also learned her lesson about dress codes for the fish company.

*****

Nick had met Bill a few weeks earlier when they worked together during the whitetail deer hunting season. Bill had informed him that each year there were cases that required investigating, everything from hunting without a license, hunting while intoxicated, firearms accidents and taking more deer (or the wrong gender) according to the license that had been issued. Both the DNR office and the sheriff's department had had their share of calls regarding deer being hit by a car. Often they were what was referred to as "hit and run." The car hit and the deer ran. In those cases it was just a matter of verifying that the dents, or worse, had been caused by a collision with an animate object and not with another vehicle. Thus, the driver's insurance claim would be considered under the "comprehensive" clause.

Chapter 14

Occasionally there were injuries to not only the deer but the driver as well, but so far neither Nick nor Bill had responded to any of those calls. They had each had to put an injured deer out of its misery, sometimes to the chagrin of the driver, but since there wasn't a deer hospital in the vicinity, they had no other option. Some of the drivers opted to take the deer with them and salvage what meat they could.

Road hunting was another matter entirely, and this past season, Nick and Bill had arrested one hunter who had been ensconced in the back of a pickup truck while the driver drove slowly down the road. Both kept their eyes peeled for a deer among the rows of standing corn not yet harvested. This method worked best when the corn rows were perpendicular to the road, and it required a keen eye as the corn offered good camouflage for the deer. The officers came upon the vehicle after they had just left a wildlife management area that was open to public hunting. While they were waiting to turn onto the main road, the vehicle cruised slowly past them, but the driver and his rider were so engrossed in their hunting they hadn't even spotted the officers until it was too late. It was fairly obvious why the rider didn't hunt in a conventional manner. Weighing close to 300 pounds, he would not have been a good candidate for climbing into a deer stand, nor would he have been able to track a deer for very far without succumbing himself. Presumably if the road hunting was somehow successful, the driver would have been the one to haul the deer back to the pickup. But as it happened, neither would be hunting for a good long while.

When Bill and Nick arrived out at Long Lake, they found it dotted liberally with fish houses of various sizes, shapes and refinement. Some who engaged in the sport of ice fishing opted to use a portable ice shelter they brought with them and set it up wherever they felt the fish would be biting on any particular day. Most, however, were more permanent structures that had been brought out as soon as the ice was thick enough and would remain until the end of February when they had to be removed.

As Bill and Nick drove out onto the lake, the first thing they looked for was litter on the ice. It was illegal to leave any litter outside one's fish house, and from past experience, Bill explained, "One violation usually leads to two."

"So what kind of violations are we looking for?" asked Nick even though he was pretty sure they would be similar to what he was familiar with in South Dakota.

"Oh, you know, too many fish, too many lines, unattended lines, no license, no shelter ID etc. etc. And lately we've been hearing of a few ice maidens who make the rounds of fish houses on area lakes."

"I'm assuming these ice maidens as you call them are hoping to land a whopper."

Laughing, Bill responded with, "As they say, it sometimes takes two hands to handle a whopper."

They both laughed heartily and then Nick said, "You're joking, right?"

"As you can see, some of the fish houses are pretty elaborate, and the owners may have a network of all kinds of associates. And now with cell phones, it would be pretty easy to line up a hooker (they laugh again at the pun) and entice one or two out to spend some time while they are waiting for the fish to bite. Someone reported they saw a fisherman hang a red flag at the corner of his fish house. About 15 minutes later a woman drove up on a snowmobile wearing a pretty glitzy snowmobile suit."

"But maybe," Nick suggested, "it was his wife or his girlfriend and she just wanted to make sure she went to the right fish house."

"Yah, I'd buy that," Bill responded. "But the next week, the same snowmobile and the same suit arrived at another flagged fish house."

"Maybe your informant is just jealous." said Nick.

"Well, I do know that he's just got a portable shelter."

"There you go." And the two laughed some more.

Chapter 14

"Seriously, though, we probably don't want that kind of activity going on on our lakes. If word gets around there are hot prospects in Isanti County, there will be way too many fish houses on our lakes."

As they drove around the lake, they could easily see if the so-called permanent houses were properly identified with the owner's name and address prominently posted on the outside. They also checked to make sure the license tag for the house was visible. They stopped alongside one house where there was a lot of litter on the ice—cigarette butts, fast food cartons, beer cans, etc. Bill could tell the house was unoccupied because the door (which had to open to the outside) had a padlock on it. He wrote up a citation and attached it to the door. It was only a warning, but usually that was sufficient since it meant the authorities had been checking the lake. Bill's leaving the warning at this particular house was also a signal to other fisher people on the lake to take care of their litter. Nick got a garbage bag from the truck, and quickly picked up the trash. He threw the bag in the back of Bill's truck for proper disposal back at the DNR headquarters.

"Luckily, most of the fishermen are pretty good about cleaning up after themselves. They seem to understand that any stuff they leave will contribute to the lake's pollution. If they want to continue fishing, they'd better leave it clean."

They got back in the truck and cruised around some other houses. On their way back to the access road leading to the lake, Bill continued, "One time at the end of the season I noticed a pile of trash by an occupied fish house so I decided to let the guy know he'd have to clean it up before he removed his house. I walked in on him as he was dumping more garbage down the hole he'd just been fishing in. When I asked him what he thought he was doing, he replied, 'I'm just going to store this stuff in the basement until next winter.' I was not amused. The contents of the empty whisky bottle and several beer cans he was trying to submerge had no doubt contributed to his glib remark. He got fined big time and I haven't seen him since on any of the area lakes."

"Maybe he got trapped in the 'basement' trying to retrieve his stuff," Nick offered and then laughed.

"The weirdest thing I've encountered, though, at the end of the season was a stray fish house. I got a call from someone in the lakeshore association that there was still a fish house on the lake. This was the third week in March, so I wondered why it took so long for the guy to call. He said he'd just noticed it because it was way down at the end of the lake where nobody lives, and it seemed to be up against the shore. I went out to check, thinking that the guy was seeing things. Since I didn't trust the ice, I had to walk in about a quarter of a mile from a county road. When I got to the lake, I saw what looked to be a big plastic industrial tank sort of listing to one side. I wondered how on earth it had ended up there. But when I got closer I could see it was actually a fish house. A door had been cut into it, and inside there was a small stove, a propane tank and some fishing paraphernalia. I could see that the tank was upside down from how it is normally used. The bottom funnel-shaped opening was instead at the top and served as the chimney. Then I remembered the big wind storm we'd had the very end of February. I could just see that tank being blown across the ice until it came to rest on the south shore. Any identification was long gone. I snapped a few photos with my phone and trudged on back to the road. The guys at the office had quite a laugh and they had to admit it was a pretty clever idea. We never did find the guy who owned it, and we haven't seen any 'copycats.'"

"So what did you do with it?" Nick asked.

"As soon as the ice was out, we went out there with a boat and were able to tow it back to the public access where we loaded it onto a trailer. It's still sitting out behind the DNR maintenance shed."

Chapter 14

"Just think what people who live in the South are missing—all these winter adventures. My dad used to tell stories about growing up in Wisconsin and how all the neighborhood kids would gather at the local lake on Sunday afternoons during the winter to go ice skating and sledding. To keep warm they lit a bonfire right on the ice of old tires and any other kind of junk that would burn. Once they were old enough to drive they brought their cars out there and tried to see how many times they could spin around. Then they'd pull the younger kids on toboggans behind the cars, and when they'd slew around, the toboggan would pass up the car if the rope was long enough. My dad said it was a miracle no one got killed."

After a couple of hours of checking out the ice fishing situation, Bill decided he'd better get home because he and his wife had been invited to a New Year's Eve party. Nick had never enjoyed going out on New Year's Eve so he was planning to binge-watch the Australian tv series *Rake* on Netflix, and he was on call in case the other deputies had their hands full with drunk drivers, accidents or both.

Before he and Bill parted, they chatted a bit about the case Nick had been assigned to. Bill had to admit it was a strange one—not only the circumstances in which the homicide occurred but also that there were no solid leads. "We'll see what this next week brings," Nick said. "I sure hope the Brewer boys can steer me to some other folks who knew Ivar, and I've got to track down that red-headed babe who showed up at the wake. Somebody's gotta know something."

As Nick settled down in his recliner and was waiting for the first episode of the series to load, he hoped the evening would pass quietly and he wouldn't be called in for some emergency. At least it wouldn't be like last Labor Day when he was also on call. He'd been on the job only a week, so each time he was on duty, he was assigned to a veteran deputy who helped show him the ropes, so to speak. He had just dozed off on the Sunday evening of Labor Day week-end when his cell phone rang. It was Deputy Hokanson telling him to get dressed because there had been an accident and he needed. Ten minutes later Hokanson was outside of Nick's apartment building, and the two took off for northern Isanti County. Hokanson explained that the Safety and Rescue team had also been dispatched to the accident, which happened to be at Lory Lake. At the time, Nick had only a vague idea of where Lory Lake was located, and now in retrospect he considered it rather odd that once again the department had been called to the part of the county that was supposed to have the least amount of crime. (Lory Lake was a mere stone's throw from the Day Fish Company.)

It seems that the accident victim—or at least one of them—had imbibed a bit more than he should have at the Dusty Eagle. When the bar closed, the waitress told him he was in no shape to drive. She suggested that she drive him, and he could retrieve his car sometime the next day or whenever he had sobered up enough to drive. The passenger was barely conscious, but he was able to communicate that he lived north and east of Day. The waitress knew where Day was (presumably because the Dusty Eagle handled herring from the fish company when it was in season), so she found her way there without any problem. The next directions he mumbled to her were to go east of Day and then turn north on Blackfoot until she got to the county line road. There she was supposed to turn east again. So as she drove along on Blackfoot, she watched for any road that might be heading east. After a mile or so, she found one, and she turned. As she was about to try to rouse her passenger for additional instructions, the road disappeared in front of her, and she drove straight into Lory Lake.

What she thought was the County Line Road was in reality the public access road to the lake. The water definitely slowed her down, and when the car came to a stop, it was halfway submerged in water. The driver's cell phone was also somewhere

Chapter 14

in the drink, but fortunately some revelers in one of the cabins had heard the splash and called in the incident. They then mobilized themselves to help get the driver and her rudely awakened passenger out of the vehicle, all of this before the two deputies arrived. Neither the driver nor her passenger were the worse for their ordeal—only a bit wet, and the driver was heard to utter more than a few expletives.

Hokanson called the Safety and Rescue team to let them know there was no imminent need for their expertise and they could wait until the next day to retrieve the vehicle. Then he and Nordin took the now somewhat less inebriated passenger to his home just a mile and a half away. They suggested he offer his keys to his kind driver so she could drive his car home from the Dusty Eagle. The deputies dropped her off at the bar, and they headed back to Cambridge. On the way Hokanson made what Nick considered to be a ridiculous speculation that the car in Lory Lake might disappear overnight. When Nick asked for an explanation, Hokanson told Nick about the Lory Monster, who might make off with it and take it to his den somewhere at the southern end of the lake.

"Really?" Nick asked. "So this is Isanti County's answer to the Loch Ness Monster?"

Hokanson replied that indeed it was. "There's even a book that's been written about it. I'll see if I can find you a copy."

Nick made a mental note to check with Madeline about such a creature the next time he visited her.

{ 15 }

WHEN NICK ARRIVED at the fish company Monday morning promptly at 10:00, he noticed that both the Brewer pick-ups were there. Luckily there didn't seem to be any customer vehicles. Waling in, he recoiled once again from the smell, but he knew from previous experience that his olfactory sense would soon become numb.

He found Jack and Bob in the office waiting for him. Bob was at the desk and Jack had taken the folding chair, so this time Nick got the lumpy sofa.

After exchanging pleasantries, Nick said it was time to get down to business. He set a small digital recorder on the desk and with notepad in hand, he began taking their formal statements. By rights he should have interviewed each one separately (and preferably at the sheriff's office), but he was aware they had already lost several days' work an d this visit coincided with his ulterior motive of being in Megan's neighborhood.

The brothers told Nick exactly what they had told him and Sheriff Erickson on the day Ivar's body had presumably been discovered, but what they said now was for the official record and would be added to the yet slim file on the homicide investigation.

At one point Nick interrupted them to tell them there was something he'd been wondering about. He didn't tell them he'd been boning up on lutefisk, thanks to the documents lent him by

Chapter 15

Ms. Moriarty. He just said "I find it somewhat strange that the tank Ivar was found in didn't have any fish in it. All the other tanks in the back room were almost filled to the brim."

Jack and Bob avoided looking at each other. Then Jack said, "We'd just emptied that tank of fish for all the last minute lutefisk shoppers."

"Yes," Bob chimed in, "We were planning on coming in the day after Christmas to clean it out. With what we have in the other tanks, we probably won't need to even start a new batch. The demand really dies down after Christmas, you know."

"I understand that," said Nick. "And let me clarify something else. You said Ivar was planning on spending Christmas Eve alone, but wasn't he going to get together with you guys on Christmas Day?"

Again Bob and Jack didn't look at each other and waited for the other one to speak. Jack finally said, "Yup, that was the plan."

"And didn't you think it was strange when he didn't show up?" inquired Nick.

"Well," Jack replied, "Ivar was a grown man and we didn't have to babysit him."

Bob cleared his throat as a signal for Jack to just shut up. Then Nick said, "But you did call him, didn't you? I remember that your number was in the 'calls received' on Ivar's phone."

"Yes, I guess I did," replied Jack.

"And you're sure you didn't try to check up on him in person when he didn't answer his phone?"

"Wait just a minute," Jack blurted. "Are you suggesting I had something to do with Ivar ending up in the fish tank?"

"Not at all," said Nick, "but I do have my suspicions that the body was tampered with before the sheriff's department was called."

"All right," Bob interjected. He then proceeded to tell Nick how Jack had indeed found Ivar's body on Christmas Day, how he'd called quite hysterical, how they'd moved the fish from

Ivar's tank to another one and how they had replaced the lye solution with fresh water.

"We didn't want to bother the sheriff's department on Christmas Day," he continued, "and we figured Ivar would be there the next day anyway."

"But I tell you," said Jack, "we just about got the bejeezus scared out of us when that cell phone started ringing."

"And what time would that have been?" asked Nick.

"Oh, I don't know, maybe about 4 o'clock. I thought we should answer it, but Bob said that would be tampering with the evidence so we just let it ring."

Nick pondered what he'd just heard, and then he remembered that the voice mail left by Marcie was at 4:00 on Christmas Day, the one that caused Sheriff Erickson to get all red in the face. He said, "Okay, I'm buying your story for now." To himself he wondered how much of what they'd told him he should include in his report. Nick checked his watch and realized he had some time before he was expected at Megan's. Since his clothes were no doubt already aromatically saturated, he figured any extra time he spent at the fish company wouldn't matter much.

"I've got a few more questions," Nick continued. "Now that Marcie seems to have a solid alibi, I'm out of suspects. Maybe you can think of who the perpetrator might be." Realizing that they were not the prime suspects, both Jack and Bob visibly relaxed. Bob opened the desk drawer and pulled out the bottle of Jim Beam with its greatly diminished contents. He pointed the bottle towards Nick, who promptly shook his head. Bob divided the whisky into two well-used and rarely-washed glasses that were sitting on the desk.

Nick looked at his notes again and inquired about the couple who had been at the wake. "That would be Carl and Mary Eng," Bob said. "They live between Dalbo and Princeton, and they're real good customers."

Nick indicated he'd want to talk to them just to see if they had noticed anything out of the ordinary when they'd been at the fish company. He also asked about the other residents of Day in case they, too, might have seen something a little unusual in the late afternoon of Christmas Eve. Jack and Bob had to admit they didn't know the names of all the people who occupied the five residences in Day. They verified that the one next to the fish company was vacant and presumably for sale. Nick had noticed when he drove by that it looked quite empty and forlorn. He'd wondered if the residents had left for good of if they decided to go on vacation to escape the lutefisk season.

The building that once housed the store had always had living quarters upstairs, but once the store closed, the first floor space had also been made into an apartment. Bob knew that Pat Brown lived by himself upstairs with his dog, at least until a few days ago. When Bob had come to the fish company Christmas Eve morning, he'd seen Pat and his dog driving away. He figured he must be going somewhere overnight. Otherwise the dog would have been left at home. The downstairs apartment was being rented to a retired couple who spent winters in Arizona, and Bob only knew that because Pat had told him. Bob had never even seen them.

"So is this Pat's dog one of the dogs I see lying on the street outside here?" asked Nick.

Bob and Jack looked at each other and then Jack said, "That would be 'saw.'"

"And why's that?" Nick asked with a puzzled look.

Bob then chimed in with, "Maybe you should check with Ms. Perry about that." And he gave Nick a wink.

Nick blushed and quickly asked about the other residents of Day. The only other one they had met was a woman named Christy, and they obviously had definite opinions about her. It seems she had worked in marketing in a suburb of the Twin Cities and hoped to transfer her skills to her new rural locale where her husband was joining his brother in a construction business.

"She waltzed in here one day and told us she thought we should have an online presence," Jack said.

"So I asked her what that would do for us," Bob interjected, "and she gave us all kinds of malarkey about how it would increase our visibility and give us more credibility among other small business owners."

"Yah, like we're worried about our reputation with the other members of the Day Chamber of Commerce," Jack quipped. And then he added, "I really got a kick out of her when she said she could help us develop a brand strategy. I guess she meant something different than what cowboys do."

"It's not like she's the first person who thought we should have a website and sell lutefisk online," said Bob. "But ever since 9-11, Homeland Security has tightened up the rules of what the U.S. Postal Service can ship, so I doubt we could even send it through the mail."

"And don't forget that one customer, the guy from Forest Lake who makes his own head cheese. He told us he'd taken a hunk with him in his carry-on when he went to visit his brother in Florida, but the TSA guys confiscated it because they thought it was C-4—I s'pose because it's kind of gray and solid, and he had wrapped it up into a nice square package."

Nick opted not to ask for any further details about head cheese. He assumed, that in spite of its name, it was yet another Scandinavian delicacy. Because Nick wanted the brothers to get back to thinking about possible suspects, he said, "Christy will definitely be on my list to visit. And then there's that Leslie woman who was at both the fish company and the Dusty Eagle and she picked Marcie up from the jail. The license number the deputy got was not registered to anyone with the name of Leslie, and I haven't had a chance to track down the car owner. You sure you don't know her?"

"Not a clue," said Bob.

Nick said he intended to talk to Marcie again, not only to find

Chapter 15

out about her driver, but also to see if she might have some ideas about possible suspects.

"Maybe one of you would like to go with me. She knows you, and it might be more comfortable for her if there's somebody with me who isn't wearing a badge."

Bob said he could probably slip away from the fish company that afternoon if that would work for the deputy. Nick quickly calculated the length of time he would need for lunch. One calculation was real—one hour that was not only regulation but was a reasonable amount of time to assist Megan with whatever task she needed help and to eat a quick sandwich. The other calculation was only a fantasy—one hour for the task and the sandwich and then some additional time for the proverbial "roll in the hay." He scratched that thought from his mind as she would most likely be repelled by his aromatic emanations.

"If you've got a few more minutes now, let's talk about Ivar. Can you think of anyone who would want to do him harm? Someone from his past who held a grudge? Some distant relative who felt he, or she, had something to gain from his demise?"

Jack, having finished the whisky, was only too eager to tell tales. He said Ivar had lived in the same place all his life, had started farming with his dad and continued after he was gone. "He never ventured very far from home, and he often said, 'I like things just the way they are.'"

"But," Bob interjected, "he did get a little more outgoing once he was completely on his own after his mom died."

"Yah, and that got him in trouble sometimes too," added Jack. "When he'd stop in at the Dusty Eagle and one of the guys at the bar would ask, 'Hey, Ivar, you buyin'?' he'd say, 'Well, I guess I can do that.' And before you knew it, Ivar had bought drinks for everyone in the place. It didn't take long for word like that to get around. Fortunately, the bartender stepped in and made it clear that people had to pay for their own drinks."

"Ivar always wanted to give my kids money for their

birthdays and Christmas," Bob added. "Five or ten bucks would have been okay, but then I discovered he was handing out twenty-five and sometimes fifty dollars. Of course, the kids didn't complain, but I had to have a talk with him. How many times in your life do you have to tell someone they're being too generous?"

"So where did he get his money?" Nick asked.

"Well, he never spent anything," quipped Bob. "And he was quite a trapper. Somebody told me he'd paid for his pickup with gopher bounties, but at one dollar that would have been a hell of a lot of gophers. I know he trapped muskrat and mink, and he may have done pretty well until the anti-fur people started making a stink."

Then Jack started laughing, and he related the squirrel story which was a classic "Ivarism." Ivar had been invited over to his neighbors one day for a picnic. One of the people there was his neighbor's cousin who lived in Minneapolis. She was complaining about the trouble she was having with squirrels getting into her bird feeders. Ivar told her to trap them and bring them out to his place. One day she showed up at Ivar's with about six squirrels in live traps. She let them loose and told him how much she appreciated his offer to help her out and give the squirrels a good life in the country. But the next thing she knew Ivar was aiming his .22 at one her squirrels. He pulled the trigger and the squirrel dropped over. Within a few minutes he'd dispatched all the squirrels.

The woman, dumbfounded and angry, asked Ivar, "How can you do that?" Ivar merely replied, "Well, city squirrels move slower than country squirrels and are easier to shoot."

While thinking this was all quite amusing, Nick tried to steer the stories about Ivar to something that might offer some clues to whoever had hit Ivar on the head. He asked, "Do you know of others besides your kids who may have benefited from Ivar's generosity and then got a little greedy?"

Bob answered, "Of course, most recently there's been Marcie,

Chapter 15

and as far as I know she's been the only woman who has had any romantic notions about Ivar. I know several people tried to talk to him, you know, just to get him to realize he didn't know much about her and there was a good possibility she was taking advantage of him. But he wouldn't listen, and I have to say it was a bit embarrassing to see how they smooched in public and carried on like a couple of teenagers."

"But Bob," Jack said, "Do you remember that red-headed kid who showed up at Ivar's—when was that, six or seven years ago? He hung around for the better part of a year. All Ivar would say was that he'd run away from something pretty awful and that he couldn't understand how people could act like that. He seemed like a nice kid and then one day he was gone. Ivar never talked about him since."

{ 16 }

Just then Nick's cell phone rang he knew from the ring tone that it was an "alert" call from the dispatcher at the Sheriff's office. "Sorry," he said. "I have to take this." He stood up and went into the customer area so he'd have some privacy. He quickly discovered that a fire had been reported, and any officers in the vicinity were requested to respond. From the address given, he realized he was definitely in the vicinity, so he let the dispatcher know he was on his way.

To Jack and Bob, Nick said, "I guess our visit to Marcie's has just been moved ahead from this afternoon to right now. Ivar's house is on fire, and the fire department is on its way."

"Geez," said Jack, "What next?"

"I'm still coming with you," said Bob. "Jack, you stay here and mind the store."

Bob grabbed his coat, and while he and Nick headed for Nick's squad, they heard Jack say, "It will be a miracle if there's anything left by the time the basement savers get there." Starting up the engine, Nick asked, "Did Jack just slam the local fire department?"

"Uh, well, you know how it is, with a fire department six or seven miles away all manned by volunteers, it's going to take a while before they can get to a fire and often there's not much they can do."

Nick, in defense of the many volunteers serving in local fire

Chapter 16

departments and other agencies, said, "Of course, in rural areas if a fire completely destroys a building, it may be because nobody noticed it until it was too late. It's a little different in more populated areas. The same goes for lots of other services that people assume are going to be available when they move to the country. That was one of the first things the other deputies clued me in on when I started here. It seems a lot of folks are looking for their five acres of paradise in the country only to discover their 'paradise' is lacking some of the amenities they took for granted when they lived in a metro area."

Before Nick could continue on his rant about those disillusioned folks, he and Bob both saw a plume of smoke in the distance, and Nick turned on the siren and accelerated.

"Looks like she's burning pretty good," Bob said. "I wonder what the hell happened."

"We'll find out soon enough," Nick replied, wondering if Marcie was now homeless or, worse, was still in the house.

Bob, echoing Nick's thoughts said, "As much as I never cared for Marcie, I'd hate to think of her being burned to death."

As they pulled into Ivar's driveway, Nick and Bob could indeed see that the house was engulfed in flames. They could also see there was no car parked in the spot where Nick had seen Marcie's car when he took her into "protective custody."

"Oh, oh," said Bob. "I bet that bitch has taken off with whatever she could get her hands on and then torched the place."

So much for having any sympathy for her, thought Nick, but aloud he said, "Let's not jump to any conclusions. Ivar burned wood, right?" Nick remembered seeing an old-fashioned combination stove in the kitchen that burned wood for heating and propane for cooking.

"Yah," answered Bob, "but he had an oil stove in the living room, and he closed off most of the rest of the house. It wasn't a real problem when he was there alone, but he did say Marcie was trying to talk him into putting in a furnace. He told her the house was so drafty it wouldn't make much sense."

"With an old house like that, there are any number of explanations as to how the fire may have started," Nick said although he had to admit to himself that the circumstances could easily lead one to suspect that the fire was intentional.

Nick's radio crackled as he notified the dispatcher he was on the scene and that apparently no one was at home at the residence. He then heard more sirens in the distance, and a moment later two fire department trucks pulled into the driveway followed by another sheriff's vehicle.

The fire fighters were quickly informed that in all probability no one was in the house, so their sense of urgency was somewhat allayed. However, they lost no time in directing a powerful stream of water at the fire even though it was obvious the house was beyond salvaging. The most they could hope for was preventing total destruction so the investigators would have an easier time determining the cause of the fire.

As Deputy Hokanson approached Nick, who was standing with Bob a safe distance away from the burning house out of the way of the fire fighters, he stopped abruptly and said, "You might want to stand downwind of the fire."

When Nick looked rather puzzled, Hokanson continued, "A little smoke would go a long way to cover up that lutefisk smell." Then he laughed and gave Nick a friendly slap on the back. Nick was not amused; in fact, he was a bit weary of Hokanson's feeble attempts at jocularity, so hoping to embarrass him a bit, Nick introduced Bob as the purveyor of the finest lutefisk in the territory. He rubbed it in a bit more by adding that the owner of the burning house had been a loyal fish company employee and a good friend of Bob's. Hokanson finally got it that this was the house that figured in Nick's homicide investigation. He mumbled, "Sorry for your loss" to Bob and then walked away as if he needed to take an urgent telephone call.

Both Nick and Bob had a number of thoughts going through

Chapter 16

their respective heads. Nick's thoughts were of an investigative nature: if it was arson, what was the motive? To destroy evidence relating to the owner's homicide? To cover up a theft? To exact revenge?

Bob's thoughts were more personal, if not vindictive: How did Marcie think she was going to get away with burning Ivar's house down? Was she now gone for good? Had she taken a bunch of Ivar's belongings with her?

Because Bob couldn't imagine that Ivar had ever taken the time (or spent the money) to get a will drawn up, Ivar's estate (or what was left of it) would have to go through probate. He did own 80 acres, of which about forty were tillable, but the house (in its condition as of a few hours earlier) did not add much to the real estate value. Now, it seemed, the only other personal property of any value was Ivar's pickup which Nick had allowed Jack to remove from the fish company prior to the so-called wake. It was out at Jack's place, hopefully out of harm's way.

Nick, looking at his watch and seeing it was close to noon, wondered if he was going to be able to keep his luncheon date with Megan. There wasn't much he could do at the fire scene, and it would be a while before he got a report from the fire investigators. Because it was just a short trip to Megan's place, he decided he could leave. He thought about asking Hokanson to stay at the site, but then he'd have to explain where he was going. Then Bob came to the rescue when he asked Nick if there was any way he could get him back to the fish company. Nick was only too eager to help, so he told Hokanson he was leaving for a bit and he'd return as soon as possible. Hokanson said he'd better hurry because one of the fire fighters had told him the auxiliary members of the fire department were bringing over sandwiches and coffee for lunch. Nick said that he had lunch covered, leaving Hokanson to assume that Nick would be dining with the guys at the fish company, a thought neither deputy found particularly savory.

After Nick dropped Bob off, he headed the short distance to Megan's. She was in the fenced area outside her barn, and she waved to Nick as he got out of his truck. He ambled down to the barn and let himself in through the double Dutch door. As his eyes adjusted to the semi-darkness of the interior, he glanced around to see the horse stalls Megan was working on, a tack area, some feed storage bins and a workbench corner. Megan came in from outside, walked right up to him and planted a kiss on his cheek. As she did so, Nick heard her inhale quickly a couple of times, and he realized she was checking out where he registered on the lutefisk aroma meter.

"Hmmm. Not bad," she said, "but what's with the smoky smell?"

As Nick described his morning, Megan said she'd seen the fire trucks go by and wondered what was going on. "Wow, I guess that puts a whole new wrinkle on your investigation."

"It sure does," Nick said, "but I won't know anything definite until the fire investigators get there and determine what actually caused the fire."

"I made some sandwiches which I thought we could eat out here, but you actually qualify for house admittance, and it will be more comfortable there."

"Gee, thanks, but I will need to get back fairly soon so I can be there when the investigators arrive."

As they headed towards the house, Nick slipped his arm around Megan, but that intimacy was short-lived when Pepper came bursting from around the corner of the barn and squeezed between them. The dog then continued on an energetic escapade, and Megan called to him to slow down. He ran up to the house and planted himself in front of the door, wagging his tail vigorously. Megan laughed and said the dog didn't often have a chance to be a welcoming committee, and he was making the best of it. Nick took that to mean there hadn't been many suitors who had come calling—a good sign since he didn't much like the idea

Chapter 16

of having to compete for a woman's attention.

Once Megan and Nick got inside, they took off their overcoats and hung them in the porch. Nick thought Megan looked particularly fetching in her bib overalls and red plaid flannel shirt. He was just about to comment when Megan said, "Nice uniform. Do you ever get a chance to choose a color other than khaki?"

Nick, who had been clothed in forest green, khaki or brown his entire working life, replied, "There are strict dress codes that apply to every area of law enforcement. Blue for municipalities and brown for counties."

"Really?" asked Meg. "What about state highway patrol people?"

"Oh, they get a color associated with their university. So in Minnesota, it's maroon." With this declaration, Nick could no longer keep a straight face.

Megan berated him saying, "You are so full of shit."

"Actually," said Nick, "I think it's the handful of folks who own the uniform manufacturing companies who have the most to do with setting the styles and colors."

"That actually makes some sense. Now sit down and help yourself to a sandwich."

The sandwiches were made with a whole grain bread Megan had baked herself and filled with a tasty turkey salad with just the right amount of seasoning and a slight crunch. While they were eating, Nick decided to ask Megan about episode with Pat Brown's dog. He started by saying, "You know those dogs that always seem to be lying out in the street in Day?" Before he even finished the question, he noticed Megan had turned beet red. "Did I say something wrong?" he continued. And then fearing that Megan was going to burst into tears, he said, "I'm sorry, but during my visit with the Brewers this morning the subject of those dogs came up. They said you might have information as to why Pat Brown's dog is no longer among them."

"It was awful," Megan said. And after she told him what had happened, Nick assured her that any dog who sleeps in the street is not very street smart.

"But just to be on the safe side," he said, "you might want to keep Pepper inside if Wes ever drives in here with the hearse." Then he grinned, and Megan's heart did a little cartwheel.

As they were finishing their meal with a cup of coffee and a peanut butter cookie Megan had retrieved from the freezer, Nick's cell phone rang. He answered it, waited a few seconds and said, "I'll be right there."

As Nick headed to the porch to retrieve his jacket, he thanked Megan for the lunch. "Okay, this is the second time you've fixed a meal for me. Now it's my turn. How about if I take you out to eat next weekend?"

"Sure. But where are you thinking? The choices around here are a bit limited—if you want anything more than a burger."

"So what's wrong with a burger?" Nick asked as he came towards her with that twinkle in his eye that Megan found quite irresistible.

He leaned down to kiss her quickly and said he'd call her. In the meantime she should be thinking about where she wanted to go.

Megan had to restrain herself from clinging to him and preventing him from walking out the door, but her better judgment took over. She simply stood where she was and watched him get into his jacket and head for his truck. As she heaved a sigh, she said to Pepper, "This is starting to get interesting."

{ 17 }

It didn't take long for the investigators to determine that the fire at Ivar's place had definitely been arson. The fire had had two points of origin, a wastebasket in the living room and another wastebasket in the kitchen. To assure that the fire(s) would not just smolder, some fuel-soaked rags had been placed on the floor next to each of the wastebaskets. The investigators estimated the fire had been burning for at least an hour before any smoke was visible, and then it was another hour before someone had detected the smoke and called the fire department.

Nick had no doubt that it was Marcie who had set the fire, and by this time she was long gone from the area. After getting the investigators' initial report Nick went back at the sheriff's department and set the wheels in motion for putting out an APB to find her and return her to the county for questioning. In all likelihood she would head to Iowa again, Nick guessed. In tracking down her license plate number, he discovered that her plates had expired in December. That violation alone might provide incentive for a law enforcement officer to stop her.

Next Nick decided to try to find out who owned the car that Leslie, the red-haired woman, was driving when she came to pick up Marcie at the jail. He found the scrap of paper where he'd written the name of the person associated with the car's license number, a woman by the name of JoAnn Hastings. He was a bit surprised when directory assistance actually had a phone number for such a person, and he was even more surprised when someone answered on the second ring. Nick identified himself and then said he was inquiring after a person named Leslie. "You too?" asked the voice at the other end of the line. "If you find him, tell him I'd like to get my car back."

Him? he thought, wondering if he'd heard right. Then Nick remembered the conversation at the fish company earlier. The guys didn't know a red-headed woman, but they did remember a red-headed boy from several years ago. Now JoAnn was referring to an adult Leslie as a male. Nick was quickly jumping to conclusions about what might have transpired in Leslie's life, but it also seemed as though he might have an auto-theft on his hands. He continued with more questions, "So you have no idea of Leslie's whereabouts?"

"Last I heard he was going to go back to that old uncle of his somewhere over by St. Cloud to try to wrangle some more money out of him."

"And how long ago would that have been?" asked Nick.

"Oh, maybe three or four years."

"And you haven't tried to get your car back during that time?"

"At first I did, but then I decided I was well rid of him for sure and no doubt the car as well."

All sorts of things were going through Nick's head: Had Marcie and this Leslie been working together to bilk Ivar out of any money he may have had? Did the two conspire to plot his demise? Did Marcie meet Ivar through Leslie? Had Leslie once been a guy but now is a woman?

It seemed crucial to contact Leslie, but Nick was certain JoAnn was not going to be able to help him. About all he could do was give her his number and tell her to get in touch with him if she heard anything of Leslie. When JoAnn asked if Leslie was in some type of trouble, all Nick said was that Leslie's name had come up in connection with a suspicious death in Isanti County.

Chaptert 17

Nick wished he could remember who Leslie was sitting with at the Dusty Eagle during the get-together following Ivar's wake. Maybe it was one of those situations where folks are sort of thrown together with the only common thread being that they all knew Ivar or at least wanted to pay their respects to a long-standing member of the community. He figured he'd stop by the bar the next evening after he had visited the Day residents to ask if they'd seen anything suspicious on Christmas Eve. Those inquiries would put him right back in Megan's neighborhood, but he'd probably best wait until the weekend for a real date. He didn't think it was necessary (yet) to inform Bob and Jack of the possible transformation to the red-haired kid they remembered.

Nick decided to stop by Madeline's on his way out to Day. He hadn't called her because he wasn't sure exactly when he'd get there, and he was sure he could just leave the documents she'd lent him on the porch if she wasn't home. As he headed up her driveway, he saw her car in front of the garage. I'll just say hello, give her the folder of lutefisk material and be on my way, he thought. He knocked on the door and when it was opened, he was greeted not only by Madeline but also by the smell of baking bread. The aroma reminded him of the summers he used to spend at his grandma's in Wisconsin. When Nick tried to apologize for dropping in unannounced, Madeline shushed him and motioned him to a chair at her kitchen table, "Nonsense. You're just in time for a nice piece of warm bread. Butter and jam?"

"Okay," Nick said. "But I can't stay long. I'm heading out to Day to see if anyone there saw anything strange during the afternoon of Christmas Eve."

"It's practically a ghost town now, isn't it? How many people actually live there these days?"

"There are still five houses, but one is vacant."

"It's such a shame. Those little crossroads communities dotted the countryside for years."

"So what happened to them?" Nick asked.

"Well, a lot of blame can be placed on the automobile. Once folks could get to a bigger town in a matter of minutes, there wasn't much point to going to the closer one that didn't have the selection and no doubt had higher prices."

"Maybe if gas prices keep going up, they'll have a revival."

"Oh, I think it's a little late for that. Nowadays even those bigger towns are having a struggle as you can see when you drive down Main Street of any one of them."

Nick laid the folder of the material he'd borrowed from Madeline on the table. "That was quite an education. You were right. I learned more about lutefisk than I ever cared to know."

Madeline chuckled. "There's usually one or two lutefisk suppers held after Christmas, so if you're lucky, you might be able to get yourself some. Otherwise you'll have to wait until next fall."

"I think I can wait," Nick replied as he helped himself to a slice of bread that Madeline had slathered with butter and strawberry jam. He continued with "Hmm. Hmm. This is good."

All of a sudden Madeline said, "Damn, I said I was going to have lefse for you the next time you came. The last piece got eaten up just yesterday. I guess you'll have to wait for that too."

"It can't be any better than home-made bread," Nick said.

"Some would question that, but I have to agree with you. A little lefse goes a long way, and it's such a bother to make. Of course, all those Scandinavian traditional foods are pretty bothersome. They all have to be made individually. I suppose you don't know about rosettes, krumkake or fattigmand either."

"Nope, but as long as lye isn't part of the recipe, they should at least be edible."

At this Madeline laughed heartily, and Nick found himself laughing along with her. Then Nick remembered to ask Madeline about the alleged monster in Lory Lake. "Oh that thing," she said with a scoff.

"But Bruce Hokanson, one of the other deputies, said there's

Chapter 17

even a book written about it."

"Well, he's right, but you know you can write a book about anything, and once it's in print, it practically becomes gospel. In the case of the Lory Lake monster, when some people read the book they actually began to believe they remembered hearing tales of such a creature."

"So you're saying it's all a fabrication?"

"Yes, not only is the monster fictitious but so are the tales of the monster."

"Wow, it kind of makes a good story though, don't you think?" Nick asked.

"Sure it does, and I'm still hoping someone will build a restaurant on Lory Lake and call it the 'Lory Loch.' In the gift shop there could be little monster salt and pepper shakers, stuffed toy monsters...." Her voice drifted off and then she said, "But I want to know how you ended up in this neck of the woods. Didn't you say you were from South Dakota?"

"Yup. My last job was in Spearfish working with the Bureau of Land Management."

"Oh, out in the Black Hills? It seems to me that area out there in western South Dakota is kind of like the banana belt compared to here."

"Oh, I liked the area just fine," said Nick.

"I see," said Madeline. "So let me guess. Girl problems, ex-wife problems, boss problems?"

"Two of the above," said Nick. "No wife, thank goodness, but the boss and the girl are kind of intertwined."

When Madeline raised an eyebrow, Nick quickly added, "Father and daughter."

"I see," said Madeline. "Didn't anyone ever tell you it's a bad idea to date the boss's daughter?"

"I know that now, so before I took this job I made some inquiries regarding Sheriff Erickson's offspring."

Madeline chuckled and said, "So you discovered that his two

daughters are presumably happily married and also considerably older than you?"

"Uh huh."'

"And that they're uglier than a mud fence?" Madeline added followed by her deep-throated laugh. And as she looked at Nick, she couldn't help think of how much he reminded her of her grandson Charlie—that same seriousness but with an engaging twinkle in his eye. At the thought of him, she got up and went to a bookshelf in the living room and came back with a photo that had been taken when Charlie had been an intern for the U.S. Forest Service the previous summer. As she handed it to Nick, she said, "He'd love to get a job in the Black Hills, but maybe I should warn him about certain persons he should stay away from."

"I doubt he'd ever get into the same kind of trouble I was in. It was a pretty unique situation."

"Now I am curious," Madeline said as she laid another slice of the warm bread on his plate.

"It's a long story," Nick said.

"Hey, I got nothing but time," Madeline proclaimed.

So Nick started in on how he had a falling out first with his boss and then with his girlfriend (his boss' daughter).

"Have you ever heard of a guy named La Verendrye?" Nick asked.

"French explorer, right?" replied Madeline.

"French Canadian to be precise. And there were several of them. The main one was Pierre, who was an explorer, fur trader and military officer. He established several forts in the vicinity of Winnipeg. Then two of his sons, Francois and Louis Joseph, decided they wanted to find a water route to the Pacific Ocean. A few others had failed, as you probably know. So they set out in 1742 from Fort LaReine on Lake Manitoba and got pretty far into South Dakota, leaving lead plate-like markers along the way in order to claim any land they'd set foot on for France."

Chapter 17

Nick continued with the tale of how one such marker had been found in 1913 by some school children near Pierre. It was dated March 30, 1743, some 60 years before Lewis and Clark made their historic expedition up the Missouri River. After more than 250 years another plate was found, this one further west at the confluence of the Belle Fourche and Cheyenne Rivers.

Madeline interrupted with, "This is beginning to ring a bell. I remember hearing about this second plate. There was some sort of controversy over it, wasn't there? Is this where you come in?"

"Yup," said Nick. "The guy who found it was from Florida, and he was on some sort of vision quest, canoeing on the Cheyenne River with his dog. At one of their stops the dog unearthed a lead plate. The guy thought it was interesting, so he put it in the canoe. When he got back to Rapid City and cleaned it up, he discovered there was some writing on it. Not knowing what it all meant, he took photos of the plate and sent them to some South Dakota historians. One was able to verify that the name on the plate was one of the explorers in the La Verendrye expedition."

Nick went on to explain that the date on the plate, March 7, 1743, was quite significant since it was 23 days earlier than the date of the plate which had previously been found. Thus, the more recent find indicated the La Varendrye expedition had traveled further west than previously thought.

"Interesting," said Madeline.

"Meanwhile, back in Florida the guy buried the plate in his back yard because his sources had had told him the plate was priceless."

"According to him," Madeline added.

"When his story was published in his local newspaper, it was picked up by one of the news wires. Soon practically every major paper in the country ran the story."

"I can almost see the vultures circling," said Madeline.

"Right. First it was the French government who thought the

plate belonged to them, then there were several museums west of the Mississippi who were interested, and presumably there were also private collectors who were offering substantial amounts of money for it. And now, finally, here's where my boss got involved"

"And ultimately you," chimed in Madeline.

Nick described how his boss decided to enforce the Act for the Preservation of American Antiquities, which states that anything found on federal land is under the jurisdiction of either the Agriculture, Defense or Interior Departments. In this case he was claiming the Bureau of Land Management would have rightful claim to the plate and it should be returned to South Dakota.

"So were you supposed to retrieve it?" asked Madeline.

"No," answered Nick, "my boss decided that the honor should go to his daughter, Marcia, who also worked for the Bureau."

"Your girlfriend," added Madeline.

"Yes, and I told him I didn't think it was very wise to send her to some backwater place in Florida to try to talk a fellow into giving up something that he obviously had quite a stake in. For all I knew, she might get into an argument with the guy and she'd end up buried alongside the plate. I also mentioned that the cost for such a trip seemed rather extravagant considering the department's continual budget problems."

"And I suppose your comments were considered insubordinate?" asked Madeline.

"Yes, and that may not have been so bad but then I also told him what one of my former history professors had said when I told him the story. He laid out some possible scenarios if the plate was turned over to the government. He said it would no doubt become like a trophy on some Washington, D.C., bureaucrat's wall, and then once that bureaucrat was no longer with the government, the plate would most likely end up in a box

Chapter 17

somewhere in a storage warehouse and be forgotten."

"And your relaying of these possibilities got you fired?"

"I didn't wait around for that. The tension in the office was so thick you could cut it with a knife, and Marcia was quite pissed that I'd dared to stand up to him. In retrospect, I realize she never had the guts to do that. So I started looking for other jobs, and within 30 days I was out of there."

"So what happened to the plate then?" asked Madeline.

Nick grinned as he told the rest of the story. "My boss did back down from having Marcia go to Florida, but he kept hammering on the idea that the plate belonged to the federal government. He badgered the guy in Florida, threatening him with a $200,000 fine if he didn't hand it over. During the time I was here for the interview with the sheriff's department, I found out that the Florida guy flew to Rapid City and hired a small plane to fly over the general area where he'd found the plate."

"Ah, yes, the bell in my mind is ringing again. He dropped it out of the plane, right?"

"Yes, indeed. So presumably it's back in the mud somewhere in the vicinity where the Cheyenne and Belle Fourche rivers come together."

"I can just imagine what it was like in your office when you returned from your sojourn here," said Madeline.

"It was pretty interesting, all right," said Nick, "but by that time I knew I was leaving. I never mentioned the plate again. But the damage was done and there was no way I could stay either in the job or in the relationship."

"That's a darn shame," Madeline said rather pensively. And then she added, "I hope that experience, with the girl, not the plate, hasn't soured you completely on women. Isanti County has some fine specimens."

The red creeping up into Nick's cheeks indicated to Madeline that Nick may have discovered a few of the county's offerings. "As a matter of fact," Nick said, "I'm pretty interested in one particular young lady but, like me, she's a newcomer to the county."

"Even better," averred Madeline with a twinkle in her eye. "Then the two of you can discover together all the idiosyncrasies of this place and be critical (or cynical) without worrying that anyone who's from here will be offended." Nick couldn't help but chuckle and then he popped the last bite of Madeline's home-made bread into his mouth.

Then Nick glanced at his watch and discovered it was already after 4:00. Thanking Madeline again for the research material and for the bread, he said he'd better get going.

"Yes," Madeline said. "I suppose if you don't get to Day today, you'll have to go to Mora."

Nick looked a bit puzzled until Madeline said, "To Mora, tomorrow."

"Got it," said Nick as he put on his overcoat and headed out the door.

When he started up his truck and headed out the driveway, he said to himself: To Mora, tomorrow. I wonder how many times that little phrase has been sprung on newcomers. He also wondered if it had been a mistake to tell Madeline his Spearfish story, but she just had one of those personalities that made him instantly feel comfortable. Of course, there was always the possibility her benevolence was all a ruse for eliciting stories to serve as the foundation for her historical writings. Of course, he hadn't actually seen any of her writings, just the files of clippings on a plethora of topics. Maybe she did her writing under a pseudonym and published them far away from the story's origin. Whatever the case, he figured she was a good source for all kinds information about the area, and she definitely was a good cook.

{ 18 }

After leaving Madeline's, Nick was soon in Day, and he was happy to see that lights were on in three of the houses. He decided to start with Pat Brown's even though Bob Brewer had said he didn't think Brown was around on Christmas Eve. Nick went to the rear of the former general store and rang the doorbell for the upstairs apartment.

A voice from somewhere above him yelled, "It's open," so Nick opened the door and headed up the stairs. When Brown stepped out from his apartment onto the landing at the top of the stairs, he did a double take when he saw that his caller was in uniform. Nick quickly introduced himself as the officer in charge of the investigation into Ivar Peterson's homicide. They shook hands and Brown motioned for him to come in. Nick explained that he was visiting all the residents of Day to find out if anyone had seen or heard anything suspicious on the afternoon of Christmas Eve or the preceding few days. Then he apologized for coming so close to supper time, but added that he figured he had a better chance of catching people at home.

"Not a problem," Brown said, pulling out a chair from the kitchen table for Nick. As he sat down, he glanced over at the stove and saw a steaming pot that had to be the source of the pungent aroma that greeted him as he entered the apartment.

"Venison?" Nick asked.

"Sure thing," Brown replied. "Nothing better than venison

chili on cold winter nights. You want some?"

"Thanks, but I'd better keep moving if I want to talk to the others here in Day. It sure does smell good though."

Brown, who had taken the chair across from Nick, said, "Terrible—what happened to old Ivar," Brown said. "It's a bit spooky now, knowing I live across the street from a murder scene. I thought I'd gotten away from that sort of thing when I moved out here from south Minneapolis."

"I know what you mean. There aren't that many homicides out this way, but I'd like to think this is still a small enough community so that neighbors keep an eye on one another."

"I'm not so sure about that. What are we, five households here in this town (at which he put his fingers up to indicate quotation marks when he said "town"), and we don't really even know each other. It's like we have to have an excuse to get acquainted. Back when I was a kid, we knew who all our neighbors were, and we all pitched in if someone needed help."

Nick nodded and then asked, "So, do you live here alone?"

Brown hesitated a bit before answering, "Yes. For a couple of days now, anyway. Before that it was me and my dog."

"Ah, yes, the Brewer brothers told me what happened. Terrible. Never easy to lose a pet."

"Well, it was bound to happen sooner or later. I tried to keep her fenced in, but she was so unhappy, and I figured that if she and the other dogs around here stayed close to home, it wouldn't be a problem. Why they felt they had to lie in the street, though, is beyond me."

"The Brewers also told me they had seen you and the dog take off sometime on the morning of Christmas Eve."

"Yes, we went over to Wisconsin to spend Christmas with my brother and his family."

"So you weren't here, then, to see what kind of cars any late afternoon customers might have had."

"No. Sorry. But I thought Ivar's girlfriend was a prime

Chapter 18

suspect."

"I thought so too, at first, but she had a rock solid alibi—for the time when the homicide took place, at least."

"What do you mean?" asked Brown.

Nick wondered if Brown had heard about Ivar's house burning, and he debated whether he should tell him. Instead Nick asked him, "Do you know her at all?"

"No, not really. I'd see Ivar and her out dancing once in a while, and I certainly heard things about her from my girlfriend and also from some of the guys who hang out at the Dusty Eagle."

Rather than get into the gossip about Marcie, Nick asked if Brown had ever seen a red-haired woman either with Marcie or just hanging out at the bar or elsewhere.

Brown couldn't remember any such woman, but he said he'd ask around and contact Nick. Nick gave him his card and before leaving for his other interviews.

As he headed down the stairs, Brown called after him, "Good luck." Then he added, "It's too bad the dogs of Day can't talk as they would have seen who came to the fish company on Christmas Eve."

"Right," Nick said as he opened the door to the outside. He then headed across the street to the only house with a clear view of the fish company. He didn't see any doorbell so he knocked on the door. Immediately a dog started barking, and soon another one joined in, more "dogs of Day." The barking grew quite loud as the dogs got closer to the door. A porch light came on, and the curtain across the glass window in the door was whisked aside. A middle-aged man was peering out, checking to see who was there. When he spotted the badge on Nick's jacket, he hollered to someone to come and get the dogs.

Then he opened the door a few inches and said, "Yes?"

Nick held out his hand and introduced himself, saying the same thing he'd said to Brown—that he was visiting all the residents of Day to inquire if they had seen anything suspicious.

Before he could finish, the door opened wider, and the man invited Nick inside and motioned for him to have a seat at the table. A television was blaring in the next room, but it suddenly went silent and a woman appeared, followed by two Labrador dogs who appeared eager to meet Nick. One put his head on Nick's thigh while the other nudged his elbow. Nick obligingly scratched their heads, and it was quite clear their bark was much bigger than their bite. Then they both ambled off to resume their naps. Nick then introduced himself to the woman who had also sat down at the table.

He took out his notebook and began asking questions, jotting down the replies from the couple. He discovered they had lived in Day for five years; Harvey Pearson was an over-the-road truck driver and his wife was a nursing assistant at the hospital in Mora. (So she goes from Day to Mora and from Mora to Day, thought Nick. He wondered for an instant if he should mention little witticism to her, but he thought better of it.) He was pretty sure if Sheriff Erickson were doing the interview, he would have brought it up and then laughed heartily, but Nick wanted to set a more professional tone.

On the other hand, Nick didn't want to seem adversarial, so he assured the Pearsons they were in no way being considered as suspects. Harvey interrupted him with, "But you would like to know where we were on the afternoon the murder took place?"

"Well, yes," Nick said as he felt his face grow a bit red.

"We should have been here," Cheryl Pearson said, "We were both looking forward to spending a quiet Christmas together. It was the first one in years one or the other of us was not working. But then we got a call that my sister in Duluth was having emergency surgery for a brain aneurysm, so we headed there immediately."

"How long were you gone?" Nick asked.

"We left about noon on Christmas Eve Day and didn't get back until 2:00 on Christmas Day," Cheryl continued.

Chapter 18

"You know, now that I think about it, I remember seeing Ivar's truck there at the fish company, when we got back," chimed in Harvey. "But I thought maybe someone had picked him up and he just left the truck there."

"And a little later, I saw a couple of more trucks there," added Cheryl, "but I just figured there was some cleaning up or some other kind of work that needed to get done."

Nick chuckled to himself because their story verified what he had earlier deduced and what the Brewer brothers had reluctantly admitted—that they had discovered the body on Christmas Day and not the day after.

The Pearsons said they only knew Ivar because Cheryl had used his telephone once when she'd had a flat tire not far from his place on her way home from work one morning. It was winter so Ivar told Cheryl she may as well stay at his place until Harvey got there to change the tire. "We had a nice chat," Cheryl said. "He thought it was strange that we lived right there in Day and had never been in the fish company. But I told him my Norwegian grandmother had lived on the west coast of Norway and always had access to fresh fish, so she turned up her nose at the mention of lutefisk. He asked me if I'd ever tried it, and when I said 'no' he told me to come over to the fish company some time and he'd give me a sample I could take home and cook. So I went over there one day, and the smell just about sent me reeling, but when Ivar saw me, he insisted that I had to have the tour of the whole place.

"I have to say he was mighty proud of his work there, and he was true to his word. I took home a chunk of the stuff. He was sure I'd become a regular customer, but no such luck. Since Ivar didn't tell me how to cook it, I went online and looked for recipes. I found all sorts of methods from boiling to baking to using the microwave. I even saw where one woman had discovered she could steam it in the dishwasher. I couldn't imagine what that might do to a dishwasher, and anyway I don't even have one, so

I settled on the baking method which was pretty easy and it didn't smell up the house."

Harvey chimed in, "I'll eat almost anything, and I generally like fish, but this was a pretty poor substitute. I tried covering it with butter, and that helped some, but a one-time experience was plenty for me. I gave the rest of my portion to the cat and after he licked off the butter, he just walked away."

When Nick asked if they had seen anything strange around the fish company in the days leading up to Christmas, Harvey said, "Besides the people coming to a hole-in-a-wall place to buy rotten fish?" Then he said, "Sorry, I don't mean to make light of the tragedy with Ivar. But I can't imagine that what happened to him was totally random."

"That's what I'm thinking too," said Nick. "But so far I haven't found anyone who would want to do Ivar any harm." Then handing Harvey his card he said, "Let me know if you think of anything." With that he turned towards the door, disturbing the dog who was sleeping in front of it. To the dog he said, "You stay out of the way of cars, you hear?" The dog thumped its tail, stood up and let Nick open the door.

At the other two houses, Nick's interviews were equally non-productive. In the one set back from the road west of the fish company, he discovered an elderly woman living alone who had both impaired vision and hearing. It was difficult to communicate to her not only who he was but also what his mission was. When she finally understood, she said her son had picked her up at around 3:30 on Christmas Eve Day and had taken her to his house near Stanchfield. The family there had gone to candlelight service at the Baptist church, had supper and then opened presents. Her son had brought her back about 10 o'clock that night, and she spent all of Christmas Day by herself. Yes, she was shocked to hear about Ivar and couldn't imagine who would want to hurt him. "Unless it was that woman he's been hanging around with," she said quite disapprovingly.

Chapter 18

"How well did you know her?" Nick asked in a loud voice that surprised even him.

"Oh, I never met her, but I certainly heard about her. You're going to interview her, aren't you?" she asked.

"Certainly," Nick replied. Smiling, he shook the old lady's hand and said, "Thank you for your time."

He let himself out the door and headed towards the only other occupied house where he hoped to find Christy, the woman who had tried to bring technology to the fish company. He hoped this would be a quick and fruitful interview because it had suddenly occurred to him that he was hungry.

As Nick got closer to this last house, a motion detector light came on, which reflected off the icy walkway in front of him. He came close to slipping a couple of times, so he was glad to reach the steps, which had been shoveled clear. His footfall on the steps roused another watchful dog of Day, but this barking indicated a smaller dog than the ones he had encountered at the Pearsons. Nick heard some shushing sounds from inside. Then, after just one knock the inside door was opened, and a terrier of some sort was being restrained by a young woman who trying to put a leash on him. When she succeeded, she held on to the leash and said through the glass of the storm door, "May I help you?"

After Nick once again explained his business in Day, the woman unlatched the outside door so he could open it and step inside. From further inside the house, Nick heard a baby crying. When he asked if this was a bad time, the woman said that there isn't any really good time. "Just let me pick him up," she said as she handed the dog's leash to Nick. The dog growled a bit, but when Nick put out his hand so the dog could sniff it. Then the dog backed away as far as the leash would allow and began barking in earnest. The woman came back carrying a baby who appeared to be about six months old. Between the baby's crying and the dog's barking, Nick was convinced he couldn't have chosen a worse time. Before he had a chance to tell the woman that he'd stop back another time, she handed him the baby, which he took with one hand while he held onto the dog with the other. The woman then relieved him of the leash and the dog. As and the dog disappeared into another room, the barking stopped. The baby, who had discovered the badge on Nick's jacket and was fingering it, stopped crying. When the woman reappeared, she looked rather amazedly at Nick and said, "Well, you may as well sit down."

She didn't offer to take the baby from him so he pulled out a chair from the kitchen table and sat down. She sat across from him said, "I'm Christy, and that's Noah. Looks like he likes you."

Nick felt a bit awkward not only because he didn't have much experience with babies, but also because it didn't seem very professional to conduct an investigative interview while holding the interviewee's baby on his lap. Furthermore, he didn't have access to his notebook.

He'd already learned a bit about Christy from the Brewers, and he wanted to determine if she could possibly be a suspect. He started right off with asking if she had been home on Christmas Eve day. She acknowledged that she had, but when he asked her if she had seen or heard anything unusual that day, she explained that the fish company was not in plain view of their house, and she had not ventured outside the entire day. She also said that her husband, who was due home from work any minute, had also been home for most of the afternoon. He'd gone to Menard's earlier in the day to pick up a door and some trim, and then he'd spent the rest of the day installing them.

"There was quite a bit of noise around here," Christy said, "and we weren't paying attention to what was going on anywhere else. I remember I did let the dog out once, and when I called him to come in, he came from the direction of the fish company. But that's not unusual because he likes to hang out with the other dogs of Day."

"I imagine you've heard that their numbers have decreased

Chapter 18

by one," Nick said.

"Yes," Christy replied. "At least Toby here seems to have figured out it's not a good idea to sleep in the street. And he doesn't like to be out in the cold for very long."

Just then little Noah had apparently decided he'd rather be with his mother so he started crying. Nick gave him up readily and was finally able to get to his notebook and pen. While Christy quieted the baby, Nick jotted down some notes. Then he asked, "Were you here all evening then?"

"No, once David got to a stopping place with his carpentry work, we bundled up the baby and went over to his brother's, a couple miles south and east of here."

"What time was that?"

"Oh, somewhere between 5:30 and 6:00."

"So on your way there you would have driven past the fish company?" Nick continued.

"Yah, we did actually, and come to think of it, I do remember noticing the light was on in the office part of the building. I commented to David that there must have been some rush orders for lutefisk if the place had to be open on Christmas Eve. And he said, 'Yup, that's another reason not to go into the lutefisk business.' And then we laughed."

"Okay, so what about on the way home? Were the lights on then too?" Nick asked.

"Hmmm. I can't really tell you because we came back here from the south. It's about the same distance to his brother's either way. So I couldn't see the fish company."

"Did you know Ivar Peterson?" Nick asked.

"Only by sight," she replied, "but since David grew up around here, he remembered him from when he was a kid. David thought he was just one of those 'local color' characters that every community has."

"And what about the Brewers? Did you know them?" Nick asked, wondering if Christy would fess up to trying to help them out with their business.

"I met them once shortly after we moved in here," Christy said. And then she explained how they had moved from the city a year ago. She talked about the marketing job she'd had in Blaine and her husband's tech job Roseville but how he had jumped at the chance to join his brother in his growing construction business in Isanti County. "I was a couple months pregnant, and I had fantasies of working from home, designing websites and consulting with small businesses."

"So have the Brewer brothers been your clients?" Nick asked innocently.

Christy laughed and said that her visit with them had been a pretty good wake-up call to the realities of life in a rural area. "Now when some of my former colleagues come out here for a day in the country, I point to the fish company as an example of a no-frills successful business. They just shake their heads."

Nick thanked Christy for her time, handed her his card and told her to give him a call if she remembered anything else or heard anything from someone who might have seen something odd in Day that day.

On his way out to his truck he managed to keep his balance on the icy path. Once back in his vehicle, he took a few minutes to digest what he'd heard from the people he'd just talked to. He decided he was none the wiser about what had happened to Ivar Peterson. It just doesn't make any sense, he said to himself. A murder of a person who didn't seem to have enemies, committed in an unlikely place, and no one who saw or heard anything suspicious. . . .

{ 19 }

Heading out of Day, Nick decided to go back to Cambridge by way of Dalbo with the Dusty Eagle as a logical destination en route. On the way he began formulating a list of questions about this case:

Was this a random killing—that is, did someone who was driving by decide to pop into a rather unattractive place and off the first person he encountered? Not likely, surmised Nick.

So if it wasn't random, who had motive and what was it? The most likely answer for "who" was Marcie, and a logical motive would be wanting to get her hands on Ivar's money/estate. But unless there was some strange sort of collusion between Marcie and an accomplice, that "who" had been ruled out because of her alibi. The fire was a whole different story and Marcie was certainly going to have to answer a number of questions once she was found.

What about this Leslie character? What was her/his relationship with Ivar that may indicate a motive for killing him? Nick made a mental note that he had to devote some serious attention to tracking him/her down. If it turned out Leslie was not a suspect, perhaps she/he could offer additional insight into associations Ivar had had previous to his work at the fish company.

Was there an old girlfriend who had dropped by the fish company and was rebuffed by Ivar, causing a skirmish that got out of hand? While Nick thought this rather unlikely, he also remembered the smoked fish that had been stuffed down Ivar's pants. That must mean something, Nick thought, but he had no idea what. He was pretty sure, though, that it was not complimentary.

The growling of his stomach jarred Nick out of his contemplations, and he turned his thoughts to the type of burger he was going to order. He fantasized about a nice glass of beer but decided he'd better nix that idea because he was technically on duty.

Since it was a week night, the Dusty Eagle wasn't very busy. As Nick took a stool at the bar, he was greeted by the bartender who was doing double duty that night by tending bar and waiting tables. "What'll you have?" he asked.

"Just a Coke tonight," Nick replied as he pointed to the badge on his jacket. "But I would like one of those mushroom/Swiss burgers."

"Comin' right up," the bartender said as he disappeared into the kitchen to relay the order. When he brought the Coke, Nick introduced himself as the investigator in charge of the Ivar Peterson case. Nick asked him if he was on duty the night of the send-off for Ivar. When he said he was, Nick then asked him if he remembered a red-haired woman who had been sitting in one of the booths with several other people.

"There were a lot of people here that night," the bartender replied. Nick detected some hesitation on the bartender's part to admit what he did or did not remember.

"I'd really like to talk to her," Nick said. "I understand she was also at the fish company for the wake before coming here, so I'm wondering what her connection is to Ivar." He went on to explain that he had just come from interviewing all the residents of Day and no one could offer any clues to who had caused Ivar's untimely death. "My next strategy is to talk to other people in the community. It seems like everyone I've talked to so far

Chapter 19

associates him only with the fish company. I think I need to find folks who knew him before he started working there."

"I'm afraid I can't help you out there," the bartender said. "I've only lived around here for five years, but it didn't take long for me to figure out that Ivar was one of the local characters, and it seemed to me everyone liked him."

"Particularly when he was buying, no doubt," said Nick, and the bartender agreed.

As the bartender went off to wait on other customers, Nick sipped his Coke and helped himself to the popcorn in paper trays on the bar. He was wondering if one burger was going to be enough to assuage his appetite which seemed particularly ravenous.

When the bartender brought the burger, Nick needn't have worried because it was more than generous. As he took the first bite, the bartender said, "About that red-haired woman, I don't know who she is, but I do know some of the people she was sitting with."

Nick put down his burger and took out his notebook. The bartender gave him a couple of names and said he was pretty sure their numbers were in the phone book.

"Are you thinking the red-haired babe might be a suspect?" the bartender asked.

Nick hesitated a bit before answering and then decided he might as well tell only what he knew so he said, "I think she's someone from Ivar's pre-lutefisk past who might have some ideas about why someone might have wanted him out of the way."

"Well, good luck. I hope the culprit is caught soon. I hate to think of a murderer on the loose. I guess it's a good thing the lutefisk season is almost over. If this had happened earlier in the fall, it would have put a real damper on the fish company's business, and this place benefits too from the extra traffic in the area."

Nick responded, "From what I've been gathering, one

homicide isn't going to keep diehard lutefisk lovers away from the source of their holiday bliss."

*****

The next morning Nick was surprised to see a visitor sitting in the reception area of the sheriff's office. This particular visitor was especially noteworthy, for it was none other than the mysterious red-headed woman he'd inquired about the night before.

As he started walking towards her, she rose and said, "Deputy Nordin?"

Nick answered in the affirmative and put out his hand, "Leslie?"

She hesitated a bit before taking has hand. "Yes, but how did you know my name?"

"Why don't we go into my office, and I'll explain. And I'm also looking for some explanations from you."

She followed him down the hall, and once inside his office, he motioned for her to sit down and then closed the door.

"I'll go first," Nick said. Then he explained how he had been told that a red-haired woman had picked Marcie up after her "detainment" and that he'd also remembered seeing a red-haired woman at the Dusty Eagle during the memorial for Ivar. Not only that, but a person by the name of Leslie had left a sympathy card at the fish company. She seemed rather amused by Nick's line of deductive reasoning, but her demeanor quickly changed when Nick said he'd traced the license number of the car in which Marcie had been a passenger after her release.

"Oh, oh," Leslie said. "I guess you must have talked to JoAnn."

"Indeed I did," replied Nick, "and I could arrest you right now for auto theft, but I might let that go if it turns out you can offer me some information that will lead to finding whoever murdered Ivar Peterson."

"Well, it certainly wasn't me, but when I heard you were

Chapter 19

looking for me, I figured I might as well stop by and get my name cleared so you can concentrate on real suspects."

"So what's your connection with Marcie Vaughan?" Nick asked.

"That's a long story," Leslie replied. She then sighed and began her tale that had a variety of adventures, none of which involved murder. She related how as a young boy, she'd been placed in foster care in St. Cloud after his single mother's drinking rendered her an unfit parent. Leslie was subjected to considerable teasing by the others in his foster home primarily because he exhibited more feminine characteristics than what was considered normal. The one highlight of his stay in foster care was a day the kids would spend at a farm, and that farm was none other than Ivar Peterson's. Somehow the foster family knew Ivar, and they would load the kids up in their van early in the morning and make the trip into the country. At Ivar's they could romp in the haymow, let calves suck their fingers, and swing from a tire swing suspended from a branch of a big oak tree in the yard. At noon they would have a picnic lunch that their foster mother had packed for them, and after several more hours of frivolity, they would tumble into the van and return to their house in St. Cloud, most of them falling asleep on the way.

However, the teasing continued and became more hurtful, so one day when he was 15, Leslie took off. He had paid close attention to the route from St. Cloud to Ivar's on those previous trips. By himself, though, it was quite a bit farther than he remembered, but after two days of walking and hitchhiking, he ended up at Ivar's place. Ivar was naturally quite surprised to see him, but when he heard Leslie's story, he let him stay, on the condition that he'd help Ivar out around the farm. Leslie was only too glad to oblige, and he was the happiest he'd ever been.

Behind the scenes Ivar had been in touch with the Stearns County Family Services folks, and at the end of the summer Leslie had to leave so he could go to school. He was placed in a different foster home where he was treated more kindly, and after two years he finished high school. He then went on to enroll in the technical college to study graphic arts. He also got his first paying job, working at Culver's. Once he turned 18 he aged out of the foster care system, but he was able to rent a room in a house belonging to Dolly, the assistant manager at Culver's who had recognized that Leslie was reliable and hard-working.

While Nick thought all of Leslie's story was interesting, he was eager to hear about his/her association with Marcie. Leslie must have noticed his impatience, and after giving Nick a "bear with me" look, she continued.

She explained that one night a visitor came to the house where he was living, and Dolly introduced her as an "old friend." However, when she said that, she winked at Leslie, so he was forewarned that something was awry. This woman was, of course, Marcie, who said she was "going through a period of some difficulties," but she didn't elaborate on what they might be. Dolly didn't ask her for details either. "I got the definite impression she was hinting around for a place to stay, but Dolly didn't make any offers because she didn't have another spare room.

"Marcie also said that she could sure use a cup of coffee, and something to go with it, which I thought was pretty forward. While Dolly was making the coffee, Marcie quizzed me a bit about how I happened to be a roomer in her good pal's house. She told Dolly that this seemed to be a bit of a departure from her old ways. All Dolly said was that she had turned over a new leaf, and it was then I realized that the two of them must have had something shady in their past. Dolly, who was usually quite congenial, set the cup of coffee and a sweet roll in front of Marcie and didn't even join us at the table. By the way that Marcie wolfed down the roll, it was obvious she hadn't had much to eat that day. While she was picking up the last crumb, she happened to notice a photograph lying on the corner of the table. I had used

Chapter 19

it for a school project and I'd brought it back home after I was finished. The kitchen table was as far as it had gotten.

"Marcie picked up the photo which was of me a few years ago earlier on one of those day trips to Ivar's. I was swinging from the tire swing and Ivar was standing off to the side with his thumbs in the suspenders of his bib overalls. Marcie was quite interested in the photo and asked me several questions about where it was taken and who the guy was. I told her about how much I had enjoyed my days there. Then she told me that if I ever wanted to go over to see the place and visit Ivar, she'd be happy to take me. I looked at Dolly, who just shrugged her shoulders."

Leslie continued her tale describing how she and Marcie made a "date" to visit Ivar the following Saturday. Leslie remembered how to get to the farm, and Marcie gave a running commentary of all of the sights along the way. "Oh, now that's a nice house." Or "I wonder how much that tractor cost." Or "Those people need to clean up their yard."

Although they hadn't called ahead, Ivar was home, and he was happy to see Leslie and hear that he was doing well. Marcie wasted no time introducing herself, and while Leslie and Ivar talked, she wandered around the place, peering in all the outbuildings and giving the house a once-over as if she was a realtor looking to list the place for sale.

Marcie didn't waste any time asking Ivar if he needed a housekeeper. She told him she was a good cook, and that it looked like the place could use a woman's touch. Ivar just grinned and said, "Yah, I s'pose so."

"After dropping me back at Dolly's in St. Cloud, Marcie drove off, and the next thing we heard was that she had moved in at Ivar's, presumably as his housekeeper."

"I'm having some trouble getting a few things straight," Nick said. "You were a guy then, but now I'm looking at a woman. How do I know you're really the Leslie who was taken in by Ivar? And I still haven't gotten a good answer as to why you're driving a car that is allegedly stolen."

"Stearns County Social Services would be able to verify that I spent a summer at Ivar's, but they only know that that Leslie was a boy. As for the car, well that's the next chapter in my story."

She went on to tell how as a male she finished tech school and got a job with the newspaper in Alexandria doing graphic design. While she was there, she sometimes went to singles group at a local church with some of the guys at work.

"That's where I met JoAnn. I didn't have much experience with dating mainly because I knew something wasn't quite right with the way I was wired. But I thought maybe I just hadn't met the right girl. JoAnn and I dated for a while, and we had a pretty good time actually, but it started dawning on me that I had some real gender identification issues. She came from a pretty conservative background, which was good in one way because she wasn't going to 'go all the way' until she was married. So naturally she started pressuring me to get married."

"I think I can fill in the blanks," Nick said. "You took off with her car and never left a forwarding address."

Leslie nodded and explained she had spent the last year and a half in St. Cloud undergoing counseling and starting on the path to becoming her genuine self. During this transformation she again lived with Dolly who also became her confidante offering wardrobe, hairstyle and make-up advice. "Marcie would occasionally turn up there (like a bad penny, Dolly said). She always reported that things were 'hunky dory' with Ivar. She said she was sure he'd be leaving her a 'little something' in his will. He'd already bought her a new car because Ivar didn't think her old one was reliable. During one of her unexpected stops, Dolly was trying to style my hair. It had grown out and was a tangled mess of red curls. Marcie was a bit taken aback by the scene, so I told her my story, but both Dolly and I begged her to not say anything to Ivar.

"So you see, that's how I knew about Ivar's passing. Marcie

Chapter 19

called Dolly to tell her. Of course, Dolly and I both wondered if she had had something to do with his untimely death, but she seemed genuinely upset. I looked online and found out about the memorial service, but I did think it was a bit strange Marcie wasn't anywhere around. Then I found out she had been 'detained' thanks to you, presumably," she said, looking directly at Nick.

Before Nick had a chance to offer any explanation regarding that so-called detainment, Leslie continued, "I wonder if the Brewer brothers had any clue I was the kid who had been at Ivar's that summer."

"I'm pretty sure they didn't," Nick said, "but there must be some folks in the area who are aware of your present identity. I can't believe it's pure coincidence that you showed up here this morning when I'd just been asking about you last night at the Dusty Eagle."

"In the 'small world' department it turns out that Joe, the bartender, has a brother who has been in my counseling group."

"I see," said Nick. "Was he in that group you were sitting with the night of Ivar's send-off?"

Leslie looked puzzled for a moment until Nick told her he had been at the Dusty Eagle that night too—in civilian clothes.

"I don't have a clue who they were," said Leslie. "It was pretty crowded, but I had claimed a booth early on. Then these three people came in and after looking around for a place to sit, they asked if they could join me. As far as I know, they were just passing through and happened to come upon a farewell party."

Then after a second or two, Leslie said, "Are you really going to arrest me for car theft?"

Nick, who had been pondering that very question during Leslie's story, said, "No, I guess not. When I talked to JoAnn, she said she would like to get her car back, so how about if you leave it here. I'll call JoAnn and tell her we've recovered her car and she can retrieve it for the cost of bringing the registration up to date."

"I'll have to do something about another, car but I guess a little inconvenience is better than doing jail time. I'll call Dolly and see if she can drive over and pick me up."

"Oh, and thanks," she said to Nick. He was afraid she was going to cry.

Then all of a sudden she said, "I think it's pretty remarkable that I've had this car for a year and a half and no one's seemed to notice the license plates have expired. What's up with that?"

Nick just shrugged and said, "It would have been quite a different story if the car had been reported stolen, so I think you were pretty lucky."

Then Leslie admitted that after making off with the car, she had parked it in Dolly's driveway for several weeks. She said she began tempting fate by driving it for short distances around St. Cloud but stayed off the main streets. The only times she took the car for any distance was when she came over to the fish company and then the next day when she picked Marcie up from jail. "I did think I was pretty cagey to drive right up to a law enforcement center with a stolen car."

Nick had to chuckle at that. As they shook hands, he wished her good luck and thanked her for giving him some insight into both Ivar and Marcie. She said she'd wait for Dolly at the library and she was happy to walk there. "Ivar used to drop me off there when he'd come into town to buy groceries."

As Leslie headed to the door, she turned back and said, "It doesn't surprise me that Marcie burned Ivar's house down. According to Dolly, she had a bit of an arson streak in her. Dolly also said that Marcie was the most stable she'd been in a long time while she was at Ivar's."

Then she was out the door. Nick watched her head down the street, her red curls swinging with every step.

{ 20 }

As Nick headed down the hall to get a cup of coffee, he heard Sheriff Erickson's bellowing voice behind him, "Nordin." Nick turned around, and as the sheriff caught up with him, puffing from the rather hurried walk of 30 steps, he said, "Say, I saw your door was closed there for a while, and then one of the guys saw this red-headed babe going back to her car. I hope this was investigative work on that Peterson case."

"You'll get my report later today," Nick said.

"Wanna give me a little heads up?" the sheriff asked.

"About all I can tell you is that I've come up empty with any leads." Then Nick told him that included in his report would be an account of his visits with the residents of Day, all of whom had not seen anything out of the ordinary on the afternoon of Christmas Eve. "I've got one more potential lead to follow up on, and if that doesn't turn up anything, I'm going to be about ready to retire the case to the back burner."

"I hear you," said the sheriff. "But I don't think I need to remind you that it's pretty important to get this thing solved. It reflects badly on the sheriff's department if there's loose cases out there, particularly when they're homicides."

"And I hear *you*," Nordin said. "There's nothing I'd like better than handing over the perp (or perps) who killed Ivar Peterson. How about if all of us in the department sit down and go over the case once I turn in my report?"

The sheriff agreed that that was a good idea and he'd get back to Nick about a time to meet. Then, saying he had a busy day, he went back into his office and closed the door.

Nick found the scrap of paper in his jacket pocket with the phone number for Mary and Carl, the couple who told him they'd been at the fish company earlier on Christmas Eve Day. When he called them, he was pleased to discover they were home so he made arrangements to visit them later that morning. He then started on the report he'd promised Sheriff Erickson. It gave him an opportunity to review the details of the case and think about what he might have missed. He still had a suspicion that Marcie was somehow involved, but that's all it was—a suspicion— because her alibi was rock solid. The notion that the mysterious red-headed person may have been an accomplice also had come to naught with that morning's visit from Leslie. Nick wasn't ruling out other possible accomplices, but at this point he had no persons of interest unless, of course, Leslie's benefactor in St. Cloud, Dolly, might be involved.

All sorts of scenarios went through Nick's head. Maybe the accomplice paid a visit to Ivar, and what began as a threat to try to extort money from him turned into an assault. Marcie got pissed over the outcome and burned Ivar's house down so her accomplice wouldn't get anything. Or maybe killing Ivar was the plan from the beginning as was the house fire, and now Marcie and her accomplice were holed up somewhere enjoying the cash that they had found hidden in cookie jars and coffee tins in Ivar's house.

However, these speculations weren't getting Nick anywhere, and he was only too eager to interrogate Marcie when she was finally found. He was a little surprised that the APBs had not been successful in locating her vehicle, but with the insights Leslie had provided, he was pretty sure that she had any number of places where she could hide her car where it wouldn't be

Chapter 20

detected. Or maybe it was time to widen the net, so to speak, and consider suspects who may lie beyond the fish company's usual sphere.

With the directions Mary had given him, Nick headed west out of Cambridge on Highway 95 and then he turned north at the sign for Walbo. Ever since he'd been in Isanti County, he had wondered about that sign which pointed to nowhere. It would be one thing if the sign had been handmade and was someone's attempt at a bit of nostalgia, but this was a bona fide MnDot sign. After a little investigating he discovered that "Walbo" referred to a general area more than an actual town. Unlike Day or Dalbo which had once been thriving crossroads communities, Walbo itself had never been much more than a store, and that store had been gone for several decades. However, he's heard folks say that they live out near Walbo, a description which, as a newcomer, he found a bit puzzling.

Nick realized that it was close to noon when he pulled up the driveway to the Eng farm. He was not surprised when Mary meeting him at the door said, "I hope you haven't had dinner yet. I'm just getting the table set, and the potatoes are about done." Nick caught himself from asking "Dinner?" when he realized that for rural folks, particularly farmers, dinner was served at noon and supper was the evening meal. Lunch was the afternoon coffee break.

Since he'd had only an order of toast for breakfast, Nick was ready for some real food which he was pretty sure Mary would be serving, so he gratefully accepted the "dinner" invitation. He was not disappointed. As he and Carl sat down at the table, Mary brought over a steaming bowl of a hearty beef stew with big chunks of meat, potatoes and carrots, all in a rich-looking gravy. On the table were slices of home-made bread. When Mary sat down, she turned the ladle in the bowl towards Nick, and said, "Help yourself."

Nick was only too happy to oblige. As they all began to eat, there were the usual pleasantries of conversation regarding the weather and how lucky they've been with no bad blizzards yet this winter but with the caution that the winter was far from over. Gradually Nick steered the conversation to what either Carl or Mary might have remembered about their visit to the fish company on the afternoon of Christmas Eve. Specifically, Nick wanted to know what time they were there, who else was at the fish company and if they had noticed anything out of the ordinary during their visit.

Mary reported that they had arrived there about 3:00. She remembered it had been a gray day with ice crystals in the air, so the roads had the potential at least to be a bit slick. She also remembered that Carl had beeped the horn at the dogs who were lying right where he wanted to park the car. Carl interjected that he had wondered who belonged to the new pickup truck sitting in the driveway. "That's right," Mary broke in, "and I said it must be a good lutefisk season if the Brewers can afford a truck like that."

"So then imagine how surprised I was when I found out that the truck was Ivar's," Carl said. "Yah, he just stood there and grinned that funny grin of his when I asked who that new truck belonged to."

"Were both the Brewer brothers there in addition to Ivar?" Nick asked.

Carl and Mary both nodded, and Carl added, "But Jack was just getting ready to leave."

Nick asked, "Was anybody else there?"

Carl and Mary looked at each other, and then Carl said, "If they were, they would have had to be in the walk-in cooler. And I didn't see any other cars around."

Nick then inquired what time they had left, and the couple agreed it was no later than 3:30. They had come only to get their Christmas lutefisk, and that didn't take much time. Mary said, "I guess you know why folks don't spend a lot of time there. It

Chapter 20

has always amazed me that the lutefisk tastes so good when the place smells so awful. One time I took my grandson there. He was probably about three, and he couldn't pronounce 's' if it came at the beginning of a word, so 'start' was 'tart' and 'swing' was 'wing.' He kept hanging onto my coat all the while we were in there which wasn't very long, and when we came out, I asked him what he thought of that place. He replied, 'I didn't like it. The 'mell kept coming in my nose.'"

Nick and Carl both laughed, but before Nick could steer the conversation back to something a bit more investigative, Mary broke in with "Oh, that reminds me. For years after the hardware store closed, the building stood there empty, and I thought it would be a good idea to put in a little coffee shop, open only during lutefisk season, you know. I figured I'd have it divided into two parts—one part for those who had been over to the fish company and the other part for those who hadn't been there yet."

Carl added, "To separate the contaminated from the uncontaminated, you mean." And then he brought his fist down sharply on the table and laughed heartily, soon joined by Mary and Nick.

Nick then asked for a few more details about their visit to the fish company on the day in question. They explained that they had simply followed Ivar into the back room and pointed to a hunk of lutefisk in one of the tanks that seemed really prime. Ivar had fished it out, took it over to the counter and wrapped it up for them. Mary paid in cash and they were on their way. Jack had followed them out of the door and got into his truck. Carl and Mary headed south of Day to return home, and Jack had turned west. And no, they didn't meet any strange cars, nor did they see anything unusual.

"And to think that just a few hours later, Ivar was dead," exclaimed Mary. "We're not suspects, are we?"

"Bob Brewer vouched for the fact that he was at the fish company when you were there, so no, you're not being considered as suspects or even persons of interest," Nick replied. Then trying to remain very serious, he said, "Unless, of course, you and Bob were in on this together."

Mary gave him a startled look, and then when she saw a smile creep across Nick's face, she realized he was joking. Carl meanwhile was close to guffawing but was trying his best to stifle it. Mary started chuckling a bit too. She thought it was worth suffering a little practical joke just to see the captivating smile of that young deputy.

"But, you know, Sheriff Nordin, I don't think we'd be even talking about a murder practically in our backyard if people looked out for one another the way they used to."

"Yah, back in the day when that lutefisk plant was the creamery, you'd know right off the bat if there was a stranger that popped up," Carl said. Then after pausing to put a big slab of butter on a slice of bread, he continued, "Now, I like my lutefisk as good as the next guy, but you have to admit that having that outfit in the neighborhood has brought in a lot of strangers."

Mary piped up with, "That's right. There's a lot of customers who drive all the way up from the Cities, and some even come over from Wisconsin. Well, that I can understand because I've never heard of lutefisk being a big thing in Wisconsin. But those city folks wouldn't have to drive way out here to find lutefisk. Those fancy stores like Byerly's and Lunds must have it. Those Lund people are even Swedish, aren't they?"

Nick decided this was a rhetorical question so he merely nodded. He then asked how well they had known Ivar. Their reply was what seemed to becoming standard—that he was a fixture in the community, wouldn't hurt a flea, and certainly didn't have any enemies. Those attributes were then followed by shaking one's head regarding his relationship with "that hussy."

Mary minced no words regarding said "hussy" and blurted, "If that woman could set fire to Ivar's house after all he's done

Chapter 20

for her—taking her in like a stray cat— she certainly could be capable of murder." Then she added, "I don't want to tell you how to do your job, but she's a cagey one, and I'm willing to bet that somehow or another she had a hand in it."

All Nick could say was, "We're certainly keeping her in our sights and looking at all possible angles that could point to her." He opted not to tell the Engs that ever since the fire at Ivar's, she had gone missing, and all attempts to locate her had been unsuccessful.

Nick then steered the conversation to the Engs themselves. Inevitably he heard more bemoaning of all the changes that occurred in the area and that nobody visits anymore.

"Visits?" Nick inquired.

Without making Nick seem terribly naïve, Mary explained that when it had been more of a farming community, neighbors would stop by to visit, maybe on a Sunday afternoon or after an evening church program. Sometimes the visitors had been invited, but more often, they just dropped in, staying for a cup of coffee and to get caught up on the latest neighborhood news.

Mary went on about how neighbors used to take care of each other, and they'd cooperate with some of the farming operations like threshing and silo-filling. Then, with resignation and a hint of contempt, Mary said, "Nowadays, we hardly know who our neighbors are, and everyone more or less keeps to themselves. They're off early in the morning to go to work, and they don't get home until dark. Then it seems like they just shut themselves up in their house and . . . "

". . . Just watch television all night or stare at the computer until they go to bed," Carl chimed in, finishing Mary's sentence.

Nick nodded, and then glancing at his watch, he realized he needed to get back to the sheriff's department if he was going to get his report done for Sheriff Erickson as he'd promised. "I need to be running along," Nick said, "but I sure do thank you for your time and that great beef stew." He fished a card out of his pocket and laid it on the table, "If you think of anything else, and I mean *anything*, give me a call. Sometimes the tiniest detail ends up being the one that solves the case."

He put on his jacket and began heading for the door when Mary stopped him and handed him a Ziploc bag that had a couple of slices of her home-made bread. "You'd better take this. It'll make good toast for your breakfast tomorrow morning."

"Thanks," said Nick, "but I may not be able to wait that long."

Then he winked at Carl who said, "Yah, it's a long ways back to Cambridge. You might need a snack."

{ 21 }

As Nick drove down the driveway and out onto the road, he thought about what the both the Engs and Pat Brown had said regarding neighbors not looking out for one another. But he recalled a couple of instances where neighbors were maybe just a little too vigilant. One Sunday afternoon in the fall when he was on duty, a call came into the dispatcher's office from a concerned citizen who was reporting that she'd witnessed a theft from the yard of one of her neighbors. She'd seen a truck drive in there and had seen a lone man loading it up with junk that had been sitting around the yard. She had been keeping an eye on the place because the owner was in the process of moving and was there only sporadically. When the truck, quite filled with automobile remnants, machinery parts and other miscellaneous scrap metal, left the place, the caller got the license number of the truck and reported that to the sheriff's office as well. It was then an easy matter to track down the owner of the truck and where he lived.

Sheriff Erickson, always eager to mobilize his deputies for a big sting operation, decided that a roadblock should be set up in order to trap the truck owner before he made it home. Because he lived in Kanabec County, the authorities there were also alerted to assist in the roadblock. While Erickson used the term "roadblock," he really meant that a squad car would be stationed on various roads the alleged thief would most likely use to get home. It was another instance of how Erickson exaggerated his image as a powerful sheriff who could conjure up roadblocks with the snap of his fingers. With the deputies from both counties at their "roadblocks," it was just a matter of time to wait for the truck, motion for it to stop, and question the driver about the contraband he was transporting. Erickson was certain the driver would be behind bars that night, and the news of the apprehension would put a stop to the rash of robberies that had been occurring in the rural areas of the county in recent months.

After more than a half hour had passed, the sheriff had to admit that he and all of his men had been outwitted. He figured the thief had either gotten wind of the sting and was holed up somewhere or that he had decided it was too risky to go home and had taken off in another direction entirely—perhaps to a drop site where the contraband would be stockpiled until there was enough for a semi load to be hauled to a scrapyard in Anoka or Minneapolis. Yah, that's about right, thought Sheriff Erickson. This guy was no doubt some low level cog in the scrap business, just hoping to get a few bucks to buy the next bottle or maybe some dope.

In the meantime, the Kanabec deputies had left their respective posts and had met up with one another. One called Erickson and suggested they could stop by the place where the supposed thief lived and see if there was anything suspicious going on. Erickson thought that was a good idea. It meant he could head for his own home, and wouldn't have to go all the way up to Kanabec County.

When the two deputies found the place, to their surprise the truck with the trailer load of contraband was sitting in the yard. As they drove up, the thief himself was ambling from the house to the barn. When he spotted the two squad cars coming up his driveway, he stopped and waited for them to approach him. The deputies figured out quite quickly that this guy did not fit the profile of a lowlife thief. He politely asked them what he could

Chapter 21

do for them, and when they told him who they were looking for, he didn't hesitate to say that's who he was.

When they further inquired about the load of scrap metal, the man explained that he had permission from the owner. He even pulled a piece of paper out of his pocket with the owner's phone number and suggested they should call him. After the deputies asked a few more questions, it became clear that the "thief" and the owner of the scrap metal were well-acquainted, and the owner had been only too happy to have his junk hauled away.

The deputies couldn't help but ask how the scrap collector had gotten home. When he told them the route he had taken, they began to laugh, and one of them said, "Well, that was one road we weren't watching." Then they had to admit that yes, they had cooperated with the Isanti County authorities in setting up roadblocks to try to catch him. The scrap collector just shook his head and said he was sorry he'd ruined their Sunday afternoon.

Another instance came to Nick's mind of well-meaning but misguided neighborhood vigilance. On the Monday morning following the closing of deer hunting season, the dispatcher at the sheriff's office got a call from a woman who had heard gunshots early that morning coming from a corner of her property, and she had seen a guy who looked like he was dragging something toward the road. A deputy who was in the vicinity responded to the call and discovered a fellow loading a freshly shot and gutted deer into his truck. The officer informed him that he was under arrest for hunting out of season and that the deer would have to be confiscated.

While, yes, the deer was killed that morning, the same hunter had actually shot the deer the previous evening just as the sun was setting. It had not been a "clean" shot, however, and the injured deer had escaped into a cornfield. The hunter had reported the incident to the landowner and said he'd like to come back the next morning and put the deer out of its misery. The landowner thought that was a good idea, but unfortunately he

Caught in the Lye

didn't tell his wife, and it was the wife who called the sheriff's office the following day. The deputy, however, was not terribly sympathetic, and following the letter of the law, he fined the hunter $500.00. He also took the deer.

By the time Nick pulled up to the Law Enforcement Center, it was after 3:00, so he knew he'd have to hustle if he was to get a report of his investigation to Sheriff Erickson by the end of the day. However, Nick hadn't specified the end of the "work" day.

As Nick entered the building, the dispatcher flagged him down and said Sheriff Erickson was looking for him. When Nick gave him a questioning look, the dispatcher shook his head and shrugged his shoulders, indicating that he either didn't know why Erickson wanted to see Nick or that he was not at liberty to divulge whatever it was that constituted the urgency for the two to meet.

Nick and the sheriff had already had their meeting in the morning when Nick was mildly reprimanded, so he wondered why two meetings in one day would be necessary. For all Nick knew, Erickson just wanted to ask him to get another canister of those sea salt caramels from Costco that Nick had given him for Christmas. If he'd already eaten the entire two pounds, that could prompt an urgent meeting.

Without even taking off his coat, Nick walked down the hall to Erickson's office. Erickson was leaning back in his desk chair with his arms folded across his stomach. He was watching something on the computer and from the smile on his face, what he was seeing was not an office memo nor a page from the Law Enforcement handbook. On his desk was the canister of sea salt caramels, still almost half full, so Nick had to revise his thoughts about the reason for the meeting.

When Nick tapped on the open door, Erickson straightened up. While pressing a key to darken the computer screen, he welcomed Nick into his office and told him he'd better sit down.

"What's this about?" asked Nick.

Chapter 21

"Well, your case just got more mysterious," Erickson replied. "You're not going to believe this, but Miss Marcie's car was spotted in a ravine near Mankato."

"Okay, that makes sense. If it really was her who set the fire to Ivar's house and then took off, she most likely would have headed south towards Iowa."

"Right," responded Erickson, now champing at the bit to divulge more information and at the same time trying to keep what he had to say a bit mysterious.

Nick just wanted the facts but knew he'd have to indulge Erickson a bit in order to discover what had actually transpired. Erickson explained that a call from the Blue Earth County sheriff's office had come in earlier that afternoon. Erickson decided to wait until Nick got back to the office so he could tell him in person what the call was about.

Nick took out his notebook and pen in order to summarize what the sheriff was relaying to him from Blue Earth County: snow in area followed by drop in temps; vehicle slid off road and down embankment; tracks partially obscured by snow; vehicle discovered Tuesday; plates matched those in APB; no driver in vehicle. . . .

Then Nick's pen stopped in midair when the sheriff's narrative revealed that a body had been discovered a few hundred feet from the vehicle. Nick immediately wondered if this had been an accident or a homicide. If it was the latter, was there a connection to Ivar's murder? But those thoughts were quickly dispelled when Erickson went on to explain that the cause of Marcie's death was hypothermia. The Blue Earth County authorities had determined that she had suffered minor injuries and most likely a concussion when the car went down the embankment and hit a tree stump. At some point she was able to get out of the car and began walking, presumably to get help. In her dazed condition she probably stumbled and succumbed to the cold. They had found her cell phone, half hidden on the floor on the passenger's side of the front seat.

Nick just shook his head, half in sympathy and half in frustration because his investigation had now really hit a dead end. Then he asked, "What else did they find in the car?"

Erickson responded, "Well, I don't know. All the sheriff from Blue Earth County told me is that it had been impounded while they were waiting for instructions from us, and the body had been taken to the morgue in Mankato, waiting for somebody to claim her."

"That may take a while," Nick said. "I didn't have much luck in finding any next of kin when she was alive. But I need to find out what was in that car because I suspect she made off with a bunch of stuff from Ivar's place. If I'm right, that stuff needs to be back here and included with Ivar's estate."

"Okay, here's the number to call," Erickson said, handing a piece of paper across his desk to Nick. "You find any wads of cash, you let me know," he continued. "I'm always looking for contributions for that new radio system I'd like to get."

"Right," said Nick as he rose to leave.

Nick looked at his watch. It was already after four. He went back to his office and sat for a few minutes trying to digest the news he'd just heard and figure out what his next steps should be. He decided he should contact the Blue Earth County sheriff's office to verify the information and see who was now responsible for taking care of Marcie's body. Normally when there's a lone fatality in an accident, the local authorities are charged with notifying the next of kin, but in this case the victim was a fugitive suspected of being a thief and wanted for questioning about an arson.

When Nick reached Sheriff Meyer in Mankato, he verified the facts that had been conveyed by Sheriff Erickson. While Nick really wanted to know about what had been found in the car, out of politeness he first asked for advice on dealing with Marcie's body. Nick explained that it might be difficult to find any

Chapter 21

relatives, in which case one of the two counties would need to take responsibility. Nick said he'd do what he could to find a relative, and he was assured by Sheriff Meyer that the body would be just fine in the morgue for a few days.

Before Nick had a chance to ask Meyer about the car's contents, Meyer interjected, "Now that we've got that issue taken care of, I suppose you want to know what we found in the car."

"Well, yes," Nick replied, "that was going to be my next question."

The sheriff chuckled a bit and said he was glad his boys had gotten to the car before some onlooker had started nosing around. Once he was informed that the car in the ravine and its dead occupant had been the subject of an APB, he had requested that the entire car be considered as evidence and taken to a warehouse where it could be secure until someone from Isanti County could go through it. He said he had personally supervised the car's transport and was sure there had been no break in the chain of custody. The cell phone was left where it had landed after the accident. He also reported what he called a twist of irony-- Marcie's coat was lying on the front seat. Had she been wearing it, she might not have succumbed to the cold. The back seat was empty except for a pair of cowboy boots and a tote bag. But half hidden under the front seat was a strong box. He pulled it out, and to his surprise, it was not locked. He got even a greater surprise when he opened it and discovered several envelopes, each containing bundles of cash.

Finally, thought Nick, he's answered my question. What is it about these sheriffs who seem to have a need to insert more mystery and intrigue than necessary into their investigations? Aloud, he said, "I guess I'm not so surprised. I figured she wouldn't have left Ivar's place empty-handed."

"Wait a minute," Meyer said, "who's Ivar?"

Without going into too much detail, Nick explained that Marcie had been a person of interest in a homicide and also the prime suspect in an arson that had destroyed the homicide victim's house. Nick ignored Meyer's comments that he wasn't aware that Isanti County was such a hotbed of crime and instead asked the current whereabouts of the envelopes of cash.

"I figured I didn't have any choice but to leave them in the strongbox in the vehicle," Meyer said.

"That was the right decision," Nick affirmed. "But now that you know more of the story, you can understand the dilemma of determining who actually belongs to that money."

He then suggested that Meyer retrieve the strong box and lock it up somewhere in the law enforcement center. In the meantime Nick would seek advice from the Isanti County attorney for any further action. Nick assured Meyer he'd be in touch regarding the disposition of both Marcie's body and the car.

"Just as an fyi, there will be a brief article in the paper here which is standard procedure whenever there is a car accident resulting in a fatality. If you want, I could send a copy to a newspaper up your way."

Nick thought for a moment before agreeing that it was a good idea. What he was really thinking was that such an article would be a fast and efficient way to get the word out regarding Marcie's demise rather than let the grapevine take its course. After he hung up the phone, he thought about how these new developments would command a considerable amount of his attention while at the same time would divert him from the homicide investigation.

The first thing he did was call Bob Brewer. He tried the fish company but there was no answer, so he tried Bob's cell phone and got an answer. Bob was naturally quite shocked at the news, but like Nick he wasn't so surprised that a fair amount of cash had been found in the car. Bob, of course, wanted to know how much it was, but Nick couldn't tell him since he didn't know either. As far as trying to find someone to claim Marcie's body, Bob said he certainly had no clues. He reminded Nick that the family she was going to spend Christmas with turned out to be

Chapter 21

a former prison mate. Nick had already considered that woman as a possible lead to Marcie's relatives and also the woman named Dolly, who Leslie thought may have been in prison with Marcie as well. But because Dolly figured in the story regarding Leslie, Nick didn't want to mention anything to Bob about her. Bob said he knew Edith would be concerned about putting some sort of obituary in the local papers, but Nick informed him that a short news release regarding the accident would be published soon. He added that he felt that the notice should suffice. After all, the little they knew about Marcie wasn't exactly good copy for an obituary.

"All right," Bob said, "I'll watch for that notice, and then get ready for all the tongue wagging. And I'd like to know what you find out from the county attorney about who rightfully belongs to that cash."

Nick assured Bob he would keep him informed. He had already written the county attorney's name on his list of calls to make, and now he added Dolly's name along with the Hudson, Iowa, woman. As he looked at the list, he decided that all those calls could wait until morning.

{ 22 }

THE LONE CAN of beer in Nick's refrigerator was a welcome sight when he got home to his apartment. It was after 6:00 because he had spent the last hour and a half finishing his report for Sheriff Erickson. He thought about asking for a reprieve, in light of the recent events, but then he realized nothing had really changed regarding the primary homicide investigation. The house fire, Marcie's disappearance and her subsequent accident had all been just energy-sucking sidetracks.

In spite of the big meal he'd had at the Engs', he was pretty hungry, but his refrigerator was pretty empty. The freezer compartment offered him two choices: a sausage/pepperoni pizza and a chicken pot pie. He chose the latter even though it would take longer to bake. Before he tossed the package, he glanced at the ingredients: only 350 calories. But a little further down the chart he saw there were 19g of fat and 930 mg of sodium. While he didn't have any handy chart to tell him the nutrition details of Mary Eng's stew, he felt somehow that it was healthier than the commercial thing he'd just popped into the oven.

As he sipped his beer, he conceded that he should eat more real food. One option was to get back in the habit of cooking himself, using wholesome ingredients, but another option, which might bring greater satisfaction, was to hang out with good cooks who don't mind sharing the fruits of their labors. That option, of

Chapter 22

course, brought Megan to mind, and the good lunch he'd had there just two days ago. Without hesitation he called her.

She answered on the second ring, and 45 minutes later when Nick's oven timer beeped, it seemed as though they had just begun their conversation. When Nick related the events of the last two days, Megan seemed more interested in the tale about Leslie than she did about Marcie's accident. She said she felt that Leslie was someone who deserved some empathy but that Marcie was a user who didn't seem to have any redeeming qualities. Nick said he agreed, but it was dangerous in his occupation to pass judgement on anyone. Megan then thought for a moment before saying that her occupation demanded the same sort of impartiality. She qualified that statement by adding that it's her *living* clients who need to be treated equally.

Nick made good on his previous promise of asking Megan out for dinner. He said he'd pick her up at 6:00 on Saturday night, and in the meantime he'd scout out a decent restaurant that didn't serve chicken pot pies.

While his pot pie was cooling a bit, he made a salad with a few greens he found in the refrigerator and some slices of green pepper that were still fairly crisp. As he sat down to eat his meager supper, he pondered the choice of restaurants in the area. There was a plethora of pizza places in Cambridge and a few breakfast/lunch places, as well as a few bars. But for this date he wanted to take Megan someplace that had some ambience as well as good food. That meant he'd have to consider places outside the county which was okay as they would be less likely to bump into people they knew. This was going to be a real date and he wanted the evening (or perhaps the entire night) for just the two of them.

At the office the next morning Nick checked his list of names of people to call. He decided to start with those who might have leads to someone who could claim Marcie's body. The sooner that could be done, the less money Blue Earth County would have to shell out for renting a drawer in the morgue. He called the woman in Iowa where Marcie had gone for Christmas. Her voice was still as hoarse as before, and their conversation was interrupted by her frequent coughing. Nick didn't think it was necessary to tell her that Marcie had been wanted for arson, so he revealed only that she had been killed as a result of a car accident near Mankato.

"Mankato?" the woman asked. "Don't tell me she was on her way down here to see me again."

That response answered the question that Nick was going to ask—if Marcie had possibly contacted her to see if she could stay there a few days. Nick said he didn't know why she was in the Mankato area. He went on to ask the woman if she knew anything about Marcie's family. She said that when they were in prison together, Marcie had said her parents were dead and she was an only child. "But who knows if that was true. Her stories had a habit of changing depending on the situation." Nick thanked her for her time and he didn't even ask her to call him if she had any additional information.

His next call was to Leslie. She was completely dumbfounded when Nick told her about Marcie's death. She asked if Marcie had taken anything valuable from Ivar's house before she took off, and Nick said that a fair amount of cash had been found in the car.

"I'm not surprised," Leslie said, "and while I suppose I should feel sorry for her, I'm more upset that she never had to answer for setting Ivar's house on fire or for taking money that didn't belong to her. I hate to say that she got what she deserved, but . . . . "

"So do you have any idea if she had family? I'd really like to help out the Blue Earth County guys and find someone who can take her off their hands." Leslie said she certainly had never heard Marcie talk about any family, but she said she'd ask Dolly who was right there with her. Nick could hear them talking in the

Chapter 22

background, but then Leslie turned on the speaker so Nick could talk to Dolly as well. She was as surprised as Leslie had been, and her sentiments were similar to Leslie's. Also she had heard the same story as the woman in Iowa had about Marcie being an only child with no parents still alive.

"I think this one's going to be on the county," Dolly said. "But, you know, I really think these last few years were some of the happiest for Marcie. She finally had someone to look after her, and she could look after someone else too. The few times I saw her during the time she was at Ivar's, her angry edge had softened. While I'm not a psychologist, I'm willing to bet her anger resurfaced once she realized that the stability she'd known had just been knocked out from under her, and in retaliation she set the fire and took off with whatever she could easily carry."

Nick could only say that he felt Dolly's summation was no doubt right on. He thanked both Dolly and Leslie and said goodbye. Then, looking at his list of people to call, he realized that he had just killed two birds with one stone, so to speak, and he had only one more name on his list, Brad Curtis, the county attorney. Although he expected that he'd either be put on hold or be told the county attorney would have to call him back, the receptionist answering the phone patched him right through when he identified himself. "I've been meaning to call," Curtis said, "as I've been wondering how the Peterson homicide investigation is going." Nick informed him of the latest developments, particularly the problem of the money found in Marcie's car and what appeared to be an unclaimed body.

Curtis, who had been a lifelong resident of the county except for the seven years or so he was at college and law school, was in his second term as county attorney. He often said he'd qualified for the post since his mother was one hundred per cent Swedish, having come from pioneer stock in the county. Marrying Brad's father who was from Oklahoma and who claimed Cherokee heritage had caused considerable consternation among some members of Brad's mother's family because they felt the Swedish purity of their pedigree had been compromised. The fact that he had Native American background was of little consequence; rather it was his non-Swedishness. Brad, on the other hand, was quite happy some hybridization had occurred within the family to avoid what he called the linebreeding phenomenon he'd witnessed among many of his neighbors and relatives. He did have to admit though that having a Scandinavian-sounding name was beneficial when running for public office. His middle name was actually Johnson (after his mother's maiden name), but he thought it would be a little presumptuous to call himself Brad Johnson Curtis, particularly if he dropped the "Johnson" after the election.

When Brad asked Nick how much money had been found, Nick could only relate what the Blue Earth County sheriff had said — that there were several envelopes bulging with cash.

"Well, depending on the denominations of the bills, the number of envelopes and just how bulging they are, we could be talking a few hundred dollars or thousands," Curtis said. After thinking for a minute, he advised that because of the circumstances, with both the finder of the funds and the presumed donor of the funds now dead, it was essential that Nick go to Mankato to retrieve the cash and other contents of the car.

"Count the money, and if there's enough to handle a cremation, and I'm willing to bet there is, go ahead and make those arrangements. As for the car itself. . . "

". . . I was told that Ivar had bought it for Marcie," Nick broke in.

"Then no doubt it's paid for and the title most likely burned up in the house. It's probably best to just haul the car to some salvage place down there. Go through the other stuff in the car and if there isn't anything that bears evidence to the case, get rid of it. Bring the rest of the cash back here, so it can be added to Ivar's estate, unless, of course, you decide to treat yourself royally

Chapter 22

on this little junket." Then he laughed and both he and Nick sat there for a moment reflecting on the strange events of the past couple of weeks.

"At least the lutefisk business will continue, won't it?" Brad asked.

"I don't see why it won't," Nick answered. "The Brewers will have several months before this fall's lutefisk season to find a replacement for Ivar, and it may take that long to locate someone who is willing to put up with the working conditions, if you know what I mean."

"Indeed I do," said Brad. "As soon as I could drive, my mother would send me to Day to get the cherished lutefisk every fall. I thought she was pretty trusting, letting me take the car by myself for the 12-mile trip, but now I know better. She wanted to inflict that contamination on me rather than herself."

On that note Nick left Brad's office and headed back to the sheriff's department. He decided to call down to Mankato to say he'd be there sometime in the afternoon. He figured he'd better take an overnight bag along just in case he couldn't get everything taken care of that day. Then he advised Sheriff Erickson that he was going to be gone at least the rest of the day and maybe part of Friday as well. The sheriff just nodded and told him to report in when he got back because he was really curious about how much money "that woman" had stolen. Nick didn't think it was worth explaining that there was actually no evidence the money had been stolen, so instead he brought up the subject of the report he'd submitted.

Yes, the sheriff had read it, and yes it was quite detailed, but it had left out one important fact—who was the perpetrator who had been responsible for Ivar's death? Nick then reminded the sheriff of his suggestion to distribute the report to the other deputies and then call a meeting to try to figure out if Nick was missing something or if there were new leads that should be investigated.

"Okay, let's schedule something right away Monday morning. I'll have Grace make copies of your report and get it out to the guys today," the sheriff said. Nick thanked him and as he walked back to his office, he wondered if the sheriff could even find the report among all the other stuff on his desk.

Once in his own office, Nick made a call to Bob Brewer to apprise him of the latest developments. Bob was not surprised Nick hadn't found any of Marcie's relatives, and he was relieved that the cost of handling her body would be taken out of the cash in the envelopes she had with her. "I was afraid I was going to get stuck with paying for her cremation too," he said. "And by the way," he added, "it looks like I've been appointed executor of Ivar's estate."

"Well, that'll keep you busy this winter," Nick said,

"Ya, it's a good thing the lutefisk season is about over so I'll have a little more time. I've already checked with almost every lawyer in both Kanabec and Isanti Counties to see if by chance Ivar had a will on file, but no luck. That would sure simplify things."

Nick agreed and was ready to end the conversation, but Bob went on to tell him what about another old bachelor who had died without a will. "He didn't have much money, but he owned 80 acres and most of it was tillable except for the area around the house, which was so full of junk you could hardly walk. The guy went to auctions and bought all the leftovers. Since the stuff had been accumulating for several decades, some of it had sunk into the ground and was half buried. The guy didn't even have electricity, but there were several refrigerators in the yard. When someone would ask him if any of them worked, he'd reply that they work real good in January. Everyone thought the property would just revert to the county, but then it was discovered that the guy still had one remaining cousin (out of a total of 47), and by law he was the rightful heir. This cousin lived in another state, was himself quite elderly, and had never even met the deceased.

Chapter 22

He had to be reminded of how they were related. So he inherited a decent piece of property, but after he took a look at it, he sold it to a neighboring farmer for less than it was worth because he didn't want to have to deal with all the junk."

Then coming back to Ivar's situation, Bob said, "Well, from what I can tell, Ivar didn't even have any cousins at all, living or dead, so if someone comes out of the woodwork claiming to be a relative, I'll be pretty surprised."

Nick, who was eager to get on the road to Mankato, said, "If that should happen, you let me know because they could be a possible suspect."

"You got it," Bob said.

After he hung up, Nick was quickly out the door of the law enforcement center, and he was on his way to Mankato within 20 minutes. He stopped briefly at his apartment only to grab a duffle bag he kept partially packed for just such junkets related to his work, or for other occasions that could keep him away from his apartment for an overnight elsewhere.

His GPS guided him through the Cities and on to Highway 169, which would take him right into Mankato. When Nick first moved to the area, it took a while for him to realize that when people referred to "the Cities," they meant Minneapolis and St. Paul, their closest major shopping/entertainment area. But then he remembered that his relatives in Wisconsin had also used that term. At the time he was too young to realize they meant the Twin Cities that were more than 150 miles away. He didn't remember hearing about the Cities in South Dakota where he grew up, but that was in west river country (meaning west of the Missouri River), which gravitated more toward Denver or Cheyenne than to the far eastern part of Minnesota. He wondered if people in North Dakota used the term "the Cities" to refer to Fargo/Moorhead. Probably not.

As soon as Nick was southwest of the Cities, he realized he was hungry so he succumbed to the allure of a number of billboards promoting Emma Krumbee's, a combination restaurant, bakery, gewgaw store and apple orchard. He knew from experience that such places were over-hyped and usually over-priced, but the place was easy to get to and he figured it offered a few more lunch choices than McDonald's and was a little more interesting than Perkin's. He was not disappointed with the French Dip sandwich, but he didn't think he'd make a special trip there to attend the Scarecrow Festival in October.

Once in Mankato, Nick located Sheriff Meyer at his office in the Blue Earth County Justice Center on the eastern edge of the city. Before Nick even had a chance to sit down, Meyer grabbed his coat and headed out the door to lead Nick to the warehouse where Marcie's car had been secured. Meyer let him into the warehouse, showed Nick where the car was and proceeded to leave, reminding Nick to turn off the lights and lock the place up when he was through. "I'll see you back at the office," Meyer said. Okay, then, thought Nick. I guess I'll be handling this all on my own.

Nick began by retrieving the cell phone from the floor on the passenger's side of the car. He could only surmise that Marcie couldn't find it after the car had gone down the embankment, or perhaps she was too dazed to even remember she had one. As he suspected, when he flipped open the phone, he saw that the battery needed charging. Then he quickly looked through her purse, coat pockets and glove box, but he didn't find a charger.

Nick thought it strange there wasn't a suitcase anywhere, but then Marcie might have been planning to use the cash she had pilfered to buy what she needed to re-invent herself in some new locale where no one would know about her past. On the floor of the back seat was a pair of Ariat cowboy boots that looked quite new and were no doubt rather expensive. He shook each one out in case there was something hidden inside and then put them in his truck. A rather beat-up zippered totebag was on the back seat. He unzipped it and saw some underwear, a hair dryer, a few

Chapter 22

other personal items and a cord that did indeed fit the cell phone he'd dropped into his pocket. He was eager to find out who Marcie called between the time she was released from jail until her fatal accident. He put the tote bag, her coat and her purse in his truck too.

The trunk held only an empty cardboard grocery tote and a couple of small rugs. He removed them and shook them out, noticing that they were rather beat-up too. Then he remembered that a lot of people keep old rugs in their trunk as they come in handy if they get stuck in the snow. Placed either in front of or behind a wheel, they can offer just enough traction to prevent the wheels from spinning. He shone his flashlight around the trunk but saw nothing that was even remotely suspicious.

Back at Meyer's office, Nick used a spare workstation to plug in Marcie's phone and go through her purse and tote bag. He was surprised that there were no messages on Marcie's phone and according to the call log, she hadn't called anyone and no one had called her since she called Leslie to pick her up from jail. What a lonely person, he thought. All the more reason to guess that she wanted to start over completely in some new destination.

Nick's thoughts were interrupted by Sheriff Meyer who came in with a square steel box in his hands. "I figured you'd want to know how much money there is in here," he said. "You'll need to know that before you can make arrangements with the morgue for that woman's cremation."

"All right," Nick said somewhat hesitantly, realizing that the order of events was out of his hands. When Meyer opened up the box to reveal its contents, Nick was quite amazed. He counted fourteen envelopes, each one "bulging with cash" as Meyer had described them. Nick took out the first envelope, pulled out the bills and began counting. To make things easier he made stacks of ten bills, and since each bill in that envelope had a picture of Benjamin Franklin and there were eight stacks, that first envelope held $8,000. He followed the same procedure with the other thirteen envelopes. By the time he was done, he had counted $112,000.

Meyer assisted by clipping the stacks together so each one held $10,000 except for the last one which had only $2,000. At some point in the process, Meyer said, "Wait a minute. We'd better make sure these aren't all counterfeit." Nick had to agree that was a good idea. While Meyer went off to look for a counterfeit pen in the bookkeeping department, Nick pondered the idea that maybe Marcie's stint in prison had to do with counterfeiting and that this money hadn't been Ivar's after all. That idea quickly evaporated, however, when Meyer's magical pen revealed that the bills were indeed real. When they had finished counting it all and had put the money back in the strong box, Meyer said, "Well, I guess you have enough cash to pay for that woman's cremation. Which reminds me," he continued, "the morgue called and wondered if you'd be able to stop by there yet this afternoon."

The money counting had taken longer than either Meyer or Nick had expected, so Nick hoped that someone was still at the morgue. When he got there, the attendant was relieved that someone had finally shown up to offer instructions for either disposal or removal of the woman who was almost a "Jane Doe." He asked Nick if he could make a formal identification. Nick recoiled a bit but then realized that even though the Blue Earth County authorities had matched the woman's car license with the APB that had been posted, there was only an assumption that the victim was the subject of that search.

Nick followed the attendant into the morgue and waited while the drawer presumably containing Marcie was pulled out. Since Nick's experience with morgues had been quite limited, he wished this opportunity hadn't been sprung on him without warning. He quickly brushed that thought aside and instead concentrated on how he was contributing a service. A quick glance confirmed that the person was definitely Marcie, and as

Chapter 22

the attendant pushed the drawer back in, Nick's next thought was of Megan and how she deals with such situations almost daily.

In the anteroom to the morgue the attendant and Nick discussed what the next step should be. Nick said that in light of no information regarding next of kin, Isanti County would pay for the cremation. He filled out an affidavit to that effect and said he'd been authorized to pay cash.

After he left the morgue, Nick realized it was too late in the day to deal with the disposal of Marcie's car, so he called Sheriff Meyer and left a message saying he was going to spend the night in Mankato and would get in touch with him the next morning.

Nick spent a restless night at the Super 8 motel. He kept dreaming about the cash found in Marcie's car. In one dream there were garbage bags full of money in the back of his truck, and as he drove down the highway, bills were flying out of the bags. In another dream he was in shackles because the money had all disappeared and he was accused of taking it. In the final dream, at least of those he could recall, he had reported only half of the money. He took the rest of it to Megan's farm where the two of them hid it in the barn for such time in order to start a new life together in some exotic place, not identified in the dream.

While the other dreams had disturbed his sleep somewhat, that last one prompted him to become wide awake. Before he was able to get back to sleep, he tried to analyze why the dreams focused on the money. Granted, it was more money than he had ever seen, but it wasn't millions. And how to get it back to Isanti County had certainly been on his mind. Did the dream about Megan mean he was actually falling for her? The other possibility was that because she had been involved in the Ivar case right from the beginning, it would be logical to dream about her. What he concluded before he drifted off was that the dreams were symptoms of his frustration over this entire case. Spending two days in Mankato, money or no money, was keeping him from finding the person (or persons) who were responsible for Ivar's being in that fish tank.

Even though Nick didn't feel very rested the next morning, he was motivated to complete his work in Mankato as quickly as possible. On the advice of the Isanti County attorney, he and Meyer took the strong box with the money to the Farmer's State Bank. Two cashier's checks later, Nick dropped one of them (in the amount of $2,000) at the funeral home with cremation instructions for the corpse at the morgue. The other check he was to deliver to Bob Brewer with instructions to deposit it in an escrow account for Ivar's estate.

Nick's next set of instructions related to Marcie's car. He'd already been assured by Sheriff Erickson that Isanti County didn't want to deal with it, so Nick authorized Meyer to go ahead and sell it at Blue Earth County's next vehicle auction. "If it brings more than what you've already spent for retrieval and storage, keep the extra and put it your rainy day fund."

With those tasks completed, Nick was ready to head back north. It gave him an eerie feeling to have some of Marcie's stuff in his truck. But he decided he'd take it with him and see if the Shalom Thrift Shop was interested in either the coat or the purse. They didn't need to know who they had belonged to. The cowboy boots were another story. They were in such good shape that he wondered if Megan might want them—if they fit, of course, and if they wouldn't serve as a constant reminder of the fish company.

{ 23 }

Nick arrived at Megan's promptly at 6:00 p.m. Saturday for their first real date. He'd gotten up that morning, ready to do some laundry, but as he went through his closet to find something to wash so he'd be presentable that evening, he realized his civilian clothes were in a sorry state. So as soon as Kohl's opened, he headed to the east side of Cambridge to do one of the things he hated most—shopping for clothes. Since his entire work career had been with agencies that required uniforms, he owned only a couple of pairs of jeans, a few sweatshirts and tees and one pair of four-year-old khakis. His shopping excursion netted him two pairs of slacks and two Oxford shirts that he figured would suffice for just about any occasion. It wasn't as if there were a lot of gala events in Isanti County that required black tie (or any tie, for that matter).

Finding a place to take Megan for something other than a burger had been a bit of a challenge. While he knew he'd have to go outside the county, he didn't want to drive a long way, particularly after he had just driven all the way to Mankato and back.

A phone call to Madeline Moriarty provided the solution. This time when he called her, she answered on the second ring. She seemed pleased to hear from him, and when he said he was looking for restaurant advice she wanted to know if he was just asking for himself or if it was for a group or maybe for someone

Caught in the Lye

special. She said "special" with a rising inflection, so Nick confessed that he wanted to impress a young lady with a place that had some ambience without being ostentatious or overly expensive.

Madeline thought for a moment and then she said, "I think I know just the place. Although it's in Anoka County, it has a connection to Isanti County as well."

She went on to tell about a place called Kendall's Tavern, named for a man named Kendall Bunker. "He came from Maine in the early 1860s and first farmed in Anoka County. Then he moved north and started farming on land that eventually was absorbed into the town of Cambridge. Some of his descendants are still around."

Madeline said she'd never been to the restaurant, but when a new manager took it over and remodeled it, he decided to use the first name of the original owner of the land where it is located, at the Bunker Hills Regional Park. "Some reporter even called me and wanted to know if I had any photos of Bunker. People often think I've got some sort of arsenal that I can just tap into for all kinds of esoteric information."

"Well, you do seem to have a lot of material either at your fingertips or in your head," Nick said. "I was pretty amazed at how you pulled together all that stuff about lutefisk for me."

Madeline laughed, saying she maybe should have suggested that the reporter call her back if the restaurant decides to serve lutefisk.

"You let me know what you think of the place," Madeline said. "And I hope both you and your lady friend like it."

She paused a bit and then asked, "Can you tell me who she is or is her identity a secret?"

"Her name is Megan Perry," Nick answered.

Before he could say anything more, Madeline said, "Oh, that cute little undertaker in Braham."

Nick was glad Madeline couldn't see his cheeks turning red.

Chapter 23

He simply responded, "That's right." Then he added that their initial meeting had had a lutefisk connection too—all in reference to Ivar Peterson's demise.

"See there," Madeline responded. "You can't get away from it—if you live in these parts anyway. You don't have to like it, but you may as well embrace it as part of the local culture."

Nick agreed, and then the conversation ended with Madeline saying she wanted him to let her know what they thought of the restaurant. She also added that if he wanted to bring Megan by sometime, that would be just fine.

Megan had been in almost the same quandary as Nick about her wardrobe. She too had a work uniform, a black suit with either slacks or a skirt and a prim white blouse, at least when she was out in public. Behind the scenes, it was quite a different story—scrubs with a disposable apron and latex gloves and a face mask. And at home her standard outfit was jeans and a flannel shirt in winter and a t-shirt or tank in the summer. Since Nick had indicated that he was going to take her somewhere "nice," she figured jeans would not be appropriate. Shortly before Christmas she'd bought a green long-sleeved pullover tunic and she decided on it paired with black tights.

When Nick arrived at her house that evening, Megan was eager to know what kind of a place he'd chosen. "So where are we going?" she asked.

"You'll see," replied Nick. "We have to drive a ways, but I think it will be worth it."

Megan did begin to wonder where Nick was taking her when, after driving for a half hour he pulled off the main road onto a secondary road that seemed to lead to a park or a golf course. Then a few minutes later a large lodge-type building came into view which she assumed was their destination. The parking area was almost full which she thought was a good sign. Because Nick had made reservations, they were seated immediately. After the server had taken their drink orders, Nick explained the history of the place and the reason it was called Kendall's Tavern. Megan was duly impressed, and in looking around at the crowd she decided that she'd chosen her outfit well.

The evening gave them a chance to learn a bit more about each other. Nick told Megan about his trip to Mankato, and Megan asked him how he felt about going into the morgue and identifying Marcie's body. He replied that in law enforcement work, seeing the occasional dead body is all part of the job. "But for you," Nick said, "it's a bit more than occasional, and I have wondered what that must be like."

"Well, as you said, 'it's all part of the job,' but I'm glad I have my little farm where I have lots of work to do that has nothing to do with my job." Then she suggested that they not talk about their jobs, so they concentrated on eating their salads. While they waited for the main course, Nick leaned towards Megan and asked her what size shoe she wore. Megan was a bit taken aback by the question, but she laughed and told him, "Seven and a half." Then she asked why and Nick, leaning towards her, whispered in her ear that he might have a surprise for her. His lips brushing against her ear caused Megan to shiver, and she felt herself blushing. She avoided Nick's eyes and turned her attention to the server, who was heading toward their table with a chicken rigatoni for her and a braised pot roast for Nick.

During the rest of the meal there were no more occasions requiring whisperings, but when Nick helped her with her coat as they were leaving, he gave her shoulders an extra little squeeze, and on the way out to the car, they walked arm in arm. While they continued their easy conversation on the way back to Megan's place, there was a bit of tension in the air as each wondered how the evening would end.

At the restaurant they had eyed the splendid array of desserts on the cart that had been wheeled by their table, but Megan said a bit flirtatiously that she did have fresh home-baked brownies at home and that she was sure she had some ice cream as well.

Chapter 23

With that announcement it was clear that Nick would not be just dropping Megan off at the door and going on his way. Even if Megan hadn't made that overture, Nick had intended to use the cowboy boot surprise to assure that the evening could be extended beyond the drive and the dinner.

When they got out of the car at Megan's place, Nick retrieved a shopping bag from the back seat and carried it with him into the house. When he set the bag down, Pepper at first recoiled but then he gingerly approached the bag and sniffed it vigorously. By this time Megan was very curious, so Nick told her to sit down and take off her shoes. As she obeyed, Nick retrieved one of the cowboy boots (perhaps illegally confiscated) from the bag. He knelt on the floor in front of Megan, who by this time was heartily laughing, and proceeded to try to maneuver her foot into the boot, ala Cinderella. Her foot went only half way, and then she had to assist by pulling it on the rest of the way. She stood up to further adjust her foot, and standing rather lopsidedly, proclaimed that yes, it fit.

Then, realizing that Nick had asked about her shoe size while he was relating the story of his trip to Mankato, Megan asked, "So were these Marcie's boots, by any chance?"

Nick, now standing in front of her said, "It's possible." And before Megan could protest, he drew her to him and whispered in her ear, "This can be our little secret."

Once again Megan felt the combination of shivering and melting. Releasing herself, she turned and hobbled towards the kitchen, saying, "I'll get those brownies."

When Nick followed her, Megan gave him the task of dishing up the ice cream which was almost rock hard. They had just sat down at the kitchen table to enjoy their dessert when Megan's cell phone rang. She glanced at the caller i.d. and said, "Oh no," and then to Nick said, "I've got to take this."

Megan got up, and with her "one shoe on and one shoe off" gait she went into the living room to take the call. The conversation was quite one-sided as her contributions were mainly, "Uh, huh," "When?" "I see," "Okay," and finally "Give me a half hour." As she hung up, she muttered, "Damn" and then returned to the kitchen.

Nick asked, "Everything okay?"

Megan explained that it had been a busy night at the funeral home. Even though she wasn't technically on call, she was needed to help retrieve a body from the hospital in Cambridge. Wes had gotten a call from the Kanabec County hospice people that one of their clients had died at his home north of Ann Lake. He was on his way there when the call came in from Cambridge.

During her studies at the U in the courses regarding funeral home administration and management, Megan had been warned that an undertaker is basically on call 24 hours a day, seven days a week. Fortunately, she didn't get calls like this one very often, but she was quite disappointed, to say the least, that she was needed at this particular time. Ordinarily Stone himself could have stepped in and helped out, but he and his wife had just left for a two-week vacation in Florida.

Megan explained to Nick that "duty calls," apologizing for having to cut their evening short. Nick replied that she was not nearly as sorry as he was and gave her a warm hug. She managed to get out the words, "Thanks for the great dinner and thanks for the cowboy boooooo. . ." when he planted a kiss firmly on her lips, stopping her both from finishing her sentence and also from breathing momentarily.

When their lips finally parted and she caught her breath again, they stood in a comfortable embrace until Nick said, "As if it's not bad enough that I could be called anytime day or night, I have to find a girl who's got the same occupational hazard."

"At least we weren't in the middle of something more important than eating ice cream and brownies," Megan said as she gave Nick a peck on the cheek. As she headed up the stairs to change clothes, she was glad that Nick couldn't see how she

Chapter 23

was blushing from what she couldn't believe she'd just said. She heard Nick chuckle as he let himself out and headed to his car.

Nick called Madeline on Sunday afternoon the next day to thank her for the tip about the restaurant. The phone rang several times before her voice mail began immediately with this recording: "Did you know that the Cambridge Woolen Mills made more than one million pairs of socks for the Armed Forces during World War II? This is Madeline, and that was your historical message for January; now please leave me a message." Nick did just that, and as he hung up, he wondered if some folks called Madeline in hopes she wouldn't be home so they could just hear her historical witticisms. He'd try to remember to have an excuse to call her in February to hear her next historical tidbit.

When Madeline called him back that evening, she said she was glad she hadn't given him a "bum steer" about the restaurant. She asked what they'd had to eat, how the service was, and if they'd tried any of the desserts. When Nick said that they had gone back to Megan's for dessert, Madeline responded with, "I see." Nick thought he'd better explain that their night had ended rather abruptly when Megan got a call to go to work. Madeline chuckled and said she was sorry to hear that. Nick mumbled something about how both their jobs require being on call almost twenty-four seven; then he asked if he could stop by sometime because he had a couple of things he wanted to run by her. "Sure," Madeline said. "Anytime. Just give me a call to make sure I'm home."

When Monday morning rolled around, Nick was eager for the meeting with the other deputies and investigators to hear what insights they may have regarding the homicide case. He hoped that after reading the report he had written, they might have seen something that had been overlooked or that required a different approach. Nick was open to all suggestions, but he hoped that as the "new kid on the block" he wasn't regarded as incompetent. The group gathered in the conference room at the law enforcement center. As Nick was about ready to review his report, Deputy Hokanson burst into the room, apologizing for being late. Sheriff Erickson asked what excuse he had this time, and Hokanson, who was grinning like the proverbial Cheshire cat, said, "Just when you think you've seen everything, you find out you haven't."

Hokanson then proceeded to tell about the call he'd answered earlier that morning from a worker at the public library. Because it wasn't an emergency, she hadn't called 911, and instead had called general number for the sheriff's department. The worker explained that she came to work at six o'clock each morning, well before any of the other staff, and lately she'd noticed a van parked in front of the building. It had been there the last three mornings. When he asked if the van was occupied, she said this morning she had driven by slowly and noticed there was a man in the driver's seat who had his head back and was maybe asleep. But what she also noticed was that he was wearing just an undershirt, and it was fifteen degrees outside.

Hokanson told her he'd do a drive-by and check it out. He drove the few blocks from the sheriff's office to the library and saw a van parked near the front entrance. He approached the vehicle from behind and noticed from the exhaust that the engine was running. His initial thought was that this might be a potential suicide. Then as he walked up along the driver's side of the vehicle, he could hear loud music coming from inside the van. When he approached the driver's door and was about to tap on the window, the guy's head snapped forward, and he looked at Hokanson with wide eyes. Getting his bearings, the man rolled down the window, and Hokanson asked him what he was doing outside the library so early in the morning. He said he was just taking advantage of the library's wi-fi. Hokanson thought that was perhaps a plausible explanation, but he asked the guy to step out of the van. When the guy said it was too cold, Hokanson told him, "Put on your god-damned shirt and coat if you've got one."

Chapter 23

The man fumbled around the front seat and found both a flannel shirt and a parka. He put the shirt on, taking a fair amount of time and then put on the parka while he was getting out of the vehicle. Hokanson then looked inside the van. He expected to see a laptop somewhere which would give credence to the guy's story of poaching the library's free wi-fi.

What Hokanson saw instead was a desktop computer setup in the back of the van complete with cpu, monitor and keyboard. He then noticed that there was a cord running from the cpu out the passenger's side window and across the sidewalk and through some bushes to an outdoor outlet on the side of the library. So not only was the guy pilfering the library's wi-fi, he was helping himself to their electricity.

Hokansan pulled his head back out of the van and asked, "What the hell do you think you're doing?" The guy replied that he had stopped in the library the previous week to use a public computer to download some music. But he was told he couldn't do that on the library's computers because of copyright infringements. When he had noticed some folks working on their laptops, he asked if he could bring in his own computer to get the music he was looking for. The librarian replied that the staff didn't monitor how personal computers were used. A few days later he returned to the library with his desktop computer, complete with cpu, monitor, and keyboard, but he was told that only laptops or other truly portable devices were allowed.

With that rebuff the fellow decided to turn his desktop computer into something more portable with the help of his van and an extension cord. He said he came to the library around five o'clock in the morning, not only because it was unlikely that anyone would be around to question his activity, but also because it gave him a couple of hours before it was time to go to work. While he waited for the music to download, he was able to catch some sleep. He kept the motor running to stay warm, and he figured he wouldn't succumb to carbon monoxide poisoning with the window open a crack. He didn't offer any reason why he wasn't wearing a shirt. Hokanson surmised that it was his usual attire when in sleep mode although he did wonder how the guy could sleep with the loud music reverberating off the walls of the van.

Hokanson's story brought many guffaws from the other men around the table, and one of them asked Hokanson if he had filed any charges against the guy. "Naw," replied Hokanson. "Quite frankly, I don't know what I'd charge him with. He wasn't trespassing, and all he was stealing was a little electricity from the library. So I suggested that he should drop a few bucks in the donation jar the next time he went inside, and I recommended that he might want to keep his shirt on to avoid scaring any passersby. He said he could do that, and he even apologized for causing any concern that required any police involvement."

Sheriff Erickson, wanting to move on to the discussion of Nick's case offered that it was up to the library to do anything further. "It would be easy enough to put a lock on that outdoor outlet if they want to prevent such happenings in the future," he said. "And they've got their own tech guys who ought to be able to figure out how to keep those wiffie rays, or whatever you call them, inside their own building."

Amid some clearing of throats, Nick got to the business at hand. He began by saying that he hoped everyone had read his report. As he looked around, he did see that everyone had a copy in front of him. He went on to say he needed to add an update and then told them about his time in Mankato, the significant amount of cash in Marcie's car, and his phone calls to both Leslie and Dolly.

"From the moment I heard Marcie's voice on Ivar's cell phone, I was sure that she had something to do with his demise. And as I learned more about her, she had all the markers—a prison record, lonely, conniver, arsonist, etc.—but the evidence doesn't support my gut feeling."

Chapter 23

Deputy Sullivan pointed out that if it was money Marcie was after, she could have taken off with that strong box at any time since she obviously knew where it was, and Ivar may not have even missed it for a good long while. The others agreed. Then Inspector Peters said he thought the fire was pretty good evidence that Marcie was not involved in the homicide. Everyone, including Nick, looked at him with some incredulity, and Peters explained his reasoning. "Look, here's a woman who's had a checkered past who finally found someone who gave her a decent place to live, provided a few creature comforts and didn't judge her. Then he's gone, the circumstances regarding his death are mysterious, and she realizes she's also lost the stability she'd had, probably the first she'd ever had in her life. Add to that, she's considered a suspect, so she gets angry – an emotion that she's most likely familiar with, but one which has been kept under the surface during the time she's been at Ivar's. She knows she has no legal right to anything of Ivar's, so she's going to make sure no one else does either. She burns the house, takes off with the money and presumably is going to re-invent herself."

"But she must have known she'd have to do time for arson. I mean that's why we had the APB for her," chimed in Deputy Hokanson. "I was out there the day of the fire. There was no way that that house burned down by accident."

Sheriff Erickson, who prided himself with short investigations that resulted in perpetrators being caught and cases wrapped up, said, "I think we can all agree there's a lot about that broad Marcie we don't understand, but if you all think she's in the clear, then we need to move this investigation in another direction and find whoever the killer is.

"Or killers," Sullivan added. "Deputy Nordin's report indicates that it may have taken two people to get Ivar into the lutefisk tank, assuming, of course, that he didn't go into that tank of his own accord." They all chuckled at that last comment, even Nick.

Deputy Dahl, who had been quiet up to this point, said, "I'm interested in the theory that it might have been a woman or a couple of women who were involved. Those things stuffed in the pants suggest some sort of jealous rage by a woman had either been snubbed or somehow wasn't getting the attention from Ivar she thought she deserved. I mean a smoked fish and a cell phone do seem a bit weird, but maybe they were just convenient."

"Okay," Inspector Peters said, "Let's go with the jealousy theory and develop a scenario that might have taken place. Two women walk into the fish company, presumably to buy lutefisk or herring or whatever. They know Ivar, so they strike up a conversation and one of them gets a bit flirtatious. He tries to ignore her but she persists. Maybe she'd had some sort of relationship with Ivar in the past, or maybe she's heard about Marcie, so she taunts him a bit, and the other one chimes in. In any case they probably make some comments about his manhood, or his lack thereof, if he's not responding the way they think he should. They start moving around the floor—doing a sort of dance with him going backwards and the two women in front of him, and then one of them starts to undo his pants."

"Whoa," interrupted Erickson again, "How much further you going to go with this?"

"Probably only about as far as the women got," replied Peters. "Continuing with this scenario, when they discovered that Ivar was not going to cooperate, they sought revenge, and one of them pulled Ivar's cell phone out of his pocket and shoved it down his pants while the other one did the same with a smoked fish that she maybe was planning on buying. Somehow Ivar got away from them, perhaps thinking he could find refuge in the fish tank room. However, at least one of them followed him and hit him on the back of the head with something. The blow caused Ivar to fall into one of the fish tanks. His lower extremities were still outside the tank, however, but with the women's help they ended up in the tank as well. The women then went on their way,

Chapter 23

leaving us with an unsolved crime."

"Good story, Peters," commented Sheriff Erickson. "Could be likely too. But it doesn't get us any closer to finding out who these women are or if that's even how it all went down."

Deputy Sullivan then addressed a question to Nick, "Are you absolutely certain that those two women Dolly and Leslie aren't involved?"

Nick replied, "I'm about as sure as I can be. They certainly have rock solid alibis for the time when the crime was committed. And there is no evidence they might have had accomplices who they conspired with, so yes, I've ruled them out as suspects."

Sullivan continued with another question for Nick, "And what about the neighbors in Day? I know you interviewed them to find out if they had seen or heard anything out of the ordinary on the day of the crime, but could it be possible that one of them is a suspect?"

"I saw nothing in any of those interviews to indicate they might be involved," said Nick. He added that the general feeling he had gotten not only from the fish company neighbors but from others as well was that Ivar was a gentle, trusting soul who didn't make enemies, but he was easily taken advantage of.

Erickson, wanting to get on with his day, said, "Okay, let's wrap up. Deputy Nordin, why don't you give us a summary of what you heard here today and if you got any ideas for how you're going to proceed."

Nick said he appreciated all their comments and if there were any conclusions to be drawn, they were that the crime was not committed randomly, but by someone who knew Ivar, either currently or perhaps from his past; there was more than one perpetrator, and they were likely female. He joked that at least the field of suspects had now been narrowed to maybe less than a thousand.

With that the meeting ended and the group dispersed. On the way out of the room, Peters took Nick aside and said that because the homicide was such an anomaly, it may be that the best strategy was to adopt a "wait and see" attitude. "Neighbors and acquaintances of Ivar may not be suspects, but they unwittingly may know someone who is connected with the crime. It may be a while before someone even realizes they know something, but since we're not dealing with a serial killer, it's okay. Sheriff Erickson wouldn't agree, but that's only because he thinks an unsolved case will damage his chances of getting re-elected."

Nick thanked Peters for the advice and returned to his office.

{ 24 }

While Nick appreciated the input from his co-workers, he had hoped the meeting would offer some hints for new avenues of investigation. Peters' suggestion to "wait and see" wasn't how Nick liked to work, but he had to agree he didn't have much choice. Being assigned to a homicide case had given him a bit of a reprieve from some of the more mundane cases that the sheriff's department dealt with.

One morning he went with Deputy Dahl on a run to Grandy where there had been a report of gunshots. What they discovered was a domestic disturbance, and one that had a rather unique twist. A shot (only one, not several as the person who called in the report had said) had been aimed at a rooster, and not just any rooster but an exotic breed and a prize-winner at that. A neighbor had finally had enough of its crowing early in the morning and decided to take care of the problem.

While the deputies were sorting out what had happened and were trying to decide if charges should be brought, another neighbor stepped out of a house next door. He said he too had heard the shot just as he stepped out onto the porch to retrieve the morning paper. He was relieved to hear the real reason for the shot because he thought his ex-wife had possibly been shooting at him. The deputies just looked at one another, and Nick wondered how long it would be before they would be called to Grandy again for another shooting. The shooter in this incident, however, offered to pay restitution to the rooster owner, so the deputies decided their work was done there, and they headed back to Cambridge.

Nick, who had been feeling that Isanti County was more like the wild west than the area he had come from in western South Dakota, asked Dahl if there weren't ordinances regarding having roosters in a town. Dahl said there were in Braham, Cambridge and Isanti, but since Grandy was not incorporated, it didn't have ordinances or any kind of city government, for that matter. Dahl went on to say that almost more interesting than a bird being shot was the guy who thought his ex-wife was shooting at him. "I know that guy," he said, "and I'm pretty sure I know who lives in that house he came out of. It may well be that his wife, who I don't think is an 'ex,' might have good reason to fire off a few rounds at him."

* * * * *

Since Nick had taken the job with the Isanti County Sheriff's Office, he had settled into a routine of having breakfast at one of the local cafés before heading to work, unless, of course, he got an early morning call that demanded his attention—in which case he kept a supply of yogurt cups in his refrigerator that he could grab on the fly. He rotated between the restaurants in Cambridge and Isanti and preferred those that were local, not the chains or fast-food. That gave him a total of three to choose from, places where he could get a full breakfast, not just a roll and coffee.

Instead of sitting at the guy table which all three restaurants had for the regular local male customers, Nick chose a table or booth by himself and used the opportunity to read the Minneapolis newspaper. When he first began this breakfast routine, he'd occasionally sense that the guys at their special table were discussing him, wondering who he was and what his position was with the Sheriff's Department. One time he overheard their conversation about that department's big budget

Chapter 24

and how back in the day there was maybe just the head sheriff and one deputy and that now there were "God knows how many deputies." That prompted someone else to say he didn't feel any safer now than he did in the past. Then the voices got more hushed so Nick couldn't hear the rest of the conversation. Soon the group had moved on to the next topic, which predictably was how they thought the Vikings would do this season.

Nick also observed that it was not just him who raised some curiosity from the regulars. They took note of anyone who came in whom they didn't recognize, and Nick got the distinct feeling that no matter how many times he patronized the restaurant or how long he lived in the area, he would no doubt be considered an outsider. Being involved in law enforcement also probably didn't help folks to warm up to him. It was not as if these attitudes bothered Nick. He wasn't the glad-handing or back-slapping type and preferred to remain somewhat aloof. Of course, if any one of them came over to introduce himself, Nick would reciprocate and welcome the guy to sit down.

With the waitresses, however, Nick was much more personable, perhaps because it was a one-on-one situation. But he was careful about how much information he divulged about himself because he knew they would report any information they had gleaned to the occupants of the "guy table." He was also aware that a couple of the younger waitresses were a little overeager to please. He treated all of the waitresses the same, cordial and polite, never asking any questions about their personal life.

Nick thought the names of the cafes were curious, particularly People's Café on Main Street in Cambridge. He'd noticed that there was also a People's Bank and a People's Realty. He'd have to remember to ask Madeline about that name the next time he saw her. The other full-service, locally owned café had an equally ambiguous name. It was called the Everyday Café. Did that mean it was open every day, Nick pondered, or did the name imply it was open only during the day and not in the evening.

The Creamery Café in Isanti at least had a name that suggested a former use of the building. It had indeed been a creamery that was a dominant landmark in the village. When it closed in the 1960s, the big butter churn and other large equipment were moved out, and the space was transformed into a restaurant. Its one drawback, both for the customers and the wait staff, was that it was on two levels. While the upper level was only a couple of steps up, it was a hazard for anyone with mobility issues, and it was an inconvenience for the waitresses.

One morning while Nick was at the Creamery enjoying his eggs over easy with whole wheat toast, he was joined by Bill from the DNR. They hadn't seen each other since the afternoon of New Year's Eve so they had some catching up to do. Nick summarized what had happened with his homicide case, and Bill was surprised it was at a standstill. He, on the other hand, had been kept busy monitoring the lakes for anything illegal, from no license to non-regulation fish houses to over-the-limit fishing. Bill then told a story about one fisherman who had a close call with an ice auger. "When I was out on Lory Lake one day, I heard some yelling coming from the other end of the lake. I looked down that way and could see someone, a guy I assumed, although sometimes it's hard to tell with everyone wearing lots of clothes. He appeared to be doing a little dance a few feet away from his truck. So I hopped in my truck and went toward the ruckus. What I saw was a guy with one pants leg ripped all the way up his outer leg. It seems he had had some trouble getting his ice auger going, and when it finally started, it had so much force it got away from him, sort of taking on a life of its own. When he tried to go after it, it spun around and grabbed onto the pants leg of his coveralls. Had he been wearing regular pants, they probably would have been ripped right off. As it was, the seam of his coveralls gave way. He finally was able to get the auger under control, and by the time I got there he was laughing

Chapter 24

rather than yelling. I told him he was darn lucky the auger didn't do more than rip his pants."

* * * * *

It was a few more weeks before Nick had an opportunity to get together with Madeline again. When he called her to set up a time to meet, he was almost disappointed when she answered because he was curious about what this month's historical tidbit might be on her answering machine. As he headed out to her place one afternoon, he wondered what kind of culinary surprise she might have for him this time. When she opened the door for him, the aroma that came greeted him indicated he would not be disappointed. It was a mixture of something gingery and fruity, he thought, and as he stepped into her kitchen, he spied a freshly baked pie sitting on a cooling rack on her kitchen table. "Wow," he said, "does that smell good!"

"I certainly hope you like it." Madeline said, "It's one of my signature pies—apricot, cranberry, ginger. It's a good wintertime pie. In fact, at one time it had the potential to become rather famous." After seeing Nick's puzzled look, Madeline said the pie had to cool a bit anyway before she could cut into it, so she suggested they start with a cup of coffee and she would explain.

"Did you ever hear of a governor we had by the name of Jesse Ventura?" she asked.

"Oh, yah, I was pretty young, but he was pretty notorious."

Madeline said that she had been asked to bake a pie, preferably a unique recipe, that would be given to Governor Ventura at a tourism conference in St. Paul. A delegation from the Braham Pie Day committee was attending the conference to promote the town's annual pie festival, and it seemed only appropriate to present the governor with a pie.

"Wait a minute," Nick interrupted, "What's this about a pie festival?"

Madeline gave him a questioning look until she realized that he had arrived in the county in the fall of the previous year – after

Chapter 24

Pie Day in August. "That's another conversation," Madeline said. And then she continued with her story, explaining that the Braham delegation was waiting at the back of the auditorium with pie in hand, ready to present the pie to the governor when he finished his keynote address. However, soon they were being surrounded by the governor's security personnel, whose body language indicated that there was no way the delegation was going to get close to the governor with their pie. Unbeknownst to the Braham folks, a pie, most likely a crème-filled one, had been thrown at the governor a few weeks before by someone protesting his budget proposal to cut funding for arts and culture. Although the Pie Day delegation was disappointed that their pie wouldn't be featured in a photo op with the governor, they did at least have a snack for their ride back to Braham following the conference.

"So now, let's sample this one and see how misguided those security personnel were."

After Nick took a bite of the still warm pie, he assured Madeline that if he had been in charge of the security detail back then, he would have fired all of them.

They both laughed. Then Nick asked Madeline if she knew why a bank, realty and café were named "Peoples."

"Actually I don't," replied Madeline, "but I do know that such names are not unique to this area. At least, I've seen Peoples banks in other parts of the country. I suspect the name might have something to do with making it sound as though the business is local and serves the people in a particular community."

"As opposed to dogs or cats or cows?" Nick asked with a twinkle in his eye.

Madeline chuckled. "Well, I know also that those names have led some folks to wondering if there had been some Communist activity in the area—you know the idea of the common people versus the ruling classes. And then there's also the People's Republic of China."

Chapter 24

She went on to tell how at a dinner party one night the conversation turned to a discussion of getting an appropriate statue in Cambridge that might be a tourism draw, sort of like Ole the Viking in Alexandria or Paul Bunyan in Bemidji. One person suggested a giant potato that people could walk through and there would be eyes that lit up. It took Nick a moment to catch on about the potato "eyes" and then he sort of groaned, which Madeline said everyone around the table had done too. Someone else suggested that because of the various businesses with People in their names, there could be a statue of Karl Marx. Everyone sat up in a sort of shocked amazement except for one fellow who had been very quiet the entire evening. He merely said, "Karl Oskar Marx."

Nick again looked a bit puzzled, but he caught on as soon as Madeline mentioned the statues in Lindstrom of Karl Oskar and Kristina, the prototypes of the Swedish immigrants to the area.

"Speaking of Swedes," Madeline continued, "dare I ask about any progress on your homicide investigation?"

"Well, you can ask," Nick replied, "but I don't have much progress to report, just some sidetracks."

"I assume you mean the fatal accident that claimed Ivar's girlfriend, or whatever you'd call her. I saw the notice in the paper about that. It took me a minute to recognize the name, but then it dawned on me who she was. So with her out of the way, are you back at square one?"

"I guess so. I'm being advised to take a 'wait and see' approach. But that's not how I like to operate. I can't believe that a prime suspect is going to just drop out of thin air."

Madeline thought for a moment. "I don't think that's going to happen either, but I think this case is sort of like an onion."

"How do you mean?" asked Nick.

"It's got several layers. You've been working on the first layer, which is the present, and any of Ivar's current associates and neighbors. But you've come up with nothing. So now it's time to peel back that layer and go to the next—somewhere, maybe 20-30 years ago, pre-Marcie at any rate, and before Ivar worked at the fish company. Talk to some old-timers around Day, find out who his friends were, if he had any other lady friends, if there are any neighbors who held a grudge or if there are any distant relatives." She paused and said, "Well, you get the idea," as she watched Nick busily taking notes.

Then Madeline continued, "After that go the next layer, further back in his life. Find out which school he went to, and what church his family went to. If you can, find a couple of his school mates or someone from his confirmation class. . . ."

Nick interrupted with, "I like your ideas, but I think I'd better start with that last layer since any of those informants are most likely dead or close to it. As far as Ivar having any distant relatives, I think I can rule that out because Bob Brewer told me that as executor of Ivar's estate, he hadn't been able to find a single one. But how would I find out about his school classmates or who was in his confirmation class? Don't tell me you have that information in your files too?"

"No, but I have some ideas of where you can look," she replied.

She told Nick that first he'd need to find the church of Ivar's youth, which wouldn't be too difficult since there were only two likely churches his family would have attended. He could contact the church to see if the confirmation photos were available. She explained that most churches, at least if they practiced the custom of confirmation, had the photos on display in a big folio hanging on the wall. It was a good public relations move as former members returning to the church enjoyed looking at the photos and would often leave a donation, sometimes substantial.

As for Ivar's country school class, she said that might be a bit more difficult, but she advised Nick to check with the local historical society. They had information on all the country schools in the county, and they might have class lists from at least some

Chapter 24

of them. He would need to find out first which of the 69 rural schools in the county Ivar had attended, but that shouldn't be difficult either because it would have been the school nearest to the place he'd lived all his life.

Madeline poured Nick another cup of coffee and moved the pie a little closer to him so he could have another piece. Nick looked longingly at the pie and then, deciding to throw caution to the winds, he scooped another piece onto his plate. He didn't know when he had tasted anything quite so delectable, if not a bit unusual. The combination of the tartness of the cranberries and the sweet apricots was wonderful, and gentle spiciness of the ginger was a great addition.

"As far as I can tell," Nick said while he was preparing to take another forkful of pie, "in these later years, at least, the Brewer brothers knew Ivar better than anybody. We talked generally about him early on in the investigation when I was trying to figure out who might want to do him harm. They said he had a tendency to be over-generous some times, but he wouldn't hurt a flea. And as far as they knew, although they had only known him about the last 20 years, he had never had a girl friend before Marcie, let alone a wife."

"I was pretty sure he was part of that Swedish bachelor farmer group," said Madeline.

"Are they kind of like the Norwegian bachelor farmers Garrison Keillor talks about in Lake Wobegone?" asked Nick.

"Yes, but around here they're Swedish. They're the guys who just never left home. They'd often take care of one or the other of their parents, and when their parents eventually died, they continued to live in the home place. Usually they continued to farm but sometimes they took up a trade. They seemed to be well-accepted in the community and were often involved things like the church, the creamery association and other neighborhood groups. Unless, of course, they took to drinking, which a number of them did."

Madeline continued, "The phenomenon has even captured the interest of some college professors. Their findings were pretty interesting once you got past the mumbo-jumbo, but they wanted to peg these guys as latent homosexuals. Well, maybe some of them were and some of them weren't. I think it has more to do with what I'd call 'luck of the draw.' In a family of several kids, some have more get-up and go than others, and they can't wait to get away from the farm to try to make their mark in the world. Others are comfortable right where they are, and by the time they figure out that they should be thinking about raising a family, the women have either all left or they are all spoken for. And then of course, there's some who would never be able to cope with anything beyond their immediate range of vision."

"I've run into a few of those," Nick said, "but they aren't necessarily bachelors or farmers though."

"I know what you mean. They tend to think that the world stops at the county line. It's quite amazing that we can be so close and yet so far from a major metropolitan area." Madeline paused and then said, "Speaking of which, do you ever get into the Cities for some entertainment?"

"I always check the Minneapolis Sunday paper to see what's going on, but the ticket prices tend to keep me away. Then when you add on parking and maybe a meal, it all makes for a pretty pricey evening, one that's beyond my pay grade for sure. But Megan and I are planning on going to the horse expo in March at the state fair grounds. She wants to look at horse trailers, and I'll just tag along."

"Great," said Madeline. "That will give you an introduction to that place so you can be ready to go there again in August for the great Minnesota get-together." She hastened to add, "the Minnesota State Fair. You must have just missed it last year. I'll bet Megan has been to it. Was she ever in 4-H?"

"Yes," Nick replied, "and she's talked about being in horse shows in Brown County, but I don't know about the state fair."

Chapter 24

"It's always good to have an escort the first time you go because it can be pretty overwhelming. If Megan's not available or if she's out of the picture by that time, you let me know and I'll be glad to show you around. I practically lived at the fair when I was a kid."

"I certainly hope Megan's still 'in the picture' but it would be great fun to see the fair from your perspective. Maybe we could make it a threesome," Nick said.

"I hope I don't have to wait until August to meet her, and I'd prefer to meet her in an unofficial capacity, if you know what I mean. So why not bring her by sometime?"

Nick said he would. He knew Megan was a bit curious about this older woman he keeps talking about.

{ 25 }

Following Madeline's advice to peel back the layers of "the onion," Nick gathered information regarding Ivar's youth. He found his confirmation picture at the Lutheran church in Dalbo and was a bit amused at seeing a tall, gangly kid who looked like he was trying to be serious, though a grin was creeping across his face. Nick wrote down the names of the other confirmands, eight in all, and then asked the pastor if any of them might still be in the area. The pastor said none of the boys, at least, were presently in the congregation. He couldn't say for the girls because they had no doubt gotten married and changed their names. He referred Nick to a man by the name of Joe Sletten, an older parishioner who might have more information. As Nick thanked him and turned to leave, the pastor asked him what church he belonged to. Nick was glad his back was to the pastor so he wouldn't see his face. He managed a smile when he turned back to face the pastor and said he'd moved here only recently and hadn't found a church yet. That was certainly true, but what he left out was that he hadn't exactly been searching for a church. The pastor merely said, "You'd certainly be welcome here. Stop by some Sunday morning and see what you think." Again Nick thanked him and said he might do that.

As he walked to his truck, he was relieved that he hadn't gotten more of a hard sell about either this church or religion in general. He had seen enough of regular churchgoers who put on

Chapter 25

a pious face Sunday mornings but during the rest of the week showed a different face either in the way they treated their family or how they ran their business. Add to that the abuse scandals in the Catholic church and the numerous tv evangelists who had confessed to infidelity, and Nick had concluded that he'd get along quite well without joining a church. Maybe if and when he had kids, he'd think differently, but he certainly wouldn't want his kids to endure the type of Sunday School he had gone to. It had been one big guilt trip that made him feel unworthy, never able to measure up to what was expected of him. He remembered crying one Saturday night because he didn't want to go to Sunday School the next day. When his mom asked him what was the matter, all he could say was that Sunday School made him feel icky. She asked if some of the other kids had been mean to him but he said, "No, it's that God. He thinks I'm terrible and doesn't want anything to do with me unless I get saved, and I don't even know what that means." The episode was still quite vivid in his memory, and what was even more vivid was the great regard he had for his mother, who told him he never had to go to that Sunday School again.

Years later his mother told him about a time in that same church when she had gone to the Christmas party for the ladies' group. The guest speakers were a missionary couple who had served somewhere in South America for a number of years. Their talk was illustrated with slides that offered a retrospective view of the time they had spent in that particular mission field. The early ones showed lush forests with chickens running wild while the recent ones showed barren land and long buildings with chickens in cages. It was not clear how complicit the missionaries were in all the changes, but they were quite proud of the progress that had taken place. They also described some of the Christmas customs in the area, among which was cooking tapioca in red wine. One of the missionaries said she had even tasted it and it was pretty good, but she hastened to add that any alcohol had been destroyed by the high heat. After their presentation there was the requisite lunch, including dishes of ice cream. Because it was Christmas time one could add either red grenadine or green crème de menthe. Nick's mom couldn't resist asking the hostesses if the crème de menthe had been well cooked. They laughed and said that of course it had. She also noticed that both the missionaries and most of the church women passed on the non-alcoholic grenadine syrup and chose crème de menthe instead. Nick's mom also remembered that the decibel level in the church dining room rose considerably while the women were enjoying their green ice cream sundaes.

On his way back to Cambridge, Nick passed a couple of churches that looked like they had just popped up on the landscape. He thought they looked like glorified pole buildings and then chuckled at his own pun. He surmised that they were most likely splinter churches as he'd seen the same phenomenon in South Dakota. A group of parishioners find something or someone to disagree with in their congregation and decide to leave and start a new church. With limited funding, they can only afford to put up a pole building, and often the ringleader of the disgruntled group proclaims himself (and it always seems to be HIMself) pastor. He heard Sheriff Erickson once refer to these churches as upstarts with a polebarn prophet. Nick wondered what the survival rate was of all of these upstart churches and what effect they had on the more established churches in the county. A pastor he had gotten to know in Spearfish had once told him that the more churches there are in an area, the lower the percentage is of church-going people. Nick couldn't help but think that because most of these pop-up churches were on private property, they were also good opportunities for some tax write-offs. Maybe they could also be considered "polebarn profits."

Nick remembered that after his negative Sunday School experience, his parents started shopping for another church. It was at the time when churches were feeling the pressure to be

Chapter 25

more contemporary, presumably to appeal to younger families in the community. One church they visited had just begun the practice of projecting the words to the hymns on a large screen in the front of the church. Nick's dad was not impressed. He thought such efforts degraded the worship experience. He'd even said, "Next thing you know, they'll be singing 'Lift High the Screen.'" Nick didn't quite understand what his dad was talking about. All he knew was that the God in that Sunday School didn't make him feel icky. His parents decided that if Nick was more comfortable there, they could put up with the screen and the occasional tambourines.

All of a sudden Nick's radio came to life, and he heard the dispatcher inquire of his whereabouts. Nick said he was about two miles west of Cambridge. The dispatcher replied that he'd just gotten a call from a farmer just west of Braham who came home to find that one of his cows was missing. "Do you suppose you can take a run up there and see what's going on?" Just then Deputy Hokanson broke in saying he was already in that neighborhood but the other deputies should be on the alert in case he needed back-up. Nick shook his head and wondered what the logical explanation would be for the "missing" cow. He was pretty sure it wasn't a case of rustling, but whatever it was, he was sure Hokanson would have a good story to tell.

Nick was relieved he didn't have to go on the call because he had made an appointment at the county historical society to try to find information on the rural school that Ivar had attended. If he didn't make it this afternoon, it would be several days before he could get there since it was open only a few hours a week. As he drove up to the building, he was quite surprised that it appeared quite new and seemed quite large for a county historical society. He'd been expecting maybe an old school or other old building that historical societies often inherit when the building had outlived its usefulness for its original purpose.

Nick didn't want to reveal a lot of details about his inquiry, but he knew there would be some curiosity because he was in uniform and presumably on duty. He asked the volunteer researcher how he would go about finding the name or number of a rural school in a particular area of the county. She disappeared momentarily and came back with a map that showed all the school districts in the county from the time before consolidation. Nick quickly found where Ivar had lived and just as quickly found the school district number.

His next question was met with a response that was not so satisfactory. He asked if the society had records from that country school and if there might be lists of students who had attended. The volunteer shook her head. She explained that if the records from that school had been turned in to the local historical society, they would have been sent to the Minnesota Historical Society. She said he was welcome to contact the state agency, but that the researchers there might consider class lists confidential unless one is looking for one's own information. "Considering the last rural school in the county closed in 1971, I guess you're not asking for yourself," she said. Nick was sure she was hoping that he would divulge the reason for his query. But, before she could ask any more questions, he flashed one of his winning smiles and thanked her for her time. On his way out of the building, he dropped a ten-dollar bill in the donation jar. It's not much, he thought, but it might pay for a light bulb or some paper towels.

When Nick came to work the next morning, there was a lot of chatter and laughter coming from the break room. As he wandered in to get his coffee Deputy Hokanson said, "Nordin, you gotta hear this." The other deputies, who had already "heard it," eased themselves out of the room.

On his way out, Investigator Sullivan patted Nick on the back and said, "Be thankful you didn't take the call yesterday." Then he winked and left Nick waiting for Hokanson's story.

Hokanson related that when he drove up to the farm in question, he was met by Ralph Bergman, the farmer who had

Chapter 25

called the sheriff's office. "So what's this about a missing cow?" Hokanson had said. Bergman explained that he was going to retire from farming so he was getting ready for an auction to sell all his livestock, milking equipment, tractors, machinery and other farm-related items. But he had one cow who was not quite up to par, and the vet had suggested she be separated from the other cows and fed a special ration. So he'd put her in a pen by herself, and each day she seemed to be improving. However, when he came home from town, having been gone only a couple of hours, he noticed some strange tire tracks in the yard and then discovered that the cow was gone.

Bergman showed Hokanson the pen where the cow had been, and he also pointed out that there seemed to be some spatters of blood on the ground. Hokanson was trying to figure out what his next step should be—put out an APB for a large Holstein named Annabel, make plaster casts of the tire tracks, call out a lab technician to analyze the blood spatters, or just tell Bergman that his cow was no doubt curtains and to count it as a loss on his taxes. However, then Bergman's phone rang, and what Hokanson could hear went something like, "Yah, yah, yah, I see, Uh, huh, You don't say, Well, I'll be damned, Thanks for calling." When Bergman hung up, he told Hokanson there was no longer any mystery about what happened to the cow, and he was sorry he'd bothered the sheriff's department with this matter, knowing that they have more important things to do.

"I stood there dumbfounded, and then I asked Bergman, 'What the hell happened?' Bergman, who had a sort of hangdog look, said it was all a case of mistaken identity. Ross Bergman, no relation to Ralph, is a farmer about three miles down the road. He had a downed cow, as in dead, and he was the one who had called the rendering company. All I could say was, 'You gotta be kidding me.'

"Ralph said that no, it was true. The rendering company got the wrong Bergman, and when the drivers came out to his place and looked around, they discovered the lone cow off by itself and assumed it had some sort of terminal illness. One of them used his pistol to put the cow out of its misery, and they hauled it away."

"So how did they find out they'd made a mistake?" Nick asked.

"That call Ralph got while I was there—it was from Ross. He explained the mix-up to Ralph. Ross said he'd gotten impatient waiting for the truck to arrive, so he called the rendering company to ask when he could expect them. When the rendering company guy said that the truck had just come back in, it was clear there had been a mistake.

"According to Ralph, the guy asked Ross, 'What did you say your name is?' And when he said, 'Ross Bergman,' the guy on the other end of the phone said, 'Oh shit. Oh shit' and a few other choice words. Then he added, 'Well, I guess we'll have to make another trip out that way then.'

"That's one for the books, don't you think?" asked Hokanson. "When Ralph told me what had happened, I didn't know whether to laugh or cry."

"So how was he taking it? I mean, a cow can be a pretty valuable piece of property."

"It was just one of those 'shrug your shoulders' type of moments. You know, kind of like 'shit happens.' But the thing that got me is that the rendering company didn't even call Ralph to apologize."

"I guess the value of a cow drops considerably once it's dead," Nick said.

"You got that right," Hokanson responded. With that they went off to their respective duties, but Nick did find himself smiling in spite of himself whenever he thought about the incident.

{ 26 }

When Nick tried to call the old timer that the Lutheran pastor had suggested, there was never an answer. Since all he had was his name and telephone number, Nick looked online and found Sletten's address in Wyanett Township about nine miles west of Cambridge. He found the place without any trouble, but the driveway was several hundred feet long and it had not been plowed. The snow was five to six inches deep, but there was a set of tire tracks, and Nick could see a car parked outside the garage. As Nick started up the driveway, he saw someone come out of the house and head toward the car. The person stopped short when he saw a sheriff's vehicle, waiting where he was until Nick stopped and got out of his truck. When Nick introduced himself and said he was looking for Joe Sletten, the man said that he was out of luck because Sletten was in Florida and wouldn't be coming back until mid-March. He went on to explain that he was just checking on the place to make sure there was still heat and that nothing had frozen up. And no, he didn't have the snowbird's phone number on him, so Nick gave him his card and asked him to call when he had it.

Of course, the man wanted to know why Nick wanted to talk to Sletten so Nick said, "Don't worry, he's not in any trouble and there's no emergency. I'm kind of new to the area, and I'm always interested in hearing stories from old-timers about how things used to be."

As soon as he made that statement, he realized it was pretty lame, but the man just said, "Sure," and he put Nick's card in his jacket pocket and continued toward the car. Nick was able to turn his truck around, and after making sure that the caretaker didn't get stuck, he headed back to Cambridge thinking that he'd no doubt be waiting a long time for the old-timer to call.

Maybe a better plan, Nick thought, to get at those layers Madeline had referred to was to attend the auction of Ivar's stuff. Bob Brewer had called him to say he had set a date for the auction. He said it had been quite a job to sort through all the old machinery and pieces of junk that were lurking in the various outbuildings at Ivar's farm. He also said he was a bit relieved he didn't have to deal with any household goods as that house had been stuffed. The farm itself was also scheduled to be auctioned at the same time. Because Ivar didn't have a will nor any heirs, the proceeds from the sale would go to the county. That information had not been made public because it was feared that prices would intentionally be deflated. Thus the auction bill would indicate only that it was a sale "to settle the estate of Ivar Peterson." In addition to some old tractor and machinery aficionados, there might be some old-timers there too, Nick thought, who could shed some light on someone from Ivar's past who might want to do him harm. He also would be on the look-out for any potential suspects.

Nick called Megan to see if she was interested in going to the auction since it was right in her neighborhood. And he told her she might find a nice piece of machinery she could hitch her horse to. She said she thought it would be fun. She had often gone to auctions with her dad when she was a kid. He called auctions Norwegian casinos—there was no fee get in, you could stay all day and you only paid when you won. But with Megan's acceptance of the invitation, there was her usual caveat—if she didn't get called to work. In addition to their dinner date that had

Chapter 26

ended rather prematurely, according to Nick anyway, there had been two more occasions where her work had interfered. She had had to cancel a movie date at the last minute because she got called to pick up a body. And another time when they had made plans to hear a jazz combo at the Hardy Performing Arts Center in Cambridge, she had called the night before to say she couldn't go because the time of the concert was the only time family members of their recently deceased grandmother could meet to plan her funeral. Because she was still the rookie funeral director, she got the short straw when it came to body pick-ups and making funeral arrangements that were on evenings and weekends. Nick understood that Megan needed to comply if she wanted to advance in her chosen line of work.

Luckily it had been a slow few days at the funeral home leading up to the auction so Megan was available. When Nick picked her up Saturday morning, she was dressed in her insulated coveralls. As soon as they got to the auction, Megan headed right over to the camper that served as auction headquarters to get a bidding number. "Are you really planning on buying something?" Nick asked.

Megan replied, "Probably not, but you always get a bidding number. It makes you seem more like one of the crowd and not just some gawker."

"I guess I'll be gawking then," Nick said. "If I find something I want to bid on, I'll just use your number."

"We'll see about that," she said. Then she added, "Actually, it might be all right to gawk. Auctions are good places for those inclined toward larceny to case the place for any items that hadn't been put up for auction." As she looked around, she said, "Not much to case out here though."

When Nick spied Jack Brewer among the auction-goers, he walked over to talk to him while Megan perused the items on the wagon. The two men shook hands, and then Nick asked, "What do you think about the size of the crowd? About what you were expecting?"

"Hell, that's hard to say," Jack said. "With auctions you just never know." Then as he looked at the people gathering around the wagon where the first bidding was about to begin, he added, "Yah, mostly a bunch of gyro-gearloose guys, you know, always looking for the odd tool or piece of machinery they might be able to use someday for whatever cockamamie project they're working on or thinking about working on."

"Nick grinned, "I know the type."

"At least we'll get rid of the stuff. That was a big job to pull everything out of those sheds. You never know what you might find. We had to rig up lights, and there were a couple of times when I just wanted to set a match to the whole thing." Then he realized he was talking to a law enforcement officer and said, "Sorry, just joking."

Changing the subject slightly, Jack continued, "I don't know why we couldn't have waited to do this until it was a little warmer. But Bob wanted to get it over with. He still wants to get to Florida for a little vacation while it's still snowbird season down there."

As the bidding got started, both men moved a little closer to the wagon. Then Jack, seeing one of the few women there, said to Nick, "Say, isn't that the funeral director lady?"

Nick nodded. Jack said, "I hardly recognized her without her black suit." Which will never be the same after its encounter with the fish company aroma, Nick thought.

At that moment Megan looked over and saw them and waved. Jack waved back and then looked at Nick, "Oh, I get it. I bet you two came together. I sure hope she doesn't have to wait for you to die before she sees you naked."

With the red creeping into his face, Nick managed a laugh and said, "Yah, me too." At that Nick said he wanted to get a cup of coffee, and he wandered off in the direction of the lunch wagon. His ulterior motive (in addition to getting away from

Chapter 26

Jack) was to eavesdrop on some conversations that might be occurring away from the seriousness of the selling.

Two older gentlemen were coming away from the lunch wagon with a sloppy Joe in one hand and a cup of coffee in the other. They looked around for a place to set one or the other down so it would be easier to enjoy their lunch. Some fifty gallon barrels nearby served as a makeshift table in spite of the grease and grime coating the surface. As Nick walked by them with his own cup of coffee and a donut, he overheard one of them say something about what he remembered when he and Ivar were kids. Nick edged a little closer to the guys, pretending to be looking at an old mower near the barrels. One of the guys asked if he was planning on mowing some hay. Nick said that he wasn't and that he didn't think anyone would, given how rusty the machine was.

"Oh," one of them said, "a couple bottles of Coke will take care of that."

"Yah," the other one said. "I used to use that stuff quite a bit, but that was back when you could buy a bottle for ten cents. When I saw what it did to metal, I was pretty damned sure I didn't want it anywhere near my stomach."

"Is that right?" Nick asked and then added, "So you guys knew Ivar Peterson then?"

They said that they had and then offered the information that only one of them still lived in the area. The other one had moved to the Cities years ago but thought he should come to Ivar's auction, mainly out of curiosity.

So one's a Swedish bachelor farmer, thought Nick, and the other went off to seek his fortune. Neither one is here to buy anything so Megan's dad was right—except in these parts auctions are like *Swedish* casinos.

"Damn shame, what happened to Ivar," the city guy said. Then he kind of shuddered and said, "Falling head first into a tankful of lutefisk, that's gotta be anyone's worst nightmare."

"But you know he had some help getting into that tank," the

other one said.

"Yah, that's what I heard. Unless you had a heart attack or something while you were leaning over the tank, you wouldn't go in there voluntarily. Did they ever catch that helper?"

"Not that I've heard. His girlfriend was a suspect for a while and then she went off and got herself killed in a car accident."

"Girl friend?" the city guy asked incredulously. "All I remember about Ivar when we were kids was that he was deathly afraid of girls. Of course, being so shy and kind of homely didn't help."

While the local fellow regaled the other one with tales of Marcie, Nick took his time drinking his coffee and pretending to study the auction bill taped to the side of the lunch wagon. He didn't overhear anything he didn't already know, but he really wanted to get the local man's name because he might have some leads to others who had known Ivar when he was growing up—or at least one "other" who may have had a motive for getting rid of Ivar. He decided against introducing himself right then and there since he didn't think that was a very good investigative technique. It would be better, he thought, to give him a call in a few days.

As the two guys wandered off to go back to the wagon where the auction was underway, Nick walked over to the mobile auction office. He asked the clerk if she could tell him who belonged to bidding number 35. When she gave him a questioning look, he quickly responded with, "Nick Nordin, Deputy Sheriff." With that introduction, she looked through her file of bidding numbers and told him that 35 belonged to Gordon Hedblom. He thanked her and went off to find Megan.

She was eyeing an old bedspring, and as Nick approached she told him she was thinking about buying it to use as a gate for one of her paddocks. As he looked at it, he realized it might have some possibilities for re-use so he said, "Sure and if that doesn't work, you could always use it as a trellis for morning glories or

Chapter 26

pole beans. What are you planning to bid for it?"

"I'm thinking it should go pretty cheap," Megan replied. "I wouldn't go any higher than ten bucks."

As it turned out, a few other people had the same idea as Megan unless, of course, they actually wanted to use it on a bed. When the bidding got to ten dollars quite quickly, Megan looked at Nick who just shrugged his shoulders. Megan meanwhile was figuring in her head how much a new gate would cost. She decided to keep bidding. In the end she got the bedframe for twenty dollars. Then she turned to Nick, "You will help me get the thing home, won't you?"

Nick responded with one of his winning smiles. "Sure, but it may cost you." Before Megan's face got totally red, she turned and walked toward the auction office to pay for her winnings. Nick picked up the bedspring and headed toward his truck. He waited for Megan, and then the two of them lifted it into the back of the truck. It was just past noon, and while Nick had wanted to see what kind of a price the real estate brought, he didn't really want to wait around that long. When he voiced that feeling to Megan, she agreed. "The land will be the last thing they auction, and that could be hours from now."

"I can call Bob Brewer next week and find out, just to satisfy my curiosity," Nick said.

"Speaking of the Brewers," Megan said, "Jack came over to me when I was looking at the bedspring and made some comment about 'hot springs tonight?' He's got a little randy streak that could get him into trouble if he's not careful."

"Yah, I know. He talked to me too," said Nick. And not wanting to elaborate on what Jack said, Nick quickly added, "Say, I've got an idea. The day is still young and so far neither of us have gotten called to work, so why don't I see if Madeline is home this afternoon, and if she would like to have a couple of visitors."

"I've been wanting to meet her," Megan said, "but don't you think it's sort of short notice. And I'm really hungry. That auction food just doesn't do it for me."

"I'll give her a call. She can always say 'no' and then we'll figure something else out. I'm pretty hungry too, so how about if we grab a burger at the Dusty Eagle and go from there?"

When they got to Megan's, they unloaded the bedspring by the fence where she was hoping to use it. "That will add a nice touch to the place," Megan said, "a little something different from the standard Fleet Farm gate."

While Megan went inside the house to let Pepper out, Nick called Madeline. He apologized for calling on the spur of the moment, but true to form, Madeline responded with "That's the only way to go" and said she would be delighted to have them stop by.

When Megan came out of the house, Nick gave her a thumbs up to indicate that Madeline was agreeable to their stopping by. Pepper had come bounding up to Nick with a stick in his mouth. They played fetch a couple times while Megan went back inside. When she came out again, she had a small jar with her. She explained that it was grape jelly she'd made from wild grapes on her property. "Madeline may have a pantry full of her own jelly, but she doesn't have any made from these grapes," Megan said.

On the way to the Dusty Eagle Nick told Megan about the possible lead he had gotten at the auction to someone who had known Ivar when he was a kid. Megan said that in her eavesdropping on a few conversations, she hadn't heard anything even remotely interesting. The talk was all about the auction items, what this thing had been used for and how old that thing was and how they couldn't believe that someone would actually buy this stuff.

"Like old bedsprings?" Nick asked.

"I guess," replied Megan, and then she grinned and gave Nick a friendly pat on his knee.

Megan said she was really eager to meet Madeline. To herself she wondered if this meeting was a sort of test to get Madeline's

Chapter 26

approval (or not) of Nick's girlfriend. However, she also wondered if she could be classified as his girlfriend because there hadn't been any acknowledgment of that status. She was not seeing anyone else, and she was pretty sure Nick wasn't either. It's not as if they hadn't tried to develop more of a relationship, but their respective jobs kept getting in the way. Although there was nothing quite like spending time together, their lengthy phone conversations enabled them to get to know each other, and from Megan's perspective, at least, what she knew so far, she liked. She was pretty sure Nick felt the same way although she wondered at times if he was still smarting from the breakup with the girl in Spearfish.

{ 27 }

As they drove up the driveway to Madeline's, Megan marveled at the tall pine trees and then at the log structure nestled among those trees. Nick parked his truck in the circular drive. And as they walked toward the house. Madeline appeared at the door and greeted them warmly. Madeline announced that she had just baked caramel rolls and they were hot out of the oven. Both Megan and Nick declared that they smelled divine, and Nick said he hoped that they could be shared. Madeline laughed and said she wondered how they knew to stop by on her roll-baking day which only happened about twice a year. "Sometimes I just get a hankering for them," Madeline said, "and I have to give most of them away or I'd end up looking like a bigger blimp than I am."

At that Megan handed her the jar of jelly, "This probably won't go with caramel rolls, but you can save it for a slice of that homemade bread I've heard about."

Madeline accepted the jar, and as they were hanging up their coats, she winked and gave him a little nod of approval. Then they sat down at the dining room table, and Megan had a chance to look around to admire all the things in Madeline's extensive collections displayed anywhere there was a wall, a shelf or any other kind of surface.

When Madeline came in from the kitchen, she was bearing a plate of the delicious-looking rolls and a carafe of coffee. All three indulged themselves. In between bites Madeline asked about the auction, and Nick was delighted to tell her about Megan's big purchase. He also told her that he'd been taking her advice about "peeling back the layers" of his investigation and looking beyond those who knew Ivar only in a contemporary context. Madeline voiced her approval. Then she turned to Megan and asked her how it was that she had chosen mortuary science as a field of study.

Nick was a bit taken aback by Madeline's directness even though he knew that she was not one to "beat around the bush." He wondered how Megan would react, but he was also curious about her answer because that was one topic they had discussed only briefly.

Megan replied that she was always interested in the sciences, particularly physiology and anatomy, and she had thought at one time of becoming a doctor. But then after hearing about the rigors of medical school, the expense and long process to become a bona fide doctor, she started looking at alternatives.

"So you opted for a different kind of rigor," Madeline said as she refilled their coffee cups.

Megan chuckled and said that yes, she guessed she had.

"And is this your first job, then, working at the Stone Funeral Home?"

"Yes," Megan replied.

"I can just barely remember when the current funeral home was built. Previously it had been on Main Street, and it was combined with the furniture store."

"Oh, that's handy," Nick said, "I suppose coffins are really just another kind of furniture, at least when they're empty. You could probably display them right alongside the beds and the sofas."

"I think it was pretty common for the two kinds of businesses to be combined, especially when families took care of their own dead. When they needed a coffin, the logical place to get one was

Caught in the Lye

at the local furniture store," responded Madeline. "At any rate, a few years ago someone was remodeling that building on Main Street to make apartments or something, and the carpenter fell through the floor into what had been the embalming pit. If I remember right, he suffered a broken ankle and had to suspend his remodeling for a time."

"That's terrible," said Megan, while wondering just what an embalming pit was.

"You're the first female undertaker we've had around here. And all I've ever seen at funerals anywhere else have been men. Are you sort of a pioneer, breaking into a field that's been traditionally for men?" Madeline asked.

"Oh, no," Megan replied. "In my class at the U there were lots of women, maybe a third of the students."

"Interesting," said Madeline. "But isn't it sometimes difficult to get those bodies loaded into the hearse and then out again?"

"There's no doubt about it that one needs to be pretty strong. But if I'm doing a removal at a hospital or a nursing home, there's almost always someone there to help. If it's a home removal, there are two of us anyway, so it hasn't been a problem so far."

Madeline seemed intent on quizzing Megan about her chosen line of work, and she continued, "You know, I'm an avid obituary reader—that's the main reason I get the local papers—and I've been noticing in the last three years or so that over half of the people listed have opted for cremation. How does that affect your job security? I mean cremations don't bring in as much revenue as a um..." she hesitated trying to find the right word.

"Full-fig funeral?" added Megan. "That would be one where the body is embalmed, placed on view for the mourners and then set into a concrete vault and buried in a cemetery."

"Yeah, that's what I'm talking about. I mean some of those funerals can cost upwards of $10,000, and the going rate for a cremation is what, $2500 or so?" asked Madeline.

"One of our marketing classes dealt with the increase in

cremations. We were reminded that the only difference when someone is cremated is that there is no embalming. The logistics of planning a funeral, arranging for the lunch afterwards, printing the memorial booklets, and so forth all need to be done, and we need to be pro-active in encouraging the family to use their local funeral home to make all those arrangements. It all falls into the category of event planning, except that we don't have weeks or months to plan. Everything has to be pulled together pretty quickly."

Then Madeline asked, "I was a little surprised when it was announced that the Stone Funeral Home was building a crematorium. Old man Stone's been around for a long time. He buried both my parents, and he was here quite a while before that. He must be well past retirement age."

"He's not that active anymore, but he's not ready to hand over the reins to someone else. And he watches the finances pretty closely. He no doubt realized that to stay in business, he was going to have to offer cremations. According to Wes, Stone's other assistant, he's had to convince Stone of a few other innovations—like a website. Then Stone resisted posting obituaries on the site, until he realized that every funeral home in the area was doing it."

"The power of peer pressure," Madeline added.

"Yes," Megan said, "but we all agreed with his decision to squelch the suggestion from one of the busybodies in town. Since she doesn't have a computer, and she must not pay attention to either the newspaper or the radio obituaries. So when she somehow missed the news of a funeral of someone she knew, she came to the funeral home and tried to convince Stone to put up a marquee that would give the name of the recently deceased along with the date and time of the service. Stone's first reaction naturally was that it would be way too expensive, but then he thought maybe it was the coming thing, so he actually called Wes and me in for a meeting to see what we thought. We couldn't believe he was serious, and we both agreed that yes, it would be very costly, and then Wes suggested that people might think it was a bit tacky."

"You think?" said Nick.

But Madeline said, "Oh, I don't know. It does have some possibilities. You could have, 'now showing' or 'coming soon.'"

"Pleeaase," said Nick again, and they all laughed.

Then Megan got quite serious and said, "Actually the biggest threat to my job security is that a lot of these small funeral homes, you know, the two or three person operations, are in danger of being bought out by a larger home. That's happened to a couple of my friends who were a year ahead of me. They got jobs with an independent funeral home in a rural area, and within months the place merged with a funeral home in the next town and they were let go."

Madeline interjected, "Yes, sometimes when I'm listening to the obituaries on the radio, the name of the funeral home handling the arrangements is a string of names of all the owners, past and present, and it's practically as long as the obituary itself. It's almost like when the school closings are given. Some of the names are a conglomeration of three or four schools that once were stand-alone districts."

Nick, listening attentively while enjoying his second caramel roll, was pleased that Madeline and Megan were enjoying themselves. While he didn't have much to add on the subject they were discussing, he decided to sit back and be an interested observer while the two women continued to chat.

Madeline, whose first impression of Megan was sealed with the jar of grape jelly, was eager to find out more about her and her occupation. Megan, who was more talkative than usual, probably from the sugar high (she, too, had consumed two rolls) and the caffeine in Madeline's robust coffee, steered the conversation away from the issue of job security. She offered the information that she wasn't sure she wanted to remain in the

Chapter 27

undertaking business indefinitely.

At this admission, Nick looked a little surprised. Catching Madeline's eye, he shrugged his shoulders, indicating that this was news to him.

Wanting to know more, Madeline merely asked, "Why?"

"It's not that the job is depressing," Megan said. "Of course, there are depressing aspects, particularly with most people's attitudes regarding death. It's more the sort of split personality that the job has. On the one hand, I'm dealing with a corpse, and that's where my interest in science comes in, at least to a degree, as one does need to know a few things about anatomy, bodily functions, et cetera. But then, on the other hand, I'm acting as a sort of grief counselor to survivors who, of course, don't want to think of their loved one as a corpse on a slab getting poked and probed, and if there is a third hand, it would be the whole event planning aspect. Each of these roles requires separate skills, and I could probably do each of them pretty well, but in having to do them all, I feel myself torn in several directions."

"So what are you thinking for the long haul? Where do you see yourself five or ten years from now? We know that Nick here will be head sheriff somewhere and maybe even heading up an investigative team for the BCA."

Nick chimed in with, "Yah, right." Neither he nor Megan had discussed future career plans. Megan, at least, had made some initiatives to commit to the area with her little farm and horses, but Nick's situation was pretty transitory. He intended to be with Isanti County long enough to gain some experience in local law enforcement and then move on. To what, he hadn't given much thought.

In answering Madeline's question about her future plans, Megan said there were some other considerations. "For one thing, it's just not a good idea to be handling formaldehyde on a daily basis. Even though we take precautions with a face guard, surgical mask and other splatter gear, there's always a chance that we're inhaling some of the fumes or getting it on our skin. With cremation becoming more popular, there's going to be less and less embalming. And that's going to affect how morticians are trained. The emphasis right now in any mort sci program is on embalming. Aside from the marketing aspect, I didn't get much info about cremation at all."

Madeline excused herself saying, "I'll be right back." She rose and went into her office. Nick and Megan heard a file drawer open and close, and soon Madeline reappeared and sat down, placing some brochures on the table.

"Look here," she said, "there seems to be a movement to start thinking about other ways to handle the dead, ways that are 'greener.'" At the word "greener" she indicated with her fingers that the word had quotation marks around it.

One brochure was advocating a modern approach to what had been standard in the days before embalming—keeping the body in the home so friends and neighbors could stop by and give their respects, and then burying the body in a simple wooden box, or no box at all. The difference with this approach and the historic one was use of dry ice to keep the body cool to retard decomposition. The philosophy was that the body should be returned to earth and allowed to join the earth as quickly as possible.

After Nick read through the brochure, he said that while it seemed like a good idea, it probably wasn't very practical because families are so scattered now. Megan said that from her experience of working with family members of the deceased, there weren't many who had such a rational approach to death. On the contrary, the idea of handling a dead person was repugnant to them.

Madeline smiled. "You're no doubt right, and that's why we continue to want our dead to look as alive as possible."

Megan's response was merely, "Yup."

The second brochure featured something called the Infinity

Chapter 27

Burial Suit, essentially a body suit one wears after death. A woman schooled in permaculture and mycology had designed a body suit that is infused with mushroom spores. After death, the mushrooms grow and consume both the body and the toxins within it. (The brochure indicated that the body is full of toxins.) All that's left behind is clean, pollutant-free compost.

"Ewww," responded Nick after he had looked through that brochure.

Megan's response was that she could understand how the mushrooms could handle the organs and muscles but from her own experience with making compost, it would take a long time for bones to break down. "My mom was an avid composter, and I'd still find chicken bones in the compost after they had been there for three years. And anyway, where would these bodies be while the mushrooms are doing their work—just out in the back yard?"

"Sure, right next to the regular compost pile, I suppose," offered Nick.

"Now here's another idea," Madeline said as she picked up a third brochure. "It's called alkaline hydrolysis, which apparently is already used to get rid of animal carcasses." She passed the brochure over to Nick who took one look at the photos and said, "Double ewww."

Megan took the brochure from Nick, and as she began reading said, "Oh, I can't wait to suggest this procedure to Stone. It says here it's legal in Minnesota, and he'd only have to invest about a quarter of a million dollars to get started."

"Why so much?" asked Nick. "I thought it was just a matter of letting some chemical dissolve the body. I guess I didn't read closely enough."

"It's a bit more than that," Megan said as she read from the brochure. "The body is put in a resomator, which is a pressurized steel chamber. Then water and alkali are added, and the temperature is raised to 350 degrees. The combination of water, alkali, heat and pressure cause a reaction that dissolves everything except bone fragments."

"So how long does that take?" asked Nick.

"It says here, two to three hours."

"And what about the left over chemical stuff? That doesn't sound particularly 'green.'?"

"Presumably, it neutralizes during the process and can be poured down the drain," Megan replied.

"I forget what chemical is used, some sort of hydroxide, isn't it?" asked Madeline.

Megan scanned through the brochure and said, "Here it is, it's potassium hydroxide."

"Now I never was a chemistry wizard," said Nick, "but isn't that just a little bit like sodium hydroxide?"

"Oh my god," exclaimed Megan. "The body is basically submerged in a lye solution, just like—"

"Lutefisk," responded Nick and Madeline together. Then they all laughed.

"Well, there you go," Nick said, "You already have some experience with that process, so maybe this green cremation or whatever you call it has some real possibilities for your career."

"Maybe," said Megan not very seriously, and then she added, "Oh, look, here's a link to a video about it. We could watch it at my place when we go back."

"Not," said Nick as he leaned over to give her a quick peck on the cheek.

Megan became serious. "I don't think any of these alternatives will catch on very quickly. It seems to me that there is still such a fear of death that people don't want to think about what will happen to them or their loved ones when they die. Then, when it happens, it's often us in the funeral industry who have to help them make decisions. I'm frankly amazed that so many people still opt for embalming and burial. Maybe it's because this is a rural area, and that's been the tradition along with church

Chapter 27

funerals and such."

Madeline said, "I think you're right. When it comes to death, people don't want to think outside the box." And then all three chuckled at her intentional pun.

While Nick had to admit he was fascinated with the topic of death and dying, he also realized he had learned more about Megan this afternoon than in all the other times they had spent together. Then, thinking that it was time to steer the conversation to another topic, he spied Madeline's collection of Dala horses on a shelf above the dining room window. He was about to ask Madeline to tell Megan about them as he thought Megan would be interested in hearing how the Swedes had turned such a utilitarian animal into a folk art phenomenon. But before he could change the subject, Megan continued with her thoughts about her chosen occupation.

"I suppose there's something comforting about staying within the boundaries of a tradition."

"Of course there is," said Madeline. "Whatever people espouse about wanting to be different or march to a different drum, there's always the need to belong and fit in."

"Even for you?" asked Nick with a twinkle in his eye.

"Yes, even for me," Madeline responded. "We're all part of a tribe, and we're kind of stuck with that."

"If you go to funerals as part of your job, you discover that right away," said Megan. "At first I thought it was kind of interesting to see how different churches conduct funerals and memorial services, but they're all pretty much the same. At one of my first funerals shortly after I started working for Stone, I was quite impressed with the pastor. He obviously had known the deceased quite well, or he'd gotten a lot of information from her family. He began by stating that in her obituary, her birth and death years are separated by a dash. He said it is that dash that is the most important part of a person's life, and then he went on to tell a lot stories about her life. Well, a month or so later, at a funeral at a totally different church I heard almost the same sermon. There must be somewhere on line where you can find funeral sermons."

Madeline then quipped, "Yes, probably on a web site called Funeral Fodder dot com."

At this they all laughed and Madeline continued, "Funerals do change over the years though. I can I remember one a few years ago, maybe ten or more by now, when it was the first time that I'd heard a pastor ask if anyone in the audience would like to say a few words about the deceased. This was really out of the ordinary. After a long, awkward silence, a woman got up, went to the front of the church and appealed to everyone to repent "because you never know when your time is up and you'd better be ready." I was certainly uncomfortable, and it appeared to me that many others were too. Then I heard afterward she was known for doing that sort of grandstanding at funerals. She kind of used them for her bully pulpit and was often not even that well acquainted with the person who died."

"I'm, always a little uneasy when there's a so-called open mic," said Megan. "When we're working with families to help them plan a service, we urge them to arrange ahead of time for friends or relatives to speak so it doesn't become a free-for-all. I think most pastors now agree that's a good idea," said Megan.

"Thank goodness," said Madeline. "I've noticed a difference in the selection of funeral songs too, particularly the solos. The one that seems to have been the tune of choice now for several years is 'On Eagle's Wings.'"

"Yes," said Megan," Wes told me that if he had a dollar for every time he's heard that song at a funeral, he'd be rich."

Madeline added, "And back a generation, it was probably 'In the Garden' and before that, in this area anyway it was no doubt 'Han har Öppnat Pärle Porten.'" When both Nick and Megan looked at Madeline, she said, "Oh yah sure, I can speak a little Swedish when I need to. That's an old Swedish hymn written

Chapter 27

actually by an immigrant who lived in this area. He wrote it 'He *has* opened the pearly gates' but when it appears in English hymnals it's 'He *will* open the pearly gates.' Just a change in the verb makes quite a difference."

"So are you saying, you'd like that sung at your funeral?" asked Nick. He felt a kick under the table and a got a disapproving look from Megan.

"No," responded Madeline. "I'm requesting Leonard Cohen's 'Closing Time.'"

"Okaaay," said Nick. "And this event will be at which church?"

"No church," replied Madeline. "The last thing I want is some sort of somber affair. I'd like a party."

"So you're talking more of a celebration of life?" asked Megan.

"Oh, God, I hope not. That implies that my life hasn't been worth much until I'm dead. If it's worth celebrating, I want to do it while I'm still alive and I'd prefer to choose who I want to celebrate with. How about if we just call it a send-off?"

While Nick was quite amused over Madeline's description of how she envisioned her own funeral, Megan was quite serious and asked her if she had these wishes written down.

"Some of it," replied Madeline. "I change my mind every couple of weeks, and in the end it probably doesn't matter much. What dead person do you know who really even cared about what kind of funeral he or she had?"

"Good point," said Megan, "and I can tell you that if they were able to care, they would often be pretty disappointed at the way their family members are acting. I didn't realize when I got into this that I'd be acting as a mediator in family disputes. Of course, it may be that grief brings all kinds of emotions to the surface, but it also seems that some families use death as an excuse to get a lot of suppressed feelings off their chest. There's been more than one time when an argument starts going, and I've had to just say, 'Why don't I just let you sort this out on your own. I'll step out for a few minutes and check back a little later to see how you're doing.' That usually does the trick, depending on what it is they have to sort out. Sometimes it's just a trivial detail like which dress should Mom be buried in, but sometimes it's quite a bit more serious and you can just feel the hostility in the air. After meetings like that, it's refreshing to spend some time with the family member who can't say anything."

Madeline handed around the plate of caramel rolls one more time, but both Megan and Nick declined. After Madeline refilled their coffee cups, she told Megan that she found her so delightful it was difficult to imagine her having to maintain the somber and serious demeanor so stereotypical of a funeral director.

Megan said, "There are times when it's difficult to keep a straight face. Sometimes unexpected things happen like one time when I was closing the lid of the coffin, my hand slipped and the lid went down with a bang. I think everyone in the church, that is all except one, jumped."

She continued, "One time a pall bearer tripped as he and the others were carrying the coffin to the gravesite. Luckily the others were able to keep the coffin from falling onto the ground."

"I get it now," said Nick. That's why the undertakers use a little Allen wrench--to screw down the lid so the body doesn't fall out if there is some sort of mishap. I always thought screwing down the lid was to seal it, you know, to help preserve the body."

"Actually," Megan said, "Caskets are now designed to burp so gases that build up during the decomposition can escape. Otherwise there's a danger of ex. . . "

Before she could continue, Nick jumped in with "TMI. That's more information than I need to know."

"Sorry, but I was only clarifying your MISinformation," said Megan as she reached over and patted his hand.

She continued, "And then there was the time when Wes and I were standing in the back of the church waiting for the funeral to begin. The organist was playing the prelude when a little girl got up from one of the pews to head to the restroom. But on the

Chapter 27

way she tripped over the organ's electrical cord and it came unplugged. Wes leaned over to me and said, 'Organus interruptus.' Believe me, any somberness went right out the window and we both had trouble composing ourselves in time for us to usher in the family."

"I hope you're jotting these things down," said Madeline, "They would make a great short story."

Megan who was sort of on a roll was about to continue with another tale of the crypt, but after hearing the clock strike five and then noticing that it was getting dark outside, she said, "Oh my goodness. I had no idea it was so late. I need to get home and check on the horses and feed my dog. "

As Megan stood up to begin clearing the table, Madeline admonished her, saying she should just leave everything. "I've got all night to do that." Megan knew better than to argue, so she and Nick both put on their jackets. Before they retrieved their boots from in the entry, Megan turned to Madeline and gave her a big hug. Nick shook Madeline's hand and she told them to come back soon. She indicated to Megan that it would be fun to have a girl afternoon and share recipes and such. Their leaving was in danger of becoming a long Minnesota goodbye, so Nick started down the walk to start the truck. Megan soon followed as Madeline called after them to have a good rest of the evening.

{ 28 }

It was almost dark by the time Megan and Nick left Madeline's house. "I feel sort of like a blimp," Megan said. "I can't even remember when I've had two caramel rolls in one sitting. They sure were good though."

"You two could be potential competitors for who is the best baker," Nick said.

"Now that is something I would like to aspire to," replied Megan.

When they got to Megan's place, she asked Nick if he wanted to help her feed the horses. Of course, he did, and once that was done, they headed to the house. After they hung up their jackets in the porch and were heading into the kitchen, Nick grabbed Megan by the shoulders and turned her around to face him. He drew her to him, and the kiss that followed was warm, passionate and long. When they finally broke away, Megan took Nick by the hand and led him upstairs.

When Nick woke up sometime later, it took a moment for him to realize where he was. The room was dark except for a sliver of light that came through the door that was slightly ajar. As his eyes adjusted, he determined that he was in a room that was not his own. His memory was quickly restored and he let out a satisfied sigh. He turned to face the middle of the bed and reached an arm out, intending to draw Megan close to him as his body began responding with both wakefulness and arousal. But his

Chapter 28

arm met only emptiness, and before he could wonder why the void existed, he began to smell coffee and bacon.

Nick had no idea what time it was, but his body clock suggested it wasn't morning. He swung his legs over the side of the bed and found the switch on the lamp on the bedside table. Next to the lamp was his watch, which he hadn't even remembered taking off. He did a double take when he saw that it was 8:30 p.m.

Just then the door burst open and Pepper came bounding into the room to greet him. "Down, boy," Nick said as he gave the dog a friendly shove and began to pull on his pants. The two headed down the stairs and found Megan at the stove in the kitchen, wearing only a T-shirt that barely covered her derriere. Nick and the dog's noisy entry into the kitchen did not deflect her attention from tending the bacon. Pepper, noticing that his dog dish was full, bounded over to it while Nick put his hands on Megan's shoulders and leaned into her.

She responded by saying, "I thought maybe you'd be hungry so I'm fixing bacon and eggs."

Nick nuzzled her ear and said, "Oh, yes, I'm hungry all right."

Megan lifted the last piece of bacon out of the pan with a fork and laid it on a paper towel. After she turned off the burner and set the pan aside, she turned around to face Nick and while she put her arms around said, "Since we didn't really have supper, I thought we'd have a little snack now and then see what the rest of the night brings."

"Food doesn't seem like a real high priority right now," Nick said, "but as long as you've gone to all this work, I guess I could eat a little something."

"Oh, that is soooo Minnesotan. You've caught on quickly," she said as she handed him some silverware to put on the table.

Nick laid out the silverware, and as Megan brought the plates to the table, she said, "I see someone trained you well."

It took a moment for Nick to realize she was referring to his placement of the silverware. "Yes," he said, "my mom said that you should always take the time to set a nice table—knife and spoon on the right side of the plate and fork on the left. She said it didn't matter what you were eating or how many were at the table."

"I had the same training," Megan said, "and I think it's a good habit. I like to think mealtimes are something special so even when I'm by myself, I take the time to set the table and sit down to eat."

"You know, I do the same thing. And when I have to eat on the run or grab something at a drive-thru, it's not the same. It's like I'm just trying to satisfy some basic hunger instinct and not savoring the experience."

"Well," Megan said as she was buttering a piece of toast, "you seem to handle some of your other basic instincts quite well."

"That's pretty easy when there's somebody else involved who responds so well to that basic instinct."

They sat for a few minutes savoring their food, and then Megan suggested that they go for a walk.

"Now?" asked Nick.

"Well, as soon as we're done eating. It's a gorgeous night, not too cold, and just look at that moon," Megan said as she gestured to the kitchen window. "Besides, Pepper needs some exercise, and so do I."

"You might want to put on a few more clothes then," Nick said.

Megan responded with "Ditto."

As she got up to begin clearing the table, Nick advised her that she'd better skedaddle up the stairs and get dressed or their walk wouldn't happen. "I'll take care of the dishes," he said.

When Megan re-appeared a few minutes later, fully dressed, she took over the dish detail so that Nick could retrieve the rest of his clothes from Megan's bedroom. He found his flannel shirt and socks but his underwear seemed to be missing. Oh well, he

Chapter 28

thought, it's not that cold outside, but he was glad he had his parka rather than a shorter jacket.

"So how far are we planning to go on this walk?" asked Nick as they started down the driveway.

"I usually just go down to the next farmhouse and turn around. Then if I feel like it, I'll continue in the other direction past my place for a ways, turn around again and then head home. This road can get pretty busy at times."

"I imagine more so during lutefisk season," Nick interjected, knowing that the road was one of the four main arteries leading to the crossroads where the fish company was located.

Megan laughed and said, "Yes, I'll be aware of that this fall and plan my walks when the place is closed. I'm just glad I live outside the odor zone."

They continued walking hand in hand. Pepper bounded ahead of them but stayed close enough to them so they could see his form illuminated by the moonlight. Nick remarked that the dog was pretty well trained to not go straying off and find his own adventures.

Megan said she had worked with him a lot when he was a puppy, and her dad continued to train him after she went off to college. "My dad instilled in me that you can't have a dog that chases cars. And that's always an issue if you've got a short driveway. Plus, Pepper is pretty protective of me. Somehow he picked up good vibes from you right away, but you'll find out in short order that he's not just a bumbling big teddy bear if you would do anything to hurt me or even act like you're going to."

"Don't worry," Nick said. "Believe me, I want to stay on both your and Pepper's good side." And he gave Megan's hand a little squeeze.

Changing the subject, Nick asked, "What do you know about your neighbors along this road?"

"Well," Megan replied, "there's a middle-aged couple living on this next farm by the name of Henderson. It's her family's farm. She grew up there, went away to college, got married and then moved back here with her husband after her folks died. She's filled me in on some of the peculiarities of the neighborhood.

"How so?" asked Nick.

"Oh, you know, how almost everyone is related and how newcomers aren't welcomed sometimes, etcetera."

"Hmm. She obviously would have known Ivar. Maybe she knows something about his early years that might offer some clues about someone who wanted him out of the picture."

"It's possible," Megan said. "She told me that everyone along this particular stretch of road had come from the same little village in Sweden. I remember she laughed when she said that it was pretty remote, and when they came here, they settled in a place that was also pretty remote."

"I wonder if Ivar came from that village."

"He wouldn't have, of course, because the Swedes came to this area in the late 1800s, but his parents or grandparents might have."

"Do you remember what the name of the village was?" asked Nick.

"Oh, it had a funny name that sort of sounded like 'vengeance.' I know it starts with a 'V.' But I'm sure Connie would be glad to talk to you, and she would know whether or not Ivar had roots there. Maybe we could stop over there tomorrow and I could introduce you."

"Sounds like a plan. But right now I have some parts of me that are starting to get cold and I'd hate to get frostbite."

"That's what you get for going commando in the winter time," Megan said as she broke away from Nick and turned back towards her driveway on a trot, laughing mischievously.

Nick and Pepper followed closely behind, and Megan soon slowed so the others could catch up to her. Nick grabbed her, spun her around to face him and planted a big sloppy kiss on her cheek. They held each other for a short time while Pepper ran

Chapter 28

around them barking. Then they continued to the house.

"I think some hot chocolate is in order," Megan said as she and Nick shed their jackets, hats and mittens and hung them up in the entry way.

"Sounds good," said Nick as he went into the living room and collapsed on the couch.

When Megan brought in the mugs of steaming cocoa, Nick asked, "What? No caramel rolls?"

"I think we both have had our quota for today."

"But a little more exercise, and I could maybe move that quota upwards," Nick offered.

Megan suggested that since the night was still relatively young and they had already had a nap, maybe they should watch a movie. Nick replied that he might be interested as long as it wasn't that video of the alkaline hydrolysis process. Megan said she didn't have that one in her library yet and that all she could offer was either *Toy Story 3* or *Friends with Benefits*.

"So are you a fan of Justin Timberlake?" Nick asked.

"Not particularly, but the DVD was on sale at Target for $5.00, so I bought it."

"And what about *Toy Story*?"

"Oh, that one I got for my nieces, but they informed me they already had it, so I just kept it."

"I vote for *Friends with Benefits*. There's nothing saying we have to watch the whole thing."

Megan popped the DVD into her player and they settled back to watch the movie, sitting close to each other on the couch even though Pepper tried in vain to sit between them. Nick draped his arm along the back of the couch, and Megan laid her head on his shoulder. She found it hard to concentrate on the movie, so at one point she said, "Popcorn?"

"No thanks," replied Nick. "I've got everything I need right here."

"Mmm," muttered Megan as she settled into him.

Their interest in the movie soon waned, however, and they found themselves entwined in a long embrace. Megan reached over and pressed "stop" on the remote for the DVD player, and then she whispered to Nick that there were places in the house where they would be more comfortable. Nick agreed, and this time, knowing the way to Megan's bedroom, he led the way. As they began to get "more comfortable," Pepper came into the room, carrying something in his mouth. Megan saw him first and began to giggle. When Nick caught sight of the dog, he exclaimed, "Why, you little shithead!"

Megan, still giggling, said, "Nick, I've never heard you use such language."

"Well, I've never had my underwear stolen by a four-legged scoundrel before."

Pepper, who seemed unaffected by the insult, dropped the underwear on the floor. Then the dog calmly turned around and padded out of the room. Nick turned to Megan and asked her if she knew what Pepper had been up to, and she had to admit that yes, she had seen a spare pair of jockey shorts on the rug where Pepper usually sleeps, but she had decided to see, first of all, if Nick noticed them there and secondly, what Pepper's plan was. She assured Nick that Pepper's returning them to their rightful owner was another sign that the dog had approved of Nick's being there.

"Are you sure?" Nick asked. "Maybe he was trying to tell me that it's time to go."

"If that's the case, he'll have to answer to me too," Megan replied as she snuggled up to Nick and nuzzled his neck. Nick responded by turning toward her and holding her close. He caressed her hair, and when she turned her face toward him, they kissed, and Nick's tongue explored Megan's mouth. As their hands began exploring each other's body, Nick's cell phone rang.

"Damn," Nick said as he reached for the phone and saw on the caller ID that it was Deputy Wyatt Sullivan. He let it ring a

Chapter 28

couple of more times while he tried to make the transition, both physically and mentally, into work mode. The conversation was short with Nick saying only, "Okay, I'll be there. Give me fifteen minutes." Then he turned to Megan and said, "Car accident on Highway 47. Possible fatalities. Gotta go. Sorry."

"Good thing you got your underwear back."

"Yah, but I was hoping I wouldn't need it anymore tonight," Nick said as he finished dressing. "I don't know how long this will take, so I'll just go on home."

"Okay, but you know where I live in case you change your mind."

"I'd love to, but I know how these things go, and I'll most likely end up back in Cambridge anyway if I have to write a report. I could stop back out tomorrow and we could continue where we left off."

"I doubt I'll get any better offers, so sure, give me a call in the morning. Oh, and do you still want to try to meet up with Connie down the road?"

"Sure, if not tomorrow, then whenever. See what you can work out." Nick leaned down and gave Megan a quick kiss. Then he hurried down the stairs and out the door to his truck. Megan pulled the covers up around her, let out a long sigh, rolled over and lay awake for several minutes thinking that she was as close to being in love as she had ever been.

{ 29 }

As Nick expected, it turned out to be a long night. On the way to the scene of the accident, he called Sullivan and got more information. It appeared to be a head-on collision, and the vehicles involved were blocking the road. The main reason for needing more officers on hand was to direct traffic around the accident. Nick was stationed a half mile north of the accident to direct the southbound traffic onto a secondary road that would serve as a temporary detour. Deputy Hokanson was stationed south of the accident to direct the northbound traffic to the detour. Thank goodness, the roads out here are laid out in nice tidy squares, Nick thought as he put on the coveralls he had retrieved from behind the seat in his truck. It was almost 20 degrees, but with a breeze coming from the northwest, it felt much colder than it was.

Sullivan himself was working with the officers from the State Highway Patrol and with the emergency personnel to get the victims out of the vehicles, dispatch ambulances and tow trucks and try to establish what had happened to cause the accident. After an hour and a half Sullivan notified both Nick and Hokanson that they could leave their posts. He reported that of the six occupants in the two vehicles, only three had survived, and they were taken by ambulance to the Cambridge hospital. Only one of them was conscious. The cars, both a tangled mass of iron, had been hauled away and the highway could be

Chapter 29

re-opened. When Nick drove to the site, all he saw was some bits of glass on the pavement and some yellow chalk marks to indicate a probable scenario for how the crash had occurred. Sullivan thanked Nick and Hokanson for their work and told them to go on home. Hokanson said, "Hell, I wasn't doing anything anyway. I was just trying to figure out which episode of *Star Trek* I should watch when you called. What about you, Nordin, were you doing your laundry, or did you have a hot date?"

Nick wanted to say, "Wouldn't you like to know?" but instead he said, "Yah, it was a pretty typical Saturday night. Had some bacon and eggs for supper, went for a walk and was just getting ready for bed when I got the call." Nick didn't wait for any response from Hokanson, nor did he really want to engage in any more conversation with him, so he just started up his truck and headed towards Cambridge.

* * * * *

Megan woke up at 6:00 Sunday morning. She lay in bed a few minutes thinking about the night before and wishing that Nick were still beside her. There will be plenty of time for that, she thought, or at least she hoped. She wondered how Nick's night had gone, and she looked forward to his call so he could fill her in on the details. She was also wondering if he would come by that afternoon. She decided she had better fix something for supper just in case. And if they were going to visit Connie Henderson, she'd better bake something to take along. Remembering how Nick had raved about Mary Eng's beef stew, she took a beef roast out of the freezer and decided that instead of a stew, she'd roast the meat together with some potatoes, onions and carrots. It could cook while they were over at Connie's, or while doing whatever else they might find to occupy their time.

Nick, meanwhile, had slept until 8:00. He stayed in bed a while longer, reflecting on the evening before. He realized that he really liked Megan, and he could envision her being in his life on a permanent basis. Better not rush things, he thought, but he was looking forward to seeing her again that afternoon.

By the time Nick had conducted his usual Sunday morning routine of breakfast at Perkins while he read the Minneapolis Sunday *Tribune*, it was 10:30, time to call Megan. She answered on the second ring. "Good morning," Nick said.

"And a good morning to you," Megan replied. "How was your night?"

"Do you mean the early part of the night or the late part?"

"I think I know about the early part. I'm wondering about what happened after you got your work call."

While Nick was filling her in on his duties at the accident, it occurred to him that Megan may be called to deal with one or more of the fatalities. When she asked if anyone had been killed, Nick said only, "Yes."

Megan's thoughts, too, went to the possibility of her being called to work, so she asked Nick if he knew where any of the victims were from. Nick didn't know, and he wondered if the highway patrol had even had time to notify next of kin for either the ones who had died or the ones who had survived.

"If any of the fatalities were from this area, I might have to go to work today. It's Wes' week-end to be on call, so he'll only call me if he needs extra help. I say we go ahead with our plans. I've got a beef roast thawing. Do you want to chance coming over?"

"Sure. Even if you have to leave, Pepper and I would have a good supper."

"And it would no doubt be your last one."

Nick smiled, realizing that he enjoyed the way he and Megan often teased one another with an easy repartee. "I'll see you about two o'clock if that's okay." Megan assured him it was.

As soon as they hung up, Megan immediately called Connie Henderson to see if she was going to be home that afternoon.

Chapter 29

When Connie said she was, Megan told her to put the coffee pot on as she and a friend would stop by about three. "I'll bring some cookies," Megan said. She had purposely not mentioned that her "friend" was a sheriff's deputy, nor that they wanted to talk to her about Ivar Peterson. Megan thought it was better to treat this as a friendly neighborhood visit rather than an investigative call.

When Nick arrived at Megan's, it was obvious that she had been baking. She greeted him at the door in her apron, and there was a smudge of flour on her cheek. He also smelled something delicious. He kissed her quickly and then headed for the kitchen before he even took off his jacket. There he saw several dozen cookies cooling on racks on the table. "Mind if I have one?" he asked, already reaching to grab one.

Megan only laughed and said, "Make yourself at home, why don't you? There's milk in the refrigerator, and the glasses are in the cupboard."

Nick, with a generous bite of chocolate chip, peanut butter cookie in his mouth said, "These are heavenly." Before he took another bite, he admitted, "I guess I'm being sort of pig, but I just couldn't help myself."

"I'm glad you like them. I'm intending to take them with us when we go over to see Connie, but there may be a few left that I can send home with you."

"Okay, I'll just have one more now."

Nick sat at the kitchen table drinking a glass of milk and eating the additional cookie while Megan peeled the potatoes and carrots for the roast. She set the oven on low and said it should be just fine while they were gone. She was cleaning up the kitchen when Nick came up behind her. He turned her around to face him, and with cookie breath kissed her warmly. She put her arms around him, and she buried her head in his shoulder. They stood in this embrace for several minutes.

"Do we really have to visit your neighbor this afternoon?" Nick asked. "Won't she be home another day?"

"Probably, but there may be other days for this too."

Nick sighed and said, "Are you always this practical?"

"Not always," Megan said as she stepped aside and then snapped a dish towel across Nick's back side. As he feigned being injured and was about to grab her again, she slipped away from his grasp and reached into a cupboard for a tin box that she filled with cookies. "These are for Connie." Next she put a half dozen cookies in a sealable plastic bag. "These are for you, but they stay here until you leave."

"Right," replied Nick.

They decided to drive over to Connie's in Megan's car. Nick had to adjust the passenger seat for his tall frame. Megan apologized, saying that the only other people who had ridden in that seat were her nieces, who were quite a bit shorter than Nick.

Because the driveway leading to Connie's house had not been plowed very wide, there were large snowbanks on either side. Nick commented that the next time it snowed, the driveway could fill in and be even harder to plow. Megan explained that Connie's husband Dan was an invalid, so either Connie had tried to plow the driveway herself or whoever she had hired had not done a very good job. "Who plows your driveway?" Nick asked Megan. "Don't tell me you do it yourself?"

Megan laughed and said that she hires Philip Randall, her neighbor to the north. "He's got an actual snow blower on his tractor, so I don't have to worry about these kinds of snow banks." As she got into the Henderson yard, she realized there wasn't a good place to turn around. "I'll just have to back out, I guess. I'm going to ask Phil if he can come over here and clear out this yard and the driveway. We sometimes get most of our snow during March, and that's just around the corner."

"I think that would be a good idea. But right now, I hope you have a snow shovel in case we get stuck trying to get out of here."

"I'm from Minnesota, don't you know, so of course, I have a snow shovel. And flares, candles and granola bars in my winter

Chapter 29

survival kit plus a blanket and a spare pair of mittens."

"All right, then," said Nick, getting out of the car.

They went up the walk, also made narrow from snow banks on either side, and Megan knocked on the door. Connie answered it, gave Nick a quick once-over, and invited them in as Megan handed her the tin of cookies.

"Thanks," Connie said, "Come on in and make yourselves at home. How about if we sit at the dining room table? I'll get the coffee." As she headed to the kitchen, she said that Dan's brother had come by a couple of hours before and was taking him to the snowmobile races in Princeton.

"Snowmobile races?" Then to Megan, Nick said, "You never told me there were snowmobile races in the area." he said.

"Sorry," Megan replied. "I guess it slipped my mind." When Connie set the coffee cups in front of them, Megan introduced her to Nick, and then she went on to tell Connie why they had wanted to stop by.

"I see," said Connie. "I don't know what I can tell you. But I've known Ivar all my life. His mother and my mother were good friends. I was so sorry I couldn't go to either the wake or the get-together at the Dusty Eagle. That's when Dan was in the hospital with pneumonia. It was a big shock to hear that Ivar was murdered. I can't imagine anyone who would want to kill him."

Nick responded, "That's what everyone says who I've interviewed so far." So now I'm trying to look at all aspects of Ivar's life, sort of like peeling back an onion," he continued, using Madeline's metaphor. "I'd like to know more about his younger days, who his friends were growing up and if maybe one of them had some old score to settle."

"Hmm," said Connie, "You realize Ivar's a lot older than I am. My mother was probably one of Bette's younger friends."

"Bette being Ivar's mother?" Nick asked.

"Yes. She was quite a character, and I always liked it when she'd come to visit because she had lots of stories. I'd pretend I was reading a book, but I was really listening to Bette. I always thought it was a bit ironic that Ivar started working at the fish company because Bette hated lutefisk and wouldn't have it in the house. She told my mother she had tried to fix it once because her husband, Ivar's father, liked it. Someone had told Bette to bake it. Several members of her husband's family were coming for supper, and they were bringing the other dishes for the meal. All she had to do was bake the lutefisk and boil the potatoes. As the women were bustling about getting the food on the table, Bette checked the oven and saw only the pan that the lutefisk had been baking in. She asked the other women if one of them had already dished up the lutefisk and put it on the table. The answer was 'no' from every one. Then Bette opened the oven door and pulled out the pan. All that was in it was a white slurry. The fish had virtually dissolved from being cooked too long."

At this point Megan and Nick were both laughing. Nick said, "The more I hear about lutefisk, the less I ever want to eat it."

"You won't ever have to worry about me fixing it, that's for sure," Megan said. "I came as close to it as I want by just being inside the fish company."

Connie responded with, "It really does taste better than it smells."

"I'll just have to take your word for it," Megan said and Nick nodded his head in agreement.

Nick, wanting to get back to the topic of Ivar's youth, asked Connie if she could remember if Bette had any stories about Ivar—maybe something about his school days, old girl friends, what he did for fun—anything that could point Nick to someone who knew what happened at the fish company on the afternoon of Christmas Eve.

Megan asked Connie about Ivar's Swedish heritage and whether or not he had roots in that same small village as so many in the area. By this time Nick had his notebook out. He'd made only a few notes about the disappearing lutefisk story, figuring

Chapter 29

he'd remember that one. But he asked Connie for the spelling of the name of the village. She said, "V-E-N-J-A-N. It's Swedish, you know, so the 'j' is pronounced like a 'y.'"

"I knew it was something like 'vengeance,'" Megan said.

Connie laughed, adding that she didn't think Ivar belonged to that clan. "I do, and I'm pretty sure I would know if Ivar did."

"You don't think there's a possibility that if his family was from a different part of Sweden that he might have been involved in some sort of tribal warfare at some point in his life—you know, like maybe he had to defend his clan's reputation against the 'vengeance' ones?"

Connie laughed again, "I can't see Ivar being involved in any kind of argument, let alone warfare. We do say, though, that a mixed marriage in these parts refers to the groom being from one part of Sweden and the bride from a different part – maybe another province or even just another village."

Megan and Nick simultaneously responded -- Nick with "Really?" and Megan with a questioning smirk and a shrug of her shoulders.

Connie took a bite of a cookie and a sip of coffee and continued, "As for girlfriends, I never heard that Ivar ever had any. But since my information about Ivar was coming from his mother, I might not have heard the whole story. I do remember Bette told of a girl in grade school who had a crush on him. She spoke with a fair amount of disdain about the girl as though she was not up to the Peterson standards. Come to think of it, she also said that the girl had an older sister, but that both were so homely she was sure they'd stay old maids all their life."

"Perhaps there's no real mystery as to why Ivar remained a bachelor. It sounds like his mother wouldn't have approved of anyone who paid attention to Ivar," Megan said.

Regarding what Ivar did in his spare time, Connie said that all she knew about was his trapping—both gophers, for the bounty paid by the county, and muskrats, which he sold to a fur company in Willow River. "I think he had a few trapping buddies, but I don't know about any other friends. Plus, I don't think he did any trapping once Marcie came on the scene. I don't know if it was because he was up in years by then and it was too hard to tramp through the swamps, or if she had a thing about trapping."

Then Nick asked Connie if she knew Joe Sletten. She said the name was familiar but that was all. Nick told her that Joe had been in the same confirmation class as Ivar and that he hoped to interview him when he got back from Florida. Connie said, "Oh, that's excellent. He's probably going to know a lot more about Ivar as a kid than I do."

"Maybe he'll know who that grade school girl was who had eyes for Ivar."

"And if she's still an old maid," Megan added.

Connie apologized for not being more helpful and said she'd let Nick know if she thought of anything else. Nick gave her one of his cards and said he'd appreciate any information.

Changing the subject, Connie said how pleased she was that Megan had moved into the Greene place. "When it came up for sale, I was afraid a family with a bunch of wild kids might buy it, and I'd have to deal with four-wheelers running up and down the road. Do you live there too?" she asked Nick.

Megan broke in, "No, he's just visiting, but you might see his truck there once in a while."

"Well, don't be strangers, either of you. The coffee pot is always on."

"And the best cookie baker is just down the road," Nick added.

Connie caught Megan's eye and gave her a thumbs up. As they walked down the narrow path to the car, Megan asked Nick just how many other cookie bakers he knew. "All that counts is one," Nick replied. She was going to give him a jab in the ribs but was afraid they would slip and fall, so she resisted.

After backing successfully down the driveway, Megan drove

Chapter 29

the short distance to her place. Once parked in her own driveway, she was about to get out of the car when Nick tugged on her jacket and pulled her back. He turned her toward him, and reaching across the console, wrapped his arms around her and gave her a big kiss.

"Yowsers," she said. "That's almost too much action for this little Mazda." She kissed him back, and when she finally drew away, she said, "We'd better check on that roast."

{ 30 }

MEGAN THOUGHT THE roast could use another half hour, so she offered Nick a beer and helped herself to a glass of wine from the box on the kitchen counter. As they sat at the table, Nick asked Megan about what she had said at Madeline's the day before. "Are you seriously thinking of going into some other line of work?"

Megan replied, "Probably not right now, but depending on what happens in the funeral industry in general and with the Stone Funeral Home in particular, I think it's a good idea to keep my options open."

"Here's a thought. I get it that you're more interested in the science behind all that stuff you do with bodies."

Megan interrupted with "All that stuff I do with bodies? You make it sound more morbid than it is."

"Sorry, I just haven't grasped all the technical terms for what you do. But what I'm getting at is that maybe you should start investigating what it would take to work in the medical examiner's office."

"I already know that to be an ME, you have to have an MD degree."

"But," Nick said, "the medical examiners all have technicians and assistants who aren't MDs. I bet you'd qualify right now with your background and experience." He took a drink of his beer and continued, "I have at least a working relationship with Ed

Chapter 30

at the medical examiner's office. Do you want me to ask him if he'd ever consider hiring a cute horsewoman with a mortuary science degree?"

At this remark, Megan was close to choking on the sip of wine she'd just taken, but she managed to say, "Or you could give me Ed's contact information, and I could call him myself. That way I'd know that there's a proper level of professionalism."

"Whatever, but it wouldn't hurt to find out. Who knows, maybe there's some apprentice or intern type opportunities where you could work part-time, and if need be, you could take some courses online."

"Yah, if I had high speed internet," Megan said. "I keep waiting for the day when this area gets connected to the twenty-first century, but so far, no luck."

"You could always come to my place. It would be a pretty sparse classroom, but there might be lots you could learn there."

"Probably not for credit though."

"Right," Nick said, "It would just count as experiential learning."

"More talk like this and our supper will have to be put on hold." Megan rose and got some silverware out of the drawer. "Here, you set the table. I'm going to pop some cheater biscuits in the oven."

"Cheater biscuits?"

"You know, the ones that come in a tube. I keep some on hand for times like this when I have more important things to do than bake."

"I'm glad you think so," said Nick as he got up from his chair and surrounded Megan with a warm embrace. They stood that way for a time, rocking slowly back and forth, both relishing the feeling of being very comfortable with one another.

In time, the roast was done, the biscuits had baked, and the table was set. Nick turned down the offer of another beer, but Megan had a second glass of wine. The combination of warmth from both the kitchen and the wine gave her cheeks a red glow. Nick pronounced the roast excellent—done just right, good flavor and tender besides. "Hard to beat farm-raised beef," Megan said. "I don't think I'll ever be able to eat meat from a store again."

"I know what you mean. I like to know where my food comes from and how it was grown. Unfortunately, I'm stuck with food that I know nothing about. But maybe that's about to change," Nick said as he reached for Megan's hand.

Megan's face got even redder. Averting Nick's eyes, she said, "I'm sure we can work out some sort of arrangement." Nick merely chuckled and took another bite of the roast beef.

Megan then segued into an entirely different subject. Realizing that it was now March, she reminded Nick that the horse expo at the Minnesota State Fairgrounds was coming up. Nick assured her he hadn't forgotten and that he was looking forward to it. "Maybe this will be our lucky month," Nick said. "You'll get your new horse trailer and I'll finally get some clues as to who might have killed Ivar Peterson. Plus, maybe you'll be on your way to starting a new career."

Megan merely replied with a "Maybe so," but she was thinking that another eventuality for the month would be the strengthening of her and Nick's relationship. Her thoughts were interrupted by her cell phone ringing. She looked at the caller ID and mouthed the word "Wes" to Nick as she swiped the screen to answer the call. Wes said he could really use some help as he was on his way to pick up two fatalities from an auto accident the night before. He started to give Megan the details of the accident, but she said that yes, she had heard about it. "How soon do you need me?" she asked. He said that if she could make it in forty-five minutes, that would be great.

When she hung up, she said to Nick, "Two nights in a row of emergency calls. One for you and one for me. Other than that it was a pretty good week-end, don't you think?"

"There were parts of it that were certainly excellent. Forty-five

Chapter 30

minutes, you say. Hmm. Twelve minutes to get to Braham. That leaves .... "

"Don't even think it. Help me with these dishes, and I think there's enough roast left over so you can take a few pieces home."

"Gee, roast beef and cookies. I can eat for most of the week."

The two quickly cleared the table, and while Nick was filling the dishwasher, Megan cut up what remained of the roast. With two plastic bags in hand, Nick headed to the porch. Megan followed him, and after he had his jacket on, he turned to her and they had a long goodbye kiss. Then Nick was out the door, and Megan got ready for a night of work.

*****

During the next few days Megan was kept busy with the funeral details for the two accident victims. As she had described at Madeline's, she was required to use science in taking care of the bodies, human relations abilities in dealing with the survivor's grief and event planning skills for both funerals. But she and Wes worked well as a team, and they kept their fingers crossed that there wouldn't be any more deaths that week, accidental or otherwise.

The beginning of the week for Nick was not nearly as busy. On Monday he and Sullivan reviewed the reports from Saturday night's accident, and Nick assisted Deputy Dahl on a call regarding an alleged robbery at a house in Spencer Brook Township. As it turned out, the "robber" was the adult son of the homeowner. He apparently had returned to his parental home to pick up some things he had left there. His mother, hearing someone trying to unlock the door, panicked and called the sheriff's office. On their way back to Cambridge, Dahl said, "Do you think maybe the guy could have called his mom to let her know he was stopping by?"

Nick replied, "And do you think the mom might have called us back when she realized who the intruder was?"

"All in a day's work, I guess," Dahl commented.

Tuesday at lunch Nick was enjoying a roast beef sandwich when Sheriff Erickson came into the lunch room. "Whatcha got there? Looks like beef." Nick confirmed that it was and that it had been locally raised. "That's good," said Erickson. "We don't need any more of those genetically modified orgasms or whatever they are. There's too much of that stuff in practically everything we eat, and they can't be good for you." Nick was glad he was the only other one in the lunchroom. If the rest of the deputies had been there, they would have had a field day with Erickson's faux pas.

Then Erickson asked Nick if there were any new developments in the Ivar Peterson case, and Nick assured him that he was following up on some new leads. "Good, good," Erickson responded. "Keep me posted. People are asking me all the time if anyone has been arrested."

"I'll let you know just as soon as that happens," Nick said.

On his way to his office Wednesday morning, Nick found the latest copy of *Minnesota Sheriff* in his mailbox. In it he noticed an article about the Sheriff's Summer Conference coming up in June. He was about to read the program to see if he might be interested in going when his cell phone rang. Jack Brewer's name appeared in the display, and Nick wondered why he would be calling. "Hello, Nick Nordin here."

"Glad I caught you. I think I've got something you're gonna be interested in."

As Nick opened his notebook and got his pen ready, he said, "Okay, tell me more."

"You've got to call this guy I ran into last night at the Pine Brook Inn. He lives just west of Day and I don't know him real well, but I think he's kind of a high roller because he drives a pretty fancy car and he's got one of those expensive watches. I saw it one day when he came into the fish company to get some pickled herring, and then I saw it again yesterday. What do you

Chapter 30

call it—a Romax or something?"

"That would be Rolex," Nick said, eager for Jack to get to the point of his story.

"Yah, that's right. Well, he said he'd been down in the Cities last week. You know, he goes down there pretty often and takes in those expensive shows. This time, it was *Annie, Get Your Gun* in downtown Minneapolis. And he doesn't just go to the show. He and his wife stay in a fancy hotel, and then they go someplace to eat and maybe spend another hundred bucks."

"Uh huh," Nick commented, drumming his pen on the desk.

"Anyway," Jack continued, "this guy Paul, he told me that they were taking a cab from their hotel to the theater, and he got to talking to the driver. He's quite a talker you know, and he'll talk to anyone. The driver must have asked where he was from. When he said he lives by a little town called Day, the driver said something like, 'Oh yah, you go to Day tomorrow and to Mora today.' Paul wanted to know how the cab driver knew about that old saying, and he said that he knew where Day was all right because he'd taken a couple of old ladies there at Christmas time. Paul asked me if I remembered any taxi cab coming to the fish company. None of our customers had ever come by taxi as far as I knew, but as Paul was telling me this, I got to thinking that maybe that cabbie and those two women had been at the fish company on Christmas Eve day. I could hardly wait to call Bob and tell him what I'd just heard, so I told Paul I had to get going. When I told Bob Paul's story, Bob said I had to call you right away. I didn't want to bother you last night, so I waited until this morning."

"I will certainly want to talk to this Paul character," Nick said. "He ought to remember the cab company, and once I know that, I should be able to track down the driver and get more details." Jack gave Nick Paul's phone number. Nick wrote it in big numbers on a page in his notebook, and he thanked Jack for the tip.

After they hung up, Nick sat for a moment staring at the phone number he'd written. He wondered if this could really be the breakthrough he'd been waiting for. He punched in Paul's phone number on his desk phone. After the second ring, a woman answered. When Nick said he'd like to speak to Paul Lake, the woman said, "Just a minute." Nick could hear her whisper, "I don't know who it is. The caller ID says 'Isanti County Sheriff.'"

Soon a man's voice said, "This is Paul. Who's calling?"

Nick identified himself and said he had been talking to Jack Brewer. He explained that he wanted to ask Paul some questions about a cab ride he'd told Jack about. "Well, there's not much to tell except that I was surprised the cab driver knew where Day is."

"But didn't he say that he'd given a couple of women a ride to Day?" Nick asked.

"Yes he did, but not to Mora." Then he chuckled at his own joke.

"I'd really like to talk to the cab driver," Nick said. "Do you remember which taxi company it was?"

"I can do better than that," Paul replied. "I even remember the cabbie's name. It was Hal, and it was a Checker cab. He's not in some kind of trouble, is he? I told him I hoped he'd be on duty the next time I needed a cab. I gave him a big tip too."

"No, actually I'm more interested in the two women passengers he says he brought out this way a few months ago."

"Okay then, I hope you can get ahold of him," Paul said.

Nick had barely hung up the phone when he was on his computer looking up the phone number for the Checker cab company. He wrote the number in his notebook alongside Paul Lake's number. After he refilled his coffee cup and was back in his office, he called the number. When Nick identified himself to the dispatcher at the cab company, the dispatcher said, "Isanti County? You're a bit out of your jurisdiction, aren't you?" Then Nick explained that he wanted to talk to a cab driver by the name

Chapter 30

of Hal who may have taken a couple of women on a rather long ride back in December. "Yah, I remember that," the dispatcher said. "I kidded Hal about it being his turn to take the old ladies on a joy ride. They'd call us every once in a while—maybe two or three times a year—and said they needed a cab for a ride to Day. Of course, we thought it was a little unusual, but hey, a fare's a fare. Once you talk to Hal, you might want to talk to Marty too because I know he gave the dames a ride, maybe more than once."

"So how do I get in contact with Hal?" Nick asked.

"He's right here—just got back from taking a fare to the airport. Hey, Hal," the dispatcher yelled, "come and talk to this guy. He wants to know about your two favorite passengers, you know, the old ladies who hardly knew where they were going and didn't know why they were going there." The dispatcher laughed and said, "On second thought, this could be a long conversation." Then to Nick he said, "I'd better not tie up the main line. Here's the number for our second line. Call that one if you don't mind."

One more phone number was added to Nick's notebook page. When he called it, a fellow answered who identified himself as Hal. "You wanted to talk to me?" he asked. Nick said that he had gotten his name from a guy named Paul, who had spoken highly of him as a cab driver. "Oh, the bull-shitter," Hal said.

Nick ignored Hal's description but instead explained his reason for calling. "I'd like to know about that fare you had around Christmas time when you had to drive all the way to Day. What can you tell me about that?"

Hal said that he had picked up the two women at their house in south Minneapolis on the afternoon of Christmas Eve. He gathered that they were sisters, but it seemed that one was a few years older than the other. They said they wanted to be taken to the tavern in Day. They'd stay there a while—they didn't know how long since it depended on who of their old friends was there, and how many drinks were bought for them. They wanted him to wait until they decided to leave, and then they wanted him to take them to where their other sister lived just a mile or so from Day so they could drop off some Christmas presents for her. They didn't want to stay too long, but they supposed they'd have to have coffee with her. I told them I hoped I would get back to Minneapolis so I could spend Christmas Eve with my family. They said if I wanted to charge extra because of the holiday, they didn't care because they could afford it. One of them had said something about having a lot more money than their farmwife sister. The only other time they had spoken to him was to give him directions. They told him about a shortcut from Cambridge to Day, and he remembered thinking that he hoped they weren't taking him on a wild goose chase.

"When we started out, they told me that the place we were going was about sixty miles away. I started to get worried when I realized we'd already gone sixty-one miles, but then we came to a stop sign at a crossroads, and one of the women said, 'This is it.' I looked around and wondered what 'it' was. Then she said, 'Wait a minute. Where's the tavern? It's supposed to be right there,' she said pointing to a vacant lot where there was some rubble sticking out from underneath the snow. The other one said something like, 'Well, now what are we going to do?' Then they saw that the fish company was open so they told me to drive into the driveway right next to that building. I did as I was told, and as I stopped the cab, one of them said, 'Wait right here.' They got out and took the bag of Christmas presents with them. I wondered if they were afraid that I'd steal them."

"Do you remember what time it was when they went into the fish company?" Nick asked.

"Yah, I remember stopping the meter because that's only used for miles. If there are layovers, we have to calculate the time from beginning to end on our own. It was twenty minutes after four when I shut the meter down. I kept the engine running so I could

Chapter 30

stay warm."

"So how long were the women there?"

"Longer than I thought they'd be. They had said they were just going to get a smoked fish for their sister. So I was surprised when they didn't come out for twenty minutes."

"Did you take them to their sister's then?"

"No, when they came out, they were in a hurry to get on the road. One of them said, 'Let's get out of here,' and the other one said something like 'Uffda, that was bad.' I just thought they were referring to the smell as they both reeked to high heaven, and I wondered if I'd ever get that smell out of my cab. It was actually okay with me that they weren't going to make another stop. As it was, we didn't get back to their house until after six, but at least I was able to celebrate Christmas Eve with my own family."

The next question Nick had for Hal was, "How can I get the names and phone numbers of these two women?"

"That's easy," replied Hal. "The cab company has those records. Give me a minute and I can get that information for you."

While Nick was waiting for Hal to come back to the phone, he wiped his brow, astonished at what he had just heard. He could hardly wait to talk to these women, his first real suspects. "Their names," Hal said, "are Stella and Amanda Lofgren, and they live on Seventeenth Avenue South. Here is their telephone number."

Nick used a new notebook page for this number, writing it larger than the other numbers he'd gathered so far that day. Then he thanked Hal and said he might be back in touch with the cab company if needed to also talk to Marty, the other driver who had some acquaintance with the long distance passengers. Hal asked why Nick had so many questions about two old ladies, but Nick merely said that it had to do with a case he was working on.

{ 31 }

Nick's exuberance at having some definite leads in the murder of Ivar Peterson was short-lived. The number that Hal had given him for the two sisters was no longer in service. "Rats," he said, but since it was still before noon, he decided he'd drive to the address the cab company had on file. He moved the marker on the staff roster to "out" and headed for Minneapolis. He put the address into his GPS and found it with no trouble. It was an apartment building that looked to have sixteen units. He walked into the entry and looked at the directory of residents. There were no Lofgrens listed. Strange, he thought. Just then a woman came from one of the units. Under her unbuttoned coat Nick could see that she was wearing scrubs, so he assumed she was going to work. When she came out into the entry way, she was surprised to see a uniformed officer. He politely said, "Excuse me, but can you tell me if there are two women here by the name of Lofgren?"

"I just moved here, but I wonder if that wasn't the name of the people who lived in my place before I moved in. The landlord is in unit eight. He might be able to help you." She held the security door open for Nick, and then she went on her way.

Nick went down the stairs and followed a hall until he came to number eight. He knocked on the door, and it was opened by a young boy who probably should have been in school. "I'm looking for the landlord," Nick said. "Would that be you?"

Chapter 31

"No, silly. That's my dad."

At that moment an older man appeared, who was also a bit taken aback by seeing a man in uniform. "What's this about?" he asked, and his next question was, "How did you get in here?"

After Nick introduced himself, he explained that a kind lady on the first floor had recommended he talk to the landlord. "I was told two women lived here named Lofgren."

"Well, I guess you're a little late," the landlord said. "They are both over in the Lilac Grove Care Center."

"Since when?" asked Nick.

"They didn't go there at the same time. Let's see, Stella, the older one, had a stroke about the middle of January, so she went there first. There was no way she could come back here. She can't talk, and her right side is still paralyzed. Then wouldn't you know, Amanda went over to visit her one day, and on the way she fell and broke her hip. She's coming along pretty well, but her doctor says she'll need to be in some sort of assisted living place once she's done with rehab. I listed their place for rent March 1, and it was snapped up just like that."

"Yes, I guess the new tenant was the woman I met on the way in here," Nick said. "That's a real shame about the two sisters. I was hoping they'd be able to clear some things up for me."

"Oh, Amanda would be happy to do that, I'm sure. Do you know where that care center is?" When Nick said he didn't, the landlord jotted down the address on a slip of paper and handed it to him.

On his way out Nick wondered what had happened to the Lofgren sisters' belongings. He'd heard about landlords who took advantage of old people who were in similar situations. As soon as it was evident that they could no longer live independently, the landlord would get them to sign a paper releasing them from their lease. Then he'd clear out all their belongings, keeping any choice items for himself, and rent the apartment quickly before any questions could be asked.

When Nick drove past a McDonald's, he realized he was hungry. He went through the drive-thru and ordered a double cheeseburger and a chocolate shake. He wolfed them both down, feeling somewhat guilty for succumbing to fast food, but since he didn't know how long his interview was going to be, he thought he had better eat something.

He found the care center without any difficulty, and while walking to the entrance, he looked around the grounds for lilac trees. Not seeing any, he thought, how typical. Build a building and then name it for something that was destroyed in the construction. Nick inquired at the reception desk if either a Stella or an Amanda Lofgren was a resident there. The receptionist looked Nick up and down, and for the third time that day his uniform caused surprise, if not suspicion. He was used to that in Isanti County, but he thought folks in the big city were more accustomed to seeing law enforcement personnel.

Finally, the receptionist said, "Yes, the Lofgren sisters are here. Are they expecting you?"

"No, I was just over at the apartment building where they used to live, and the landlord told me to come here."

"I see. Let me check if they are in their rooms." She called a room, and after letting the phone ring several times, she hung up and then tried another number. When someone answered, the receptionist said, "Amanda?" Then she turned to Nick. "Amanda is visiting Stella in her room. Who should I say wants to see her?"

Nick thought for a moment before saying, "Deputy Sheriff Nick Nordin." He wondered if he should have identified himself as a deputy, but he was pretty sure that even if that title alarmed them, neither one would be making any hasty escape.

After the receptionist relayed Nick's identity to Amanda, she immediately hung up the phone and told him how to get to Room 138 in the Apple Blossom wing. Nick thanked her and headed down the hall. Passing the Cherry Blossom wing and then Orange Blossom, he finally came to Apple Blossom. A woman in a wheel

Chapter 31

chair was sitting outside one of the rooms, and as Nick approached, she said, "You Nordin?"

Nick said he was and asked if she was Amanda. She didn't even answer but turned herself around and went back into the room. He followed her saying, "I'd like to ask you a few questions. Mind if I sit down?" There was no answer, but Nick took a seat on the lone chair in the room. As he did so, he looked at the other woman in the room who lay in bed facing both his chair and Amanda's wheel chair. "You must be Stella," he said to her.

An expression that was a combination of a frown and a sneer went across the woman's face, and then Amanda in a loud voice said, "She can't talk. So anything you want to say, you'll have to say to me. What kind of questions you got?"

"I'm wondering if you can tell me where you were last Christmas Eve."

"We were home—in our apartment where we'd lived for 35 years." Her answer elicited a muffled but agitated sound from Stella, who glared at Nick with wide angry eyes.

"Are you sure?" Nick asked as he flipped open his notebook. "I have information from the Checker cab company that you hired a cab that day to drive you to Day."

"They must have us mixed up with somebody else," Amanda said. Stella made the same agitated sound as before. "Just be quiet. You're not helping any," Amanda said to Stella.

"I know that a cab showed up in Day that afternoon ay, and the next day, Christmas Day, Ivar Peterson was found floating in a tank at the Day Fish Company."

"We know about that, all right. Our other sister wrote and told us."

"So you knew Ivar then?" Nick asked.

"Well, yah, we went to school with him."

Nick, remembering what Connie Henderson had said about the two sisters who Ivar's mother had been critical of, said, "You didn't have a crush on him, did you?"

"No," Amanda answered adamantly while Stella grew even more agitated.

"Have you or Stella ever been married?"

"None of your business."

Actually neither of his last two questions were relevant to Nick's interview which had quickly become an investigation in his opinion. He decided to go on the offensive and said, "Look, why don't you just tell me what happened at the fish company when you went there on the afternoon of Christmas Eve? Was it an accident? Was it self-defense?" Nick almost choked on that last question. "Do you want to go to your own room so you can tell me in private?"

Amanda looked over at Stella, who raised her left hand slightly and turned it over to indicate that it didn't matter. Amanda then hung her head, and when she raised it a few seconds later, there were tears in her eyes. "All right, all right."

Nick pulled his digital recorder from his pocket and switched it on. Then he said to Stella, "If she says something that you don't agree with, you put up your hand, okay?" Stella blinked at him, and then Amanda began telling the story of what had happened on that fateful day in Day.

Just as the cab driver had said, the pair intended to go the tavern, but when they discovered that it was no longer there, they decided to go to the fish company instead. Amanda said that they had been nipping a little on the way to Day (a detail that the cab driver had omitted, presumably since he didn't know, or because he might get in trouble with his boss). As they went into the fish company, no one seemed to be around. Stella chose a smoked fish from the counter, and then she called, "Yoo hoo." Ivar came out of the fish tank room, mop in hand. Stella held up the smoked fish in one hand, and in the other she had the bottle from her shopping bag. She asked Ivar if he wanted a little Christmas cheer. When he declined, Amanda then moved toward him and

Chapter 31

said, "Merry Christmas, you old coot. Give me a kiss for old time's sake." He resisted that invitation too by turning his head away from Amanda, but then both women kept getting closer to him.

Stella set the bottle down and grabbed Ivar by his belt. As Ivar was squirming to get away from the women, his cell phone rang. When he said it was probably his girlfriend calling, Amanda grabbed the phone out of Ivar's shirt pocket and with Stella still holding Ivar stationary, Amanda shoved the phone, plastic bag and all, down his pants. Stella, still holding on to the smoked fish with her free hand, jammed it down Ivar's pants too. Ivar doubled over, but the women kept coming at him, forcing him to shuffle backwards into the fish tank room. Then Stella slipped on the wet floor, and while she was regaining her balance, Ivar was able to turn around and stand up. He attempted to maneuver himself around the fish tanks and get back into the customer area. But Amanda, still begging for a Christmas kiss, was on one side of a fish tank and wouldn't let Ivar get past her.

Stella, back on her feet, went into the customer area and came back with the shopping bag. She pulled out a rolling pin intended as a Christmas gift for the sister they were planning to visit. When Amanda saw the rolling pin, she yelled, "No!" but Stella came up behind Ivar and hit him on the back of the head. Amanda insisted that Stella had only wanted to threaten Ivar with the rolling pin so that he'd comply with their wish to give Amanda a kiss. However, the blow knocked him out, and he fell headlong into the fish tank with his torso half-submerged. The sisters realized then that their day in the country had taken an ill-fated turn. They took a look at Ivar's still form and without even saying anything to each other, each sister grabbed a leg and lifted the rest of Ivar's body up and over the rim of the tank. They grabbed the bottle of whisky and returned it and the rolling pin to the shopping bag. Before they went out the door, Amanda noticed the mop on the floor. She picked it up and put it back in the fish tank room. They told the cab driver to head back to Minneapolis, and they gave no explanation why they weren't going to visit their sister.

When Amanda finished her tale, Nick turned off the recorder and was at a loss for words. He remembered something he'd read in a James Lee Burke novel* about there being three essential truths about law enforcement—most crimes are not punished; most crimes are not solved through the use of forensic evidence; and informants produce the lion's share of information that gets convictions. In this case the last statement was certainly the truth even though the informant's information had come about by sheer coincidence. It didn't matter, thought Nick, but it was the first truth about crimes not being punished that bothered him. He looked at Amanda and Stella and thought there was no way either of them could stand trial. In their condition it was highly unlikely either was a threat to society. About all he could do was turn his notes and recording over to Brad Curtis, the county attorney, and hope for some clemency.

*Creole Bell by James Lee Burke. Simon & Schuster, 2012

{ Epilogue }

When Nick returned to Cambridge after his interview with the two sisters at the Lilac Grove Care Center, he went straight to Sheriff Erickson's office. Since it was almost 4:30 in the afternoon, Erickson was getting ready to head home, and he suggested that whatever Nick had to tell him could wait until morning. But when Nick said that he'd solved the Ivar Peterson murder, Erickson sat back down. By the time Nick had finished relating the events of the day, it was nearly 6:00.

By noon the next day, Nick's news had traveled throughout the Law Enforcement Center and beyond. He was slapped on the back, told he was a hero and commended for his crime-solving ability. Nick, however, did not feel any particular sense of elation. Yes, he was glad to have finally discovered who was responsible for Ivar Peterson's death, but he had expected that such a discovery would stir up feelings of anger and hostility toward the murderer who had committed the crime. Instead he felt mostly sad – at the women's poor judgement that day at the fish company and at their current physical condition. He couldn't help wondering if Ivar would still be alive if the sisters had been totally sober when they got to the fish company, and he also wondered if the events of that Christmas Eve afternoon had been a factor in causing Stella's stroke.

When he shared these thoughts with Brad Curtis, the county

attorney said he could certainly understand how Nick felt, but the law needed to be upheld. He said he'd have to file charges, but he assured Nick that the case would never get to trial. Brad felt there wasn't any urgency to set an indictment process in motion because there was no indication that the women were going to commit any additional murders. As it happened, there was even less urgency because Amanda had a heart attack a week after Nick's visit. She lingered in a coma for a couple of days and then died. It came as no surprise to Nick that Stella joined her sister in less than a month. After all, they had been together their entire life. They lived together in Minneapolis for over 50 years; they worked in the same bakery; they rode the bus to and from work together; they retired on the same day; and as far as anyone knew, they had committed their one and only crime together.

Meanwhile there were other crimes for Nick to deal with in Isanti County (although luckily there were no more homicides), so he was kept busy for the rest of the winter. On occasions when he was in the northern part of the county, either on business or to visit Megan, he would drive through Day and try to imagine what the town had been like in its heyday when it was a bustling crossroads community. Whatever he imagined was a far cry from its present reality. Because it was the off season for lutefisk, there was little activity in the small hamlet, and except for the dogs lying in the street, it was practically a ghost town.

Nick and Megan continued to get together as often as their respective jobs allowed, and more than once their trysts were interrupted by one or the other being called to work. There was a mutual feeling that their relationship was heading towards something permanent. Even though they had known each other only a few months, there was a camaraderie and closeness that neither had ever felt before.

During their excursion to the Minnesota State Fairgrounds for the Horse Expo, Megan found a reasonably priced horse trailer, and they had had a good time looking at all the horse gear.

Epilogue

Nick was amazed at the size of the Fairgrounds, quite different from what he remembered at the South Dakota State Fair in Huron. From that introduction, he was eager to return to the fairgrounds in August for what Madeline called the great Minnesota get-together.

Madeline had been very interested in Nick's account of the interview with the two sisters. She hadn't known them, but she had known other spinster sister pairs who had lived together. They often died within days of each other, she said, not unlike when a spouse dies and the surviving mate dies soon after. She commended Nick for taking a sympathetic approach to the two sisters rather than feeling that they must be punished to the extent of the law.

Megan's exploration of career options led to a discovery that she needed only a few courses to qualify as a medical examiner's assistant. The news that high speed internet service was being installed along her road and would be available by September meant that she could take the courses online. Once she completed them, the ME's office in Anoka had promised her an internship that had the potential for becoming a part-time job. When Megan told Wes of her plans, he said he was relieved because Stone's business was suffering due to the newly-expanded Cambridge funeral home. Stone had advised Wes that Megan's hours were going to have to be reduced, and Wes was worried how he was going to break that news to her.

On a late spring visit to Madeline, Nick announced that he was going to be moving in with Megan. Madeline inquired if that meant they were getting married. When Nick replied that they were thinking of a late summer or early fall wedding, Madeline suggested, "Why not get married at the state fair?" Even though most state fair weddings are booked more than a year in advance, Madeline said she was sure she could get Nick and Megan a time slot as one of the fair's wedding planners was her niece.

So at 8:00 a.m. on the Sunday before Labor Day, a small group assembled at the Horton Pavilion on the Minnesota State Fairgrounds: Nick and Megan, the wedding couple; Madeline and Wes as witnesses; and Brad Curtis as officiant. After the brief marriage ceremony the group walked from the pavilion to the Food Building. There, amid cheers from the fair's early birds, the bridal party had wedding cake—one of the first funnel cakes of the day. And because Megan and Nick were scheduled to work on Tuesday, they had only a short honeymoon. Stone had insisted on paying for a villa on the North Shore for them as a wedding present. It was a lovely place, and no doubt most newlyweds would have been thrilled. Nick and Megan, however, would have preferred spending the rest of Sunday and Monday at the fair.

September also saw some changes at the fish company. The firm's accountant had informed Bob and Jack that the previous year's business had turned a significant profit—the largest ever. Because Bob no longer needed a new truck (he was granted Ivar's, which was practically brand new), Bob and Jack considered options for ways their profit could be turned back into the business. They decided to build an addition to the fish company that would accommodate a drive-thru for those customers who did not want to come inside. They could remain in their vehicles, place their order at a window and wait while their order was being filled. Nevertheless, when the lutefisk season opened in October, it seemed that most customers still preferred to come into the fish company. Apparently, that was a fundamental part of the lutefisk-buying experience.

The brothers had wondered how they would find someone to replace Ivar, so they were pleasantly surprised when they got a call from a man who had recently moved to the area from Norway. He had married a woman from Ogilvie whom he met while she was in Norway studying rosemaling. Since he'd worked in Norwegian fisheries most of his adult life, he fit in well at the fish company, although Jack and Bob often said, "He's not Ivar."

Epilogue

The brothers also wondered if their business would be adversely affected because a murder had occurred at the fish company. But they need not have worried. If anything, their business increased, and the two brothers, together with their new helper, Sven, had all they could do to keep up with the demand for not only lutefisk but also for herring and smoked fish.

However, more than one customer commented that it seemed as though Ivar Peterson was still on the premises. Stories were told that while waiting for their fish to be wrapped, customers would sometimes see a ghostly image floating in the vicinity of the doorway leading to the fish tank area. Other customers said they had seen a shadowy figure of someone resembling Ivar holding a mop, an image that lasted only a few seconds and then dissolved into the wall. Whatever the images meant or whether they existed at all were no doubt indications that those who made such observations had strong and lasting memories associating Ivar Peterson with the Day Fish Company.